DANA EVYN

THE
MIRROR
IN THE
MOUNTAIN

THE MIRRORED TRILOGY

THE MIRROR IN THE MOUNTAIN
The Mirrored Trilogy, Book 2

CITY OWL PRESS
www.cityowlpress.com

Cover Design by MiblArt. All stock photos licensed appropriately.

Page Edges by Painted Wings Publishing Services.

Edited by Danielle DeVor.

For information on subsidiary rights, please contact the publisher at info@cityowlpress.com.

Paperback Edition ISBN: 978-1-64898-498-3

Hardback Edition ISBN: 978-1-64898-499-0

Digital Edition ISBN: 978-1-64898-497-6

Printed in the United States of America

For anyone who ever opened the wardrobe, tapped the traveling stone, or touched the mirror...just in case.

AUTHOR'S NOTE

Your mental health matters. Please be mindful that *The Mirror in the Mountain* includes the following themes: sexual assault, violence, suicidal thoughts, loss of loved ones, near-death experiences, death, and explicit sexual situations. For a full list of warnings please visit danaevyn. com/content-warnings

CHAPTER I
ESTELLE

The High Queen had always stared at me in an unblinking way I didn't like. Perhaps she was staring at my eyes—at the crown of gold around my pupils—that marked me as the one who would ultimately usurp her rule, as she herself had foretold. But I couldn't shake the feeling that Queen Amerie's cloudy blue gaze was staring even deeper than that. As though she could see straight through me into my very soul.

The great hall was filled with twirling streamers of pure silver that hung from the high ceiling, silver feathers that matched the mirror gateway that had brought us all to Morehaven drifting endlessly above the heads of onlookers, and music and merriment so loud, it felt suffocating. Yet even across the room, those milky eyes found mine with an utterly unnerving accuracy. I threw back the remains of my drink, its bubbles stinging my throat as I swallowed. Then I ducked behind a giant vase of cascading flowers as though it might do something to shield me from that all-knowing stare. Slowly, I backed away toward the wall of windows and the cracked doorway of my escape.

As I snuck out onto the balcony, my mouth twitched in irritation as I found someone already there. His raven black hair brushed against his high, bronzed cheekbones, casting a shadow across his intense gaze. There was an air of purposeful dishevelment to his courtly clothes. A fitted jacket clung to his broad shoulders and nipped in at his narrow waist, the buttons of his shirt undone enough to display the dark hair of his chest. Then his eyes flicked up to meet mine, his full lips pulling into a devilish smirk at my obvious annoyance that someone else was out here, even though I was the one who had technically intruded upon *him*.

Obviously, he was also trying to escape the monotony of the function, for which I couldn't blame him. Stepping forward, I noticed he was watching me as closely as I was watching him; his golden-brown eyes brazenly looking me up and down. He had the look of someone who knew his way around a fight, muscled in such a way that his fine clothes clung to the bulge of his biceps. Not that I couldn't take him…but that was the last thought on my mind as he smiled at me. My heart was suddenly hammering as one dimple appeared lopsidedly on the right side of that crooked grin.

"Hello there," he said with a lilting accent, marking him as a subject of Esterra—that dry desert fae kingdom in the East. He leaned forward in a graceful bow that had likely been drilled into him since his birth.

My answering curtsy was a short rustle of my voluptuous pale pink tulle skirts, their layers see-through save for the beaded sheath underneath. The quickness of the dip verged on rude, especially as I narrowed my eyes rather than looking demurely downward as I had been taught. "Hello."

I glanced toward the other end of the balcony, wondering if I could make a quick exit to the gardens below. He looked at me askance, his dark hair falling over one eye. "Why does it feel like I'm the one intruding on your moment of solitude when it's the other way around?"

I started slightly, surprised at his bluntness. "I imagine you also weren't looking for company if you escaped out here."

He smirked, that second flash of dimple making an appearance as equally diverting as the first. "Escaped is one word for it. But I'm not against company if *you're* what it entails."

I rolled my eyes. "You don't even know me."

He laughed, and my heart skipped a beat despite myself. "What if I'd like to?"

"Because I've made you feel so welcome? Or do you enjoy a companion who's annoyed by your very presence?"

He smiled wider, the corners of his eyes crinkling, but his dark gaze flashed with a hint of danger that made my stomach dissolve into concerning flutters. My overbearing father rarely left me unchaperoned, but it wasn't like I didn't have friends of the opposite sex, even if most were clearly under my father's thumb. And yet...there was something about him that made me uncomfortable in a curiously pleasant fashion. An innate connection I found myself yearning to investigate further.

Or maybe, despite my evasion of the simpering, soulless courtiers, and watchful eyes following my every move, it wasn't true companionship I was trying to avoid.

"I enjoy a companion with spirit. You obviously have *that* in abundance." His voice was low, his gaze never leaving mine. "One that prefers fresh air and enough space to breathe to the courtly politics and drunken revelry of this function. And one who might be the most beautiful person I've ever seen."

I pressed my lips together, acting as though I was unfazed even as that flutter in my belly multiplied. "You're very forward for someone I've only just met."

"And yet it feels like I do know you, somehow." He shrugged. "Tell me I'm alone in the feeling, and I'll leave you to your solitude if that is your wish."

I opened my mouth, but when nothing came out, I slowly closed it again.

"Your name, lady," he demanded, his voice deep and sinful.

It was rare that someone didn't know who I was, and him not knowing made my pulse climb with excitement. Because I was the Princess of Soleara and likely heir to all faeriedom considering the blistering force of the Celestial magic that had appeared to me two years ago on my Seventeenth. Though many already speculated about the obvious path of my future, no one was supposed to know about the prophecy since the High Queen had commanded I share it with no one.

"Yours first."

Before I could so much as protest, he walked forward, catching my hands in his larger ones. I jolted at his touch, at the strange shock that sizzled between us the second his skin touched mine. And maybe that was why I didn't pull away. Maybe that even explained why I leaned in to breathe him in —some intoxicating mix of citrus and anise that seemed to sear into my brain.

"Perhaps we can bargain then. For there's one thing I want even more than your name."

A shiver of anticipation ran through me, and I hoped he didn't notice. Though the way his hands tightened on mine said otherwise.

"Oh?" I hoped my voice sounded as composed as I wished it did...but something about him was making calm hard to find.

Why was my heart pounding like it might break free of my chest? For a fanciful moment, I wondered if he could hear its loud staccato.

"Your name, or a taste of those rosy lips, are all I could ask for, lest they haunt my dreams more than they already will."

My jaw might have dropped at his forwardness, at the heated look on his face as I felt an answering blush on my cheeks.

Coolly, I raised an imperious brow. "You'll have to do better than that. But I suppose it's only fair to give you a chance to earn it."

I spun around, a destination already in mind. I shouldn't do this. Yet the warning bells that should have been blaring in my mind at slipping away with a stranger were strangely silent. Blindly, I reached behind me on instinct, not bothering to look back because somehow, I knew I wouldn't need to. His hand found mine, nearly swallowing my own, before I could make it off the balcony.

The High Queen's fete nearly deafened me as we reentered the ballroom, the merriment seemingly rowdier in the mere minutes I had missed. I ducked behind the tables overflowing with ostentatious piles of food and drink, unwilling to attract the attention of my father, or one of my ladies now twirling on the dance floor. No one looked our way as I quickly led us into a back hallway, the sudden silence now that we were far enough from the lively, enchanted music making my ears ring. My body heated at the steady presence behind me. There was something so forbidden about sneaking away with his hand entwined in mine, especially now that we were truly alone.

"You know your way around," he said slowly. There was an unasked question there. But a familiar voice broke through the silence, echoing down the hallway.

In a flash, I shoved the Esterran into an alcove, pressing myself back against him to keep out of sight as Queen Amerie's nasal voice answered my father's demurring tone. Likely another monotonous conversation about their plans for me, with my father trying to twist my life to his own benefit. They were the last two people I wanted to run into, let alone in such a compromising position.

I jolted, suddenly innately aware of how close I was to a virtual stranger. He had circled his arm around my waist, his fingers firm against my stomach. The heat of his breath puffed against the nape of my neck, and a shiver coursed down my spine in stark contrast to the warmth of his body wrapped around mine.

He bent his head, the tip of his nose just barely brushing against my skin before his low, deep voice rumbled between us. "I think they're gone now. Though I'm happy to pretend they aren't should you like to stay like this a bit longer."

I jumped away from him, feeling my cheeks heat as I whirled around.

He was smirking at me, that one-sided dimple teasing. "Was that not the destination you had in mind?"

My jaw worked as I forced my thoughts away from the way I had perfectly fit against him. "Hardly. Keep up, will you?"

Turning on my heel, my layered skirts twirling against my slippered feet, I hurried down the hallway, light bouncing off the sparkling beads decorating the corseted bust of my gown. My companion caught up in a few long strides, his fingers brushing against mine. I jerked my hand back as that strange energy danced between us yet again, leaving a tingling static in its wake. Was it his magic reaching out to mine? If so, I was hardly going to give him the satisfaction of asking if he felt it too, let alone if he understood its meaning.

The hallway remained thankfully empty as I took us down a spiral staircase that led to the training yard, a regular haunt of mine during these courtly visits, of which there were far too many. The High Queen was adamant in her demand to 'watch my progress' in both my magical and my courtier's training, and my father all too eager to mingle at court.

Wordlessly, I grabbed two time-worn practice swords, then headed toward the outdoor sparring ring, my body thrumming with anticipation from the unspoken challenge. The fading sunshine filtered through the treetops, bathing the ring in an otherworldly glow. My companion dutifully followed a half-step behind. His eyebrow raised as I lifted a sword and pointed it at him, before smoothly flipping it downward to offer its hilt.

"I hope you know your way around a sword." The statement was casual, though the teasing timbre of my voice was perhaps a bit more sensual than I intended. I saw the flash of delight in his eyes as I tossed the sword to him before he could respond. He caught it easily, then settled into a fighting stance to match my own. "Because the first one to disarm the other gets what they asked for."

His eyes darkened when he realized I hadn't specified between my name and a kiss. But I was the Faerie Princess of the North, so it hardly mattered what he wanted as I wasn't going to let him win.

We circled each other, and instead of waiting for an opening, I lunged in eagerly, our swords clashing as he parried my blow. I tried to ignore the intensity of his gaze as we fought yet found myself unable to tear my eyes from his. We exchanged strikes in a relentless dance, neither gaining the upper hand. My respect for his swordplay was rapidly growing, as I had been trained by the best, and yet he was proving to be a worthy opponent.

When we came apart, I feigned a high parry before ducking under his sword arm. My opposite hand slipped through the folds in my skirt, nimbly unsheathing the small dagger I always kept on my person as I twisted to face him. My blade was at his neck before he could react. In response, he dropped his sword to the ground with a hollow thump, and then hauled me into his arms. He held me against his hard body, only my dagger between us, both of our chests heaving.

"My name is Adrian," he whispered, his warm breath tickling my mouth.

I didn't bother to drop my weapons when I kissed him, hard. His mouth eagerly met mine, our mouths parting, tongues parrying in a different sort of battle. But even as I was swept away from the force of the kiss, his name sparked in the recesses of my mind. I pulled back, keeping my dagger firmly at his throat.

"You're one of the princelings from Esterra."

Adrian frowned slightly, his throat bobbing against my blade, but carefully nodded, his eyes still on my mouth. His hand curled against my cheek, the other tightening against the small of my back, like it was all he could do to stop himself from pulling me back against him.

"I'm afraid you have me at a disadvantage in more ways than one," Adrian murmured in that sinfully accented drawl. "For while it feels like my soul knows yours, I still don't know your name."

I smirked, lowering my sword to my side. "Now, those weren't our terms. Unless you'd like another round?"

"That's exactly what I want," he confirmed bluntly, pure longing darkening his gaze.

Adrian's thumb brushed my bottom lip, and I gasped when he tugged me back against him, his lips taking their place. I moaned into his mouth as I dropped my sword with a thud so I could drag my fingers through his hair. A flare of heat roiled through me as I finally pulled my dagger away, holding it limply at my side. He groaned, his fingers twisting into my dress, hitching it up slightly like he needed me closer—

"Princess Estelle!" The shocked voice of one of the queen's ladies cut through our embrace, and I jumped back, though not before Adrian caught my free hand. I could feel the moment the name registered, his grip tightening slightly as he froze, my name a whisper on his lips. And I looked at him—at the shock slackening his features as he realized exactly who he had kissed.

His wide eyes crinkled at the corners. "Princess, huh?"

The way his low voice sinfully stretched out my title, each syllable enunciated, sent shivers down my spine. My mouth quirked. "Took you long enough, Princeling."

The ladies' maid was still squawking something about propriety from the doorway, and I nodded my head placatingly at her lecture as I collected myself. Still appearing scandalized, she shrilly screeched, "The

High Queen requests your presence immediately, Princess." With a bobbed curtsy, she turned to lead the way.

"Then we'd better go," Adrian said, his hand still in mine as he led me toward the door, that devilish smile firmly back in place.

As we walked up the staircase, Adrian tucked my arm in his without releasing my hand. We stayed silent, though I couldn't keep from tensing the closer we got to the ballroom. Adrian's thumb rubbed gently against the back of my hand, and I knew he had noticed.

We reached the ballroom with our fingers still entwined. And though I *should* let go of his hand, I didn't just yet, letting him lead me toward Queen Amerie's ancient throne. Reluctantly, I removed my hand from his as we got closer, not missing the queen's raised eyebrow as she took in the movement.

I stopped in front of her and dropped into a low curtsy. Adrian bowed low beside me.

"Good." The High Queen's blue eyes twinkled as we rose together, a rare smile on her wrinkle-lined lips. "You've finally found your *anima*."

CHAPTER 2
EVA

I woke up chained to an all too familiar bed, trapped in a living nightmare from which I was desperate to awaken. My eyelids were unbearably heavy from the remnants of the drug that had finally released me from its cloying grasp, and I was too drained to open my eyes more than a crack. Everything inside me felt bruised and raw from the aftereffects of the battle against Aviel, the hammering in my head worsening as I silently screamed at myself for what I had done.

But I would sacrifice myself for them again in a heartbeat. For my *anima*, my faerie soulmate, Bastian, though he had always been Bash or a teasing 'freckles' to me. For our friends, Yael and Rivan—the latter of whom had been barely breathing when I last saw him. For Tobias, my twin brother who had survived the fire I had assumed he had died in. Instead, he had made it to the faerie realm of Agadot first, where he had learned that our parents were truly Queen Estelle and King Adrian...and they had fled to the human realm because I was the heir not only to the hidden northern kingdom of Soleara but to all of Agadot. That was why the False King had hunted me while hiding in plain sight pretending to be his own son, Prince Aviel. It was why he had spread the lie that the curse warping the magic of the land was due to the need to find his lost *anima*—leading to my true fae soulmate bringing me to him. And it was why Aviel had grown obsessed with claiming me in order to somehow use my power to become High King.

My sacrifice had been worth it, even if I was left to face the consequences.

Determinedly, I forced my eyes fully open. Then let out a short, relieved breath. I appeared to be alone...for now. Though the reprieve was likely Aviel trying to make me squirm from the dread of anticipating his arrival—a monster playing with its prey.

Fear unfurled in my stomach, cords of apprehension lacing around my lungs, binding each breath. Closing around my throat as surely as if he were strangling me.

I curled into as tight of a ball as I could with my hands bound above my head, manacles securing my wrists, the gleaming silver headboard they were shackled to shining dully. Ignoring the pain radiating down my side, I squeezed my eyes shut as I tried to hold back my sudden rush of tears. One slipped out anyway, rolling across my temple.

Big breath in, my father's voice commanded me as I attempted to inhale. *Count each second.*

There was a sharp, stabbing pain in my ribs as I finally managed to suck in a shaky breath, my wounds struggling to heal with the band blocking my magic. On instinct, I reached out for Bash...and came up against an adamant wall where our bond should be, his calming presence entirely out of reach. Then cringed at the yawning emptiness where my darkness should live. At the static where I should feel my magic roiling.

It was horrifyingly silent to be alone inside my head again after growing used to that constant flow of love and warmth. My heart throbbed, painfully aware of the half it was missing.

At least he was safe. They were all safe for now, having been forced back through the mirror to Imyr, the Southern kingdom, before Aviel had closed the gateway to Morehaven to them. And assuming Marin had been able to heal Rivan after Aviel had suffocated him with the light magic he had leeched from my brother. They were *safe*, I repeated to myself firmly, though I doubted they would be content to stay that way.

As much as I ached at Bash's absence, we had been lucky in that one small instance. I hadn't been sure if Aviel would really let him go—not when he could use him, or Tobias, or any of my friends as leverage to control me. He could have easily used their presence and continued safety to force my obedience, even though I had already promised it.

Unfortunately, something told me Aviel had something more sinister in mind for me. Pulling fruitlessly at the shackles binding me, I suppressed my mounting dread and desperation before it could escape me in a cry of despair. I would never forget that feeling of being held down against my will in this bed, never forget that utter helplessness, but I couldn't let my mind take me back there. I needed to stay strong, stay vigilant for any chance to escape. To hone my rage into a weapon that would ensure I would *never* feel that way again.

I uncurled from my fetal position, wincing as the shackles dug into my wrists as I tested their limits, the scarred skin stinging. It had been too much to hope that Aviel would trust me at my word to stay in line after I had agreed to do so to save my friends. Nor should he.

My upper teeth sank into my dry lower lip as I glanced at the doorway. Where *was* he?

The waiting almost made it worse…so much so that when I did hear footsteps, I was almost grateful for a reprieve from the anticipation, my heart racing even as I braced myself for what came next.

Aviel had come for me, and the time had come to fight with everything I had left.

I bit the inside of my cheek, the iron taste of my blood grounding me as I lay on that cursed bed I had so recently escaped. My hands had started to tremble at some point, and I found myself unable to stop the shaking that overtook me. I closed my eyes, willing my body to stop but failing. The footsteps neared and I held my breath, tensing to strike when the opportunity best presented itself.

But the hand that stroked my face was soft, female, and familiar.

"Poor little bird, caught in the serpent's nest once again," said an annoyingly sing-song voice. "You don't need to pretend you're asleep. He's not here."

I cracked one eye open, groaning at the jolt of pain from my broken rib as I tried and failed to take in a deep enough breath. "Where is he?"

"He's gone to feed from the land like the vampire he is," Alette half-sang in my ear, her voice raising the hair on my arms. She had helped me escape the last time I had been trapped here after I had convinced her to stop doing Aviel's bidding. I had no doubt that her strange resemblance to me was the reason he had enslaved and abused her, and I held back my wince as her gaze met mine, a hint of madness in her too-wide eyes. "He used too much magic fighting you and yours. But at least we have some time alone." Her grin was maniacal as she tugged on a loose strand of my hair, the chestnut brown a match to her own. "Should have flown further, little bird."

My lips parted, but I bit back my retort as I glared at her. For all the good it would do as she closed her eyes, humming four eerie notes over and over.

"What do you mean, feed from the land?"

Her wild gray eyes flew open, her expression almost pitying. "From the Source, of course. The lake of magic that lies deep beneath this very castle and branches out throughout this realm. Or did you think he got so powerful from feeding off your brother? Not to mention the others who weren't so lucky as to get away with their lives…"

She clucked her tongue at me disappointedly as if I should have known this already.

"He's stealing magic from the realm itself?"

I couldn't seem to stop shaking, whether from the drug leaving my system, being back in Aviel's bed, or the shock of what Alette was telling me.

No wonder we weren't able to stop him.

I swallowed; my mouth painfully dry. "Who knows about this? How do you—"

"Oh, I know a lot of things I shouldn't, little bird," Alette said, her unblinking gaze unnerving as she slowly cocked her head to the side. "No one notices the fly on the wall."

Looking at her more closely, I realized the shadows beneath her eyes had multiplied, her complexion sallow like she hadn't seen daylight in far too long. She had always been willowy, but now her skin seemed too loose, like she had lost weight too quickly, her simple black linen dress billowing on her thin frame.

"How are you even alive? After you freed me, I thought he would kill you."

Her head slowly tilted to the opposite side, a blank sort of smile plastering across her face. "No one notices a fly *in* the wall either."

I thought of the hidden passage she had taken me through to escape from Aviel the last time I had been trapped here in this bed. Its faintly glowing stone, leading downward. Of course it wouldn't be the only one of its kind.

Would I be able to use the same escape a second time?

"Alette—"

"The first thing you need to do is get him away from the source of his might. Or, well, you *should* have." She giggled, repeating "would've" and "should've" a few more times in a possessed-sounding chant that had my already bleary head pounding.

"*Alette*, please," I urgently interrupted her, earning me an annoyed pout. "I need to get out of here before he returns. Do you have the key?"

She shook her head as she leaned closer. A manic gleam reflected in her too-wide eyes as she started stroking my hair. "But don't worry, little bird. We're friends now. So I'm going to help you."

The words sank in strangely, like the other shoe was about to drop, just as I realized the light gray of her eyes had morphed into the reddish orange of an ember. A nonexistent fire reflected inside them—an inferno blazing to life like a backdraft given oxygen.

I opened my mouth just as all the air seemed to suck out of the room.

And then everything exploded.

CHAPTER 3
BASH

The not knowing was torture. Not being able to feel her through our bond. Being left to imagine her suffering in Aviel's hands. Knowing that the bastard sought to claim her against her will had long since ignited my fury into pure, unadulterated vengeance.

My shadows eddied around me in agitated circles. I clenched my fists, feeling them stream between my fingers—wishing I wasn't so damn helpless to help her in this moment.

The people I loved tended to be taken from me. I had been a fool to think she would be any different, not when it was the same perpetrator that haunted all my nightmares.

I couldn't draw a deep enough breath as that soul-crushing fear threatened to destroy me. She was gone, she was *gone*—and I had been unable to save her, despite my promises that I would keep her safe. My stomach turned over as I remembered the sight of how shattered she had been after the last time he had held her captive. The marks he had left, the shadow behind her eyes…it wasn't something I could ever forget. And now she had given herself up to him to save us with the full knowledge of exactly what he would demand in return.

I hadn't been able to stand the sight of the way he looked at her—like she was *his*. The greedy way he had held her against himself, that proprietary hand stroking her cheek making me go blind with rage. Yet she had held firm, her determination unwavering as always as she stubbornly saved the rest of us—even as I saw the slight quiver to her lip, the terror in her eyes I could no longer feel across our bond. I had been helpless to stop it as she laid down her freedom for ours.

I had to get her back, to save her from the very fate from which she had already saved herself once before. There was no me without Eva, no future I would consider without her in it. When I thought about a world without her, I wanted to burn it to the ground, everyone else be damned.

Something wretched burrowed into my gut, a mixture of rage and bitter grief that knocked the breath from my lungs at how thoroughly I had failed her. I couldn't leave her there with him. Just as I knew we couldn't risk going back unprepared and make her sacrifice be for nothing.

But one thought managed to break through the chaos of all the others, silencing the storm in my mind.

She's alive. And as long as she still breathed, I would come for her.

As I made myself eat something to maintain my strength, each bite tasteless on my tongue, Marin placed our mother's invention on Tobias's still-collared neck that would absorb its magic, Yael and Rivan looking on. Tobias closed those familiar eyes as the stone hummed, his chestnut hair falling across his gaunt face. His body shuddered as the band fell to the floor.

My shadows wrapped protectively around my arms, painting them like a living tattoo as I stared down at the broken collar. I prayed I would never know the agony of being separated from my magic as he had been for so long. My shadows had always been with me, as much a part of me as breathing. I could barely imagine not having access to that intrinsic part of me, let alone the pain of having them repeatedly stolen and used against those I loved.

Tobias's eyes were haunted as he stared down at his hands, stretching his fingers out and then curling them into a fist before he deliberately turned his palm upward

Slowly, one fingertip began to glow, then another. The light spread through his body, as if stretching after a long slumber, carefully getting reacquainted before bursting out of his hands in a dazzling display. The shower of white embers faded quickly. I knew he would need more time to rebuild his strength, along with his well of power.

There were tears in his eyes as he looked at each of my friends in turn. "Thank you."

I noted that he skipped me in his gratitude. And I knew it would take a long time, if ever, before my *anima*'s brother fully forgave me for my role in his imprisonment. For being part, however unknowingly, of what had taken his magic from him in the first place.

Would she *forgive me?*

There was a stabbing sensation in my chest as I recalled how horrified Eva had been when she realized I had unwittingly helped in her brother's capture, just as he had been on the way to find her. It had shattered me to feel the moment her trust in me had cracked, her stunned hurt slicing like shards of glass through our bond.

But her forgiveness wasn't what was important right now. I had felt her love for me across our bond before it had been muted, mingling with her utter resolve to save everyone but herself. And once I got her back, I would do everything I could to make it up to her. To both of them. Preferably by killing the bastard who was to blame for their torment in the first place.

"So about that plan," Tobias whispered hoarsely. "We need to get Aviel away from Morehaven. We don't have a chance of succeeding with him there."

Everyone looked at Tobias expectantly. I stilled as I remembered his bold declaration that he knew how to stop Aviel. With Eva's capture playing in a loop in my mind, I had nearly forgotten. Rivan obviously hadn't, nodding impatiently from where he had been gingerly sipping on some tea. The red lines on his cheeks, where Marin had healed the slices where Aviel's light had gagged him, had faded slightly but still looked painful. He had refused to go upstairs to rest, despite Marin's urging, but his brush with death was obvious in the way he held himself. Even my sister's magic wasn't enough to fully heal that level of trauma immediately.

Tobias's face was grim. "There's a lake deep under Morehaven...it's where he's drawing his power. The reason why he's so powerful."

Yael cocked her head. "I thought the Source was a myth."

"I was told the same," I added.

Tobias's eyes narrowed as he looked at me, his grievance with me apparent despite our casual truce. "That's exactly what they want you to think. But it's not." He cleared his throat, his voice gruff from disuse. "It's a secret passed from one ruler to the next. Or tortured out of, in Aviel's case, from the former High Queen. *That's* the reason behind the so-called curse, not whatever nonsense he made up. He's sucking the magic from the realm itself, deep beneath the earth, from the very Source. That's the true reason behind the depth of his power."

There was a silence so deep, I could hear the wind whistling through the streets before battering in vain against the gray stone wall protecting my city.

"So, to stop him and save her, we just have to cut him off from that magic?" Rivan leaned forward, his lavender gaze resolute. "Or..."

"He was ready for you when you came for me," Tobias said matter-of-factly. "Fully powered up from the magic of the land and practically unstoppable. But the magic he steals drains quickly with each use." He started pacing, a heartbreakingly familiar gleam of determination in those two-toned eyes. "We need to cut Aviel off from the Source. Take the inevitable battle away from Morehaven and the seat of his power. If we can lure him away for long enough to take the castle and drain his stolen magic, he'll be helpless except for what he can take from others. Without the Source to draw from, he'll be stoppable."

Rivan frowned. "We'll have to wear him down enough to pull that off."

"And he'll be expecting us to attempt to rescue her," Yael added grimly. "For us to try to lure him away."

I closed my eyes, trying in vain to feel a spark of anything across our silent bond. Trying and failing to keep my growing desperation under control. "Then he'll be right. I'm not waiting to save her any longer. As soon as our rangers are ready—"

"I understand what each second could cost her, Bash," Rivan said quietly. "But if we go against him without a plan to separate him from the

Source, we entirely ignore what Eva did for us. He'll be ready for us this time, just as he was the last."

He was right. But I didn't care. Not if it meant waiting when she needed me.

"I'm *not* leaving her to face him alone."

Yael let out an exasperated breath. "The only thing that could make this situation worse is if you get captured right alongside her."

My shadows dug into my arms, and for a second, I saw the shackles that bound her in their place. "There has to be something we haven't thought of, some way to rescue her before—"

A message appeared in front of Yael in a flash of green light. She snagged it from midair and unfolded it, sucking in a sharp breath as she read. "There's been an explosion at Morehaven."

The air seemed to solidify in my lungs. With our bond blocked, she could be hurt, and I would have no idea. All I could see was the fear in her eyes, the fire surrounding her just as it had all those years ago as she fought to free herself…

"Breathe," Marin commanded. But her gaze wasn't on me. Tobias sucked in a measured breath in a familiar four-count I attempted to copy to slow the frenetic beat of my heart.

"I can't write back," Yael whispered into the blaring silence. "It could blow their cover."

I knew the explanation was for Tobias's benefit. Rivan, Marin, and I all knew and had used the codewords intermingled in a message that let its receiver know whether the coast was clear to respond or not. My pulse thundered as I stared at the spot in the air the message had appeared like I could will another update into existence.

There was a roaring in my ears. My friends' voices merged together in a distant murmur as my trembling finger traced iridescent letters atop the clammy skin of my palm.

You saved us, and now it's our turn to save you. Hold on, hellion.

CHAPTER 4
EVA

I *should have known Alette had fire magic.*

Maybe I should have been more surprised. But I could only look on with detached horror as Alette blasted the False King's quarters apart, a fireball tunneling down through the floor until the hole it had formed looked like the yawning entry to hell itself. Flames flickered at me from every surface, and it was all I could do to quash my terror as my mother's screams filled my mind, my two worst nightmares merging to become reality.

I was almost grateful Bash couldn't feel my distress as I lay rigid with fear, trying not to let my panic overwhelm me.

But there was a faint reddish glimmer around the bed that not even the smoke penetrated, the shield the exact shade of the fire I had seen in Alette's eyes. Shaking, I desperately focused on it, forcing my mind to calm.

I hadn't so much as breathed in before four guards, who must have been stationed outside the door, burst into the room. Alette, however, was gone, as if she had disappeared into the hole she had made in the earth. I pretended to be stunned as one of the guards unlocked the chain extending from my manacles to the bedframe, their metal now steadily heating around my wrists.

Sucking in a scorching breath, I readied to make my move. As two of the guards yanked me up by my forearms, I kicked out with both feet at the third in front of me. His eyes flared as he seemed to hang in the air for an extended moment. Then he fell into the flaming hole with a scream that was swallowed by the roar of the fire.

Taking advantage of their shock, I stomped on the foot of the guard to my left, yanking myself from his hold. The other guard roughly twisted my arm, trying to subdue me. I slammed the crown of my head into his face, feeling the gush of his blood on my hair as it cracked his nose.

I screamed as something hit me from behind. A stream of water turned to ice as it pinned me against the double doors. The fourth guard prowled forward, a sneer curling his lip. With all my limbs frozen in place, I could do nothing to stop him as he pulled that too familiar syringe from a small metal case and stabbed it into my arm.

A burning sensation spread like a fire through my veins. The flames swam concerningly.

No.

Past and present merged together. Smoke blurred my vision. And then I could feel my mother's hand on my chest pushing me into the void—

But there was no mirror to fall through. There was nothing at all.

CHAPTER 5
BASH

My heart pounded loudly in my ears; each beat a thunderous drum in my chest. Every instinct screamed at me to do something, even as I stood rooted to the spot, the room closing in around me as I stared at the space where the last missive had appeared.

"She's alive," Marin said firmly. "You would know if she wasn't."

I swallowed hard; my mouth dry. Ignoring the voice that whispered, *Would I?*

Tobias's hands curled into fists. "We can't just sit here and—"

Another flash, and Yael snagged a second message from midair, a frown crossing her face before her eyes met mine.

My heart caught in my throat. "Is she—"

"I don't think so," Yael said, her features tight. "Our people there say the prince—" She shook her head, correcting herself. "The False King is gathering a contingent. He's leaving the castle. Which means someone's doing our job for us." She frowned, worry lines etching her forehead. "We have to assume he'll take Eva with him."

"Whatever happened, it at least bought her some time if Aviel now needs to move her," Rivan said grimly.

"We need to let him get farther away from Morehaven so there's no chance he can quickly return to the Source when we do attack," Yael said, then winced. "Even if that means Eva's trapped with him longer. But if they're on the move, and in a hurry—"

"—whether anticipating retribution from us or running from whomever orchestrated that attack," Rivan interjected.

"Then this may work in our favor," Marin finished.

I forced myself to swallow my immediate retort. They were right—though I noticed Tobias looked no happier about that than I did.

Only when Marin took my hand did I realize it was shaking.

"So we wait," I gritted out, the word tasting like ash on my tongue.

"And recover," Marin said, giving Rivan a pointed look before spearing each of us with one in turn. "We'll all need to be at full strength when the time comes to save her."

"A full-frontal attack on Morehaven was never a good option anyway, even without the Source as a factor," Rivan muttered. "It's too well fortified. But if we can catch up to them in transit or find a way to head them off at their end location..." I could practically see the battle plans being devised behind his eyes. "This needs to be a surgical strike."

"Marin and I can make sure everything is ready to go when the time comes and keep an eye on any communication about where they're going," Yael said. My sister nodded in agreement.

I let out a long breath. "I'll see if I can find anything else about the Source. Something that could help us."

Yael shook her head, gently taking my hand. "We can do that too. You need to try to sleep and see if you can find her."

My mouth dropped open as I stared at my friend. I should've thought of that. Though being able to calm my body enough to sleep when my *anima* was the False King's prisoner—when she needed me—would be another battle entirely.

But if it gave me the chance to talk to her...

"And you two need to rest and heal," Marin chimed in, staring down Rivan before turning to Tobias. "Especially if you want your magic at full strength when it's time to fight."

He looked ready to argue but seemed to think better of it, giving my sister a short nod as a muscle flexed in his jaw. Yael helped Rivan to his feet, Marin on his other side as they brought him toward his room.

Tobias followed me, the stairwell painfully silent as we ascended. Tilting my head at the correct hallway, I led him to Eva's old room, which the house had long since magically cleaned. Though the scent of her on the sheets was long gone, it still held the memory of her within its walls, and I couldn't help my surge of longing for her. I saw her everywhere. I could almost hear the sound of her laughter, still feel the touch of her fingers against mine as we all gathered for breakfast at that table by the window. Could practically see the way she had looked in the moonlight— wide-eyed and far too stunning for having just woken up from a nightmare. The one about the monster who now held her captive.

Tobias was looking at me strangely. I realized I was just standing there, staring blankly ahead, my hands slowly clenching and unclenching.

"You love her, don't you?"

It wasn't a question, but I nodded, not trusting myself to speak.

"We'll get her back," Tobias said in a low voice, eyes glimmering with deadly promise.

"Or die trying," I swore hoarsely. "But I *am* s—"

"Don't apologize again. I heard you the first time," Tobias said coldly. "I may not like what you did, but if we're both going to be in her life, I can try to forgive you for it."

"If you need to take a swing at me first, I won't stop you," I said, meaning it. I dropped my hands to my sides, steeling myself in case he decided to take me up on the offer immediately.

Tobias stared at me before letting out a short, rough laugh. "I'd prefer to do so in a fair fight."

"We'll train together soon then," I promised, relieved to have moved past at least some of the discomfort between us. I walked toward the door just as my sister arrived, carrying a tray of food: a hearty-looking soup, boiled eggs, and some thick, crusty bread coated in butter, alongside a pot of tea.

Tobias was too thin, a testament to his treatment while in captivity, but to his credit, muscled in a way that showed he hadn't let himself languish. I pondered how lonely, how isolating it must have been exercising alone in that cell after an entire childhood of having Eva train at his side.

He thanked Marin as she set the tray down on a table, dunking the bread in the broth of the soup before tearing the piece off with his teeth like he was starving.

Marin looked at me expectantly, and I felt the muscles in my jaw flex.

"If anything changes, or if you find out anything useful, wake me," I demanded.

"Of course. Rest while you can," Marin ordered in return. I barely resisted my retort that it would be easier said than done, though she seemed to understand the sentiment from the look on my face. She poured a cup of faintly steaming tea from the kettle on Tobias's tray, holding it out to me. "This should help."

"Thank you," I said wholeheartedly, the scent of chamomile and mint filling my nose as I brought the cup to my mouth.

"If you find her, tell her thank you," Marin added softly. "And to give him hell."

She squeezed my hand before leaving the room. I stared at Tobias, who was now methodically polishing off the eggs one by one, his soup bowl empty. "Can I get you anything?"

The kettle shook slightly as he poured himself some tea. "No."

I turned toward the door.

"Tell me about her?"

The question wavered, like he hadn't entirely meant to say it out loud. But he hadn't seen his twin sister for more than a few minutes since they were seventeen. I could at least do this much for him.

Walking over to where he sat, I pulled the chair from the desk along with me. Turning it around, I sat with my arms folded over its back, facing him.

Tobias's hazel eyes were so like hers I felt a pang in my chest as he murmured, "The last time I saw her, my mother had just pushed her through that mirror."

"The mirror took her to Quinn's house. Who is also likely fae, by the way," I said, sharing some of what we had spoken about during those long nights in the woods. Tobias jolted slightly at the name, though his face betrayed nothing—like that mask he had worn for so long had slipped back into place. "After that…well, it took her a while to move on from what happened to your parents. What she thought had happened to you. But she went to college with Quinn, which likely saved her from Aviel tracking her down sooner. And despite everything, she never lost her fight, nor stopped her training. She went to college on a full fencing scholarship…"

Regurgitating the little details Eva had told me in the woods before we had known what we were to each other made an ache burn in my chest. But I forced myself to continue, weaving the story of her life since he had disappeared between sips of tea.

Tobias's face remained unreadable. But I took his silence as a plea to keep going. So I told him how we met—how it had been fate or luck that when the False Prince's lost *anima* had finally been found after so long with nothing to go on, Yael, Rivan, and I had been closest to retrieve her. The fight against the golem after Eva had returned to her hometown. The trek through the Faewilds and how I fell for her long before I realized what she was to me. How I failed her by doing the same to her as I had to him: by bringing Eva to the monster they had spent their whole lives unknowingly trying to escape. How smart she had been in Morehaven, trusting her instincts instead of the lie we had all believed. And how she had discovered Aviel's deception, leading to her imprisonment before she had managed to free herself.

Tobias sighed heavily. "If I'd only gotten back to her before my capture, she would've always known what Aviel was. He would've never gotten the chance to deceive her, let alone the rest of it."

I flinched, knowing the part I had played in Tobias's capture had made me every bit as complicit as his delay in returning.

"When I saw her in that dungeon baiting that guard to attack her—"

I nearly dropped my mug. "She did *what?*"

Tobias winced. "There was a guard who liked to prey on the female prisoners. I didn't even realize Eva was there until she lured him away from someone else." His darkening expression was a reflection of my own at the danger she had knowingly put herself in, even if I understood the reason behind it. "She succeeded. Goaded him into getting close enough for her to knock him out and take his keys. If she hadn't stopped to try to save me, maybe she would've made it out before Aviel had a chance to stop her." He shook his head. "Too many what ifs. What happened after that? All I know is Aviel ordered her brought to his bed."

His eyes flashed with a familiar white light. I flexed my jaw, trying not to remember the way that same light had entirely incapacitated us all.

"She got away," I whispered. "She outsmarted him and convinced one of his servants to help her flee. When I reached her, she was already in the forest."

The haunted look in Eva's eyes after her escape flashed across my mind.

And now she's right back there.

On instinct, I reached for that stagnant bond, cursing it for being blocked so thoroughly that I had no idea what she was going through. I finished my tea in a gulp that burned my throat, finally starting to feel the effects.

Tobias blinked, the only sign of his confusion. "How did you know to come for her?"

"I grew concerned when I hadn't heard anything from her. And then she dreamwalked to me." I blew out a breath. "I should've known far before then that she was my *anima*. It wasn't long after that she accepted the bond between us."

Tobias's mouth twitched in what might have been distaste. "I suppose we're going to have to learn to tolerate each other then."

I winced. "It took her a bit to come to terms with the bond too. Between what happened with Aviel, how he used the *anima* bond to lure her in, and how wary she was to open herself up in the first place..." My voice cracked, on the verge of giving out entirely. "He put that band around her neck, which blocks our bond. I can't...feel her. But there's another way to reach her, one that Aviel doesn't know about, provided she can see it."

I lifted my hand, my mother's quill shining where it wrapped from my pointer finger to my palm. A curl of feathers circled around the pulse point of my wrist.

His eyes fixed on its iridescence. "Can I write her a message?"

The hesitant question took me by surprise, but I quickly nodded.

"Even if she can't read it, it will let her know we're here," I said firmly. "I haven't been doing it too often in case someone's watching. But I know she'll want to hear from you if she can."

I held out my hands, extending my right pointer finger and my left palm. Then I looked pointedly to the left to let him know I wouldn't look over his shoulder at what he wrote. But he held out my palm to me when he finished.

It's me, sis. Eyes up.

"Our mom used to say that." Tobias dropped my hand, his voice choked. "Eyes up, stout heart. The only way out is through." Quietly, he added, "It's one of the last things she said to us, actually."

I nodded, unable to speak through the lump in my throat. But I swallowed it down.

"Get some rest," I said shakily. "Tomorrow, we're saving your sister."

CHAPTER 6
EVA

I groaned as I woke, my head pounding. It was too dark to see anything, though the world moved strangely around me in sickening jolts as my back slid against the cool metal beneath me. Pain radiated up my ribs as my side collided against something hard, threatening to pull me back into unconsciousness.

Of course Alette had disappeared before she could be of any help against the guards who had taken me, leaving me in the middle of whatever her half-cocked plan had been. But she *had* gotten me out of that room, and delayed Aviel from his plans for me, though I could only guess for how long.

Perhaps freeing me hadn't been her goal this time. After all, she had succeeded in getting Aviel away from the Source, if the sounds of soldiers and horses cutting through the darkness were any indication.

Now it was up to me to save myself.

Based on the rocking motion and jarring bumps, I was confined in the back of some sort of carriage as Aviel transported me to gods knew where. I shifted only slightly in case I was being watched...and felt iron biting into my wrists and ankles. I was shackled, even here in this new prison.

Aviel was taking no chances I would flee again.

Reaching out with my hands and feet as far as I could, I felt around the corners of my cage, even as my blood dripped down my arms from where new cuts sliced into old scars. It was a box, barely bigger than I was, my flexed fingers brushing against it where my hands were secured at my sides. The cold of the metal bit into my back, one shiver turning into another as it leeched away any sense of warmth.

Aviel might be taking me away in a coffin, but I refused to be reborn into the new life he imagined for me.

My own choppy breathing echoed loudly in the box—still so dark that for a second, I wondered if I had gone blind without realizing it. My head ached, my ears still ringing from the aftermath of that explosion. The toxin stubbornly clung to my mind, making my thoughts sluggish. My eyes strained, failing to make out even the faintest outline. Surely, if I waited long enough, they would adjust.

And yet, the unfamiliar darkness only deepened, the walls pressing in more tightly with every passing second.

Gasping, I attempted to suck in a full breath—trying to calm my mind, my heart. Trying not to think about how I was never going to escape this time. I yanked futilely against the shackles binding my wrists, only succeeding in making myself bleed further as the cold iron didn't budge.

There was a crushing weight in my chest, as if an invisible force was squeezing the life from me. Despite knowing it was the worst possible thing to do, panic tore through me like a creature clawing at my ribcage as it tried in vain to escape.

Breathe. I had to breathe.

But there was no air, the darkness suffocating. The rising tide of pain and fear and dread threatened to swallow me whole.

I couldn't *breathe.*

I could almost appreciate the sadistic irony. That the core of my own magic, the one thing that had always helped me breathe easier, was now being used to break me.

A bump in the road bashed me violently against the too-close walls of the box, and I bit back a cry, the claustrophobia setting in worse than before. I was dangerously exhausted, choking as the stagnant air seemed to solidify in my lungs, my broken ribs screaming as I gasped for breath. Staring into the rocking darkness as it ate me alive.

There was such silence in my heart—utter, awful silence, without Bash sharing it, the lack of him a torture all on its own. It blared like an alarm in my head, drowning me in his absence. Like, without him, some intrinsic part of me had stopped working. The gaping place where he should be pulled what was left of me toward it like a black hole ripping apart a star trapped in its orbit.

I was alone. Utterly alone…and I was scared, both of what was to come and how little control I had over it.

Misery crawled up my spine. With every lurch forward, the seams holding me together unraveled a little more.

Breathe, I heard my dad's voice say, and I clung to the memory. *Now hold. Breathe out. Hold again.*

Clenching my fists, I forced myself to heed that voice's command. It took far too long to do so in my clattering cage, but I finally managed one deep breath, then another, my breaths still too loud and shallow. Counting each second.

I breathed until the buzzing cleared from my head, trying desperately to center myself. Forcing myself to focus on anything other than my enclosed tomb. Centering myself on revenge.

Aviel had taken everything from me. I would make him regret it.

You need to make a plan.

My mother's strategy lessons came back all at once, her tone as no-nonsense as always.

Focus on the facts. What exactly do you know and how can you use it?

I reined in my breathing with single-minded determination. I knew that Aviel was the False King masquerading as his own son and had done so to gain the will of the people after his hundred-year war. I knew that he could leech magic from other fae, and from the very land itself, drawing it from the Source deep beneath Morehaven to give himself unstoppable power. And I knew he must be the true cause of the so-called curse in doing so.

Thanks to my brother, I now knew that the former High Queen had foretold that I would be her heir—and that was why Aviel had sought me out. And I knew Tobias was alive. Safe with my friends, and my *anima*... who was definitely blaming himself for my capture, even if I couldn't feel his self-flagellation through our silent bond.

I might not know where Aviel was taking me. But I *did* know if I could get my pointer finger to my opposite palm, I could write Bash a message and tell him where to find me...assuming I could figure that out myself. Because the shackles on my wrists weren't the same as before: there was nothing covering my hands this time. Perhaps Aviel had realized the band was enough to block my magic and had never noticed or understood what the silver quill on my palm meant. For now, my hands were forced apart, each attached to the box I was trapped in. That didn't mean they would be forever.

When I got the chance, I had to reach Bash. Relying on him getting to me in time couldn't be my only plan for escape, especially without any idea of how long we had been traveling while I had been unconscious, or if there would be a mirror that was safe to travel through when we arrived. Yet what else could I do, chained and magicless, beyond relying on my wits to find a way out once we reached wherever Aviel was taking me?

I lifted my head, grateful my collar hadn't been attached to the iron behind me, only for my forehead to kiss more cold metal. Something warm and wet trickled down my face. It wasn't until the saltiness touched my lips that I realized I was crying, silent tears tracking down my cheeks. A sob gurgled up my throat, but I choked it back in case my captors were close enough to hear me break. The urge to scream rattled around within me; tearing into my lungs, my chest suffocatingly taut as the walls pressed in again.

Blinking back the useless tears, I forced myself once more to draw a ragged breath. To pretend I was tightly wrapped in the darkness of my own making, even though the collar made that impossible.

I will endure this too. The only way out is through.

I repeated the words to myself, over and over and over as my prison rumbled forward, wincing as I was knocked against the cold metal sides of the box with each bump in the road. No...not just metal. *Iron.* That deadened, dissociated feeling reminded me of the cell back in Morehaven.

Though the iron's effect on my magic seemed like overkill with a band already on my neck and shackles around my wrists and ankles.

My stomach swooped as I felt a tingle on my palm. I craned my neck, contorting my wrist around painfully. Something warmed in my chest when I saw a familiar silvery glimmer breaking through the darkness.

You saved us, and now it's our turn to save you. Hold on, hellion.

Saved *us.* Cursing my inability to write back, I dug my fingernails into the rose-shaped scar on my palm, wishing I could confirm if that included Rivan. Would Bash even tell me if he had died? If I had failed to save him in time?

A drop of something wet ran down my palm over the words, and I realized my nail had drawn blood, a dark half-moon now cutting into Bash's silvery scrawl. I looked away, hoping it wasn't a bad omen—a sign that my fears were right.

I bit my lip as the message faded, returning me to the endless blackness.

Pins and needles spiked up my legs. Shifting, I methodically moved my limbs, welcoming the prick if only as a brief distraction. I needed to relieve myself, and I suddenly realized that that urge could help me, perhaps even give me an opportunity to escape before Aviel could get his hands on me. Heat stung my cheeks as I let my bladder loose, cringing at the warm, wet puddle spreading beneath me.

If it bought me time, I wouldn't waste the tactic to my own embarrassment.

Because they would eventually take me out of this box—and when they did, I needed to be ready. Preferably to find a way to escape before I got to wherever we were going, and Aviel chained me inside another bedroom.

My stomach lurched at the memory of him holding me down. At what I very well might not be able to stop this time. But I wasn't defenseless, not now, not ever. I had survived him this far. And I couldn't let myself worry about that until I had to if I was going to stay sane. Not when the only way I was going to get through this was from sheer will alone.

With one last jolt, the carriage came to an abrupt stop, my body thrown against the side of the box. I gasped aloud as my ribs screamed.

Were we at our destination? Or merely a stop along the way?

There were footsteps, and the echoing click of a lock. Then light. Blinding, blinding light burning my retinas like a reflection of Aviel's stolen power.

The lid screeched open. I blinked over and over as the world burned in the daylight, a shadowy figure leaning over me.

You missed your chance, I thought determinedly. *You missed your opportunity to find me defeated, if only for a moment. Now, I am ready.*

Aviel's face came into focus, though it might as well have come straight from my nightmares. His mouth twisted in a smug, sickening smile as I stared into those pale, depthless eyes, not bothering to hide my revulsion. How he had ever managed to pretend to be my intended, let alone the rightful ruler of this realm was beyond me. All I could now see in those dead eyes was the sort of murderous madness not so easily masked.

"Welcome home, darling."

Even the sound of his voice made me nauseous, a blatant antithesis to my reaction to Bash's ever-teasing drawl. But his nose wrinkled at the smell of piss, and I couldn't help a grim little smile.

"Get her cleaned up and ready as soon as we're inside," he barked to someone behind him. Silvius, likely. That weasel was never too far away from his master.

There was a turn of a key and a few more loud clicks, the noise reverberating down my chains. I barely had time to register my manacles falling open before rough hands dragged me upright. Sagging forward, my legs unused to standing after so long, I breathed through a rush of dizziness—those rough hands pinning my arms were the only thing holding me up. While I might now be in even worse danger, at least I was free of that godsforsaken box and the blood-crusted chains that bound me. And, more importantly, my finger could reach my palm. I just needed to wait for a moment when I was sure no one was watching.

One guard made a noise of disgust, either at the sodden back of my clothes or the acrid smell, but I acted as though I was too out of it to notice anything, keeping my eyes half-lidded. Though I couldn't keep them from widening slightly as I was dragged from the carriage and finally took in my surroundings.

We were in front of the drawbridge of a familiar bronze castle that glinted in the setting sun. Exactly as I saw it in my vision, down to the very last spire.

Aviel's words finally registered.

Home.

Soleara.

A snow-topped mountain loomed up behind the castle, its two magnificent blue-gray peaks dark against the sunset sky. We were surrounded by dark green hills, snow dusting the tops of towering evergreens, the still flowering plains covered in burnt orange and lush violets. There was a great rushing river underneath the drawbridge, as if the land itself had decided to form a moat, though the castle had obviously been built around it. A swift, cold breeze whipped around me as if welcoming me home.

There was something like hope in my chest at the sight of it, but I forced myself to continue my feigned dazed state as we neared the castle entry. Let them underestimate me as I waited for the right moment to strike.

"Bring her here," Aviel ordered from the doorway. "We need her blood to open it."

One of the guards shoved me forward, extending my hand in offering. Another pulled out a dagger. I cried out as it sliced across the rose seared into my palm. Aviel grabbed my wrist, and I flinched at his touch, unable to stop it. He pressed my bloody hand onto gleaming writing I could've sworn hadn't been on the enormous castle doors a moment ago. They immediately swung inward, though no one pushed against them, revealing an airy entryway.

A magnificent staircase crafted of polished bronze led down to the enormous greeting hall, where the agate flooring gleamed as though freshly mopped. The grand chandelier covered half the ceiling, adorned with hundreds of tiny bronze leaves that matched the aspen trees outside. Each leaf sparkled like gems in the light, as if an enchanted wind fluttered through its foliage.

I purposely staggered into the guard to my right just as he slid his dagger back into his belt, remembering all those times Tobias and I had practiced pickpocketing each other. As the guard lifted his hands to brace me, I fell against him, pretending to be too unsteady to stay upright. The other guards were distracted enough by our new surroundings to give me a split second to unfasten the short blade, sheath and all, from his belt. Before he had even pushed me away, his dagger was safely tucked into the back of my leather pants, hidden beneath my now untucked undershirt. I could only hope no one would look too closely at the slight bulge beneath the sodden fabric as the guards hauled me inside.

Suddenly I was five years old and sliding down the banister on the staircase. Tobias was at the bottom, his arms outstretched. But I was coming in too fast for it to end well, careening toward the edge—

Then my dad was there, pulling my brother back with one arm and catching me with the other as he swung us around from the resulting momentum. We ended up in a giggling pile on the floor, my father's booming laughter the loudest of all.

His laugh was still ringing in my ears as I was literally yanked back to reality. The tops of my boots skidded on the shining floor as I was unceremoniously dragged toward that very staircase before my feet bumped against each step. I let my head loll to the side to get a better look around while continuing my charade, holding back a gasp as I got a glimpse of the enormous mirror at the bottom of the stairs. It was a near replica of the one I had grown up with, bronze roses gleaming along its curved, filigree edges, though nearly twice as large. As we reached the top of the staircase, I was taken down an endless hallway and through the double doors of a large chamber.

The room was long and ornate with an enormous bed taking up the opposite wall. A colorful, forest-themed rug lay across the stone floor, somehow magically devoid of the muskiness of disuse. The mahogany armoire and matching bedside tables were bare except for a small bronze table mirror edged in gilded leaves. Pillars and portraits adorned the walls, and a bronze wax-dribbled chandelier hung from the high ceiling, its numerous candles flickering a hello. One wall was covered in arching windows, the vast mountains outside darkening into shades of blue in the waning light.

I might have thought the sight beautiful if my guards weren't chaining my wrists and ankles, hindering any hope of an immediate escape.

"Clean her," Silvius ordered from behind me to a pair of servants in matching silver shifts, both shivering in the cold of the room. He turned to me, the annoyance on his face plainly telling me he hadn't bought my act. "If you make any trouble, I'm sure your guards would be happy to bathe you instead."

I glowered at him. He held my stare for a second, sneering, before he turned on his heel, shutting the door behind him. I supposed I should be thankful he hadn't drugged me again. The servants began running a bath and lighting a fire in the hearth. One stern-faced guard patted down the bed before moving around the room, carefully inspecting each nook and cranny, the other watching me from the doorway, a flicker of flame in his open hand. His mouth curled in cruel satisfaction as I backed against the bed, the fear only too easy to call upon. When his gaze darted away, I surreptitiously slid my pilfered blade from behind my back—sticking it between the headboard and the mattress as quickly yet as silently as I could with my chains.

Once again, I was thankful for my less than normal childhood. My mom had turned pickpocketing into a game of dexterity and misdirection, where we would compete to see who could swipe the largest item from the other. Tobias always seemed to win, but I hadn't been a fan of being in second place and worked all the harder for it. I remembered one school day when we had switched off who could hide our car key in harder and harder to reach places—including the principal's back pocket, and the fake skull on the drama teacher's desk—while challenging the other to retrieve it.

There was a prickle on my palm. Tears pricked my eyes when I glanced down and saw my brother's scribble, recognizable even after all this time.

It's me, sis. Eyes up.

Hope blossomed in my chest at our mother's words written there—and that Tobias was safe, and with my friends. With Bash. I smiled despite everything at the mental picture of the two of them together, even with the reason behind my brother's animosity.

I saved them. Now to figure out how to save myself.

Before I could attempt to write back with my location, a guard motioned for me to walk forward, leading me to the already full bath. The servants walked up to me, one wrinkling her nose as she cut my clothing away, before muttering to the other to throw my bloody, soiled leathers directly into the fire. The guard watched from the doorway, but she averted her gaze in a rare show of empathy, though I couldn't be sure if it was at my nakedness or at the bruised skin it revealed. Proof of my torment at the hands of her master. I set my jaw as the servants' hands clasped around the bruises on my arms and legs, clumsily lifting me into the copper bathtub.

The water burned against my freezing skin, but I sank into it, letting it cradle my battered body. I leaned my head back, so its surface covered my face, washing any remains of my tear tracks away. The cold, impartial hands scrubbing and tugging at me had me grasping for the unreachable pit of power inside me, wanting to throw everything I had at them. To scream at them before I tore them apart with sharp spears of darkness. Because there was no way they didn't know *exactly* what they were cleaning me up for...and for whom.

But I knew I had to pick my battles. Especially when I couldn't afford to lose.

"Why are you helping him?" My first words in too long a while were strained, hoarse.

They ignored me, scrubbing and grooming me until my skin was bare and chaffed, and I had given up at not cursing at them.

I debated turning on them now, but I knew it would earn me a prick in the arm and me losing any chance of escape. So I waited, bristling with rage as they pulled me from the water. Even as they dressed me in a pale blue dressing gown, a painstaking process in which one guard unlocked, removed, and relocked my chains one by one while the other brandished his threatening ball of flame, all while leering at my half-naked body.

Refusing to shrink back from his gaze, I carefully noted that the female guard held the key to my chains, my eyes zeroing in on the small pocket of the waistbelt she returned it to after making sure each bond was secured.

But I didn't struggle yet, didn't make a move to escape knowing I would only have one shot at this.

"Chain her to the bed," the leering guard ordered. "I'll let him know she's ready."

Right as he closed the door behind him, I lunged, shoving the hard shackles into the remaining guard's face. Her knees buckled, her eyes rolling back in her head, and we fell to the floor. The servants cried out for help as I pretended to pummel her unconscious form while quickly palming the iron key to my locks, before carefully closing her pocket. The door flew open, but I was too busy shoving the key in between my cleavage as I turned away, the servants fleeing like I would attack them next. I was suddenly thankful they had dressed me in a ridiculously lacy bralette, as the key snagged in the fabric. I wrapped it around the lace, hopefully securing it.

I was already out of time. Rough hands grabbed my arms, yanking me back before smashing my face into the cold stone floor. Pain radiated down my side as I fought back, panic flaring through me as a knee rammed into my spine, holding me down.

Silvius tutted as he readied a syringe. "A shame you haven't learned to be better behaved for His Majesty. All in due time, I suppose. Perhaps I'll figure out a serum for that too."

His grip closed like a vise on my upper arm as I tried to twist away.

No...not again.

I couldn't breathe as I saw that syringe, a wave of dread shuddering through me. Silvius's lips curled into a smirk of satisfaction before he stabbed me with it. I gritted my teeth, looking away from the sight of the needle piercing my skin, trying to stop myself from hyperventilating.

Anger ignited within me as I felt the toxin dragging me into nothingness. I latched onto its flame, letting it burn away the fear and hopelessness even as my limbs grew heavy.

"I'm going to kill you," I promised, my words slurring as Silvius backed away.

I needed to write something, anything to Bash in the seconds I had left before I lost consciousness. To let him know where I was, that I was alive…knowing he would be frantically trying to find a way to save me. But the guard's eyes remained on me, tracking my every movement.

Then I froze as my gaze fixed on a large portrait behind the guard. The young couple was familiar even if I didn't recognize the crowns on my parents' heads.

Seeing them there, so young and lifelike, made my heart clench. It was strange to see their faces when all I harbored were the watercolor memories of them; the details fading with time. The picture I had of them in my head had grown more intangible over the years as I lost the memory of those little things that made their faces theirs, replaced by an amalgamation of the photos I had left behind in another realm. To see them like this, an image of them that was *new*, made my breath catch, a sudden wave of grief slamming into me before I could steel myself against it.

The world tilted as their faces went slightly blurry, intangible in a way that made it feel like I could reach out and touch them.

Desperately, I refocused on Bash as unconsciousness tried to take me once more. Maybe…just maybe, I could find him in the space between our dreams.

Bash's name was the last thought in my head as my mind finally gave into the drug coursing through my body. And then I was gone.

CHAPTER 7
BASH

I didn't want to fall asleep. Couldn't—not when every cell in my body screamed that I should be going after Eva, my heart bellowing at me to *go get her* without wasting another second. Torturing myself with everything that could be happening to her while I lay here, safe in my bed, because of what she had given up.

I couldn't stand it, being apart from her. Not for one more heartbeat.

But I knew there was a chance she would be able to dreamwalk to me if I could only get my body to cooperate. It took much longer than I wanted to calm my mind enough to fall asleep, despite Marin's tea. Especially as I kept startling awake every time I silently begged our bond to reach her, to find her.

Where are you? Where are you? Where—

I shouldn't have worried about the logistics of it. My mind found hers as easily as breathing.

Here I am, it seemed to say. *Come to me.*

I obeyed.

My eyes were still closed, and for a moment, I forgot about everything except the feeling of her in my arms. When I opened them, I found myself in a forest glen, sharing a familiar sleep mat. The night glittered strangely, and I realized that the trees surrounding us faded quickly into a deep, rumbling fog.

For a second, Eva stilled, barely seeming to breathe as she stared at me. "*Bash.*"

The way she said my name made my heart stop for a second, more of a sob than a word. Her lips found mine in an instant, so quickly I couldn't tell which one of us had reached for the other first. Then she was everywhere—her hands in my hair, her leg hitching around my waist, her body molding against mine.

Even forced apart, we still belonged to each other. But while I couldn't help but savor the taste of her, we didn't have time to waste. As if we had the same thought, we both pulled away, though my arms remained around her waist, her hands clasped around my neck.

"You insanely reckless—"

Eva's eyes flared. "I wasn't going to let any of you—"

"—selflessly noble, irresponsibly brave love of my life."

"...die."

She blinked as my words registered, and I held her tighter, wishing this was truly real.

"You saved us, hellion," I said, my voice raw.

Eva took a gasping breath. "But Rivan—"

"He's okay. Thanks to you."

Eva let out a sigh of relief that permeated throughout her entire body.

"Tell me what's happened," I demanded, my tone softly murderous. Unable to wait any longer for the answers that already haunted me.

Her teeth sank into her lower lip, and I knew she would try to hide the worst of it from me to spare my own feelings.

The rage roaring through my veins stumbled as I captured her face in my hands. "Please, Eva. I need to know everything."

"He hasn't touched me," Eva said quickly, as if realizing we were on a timer that could run out at any moment. "Not yet. He hasn't had the chance. Alette tore a hole through Morehaven...well, she sent a fireball through it."

I was also speaking swiftly, all too aware of the fact that we were on borrowed time. "Whether or not she realized the benefits of drawing him out, Aviel won't be able to draw power from the Source while we're away. It's—"

"Under Morehaven," Eva finished, and I stared at her in silent question. "She knows. Alette told me what it is. I assume Tobias told you?"

I nodded. "If he's already away from the castle, that can help us. We need him separated from the Source so we can drain his power long enough to defeat him." I stopped and then realized I missed an important question. "Wait. Where are you now?"

"Soleara," Eva said solemnly. "We just arrived. I'm not sure why we're here, but I think I might have a way out. Or at least the start of one."

My heart jolted at the certainty in her voice. "I should have realized you'd have a trick up your sleeve. But—"

I lost what I was saying as I heard the clank of chains. My heartbeat faltered, then stopped altogether when they appeared, binding her as they were conjured from the waking world. Her wrists were rubbed raw under the shackles, and I realized, with a mounting need for vengeance, that there was also a pair tearing into the skin of her ankles, hobbling her. That band was still around her throat where I watched Aviel place it during those achingly horrible last moments together.

We both knew what the waking world shoving its way in meant. Our time together was already dwindling.

It was only when I felt her body stiffen in my arms that I realized she was letting out a wordless cry of pain. Quickly, I loosened my hold on her, unable to breathe past the sudden pressure ballooning in my chest as I took in her injuries. The left side of her face was shadowed by a dark bruise, cuts that should've been healed by now were barely scabbed over without her magic. Yellowing bruises blotted her body from our fight with Aviel, newer purple ones covered her arms and legs. She winced as she breathed in, her ribs likely broken. But what made me go blind with a primal rage was the bite mark on her neck, freshly bleeding over the scar already there.

Claiming what was mine.

"He needed my blood to open the gates to Soleara, Bash. I think we're here for a reason, that coming north was Aviel's plan all along, even if

Alette made him move it sooner." Eva's words ran together. Like she needed to get them all out before she was taken from me again.

"Then we'll find out why," I assured her, even as a cold wave of dread washed over me. "And I'll be there soon."

"Be careful," Eva whispered, her arms tightening around my neck.

"I'll always come for you, hellion," I vowed. "Just hold on."

Gently, I held her against me as if I could somehow keep her here. I could feel her shaking as I kissed her forehead, her cheeks, her hair. Her fingers dug into me as if trying to anchor herself to me. To stay with me as long as she could.

"Bash—" Her voice cracked as I felt her become as impermanent as the fog around us. "No matter what happens…"

"I know," I whispered. "I love you too."

"Bash…"

Tears started to roll down her cheeks, the fear in her voice cutting me to the bone. I cursed under my breath as I tried to wipe them away only for my thumbs to go right through them.

"Stay with me," I pleaded.

The tiny noise she let out broke something inside me, my soul splintering as she faded away. My arms slipped through the empty air in front of me before I slammed them to the forest floor.

CHAPTER 8
ADRIAN

The entire room seemed to be looking at me except for her.

After the High Queen's pronouncement, the hall had exploded into an uproar—our parents loudly exclaiming about how fate had ensured this meeting, my mother already planning the royal wedding of the century.

No one but me seemed to notice that my betrothed had gone cold as ice, pulling away when I attempted to hold her hand once more. And she remained that way as the High Queen demanded we all stay here in Morehaven, the bonding ceremony to be held while everyone was gathered.

"Estelle…"

She didn't so much as look at me, though a muscle in her jaw clenched before she turned away, slipping through the crowd as I tried to follow. One of the queen's courtiers stepped in front of me, blocking her hastily retreating form from my view.

He cleared his throat as I tried to step around him. "Let me show you to your room. Preparations will need to be made quickly of course."

"Of course," my mother said, coming up to my side and patting my arm.

I craned my neck, looking for any glimpse of my soul bonded who had somehow disappeared into the crowd in mere seconds. "I need to talk to—"

"Plenty of time for 'talking' later," my father said with a loud guffaw. My mother pursed her lips.

"As I was saying," the courtier continued. "You have been granted rooms here until the ceremony."

He prattled on as he led us into a sparkling white hallway teaming with people, many too inebriated to walk in a straight line. A few clapped me on the back, shouting words of congratulations that I barely heard, wondering how I was going to find her in this maze of white marble and shining silver.

A throat cleared beside me, breaking into my thoughts. "Your room."

From the way the courtier was looking at me, it wasn't the first time he had said it. Hastily, I nodded my thanks, pressed a kiss on my mother's cheek, and, after promising to help my parents plan in the morning, closed the heavy door behind me.

As soon as it shut, I leaned back against it, my head hitting the wood with a thud. My *anima*. I had finally found her. She was smart, quick-witted and even quicker with a blade in her hands, effortlessly charismatic, and so beautiful I hadn't been able to look away from her the moment she had walked out on that balcony.

The thought that she was unhappy about our union in any way brought my delight crashing down around me.

I barely looked around my room before leaving it, heading back into the now-darkened hallway. There was a buzzing under my skin, my throat dry as I swallowed. I knew I wouldn't be able to sleep with her reaction on my mind. Not until I got to the bottom of it.

A few drunken revelers were still stumbling away from the festivities, some mumbling toasts as they recognized me. I nodded serenely, even as the hallways blended together. For some reason I thought I would be able to...find her. Like a magical golden arrow would point me to her room. Instead, I was only getting hopelessly lost and increasingly frustrated with myself, my elusive *anima* feeling more and more like a mirage.

Take a breath, I told myself. *Count each second. Breathe out. Now count the same.*

Without the crowding of my thoughts and the frenzied pounding of my heart, I felt the faintest of tugs. Not within the castle, but outside it. My hand trailed against the wall next to me as I rounded the corner, the feeling getting stronger.

I didn't question that pull, just obeyed it. Perhaps our bond would take me directly to her if I just got out of my own head.

Silently, I snuck through the now empty ballroom, the formerly festive scene now faintly ominous in the cool moonlight. An enormous, ostentatious mirror covered in shining silver feathers rippled inquisitively as I passed, following that tug to the balcony outside.

I was entirely unsurprised to see Estelle standing in the very spot we had first met, wearing a pale silk nightdress that made me want to fall to my knees. It fluttered gently in the breeze; a matching silk robe had fallen from her shoulders to reveal the gooseflesh on her upper arms. Her golden eyes met mine. My heartbeat picked up so quickly I pressed a hand against my chest as if to keep it in place, its frenetic pulse urging me onward.

You've finally found your anima.

Her eyes narrowed. "What are *you* doing here?"

"Looking for you," I replied baldly.

Estelle's mouth twitched in annoyance, whether at my presence or how easily I had been able to find her. Her obvious reluctance slowed my stride.

"I wouldn't lie to you, Estelle." I drew out her name, loving the way it felt on my tongue. Dying to get another taste of her mouth. My gaze dropped to those rosy lips unbidden, and I saw the answering flush in her cheeks creeping up her elegant neck.

She flinched almost imperceptibly, taking a small step back. I froze, taking another deep breath as I forced myself not to run to her.

Whether it was me, or who I was to her, something about this scared her. Based on our easy banter prior to the discovery of our bond, I had a feeling it was the latter. But we could work through whatever it was that was stopping her from giving in to this—to *us*. I just needed to get her to talk to me.

"Come on," I said, reaching out my hand. "My turn to take you somewhere."

Estelle eyed my hand like it was an asp waiting to strike. "Just because you're my *anima* doesn't mean I can trust you."

"I'm pretty sure that's *exactly* what it's supposed to mean," I retorted wryly, even as something twisted in my chest.

Her eyes flared, then fell to where my hand was still reaching for her.

"Come on, Princess," I chided, trying to fall back into that easy rhythm from before. "It's only fair. But if you get there and want to turn around, I'll return you to your self-proclaimed spot and then leave you be. I promise."

Estelle stared at me appraisingly, the silence so long I was sure she was about to say no, until...

"Fine."

She ignored my outstretched palm but took one step toward me, that fire in her eyes making my blood heat. I swallowed against my dry mouth, not even daring to smile should it scare her off.

Dropping my hand to my side, I discreetly rubbed my damp palm against my thigh as I turned toward the exterior stairwell that I had noticed earlier. Before she could change her mind, I started walking down to the gardens, silently praying she would follow. I was grateful she couldn't see my face as I heard her footsteps behind me, or hear my soft, shuddering sigh of relief as she hurried to keep up.

"I thought we'd take a walk, Princess," I drawled, only turning to look at her when we reached the bottom. "Get to know each other a bit."

She followed as I stepped onto the cobblestone trail. Night blooming jasmine lined the path, and I took in a deep inhale, letting its sweet scent calm my nerves.

"Why?"

"We're bonded until eternity, and you don't wish to learn more about me?"

Estelle paused. "And if I don't want to accept the bond?"

My stomach dropped, but I forced myself to keep walking, trying not to make it obvious how much that question terrified me as I carefully asked, "Is there some reason you're so against finding your soul bonded?"

She flinched away from my gaze, then threw her hands up in exasperation. "I don't need another person to control me. And maybe there are a few things I want to do before being tied down in matrimony."

"Do you think I plan to stop you?" I came to a stop so quickly I put my arm out to steady her as she almost crashed into me. She stiffened at my touch, and I knew she felt the crackle of energy that passed between us before I let go of the bare skin of her arm. "Perhaps you'll even allow me the honor of tagging along."

She stared at me, a bit dumbfounded, and I found myself lost in those ethereal eyes—hazel with flecks of gold that encircled her pupils like a crown. I drank in the sight of her, forcing myself to drop my hand back to my side, even as I ached to touch the chestnut curl that perfectly framed her heart-shaped face.

"I'm not sure where you got the idea that an *anima* bond was a prison sentence, but I happen to be quite happy about the thought of accepting it with you," I said, acutely aware of how vulnerable I was making myself. "Or I *was*."

"Of course you are," Estelle sniffed, brushing past me to continue down the trail.

It took a second for her words to register, having been distracted by the view of her sauntering away.

"What's that supposed to mean?" I caught up to her in a few long strides, resisting the urge to spin her around and make her look at me. "Of course I'm happy about finding the person who I get to spend my life with. Doesn't everyone dream about getting to know the other half of their soul?"

So why aren't you? I bit the words back, knowing my hurt feelings wouldn't help me here. But if she meant what she said, and she didn't accept our bond...it was unthinkable.

She stopped walking, warily crossing her arms as she looked downward. "And the fact that I'm the Solearan heir has nothing to do with it?"

There was something heartbreakingly soft behind her question. An uncertainty she was failing to hide.

Gently, I lifted her chin with my forefinger, bringing her eyes to mine.

"What exactly are you implying? Because you seem to forget I wanted you before I knew anything about that." I swallowed hard. "Or do you find me so unfit to rule at your side?"

Estelle blinked, looking at me strangely. "That's not—It's not about…"

"Then what's it about, Princess?"

Her eyes narrowed. "Where shall we live? Do you plan on taking me back to Esterra?"

I laughed. "I'm the second son of the Eastern King, and you're the Northern heir. I'll take you home with me if you wish, but it's entirely up to you." I took a small step toward her, closing the distance between us, just as she took a matching step back. "If it means spending our lives together, I'll follow you wherever you want to go."

"So your plan is to come to Soleara and…" She cut herself off, looking upset at herself.

And suddenly I realized what this was. The reason she was pushing me away.

"I'm not planning on usurping your throne," I said in a low, urgent voice. "Though I think the best partnerships are the ones that learn to share the load—who work together. And while I'd like to rule by your side, it's your people. Your kingdom. Even though I hope they might one day be ours."

She gave me such a startled look I was certain I had guessed right.

"I thought…"

"Are Solearans so puritanical that a female in charge is such a strange thing, even with a High Queen as the leader of our realm?" I smirked at her. "Because Esterrans have no such idiocy. Or if they did, my grandmother sorted it out long before I was born."

"My parents have always been…protective. The High Queen told them at my birth that…" Estelle trailed off, shaking her head. "We lost my mother before she could produce another heir."

I frowned. With heirs determined by power, not birth order, was her magic not…strong enough? Somehow, I couldn't imagine that. Especially not when our every touch seemed to spark with whatever lay beneath her skin, like her magic was trying to reach out to mine. But if that wasn't it, what had the High Queen told her parents that had scared them so?

"My father has been committed to finding me a strong match, a strong alliance ever since," Estelle continued softly. "Someone he felt could lead."

That careful admission, and what it implied, set my throat on fire. "I'm very well aware you can rule Soleara all by yourself, Princess, and I barely know you." Though I tried to keep the anger on her behalf out of my voice, I only somewhat succeeded. "How your father can't see that is beyond me. Or perhaps he's afraid. I knew how strong you were even before you bested me with your sword. And even if I didn't, I have no desire to control you, now or ever." I held out a hand, pleading with her silently to take it this time. "But maybe you can find some use for me, anyway."

Her eyes fixed on my outstretched hand for an endless moment, like she could see the heart I held out to her in offering.

Something swooped low in my stomach as she took it.

CHAPTER 9
EVA

A tear trickled down my cheek as I kept my eyes squeezed shut, trying in vain to prolong my dream—that stolen moment with my *anima*. But when I heard someone moving nearby, my eyes flew open, my muscles tensing for a fight.

There was a servant tending to the fire in the hearth, but she wasn't looking my way, nor was the new guard at the door. My neck stung, and when I gently pressed against it, my fingertips came back bloody. Aviel must have been here…must have bitten me sometime after I had been knocked out, when my drugged sleep was so deep, I hadn't woken.

I couldn't stop the shudder going through me at the thought of how helpless I had been, unconscious and chained to his bed as he left that mark behind. I was still clothed, but he had undoubtedly put his hands on me. Could have…I cut off the thought with a harsh exhale. There was nothing I could do about what had already happened. Only fight now that I could.

With a jolt, I realized that my shackles were still only locked around my wrists, with nothing covering my hands. Aviel was apparently confident that my collar was enough to suppress my magic.

Or maybe he didn't want me to hide a syringe in the bulb this time, I thought with grim satisfaction.

I was still in the same blue dressing gown as—from what I gleaned from the daylight streaming in—last night. Chained to the headboard by the shackles on my wrists, a chain securely looped around a hardwood spire at the top of it, though with enough slack to comfortably move around, at least for now. My ankles were still shackled together but weren't attached to anything but each other. There was a chamber pot next to the bed, and I smirked, knowing it was a warning not to try the same thing twice or face the consequences.

Having no desire to face the indignity of being scrubbed down again, I relieved myself, my chains going taut as I sat down. As I hoped would happen, the servant turned her back to give me privacy, and the new guard uncomfortably averted his gaze. Carefully, I extracted the key to my shackles from under my arm, wincing as they pulled against my bloodied wrists even as I thanked my lucky stars it hadn't fallen or been found when Aviel visited me. I closed my hand around it just as another guard walked into the room and came toward me.

He looked bored, like whatever he was about to do was just another chore on his to do list. I wanted to scream at him, demand to know why his first thought wasn't to help me, but I clenched my teeth, knowing it would only be wasted breath. He gestured for me to move back, the flash of flame from the guard behind him a silent threat if I disobeyed. Without breaking eye contact, I crawled backwards onto the bed as a servant scurried forward to retrieve the chamber pot.

I tensed as the guard reached the edge of the bed. A tight smile curved his lips, then he grabbed the chain that attached to my wrist shackles, pulling it taut. I yelped as my hands were painfully yanked above my head. But I kept my hand clenched as he refastened the end of the chain to the side of the headboard, the key digging into my palm as I twisted my wrist to keep it hidden.

The guard finished fastening my chains as I glared at him, silently vowing vengeance. Even as my panicked, stuttering breaths gave my fear away.

I knew what it meant.

I'm running out of time.

A wave of fear swelled inside me, threatening to turn into a flood. I didn't dare give in to it, forcing myself to quell the rising panic in my chest, the powerlessness clawing up my throat. My nails dug into the scar on my palm as I sucked in a slow breath, then let it out in a careful cadence.

Waiting until my guards turned away to do a sweep of the room, I slowly opened my hand, moving the key from where I could feel its shallow indent on my palm to between my trembling fingers. I rattled my chains, but the guards didn't so much as turn around before they left the room, the servant following quickly behind them.

Aviel was coming. I only had seconds.

Each turn of the lock felt like it echoed in the silent chamber as I swiftly unlocked one of the shackles around my wrist, then the other. Before I could attempt to free my ankles, I heard footsteps approaching outside the door. Quickly, I made sure the shackles on my wrists appeared closed, praying Aviel wouldn't be looking for the same deception a second time.

The click of the door opening made me flinch.

Aviel stood there, dressed in gold and white, the vision of every fairytale prince except for the sadistic glee in his eyes. Despite my plan, my heart thundered like it was attempting to escape at the sight of him— at the way his gaze trailed down my body as if he owned it.

I forced myself to meet his eyes, trying not to betray the fear that threatened to consume me.

He was obsessed with me in the sort of way the worst sort of monster felt they had a right to another. But Aviel only loved what I could be for him; he was incapable of wanting me in a way that wasn't intrinsically linked with what my magic and birthright could do for him. Still, *he* thought he loved me, and that delusion was one of the few defenses at my disposal, albeit a fragile form of power.

The door closed behind him with a bang that made me jump. His lips curled into a smirk, that slight movement somehow sucking all the air from my lungs, his pale eyes devouring me as I focused on holding myself together.

"Eva, darling. I hope you slept well. You look lovely waiting for me."

I hated that his voice sent a shiver of fear down my spine. My nails bit into the rose on my palm as I clenched my fists against the shaking of my hands, not wanting to give away just how much he scared me. While I debated remaining silent, I wouldn't let him think me cowed, even if a part of me desperately wanted to shrink away; wanted to scream aloud at being forced into this situation yet again.

I wasn't used to not being able to defend myself. To lay in wait, desperation mixing with my panic yet again. Weaponless beyond my own defiance...and the dagger I had hidden just out of reach. I was looking forward to using it to inflict even a fraction of the pain and terror he had caused me.

"I think the box was better company."

He laughed, cold and cruel. I tried to act as though his very presence wasn't causing my lungs to falter in my chest.

Breathe.

"That can be arranged." Aviel smirked as he unhooked the dagger from his belt, laying it on a dresser across the room. My mouth twitched—at least he knew better than to practically hand me a weapon to use against him. "But we have some unfinished business first."

He walked toward the bed as though savoring the time it took to get to me—a predator stalking its prey. And I knew the bastard knew exactly how terrified I was beneath the bravado. My heart beat in terrified anticipation as he reached me.

When he pulled himself over me, it was all I could do not to struggle too hard. To keep my hands in place so as not to give the game away. To wait for the right moment, even as nausea simmered in my stomach.

Stout heart, I reminded myself as I tried not to tremble.

I remembered telling a drunk guard in a dungeon not too long ago about the sort of worthless, dickless type of bastard it took to force someone against their will. And I knew I needed to keep this monster talking—too distracted to notice the crack in the iron around my wrists hinting at my freedom. Too caught up in his fixation of me to notice the trap I was laying for him.

It felt strangely fitting using a trick I had already used to escape. If he hadn't been so arrogant, so assured of his own victory, then maybe he would have learned to double check my bindings.

He would learn not to underestimate me.

"I can see you waiting to strike, darling," Aviel purred, his hands roving my body as his leg shoved between my thighs. I jerked back into the bed but couldn't wriggle away enough to do anything other than encourage him, based on the feral gleam in his pale eyes. "Don't think that I'm fooled into thinking you'll keep the promises you made to me to save your little friends. Besides…what, precisely, do you think you can do to stop me, when all of you put together failed to keep me from getting exactly what I wanted?"

I refused to think about how he had forced them down, bleeding and prone and suffering. But he hadn't killed Rivan, hadn't prevented us from freeing Tobias. And I wouldn't let him win.

"If you think I'm going to stop fighting you, you'll be sorely mistaken."

Aviel laughed coldly. "And where would be the fun in that?"

My chest constricted to the point of pain as his fingers played with the collar, his thumb dipping into the hollow of my throat.

"I told you already that you've always been mine," Aviel said softly. "Even if it takes another century, I will own you, body and soul. And you will learn to stay willingly at my side."

The only way out is through, I repeated in my head, willing my mother's strength to be with me now.

"And what makes you think I will ever be willing?" I lifted my chin as I stared him down. "I know exactly who you are. My brother told me *everything*. And now he's going to expose you."

Aviel waved a dismissive hand. "It doesn't matter now. Once I go through the Choosing with your power, I will finally become High King, and there won't be anything anyone can do to stop me then. Even if your brother tells the whole realm exactly who I am, and what my powers really are, I *want* them all to know exactly whom they bow to." He stroked my cheek, and I suppressed a shudder. "All my life I've had to take what I wanted. You, my darling, are no different."

His eyes darkened as his hand flattened at the base of my neck. I jerked away from the possessive touch, but there was nowhere to go.

"I almost kept your *anima* to force your obedience. But I far prefer to break you to my will myself." Aviel's fingers tightened savagely, and I couldn't help my hiss of pain. "And when I break you, when you learn you are mine, we will remake this world together." He smiled cruelly. "It's almost time now."

"You're insane."

Rage contorted his features. Then he pressed into the band blocking my magic, choking me as he pushed me down, his hand squeezing like a vise. He barely seemed to notice I was writhing underneath his grip.

I steeled myself to pull my hands from the shackles and retrieve my stowed blade. But something sharp and slithering slid along my mind, my...magic. Trying to get *in*—

A scream tore from my throat, then another. There was a tearing inside me, an inexorable tug that felt like Aviel was slowly wrenching out my spine. Like my very consciousness was being flayed, and I was about to break right open. My body shook in agony as a black essence trailed from my eyes, my mouth, my nose, merging together to flow into Aviel's hand on my throat.

Aviel stared into my too wide eyes as I screamed, those pale irises turning black as he sucked my darkness into himself. Licking his lips as the last of it disappeared, he gently stroked my collar before releasing it. Even so, I could barely manage one shuddering breath in—my exhale a choked, strangled sob.

"Gods, how I've missed your screaming."

I was shaking so violently I was worried my wrist shackles would fall open. Had he done this the whole time I was captured and drugged back at Morehaven? I didn't know if I would have noticed while unconscious, not with the collar blocking my magic. Though he had never used my darkness against me.

Aviel leaned forward, and I flinched as he ran his lips along my cheek —barely able to manage even that movement, my entire body still stiff and unmoving. His fingers found my neck, and, with a click, I realized with shock that he had unlocked my collar.

For a half-heartbeat, I thought my magic was about to come back. I strained to reach my darkness, seeking it in the chasm inside myself—

There was only a nauseating nothingness where it should have been, that well of power entirely drained. I thought I might be sick.

My stomach lurched as Aviel pulled back a bloodstained finger, and I realized my collar must have been somehow bound with his blood. Even magicless, this was it: the moment I needed to get away.

If only I could move.

"The only reason I left your *anima* alive at all," Aviel said with silken menace, "was so he can feel *exactly* what I do to you through your bond." He leaned in, slowly drawing out every word. "As I make you *mine.*"

As if summoned by his words, I felt that bond flare back to life without the collar constricting it. And I knew Bash could sense it too.

Aviel had only freed me from my collar so that my soul bonded would feel my terror, my helplessness as he raped me, my magic no help before it could replenish.

But I had never been helpless, even before I found out what I was.

I reached for the bond like a lifeline, feeling Bash's turbulent mix of confusion and hope like a bubbling wave...then his frozen horror trickling down my veins as he sensed the fear and pain I was trying to control. His dread wrapped around my chest like a vise, his panic for me compounding my own.

Aviel leaned forward, his lips brushing my breast before sucking against my neck. I let out an unintended cry of pain when he bit down on the fresh wound he had left there before forcefully kissing me. The taste of my own blood lingered on his lips as he drove his tongue into my mouth, rough and claiming. Groaning into my mouth as one hand roved down my body, his touch proprietary as his fingers pinched my nipple so hard I gasped.

I couldn't do this again. Couldn't endure it, especially with my *anima's* helpless desperation breaking me inside.

But I knew he could feel my resolve, too, even as I shoved everything away, slamming a hasty wall down between us as I forced myself to focus.

"Your blood tastes delicious," Aviel said in a throaty whisper.

The entitlement in his words spurred me to action. Shaking off my stupor, I pulled my hands from my bonds in one sharp tug and punched him squarely in the face. Blood spurted from his nose, and his pained shriek echoed throughout the chamber.

Reaching behind me, I grabbed my plundered blade, leaving its scabbard stuck between the headboard and the mattress as I stabbed downward in one smooth movement.

Aviel was too fast, despite the shock and the injury, rearing back with superhuman reflexes. Instead of hitting the artery I had been aiming for in his neck, I merely sliced a line down his chest, cutting his shirt wide open. I got my knees under me, my ankle shackles yanking painfully as I lunged toward him. But Aviel gripped my wrist with unnatural strength and twisted—the blade clattering uselessly across the floor.

There was a flurry of movement outside the door, but no one entered. I fervently hoped the guards were chalking up the sounds of my attack to a different kind of struggle.

I tried to twist away, but Aviel backhanded me so hard my vision went black for a split second. On reflex, I used the momentum of the blow to roll off the bed, my ankle chains forcing me to land awkwardly on all fours. Faster than I could track, Aviel was on his feet before me.

"Don't you understand what we could be together?" Aviel's head tilted to the side like he was truly perplexed at my reticence. "With my power and your birthright, we will rule both realms. I will give you the world, darling. You only need to give in to me."

"Never," I spat. "I'm not yours, and I *never* will be."

My head swam as he stalked toward me. Blood ran from my nose and my split lip, the taste of iron coating my tongue. I rose unsteadily to my feet and took an involuntary step back, stumbling as my chains stopped me from retreating any further. Prince Aviel might have been about my age, but the False King had been around for far longer. And he was a trained fae warrior, who had survived and succeeded this long for a reason.

And I was trapped, bleeding, and magicless. Something like despair shot through me, and I felt Bash's answering echo of it. I wished I could hide this from him. But I forced myself to push it all down, blocking Bash out as best I could. Becoming the weapon I had been trained to be.

I wouldn't give in. Not ever.

Gathering my strength, I braced my feet apart despite the chains rattling between my ankles. Then sunk into my heels, raising my arms in a long-ingrained fighting stance. Settling into my battered body as I readied myself for this fight.

Aviel laughed mercilessly. "You truly think you can stand against me?"

"Oh, I doubt you know how to win without stealing someone else's magic to use against them, you *little* leech," I said with a mocking hand gesture, my thumb and pointer finger moving an inch apart.

If he used magic, I knew I wouldn't last long without mine. But maybe I could bait him into a situation that would give me a chance. No matter what, I wouldn't give up without a fight.

A slow smile formed on his face. I suppressed my own as he raised both hands, rudely mimicking my stance.

Thank the gods he's arrogant enough to take the bait.

"I have hundreds of years on you, foolish girl," Aviel scoffed. "But I can't say I mind this particular form of foreplay."

I tasted bile in my throat. Aviel took a step toward me. Before he could use either of our magics, I threw myself at him, swinging out to strike him in the chest with my forearm. He dodged, but I was already moving, rotating my body into my uppercut. My fist connected with his chin with a satisfying thud, the blow reverberating up my arm. Aviel's head snapped back. I kicked at his side, but he caught my leg with a snarl, wrenching me toward him before throwing me against the wall.

I let out a small cry as my head slammed against one of the pillars. My vision blurred at the impact, my injured ribs screaming. I let my eyes flutter closed as if stunned, and Aviel stepped forward to press his advantage. Coming to life, I reverse scissor-swept his legs, using my knee to tackle his forward leg and taking him to the ground.

Before I could make another move, my own darkness slammed into me, shoving me down. Bands of my magic wrapped around me, holding me prone as I struggled in vain. Slowly, Aviel got to his feet, calmly straightening his shirt as he placed his foot onto my broken ribs. I screamed as he pressed down, white-hot pain tearing through me as I tried to twist away. But there was nowhere to go.

I should have known it would only be a fair fight until I had the upper hand.

"You will learn to remember your place," Aviel said with one final press that left me gasping.

"Fuck. You."

I stared daggers at him as my own magic turned on me. Tendrils of darkness forced me around like a doll, twisting around my torso to pull me upright before shoving me back onto the bed.

He advanced, smirking at me. "I'm going to enjoy this."

CHAPTER 10

BASH

My dreamwalk had ended in a panic, every fiber of my being yearning to go to her. I had no more patience for waiting. Not when I could still hear Eva's gasp of pain in my ears, the vision of her bruised cheek so fresh in my mind. Not when she was with *him*.

Waiting would be the death of me...or her.

My friends were already gathered around the round wooden table in the war room, grim-faced and fighting leathers donned, dark circles under their eyes betraying their similar lack of sleep—if they had slept at all. But despite their obvious weariness, the determination in their gazes was a testament to their unwavering resolve. The low din of voices and sharpening swords as my rangers gathered in the great hall leaked in through a crack in the door, Marin's voice cutting above it to shout orders. They had amassed a small arsenal of weapons as I slept, more of my people joining their contingent with every passing minute. The enormous rectangular mirror loomed over it all, its polished surface reflecting the controlled chaos around it, rippling as if in anticipation.

My fingertips drummed on the ancient grain of the oak table, worn smooth from years of use, a silent witness to the strategic deliberations of more than one war. Rivan had gathered as much as he could about Soleara's defenses as soon as I reported the reason behind Aviel's journey north—which wasn't much. He looked markedly better, the cuts from Aviel's magic mostly faded. His neck was still mottled with faded bruises, his voice less hoarse as his vocal cords healed. Tobias was as helpful as he could be, roughly sketching the schematics and surrounding area of the castle, as the two of them pored over them, looking strangely conflicted as he did so.

He had the same look on his face as Eva did when she was hiding something. The same tightening of that familiar, downturned mouth, the carefully smoothed expression. But I knew I wasn't the right person to press, even if we had reached a reluctant truce.

I was only half-listening as Tobias explained the magic that had kept Soleara hidden, flipping through an ancient tome my sister had found in the castle's library about the Source. It was hard enough to stay focused on the tedious, faded text, my every thought returning to Eva. Especially as the book had only yielded more conjecture about the magic of the land and its bond with the High Queen or King, rather than anything that could actually help her.

"It was a precaution to keep the enchantment while the False King ruled. To keep Soleara protected and out of sight." Tobias swore. "That Aviel even knew where to look..."

Marin frowned. "Perhaps it was your blood. If it breaks the magic hiding Soleara, then when he took yours to find Eva..."

Tobias grimaced. "Then he's known about it all this time."

I paced, wanting to walk right through the mirror Tobias had described in the main hall of the Solearan castle and run to her.

"Don't you dare," Rivan rasped.

I had walked to the doorway without even realizing it, my eyes fixed on the rippling looking glass. Whether Rivan had seen the look in my eye or had simply seen the direction I was going, it was obvious he had tracked my thoughts.

"I was just—"

"Don't bother lying to me." The glower on my brother's usually amused face was enough to stop me in my tracks. "Besides, we don't even know if their mirror is blocked."

If the gate was closed to us, our other option was to go by horseback on a too-long journey. Far too late to stop Aviel from doing what he wanted to Eva. Especially if we dragged an army along with us.

To check would be to engage the magic of the mirror, and if someone was watching it from the other side and saw the warning of the ensuing ripple...

"Then give me a better option. Every second we waste—"

Rivan slammed his fist down on the map in front of him, the outburst so unlike him I jumped. I knew that half his frustration was from wanting to follow me through—to save her by my side.

Yael's eyes widened in surprise. "Rivan..."

"We all want to get her back," he said, slowly uncurling his fist. His fingers shook slightly. "To save her the same way she did us. But we only get one chance to do it right, otherwise, we're just failing her all over again."

"If it *is* open, I can hold them back long enough for our people to follow and make it a fair fight."

Rivan got to his feet, hands scrunching the map as his fingers curled. "Fair until Aviel arrives, and we're back where we started with no one to bail us out this time."

"It's our only chance of getting to her quickly. Otherwise—"

Rivan swore under his breath. "We still need a way to drain Aviel's power before we rush through that mirror. Or it'll be just another trap."

He was right. Side by side, we could maybe fit four at a time through the mirror at once. Stealth would be useless when walking into the bright entry of a palace. Even with my magic, it would be a slaughter, and that was if we could even make it through.

"We'll have help," Tobias cut in. "We just need to get there. I've already let the Solearans know."

All eyes snapped to him, though Yael spoke first. "I thought you said the Solearans went into hiding when your parents left."

"Yes and no," Tobias muttered. "But I don't have time to explain now.

They're ready to move on my word. To provide a distraction when we need them to."

"And they're close enough to do so?" At Tobias's nod, Marin raised a brow. "How many?"

Tobias shrugged slightly. "Enough. Based on the numbers your spies saw leaving Morehaven."

"This still only works if we can get through the mirror," Rivan grumbled. "If not, we won't get there quickly enough to change anything."

Tobias grimaced. "I have another way in if we can't. But we'll be wasting time."

Rivan's gaze sharpened on him. "One you didn't think to mention before?"

Tobias's brows drew together. "It wasn't—"

"Not now, boys." Yael put a hand on her hip. "Main mirror plus the Solearan distraction, then Tobias's backup route if it doesn't go to plan."

Nodding, I rested my hand on my sword. "Then let's—"

I staggered on my feet. Then my heart stopped beating entirely as I realized I could feel Eva again, the bond between us flickering to life without preamble. If I could feel her, she must have gotten the collar off. But there was no sense of relief, nothing that felt like freedom or safety. Cold sweat broke out on my skin, my grip tightening around my pommel.

Everyone's eyes sharpened on me, my sister stepping forward as though her magic could fix whatever ailed me.

"I can feel her," I gasped out, my blood roaring in my ears. Then sucked in a breath as her fear ripped down our bond, as sharp as a blade as it sliced me apart. Whatever had caused this, she was far from safe. Her terror was multiplying despite the grit of her resolve.

Marin grabbed my arm. "Did she escape?"

"She's...I think she's fighting." I choked as pain tore through our bond, the feeling of it so excruciating I nearly dropped to my knees with a howl. My horror hardened into molten rage. "She's fighting him."

Panic that wasn't my own skittered down my spine paired with a resilience that made my chest heave. My stomach lurched sickeningly as I realized I was about to feel my *anima* be forcibly taken by another. My hands balled into trembling fists, my fear mirroring her own. I could barely think, barely breathe—about ready to fly out of my skin.

Tobias stood, shaking with rage. "We need to help her."

There was another wave of stinging distress and pain so acute it was all I could do to stay upright. For a heartbeat, I felt the suffocating sensation of being caged...of being trapped. Then there was only her fear paired with the heaviness of resignation.

"We go *now*," I growled, unable to fathom failing her yet again. "We have to try. I'm not leaving her to fight him alone. My magic can block enough of whatever's waiting for us there to get enough of us in. Then we take down whatever we find when we get there. And get her out."

Rivan's gaze fixed on me. "And the False King?"

"I'll distract him long enough for the rest of you to save her. Maybe between our forces and the Solearans, it'll be enough to defeat him this time."

Yael stared at me. "You'd better mean we. *We'll* distract him."

"She won't forgive you if you trade your life for hers," Tobias murmured, his gaze shrewd. "Or those of your people."

"And he'll just use you to get to her," Rivan added, understanding dawning on his face.

"I can deal with that," I countered stonily. "As long as she's free."

Rivan was already shaking his head. "*Bash—*"

"We don't have time to come up with a better plan," I gritted out. She was blocking the worst of it from me, I realized, as a muted shock of pain still reached me despite her efforts to keep me out. "He won't kill me, not when he can use me as leverage."

"Absolutely not," Marin hissed. "You don't know that. He very well might."

"And it'll give the rest of you and her enough time to figure out how to weaken him," I stubbornly continued.

Yael grabbed my arm, fear and concern warring on her face. "You're not thinking clearly. You need to slow down, block her out, and think this through."

"If this were Marin, you'd already be through the mirror," I said accusingly. Shadows streamed from my fingertips, prying away the hand holding me back.

Her jaw flexed. "We're not letting you trade yourself for her. Eva wouldn't want that."

But I was already walking toward the door, my heart pounding so hard I thought it might tear through my ribcage and find its way back to her. "This isn't up for debate."

CHAPTER II
EVA

I couldn't breathe as my darkness tightened around my neck. Couldn't *move*, even as something inside me frantically urged me to fight—a compulsion I could no longer distinguish as Bash's or my own. Aviel drove his fist into my gut, crowing with mirthless laughter as I doubled over with a cry.

I let Aviel think he had me as I slumped back onto the covers, closing my eyes as my own magic choked the air from my lungs. Let him think he had already won, if only to give myself leeway for one last shot.

And then he was on top of me, flattening me to the bed with the full force of his body. Dots danced in my vision as he wedged a leg in between mine, parting my thighs. My body was growing heavier, my struggles for breath weaker, even as my fingers searched blindly for a way out. With a cold laugh, Aviel licked the wound he had bitten on my neck, one hand reaching down to lift my dress.

I felt his arousal press into my hip, just as I felt what I had been searching for pushing against my side, inches from my hand.

Springing to life, I kneed Aviel in the groin with every ounce of strength I had left. He fell against me with a cry. Before he could do anything, I snapped the cold metal band in my hand around his neck with a loud click, my blood still dripping from the clasp.

His eyes went wide as his magic slipped from his hold—that collar taking from him exactly what it had taken from me.

I didn't give him a chance to recover. Before he could call for help, I snapped my neck forward, slamming my forehead into his face. His nose crunched against me as it broke, his blood splattering down my awful sheer dress.

Aviel slumped on top of me, unconscious.

Gasping for breath, I pushed him off me, scrambling away. I half fell off the bed, crawling on my hands and knees to where the key to my ankle shackles had fallen next to the footboard. There was a splitting sensation in my side where I was sure I had rebroken a rib. My head throbbed, and the room swam concerningly, paired with a sickening sense of déjà vu.

Scooping up the key, I staggered over to a pillar on the far side of the room. Needing to put as much distance between me and Aviel as I possibly could, as I tried to suck down a breath.

I slid down the pillar to free my ankles, turning the key with shaking hands. My heart pounded in my throat, Bash's blaring panic only exacerbating the issue, but I pushed all of it aside for now.

Because I needed to kill him. To stop him from hurting anyone ever again.

My injuries were worrying enough that I dared not climb out the window. Aviel had been too overconfident to call for help, but someone would come soon, and they would have no qualms about killing me when they found him dead. I could perhaps get past a few of his guards, but in the state I was in...

Was I willing to sacrifice myself for a better world? I already knew the answer as I pushed up to stand on shaking legs, leaning against the pillar for support. Resolutely, I reached for the dagger he had foolishly left in the room with us.

Then froze as my fingers brushed its hilt, a familiar black diamond shining up at me from a polished silver handle etched with intricate, latticed designs. This was *my* dagger. The twin to the one I had returned to my brother. The blade I had thought was lost in that fire. The one Aviel must have stolen that night after he had murdered my parents.

Pure shock hit me as my fingers tightened around it, that diamond seeming to warm in my hand as my thumb brushed against it. But I felt less panicked, less vulnerable with it back in my hand.

Perhaps it was fitting that this blade had returned to me just in time to use it to end the one who had taken it from me in the first place.

Bash's face floated to the front of my mind, and I glanced down at my hand, suddenly at a loss at what to say. I wondered what my trembling acceptance felt like over our bond as my eyes moved from my scarred palm to the sharpened edge of my blade, trying to find the words for goodbye.

Two hands reached around my chest from behind and yanked. I screamed, railing against the arms holding me, but they immediately let me go.

"You must be quiet, Princess," said a low, frantic voice.

For a second, I was stuck with how similar this moment was to when I first met Bash not so long ago in a shadowy doorway outside my apartment. Before I believed in any of this—magic and fae and realms beyond my own. Before I even knew who I truly was.

I lifted my dagger in warning, the slender blade seeming to pulse with an inner light even in the dim. But her hands were already raised in surrender.

The fae in front of me had short, silvery hair that contrasted beautifully with her dark skin tone. A slashing scar ran across her cheekbone, barely missing her right eye before slicing through her arched eyebrow. She was smaller than me, but from the look on her face, the strength of her arms, and the cache of weapons at her sides, I immediately knew better than to underestimate her. She took a step back, her deep brown eyes imploring, but it was easy to see she was here to help, especially since she had saved me from that room.

I realized that I could see Aviel through the wall behind me, still slumped forward on the bed. Not the wall...I was looking *through* the portrait next to the pillar where I had stood just a moment before.

It was almost funny that my old fear of being pulled through something had just helped save me for a second time, even if it had been a glamor and not another mirror.

Her voice cut through my thoughts. "We need to—"

"No." I took a step toward the bedroom, my hand tightening around my dagger. "I can end this right now."

Loud voices rang out from the hallway. I swore under my breath as Silvius rushed into the room, a contingent of guards in tow. He cursed when he saw his king, the servant quickly running to Aviel's side.

"Search the castle and the surrounding grounds," Silvius screamed. "She can't have gone far."

There was a rustle of wind, and I turned to see a note disappear from my companion's hands in a whirl of air magic. I opened my mouth to demand an explanation, but she raised a finger to her lips, then held out her hand with unspoken intention. I stared at it, silently berating myself about missing my chance to finish this. Then my hand clasped around her own.

With the surefooted steps of someone who had taken this path many times, she led me into the dark. My ears rang as I followed her deeper into the tunnel, powering through a wave of dizziness as we reached steps that spiraled downward—not daring to make a noise beyond my own ragged breathing. A faint light glowed at the bottom, barely illuminating our way.

Each step was a struggle, and I leaned against my companion more and more heavily the farther we walked. She gingerly took my elbow to steady me as we came to a stop, and I swayed on my feet.

It felt like forever before she finally spoke, her voice barely a whisper. "We saw you being brought into the castle and knew who you were even before they used your blood to gain entrance. Only a member of your lineage can open the castle doors due to the protection your parents put on it before they left to the mortal realm." Her eyes scanned my face, but I could only stare at her, my adrenaline crashing in the aftermath of my escape. "Our people haven't been able to access it for years. Even before your brother's capture, he was careful to leave its protections in place. I had just made it through the old passages when you almost backed right into the portrait hole...though I'm a little sad I missed you taking down that piece of shit." She gave me a small smile. "I'm Pari, by the way. Welcome home, Your Majesty."

My throat was raw from screaming but I managed to whisper, "Eva," though she obviously knew that already. "There's no need for titles. But you should know that Tobias is safe. We freed him."

Her lack of surprise told me she already knew. "He was the one who warned us of your arrival. Though when the False King's army breached the castle's wards like they weren't even there, we knew he had you. But Eva—"

I tripped over my feet as our descent reached a long, musty hallway. Two fae stepped out of the shadows, and I flinched back, though I should've known that Pari hadn't come alone. They were smiling as they walked forward, their lean, muscled forms silhouetted against the faint light of the glowing tunnel. One was dark-haired, one light, both moving in unison as they hurried toward us.

The glint of their blades on their belts sliced through the darkness. One held up a hand and a small fireball appeared, reflecting against the flaxen skin of his razor-sharp cheekbones and his shoulder-length black hair. His companion's shockingly white hair was pulled back with a leather tie, and I had to suppress a shudder at the pale blue of his eyes. The fact that they were both warriors was obvious, even without the collection of blades adorning their muscled bodies.

As one, they dropped to a knee.

"All hail the rightful Queen," they said in unison.

"You seem to have me at a disadvantage," I said dryly, grateful that their eyes didn't linger lower with the sheerness of my dress. Though perhaps they were just distracted by the blood still drying on my face. As if reading my thoughts, the dark-haired one took the cloak off his back and offered it to me. I tugged it on gratefully.

"I'm Akeno," he said softly. "And that's Thorin."

"We're here to take you home to your people," Thorin said, his deep voice gentle. "To the heart of the resistance."

CHAPTER 12
BASH

My hand shook as I reached for my sword, the cool hilt against my damp palm doing nothing to halt my nausea. Sweat dripped down my back as I started toward the mirror, battle-ready soldiers coming to attention as I passed. Most were already lined up, too well trained to show their nerves even as the impending countdown hovered thickly in the air, charged like the moment before a lightning strike.

A flare of Eva's terror broke through her hold, her pain twisting my insides like it was my own as I strode toward the enormous silver mirror. I could barely breathe as my own panic overwhelmed me, even as I tried my best to master it—only too aware of how my emotions could affect her in return.

Turning to face my people, I drew my sword as Rivan, Yael, Marin, and Tobias took their places by my side. "We don't know what we'll find on the other side of this, so be ready. But leave the False King to me."

Lowering my voice, I murmured to Tobias. "Let the Solearans know it's time, whether they're ready or not."

I thought my heart might beat out of my chest as I felt her desperation giving way to…was that relief? Tobias held up a pre-written piece of parchment, his hand starting to glow with pure white light.

"Wait," I gasped.

I reached out through our bond, but all I could discern was a strange sense of regret. The fear was gone, that light, floating feeling definitely a wave of relief.

Had she fought him off? Had she gotten away from him? Was she hurt?

Not knowing what was happening was going to drive me mad. I wrote her yet another message, praying she would see it.

Eva, please, I need to know what's happening.

Marin took my arm. "Is she..."

Tobias snatched a message from midair that appeared in a bubble of wind. "She's okay," he rasped. "The Solearans have her. She's safe."

My relief was so potent it brought me to my knees. But I shouldn't have been surprised that Eva had managed to escape. I had long since realized there was very little she couldn't do.

Rivan's eyes met mine as he helped me up. "How did she—"

Tobias shook his head. "That's all I know."

She's safe. I could feel her on the other side of our bond, calm, despite the bite of her pain, her very presence soothing.

Marin cleared her throat, addressing the surrounding soldiers. "This gives us more time to prepare, but that doesn't mean we won't be needed sooner than later. Spread the word. And get some food and rest while you have the chance."

I shot her a grateful look as they bowed in unison, unable to find the words to even thank her. A clamor once again overtook the hall as swords were sheathed and armor removed. Staring at the rippling mirror before me, I breathed in, counting each second. Trying to find a semblance of calm while I waited impatiently for her response, distantly aware that my friends were discussing the next steps around me.

But there was a tingle on my palm, a message waiting there.

I'm safe. I got away. Don't go near Soleara, they're searching for me.

I could feel everyone's eyes on me as I wrote back as quickly as I could. Yael stepped closer, craning her neck to read my response over my shoulder. Tobias's gaze bore into the back of my hand.

Hellion, I'm going to need more than that. Where can I find you?

Iridescent words appeared on my palm as I held it up for her twin to read.

Tell Tobias the gate will be open to you soon. He'll know the way.

CHAPTER 13

EVA

Bash's worry for me was a ringing bell in my head as the tunnels started steeply climbing. That and a persistent shiver on my palm finally made me realize there was a message waiting for me. I looked down, trying my best not to trip over my feet. Pari reached out and gripped my arm as I staggered. I couldn't blame her for not letting go.

Eva, please, I need to know what's happening.

My heart sank as I realized I had left Bash with only my tumult of emotions after my struggle with Aviel. Cursing under my breath for not thinking about sending an update sooner, I stopped to jot a message on my blood-stained palm.

I'm safe. I got away. Don't go near Soleara, they're searching for me.

His relief was palpable, airy, yet almost painfully hesitant through our bond.

Hellion, I'm going to need more than that. Where can I find you?

I glanced up at my companions, who were watching the exchange curiously.

"That's new," Pari said dryly. "A magic I haven't seen before."

"My *anima*," I explained. "Bash."

"The Southern King," Akino said, without a hint of surprise.

I watched as his lanky scrawl faded from my hand. "He wants to know where to meet me."

As we rounded the corner, the narrow tunnel suddenly gave way to a vast cavern. Its walls were adorned with the same gleaming blue stone that I remembered from my escape from Morehaven, its soft blueish hue bright enough that I could see almost the entirety of the massive space, even in the gloom. Stalactites hung from the ceiling like the jagged teeth of some ancient beast, casting distorted shadows on the ground below.

My adrenaline was fading, my injuries flaring with renewed strength, and I stumbled, breathing hard. Pari gripped my arm tighter. She obviously had already realized how hurt I was, our frantic pace having long since slowed to a crawl.

"Tell Tobias our gate will be open to them as soon as we can," Thorin said, taking my other elbow. "He knows the way."

I relayed the information as succinctly as I could. "And *where* exactly are we going?"

The three exchanged slight grins.

"The North has been an Allied stronghold ever since the beginning of the war," Thorin said matter-of-factly. "The False King's supporters never gained a foothold here because we have long been wary of outsiders, our people hidden away even before the war began...though that hasn't always been to our benefit. While the castle has wards to keep unwanted visitors away, the city itself is protected both through magic and—well, you'll see in a moment."

We had reached two gigantic wooden doors hewn directly into the rock of the earth itself. They swung open with a groan of hinges as though they were expecting us, and I squinted into the sudden light after being underground so long. We were inside an enormous crater, and I realized with a start that I could see the tip of the mountain's majestic blue-gray peak not very far above us. A wispy cloud blew past the edge of the chasm, briefly obscuring the summit from view.

Colorful buildings nestled into the rocky mountainside painted a vibrant scene against the rugged backdrop, their lustrous copper roofs gleaming in the sunlight streaming through the clouds. My gaze was drawn to a towering wooden house with intricate copper accents built by a substantial natural lake. Despite the biting chill in the air, the lake remained unfrozen. Steam rose from its surface, and I realized it must be a hot spring.

An entire city—a hidden oasis—was built into the mountain. No wonder we had walked so far uphill.

It all seemed so familiar, so much so that it somehow immediately felt like home. Sometimes it seemed odd how quickly I had gotten used to this realm, like I was never meant for the other one. But this renewed sense of belonging was on a deeper level, as if I had always been meant to be right here.

Pari laughed delightedly, and I realized my mouth had fallen open.

"Soleara has always been here," Pari said with a knowing smile. "The castle is just a figurehead. The whereabouts of our people have long been a mystery to outsiders, as we have kept the secret of this location for generations. Only a chosen few were allowed inside our sacred mountain." I didn't miss her frown at that. "When the False King targeted you, your parents bound the castle so it could only be entered by their blood before they spirited you and your brother away to the mortal realm. That magic made the rest of Agadot forget about us as our people stayed here in our hidden kingdom. Though our spies and soldiers found ways to be useful to the resistance effort."

We slowly walked forward through the cobblestone streets. I leaned heavily on Pari and Thorin, unabashedly using them to remain upright, my feet dragging with every step.

"When the False King tricked the realm into believing his son had vanquished him, we remained here, working against him," Akeno added. "Trying to buy you and your brother time to come into your power as we waited for your family's return. But after the loss of your parents, we were unable to find you with the protections guarding you until your brother showed up in our realm."

We came to a stop in front of the giant wooden house, and I let out a weary sigh of relief.

"There's a healer already waiting for you," Akeno said with a smile.

"And there's a mirror here? A gate?"

They all nodded.

"While most mirror to get here, those tunnels are an ancient trail system some say are as old as the mountain itself." Pari cocked her head to the side. "Perhaps it knew they would one day be needed to save you."

CHAPTER 14

ADRIAN

Estelle's fingers threaded through mine, tugging me forward. She didn't look at me as she silently led me toward the pond. And I didn't say a word as I followed her under the curved branches of a willow by its shore.

She turned slowly, the moonlight refracting from the calm waters glistening on her cheekbones, lighting up those stunning, gold-flecked eyes.

"You don't have to fight this," I whispered, the world around us so still, it felt like we were under an enchantment. "I'm not trying to use you. And if you never want me to help you rule Soleara, I'll be content to spend my days learning all the ways to make you smile, make you laugh…and make you moan, if you'll let me."

The corner of her mouth quirked up in an almost smile, and I reached up my hand without thinking, cupping her chin as I traced the edge of her lips with my thumb.

My heart leapt when she didn't pull away.

"So, what *is* it that you want then, Princeling?"

"You," I said baldly. "I want you to give me a chance. Give this *anima* bond between us a try before denouncing it to crueler intentions." My hand traced down her jaw, wrapping behind her neck as my fingers threaded in the waves of her hair. "I won't rush your decision. And if I need to tell the High Queen herself that we need more time before the bonding ceremony, then I will, if that's what you want."

Her eyes widened. "There's no way—"

"This is your decision," I said firmly. "And if it's not me, I'll find a way to accept that too."

"It's your decision too," Estelle whispered.

I gave a small shake of my head. "I already know what I want. I don't need time to deliberate because there's no question that it's you." My fingers stroked the back of her neck as her lips parted in surprise. "I know you don't know me yet, but somehow, I feel like I've known you forever. Like I've always been waiting for you. And I think you feel that too."

Those flecks of gold in her eyes glinted as they narrowed. "Bond or no, I have no intention of losing my head just because I met my *anima*."

But I felt her shiver as my other hand traced down her back. Felt the way she arched into me as my hand wrapped around her waist, drawing her flush against me.

"We'll see about that."

I leaned forward, my mouth brushing hers in the barest whisper of a kiss. Over before it had even begun—waiting for her response before giving in to the desire to take her exactly as I wanted to and never let her go.

She sucked in a faint breath. Then her lips crashed onto mine, frantic and rough and claiming. Like she'd been holding herself in check and was finally giving in to reckless abandon. I lifted her up, and she immediately wrapped her legs around my waist, her nails digging into my back like the remaining room left between us was as intolerable to her as it was to me. I backed her further under the willow, away from the prying eyes of any guards that might happen to patrol above us. Pushing her against the rough bark of its trunk as I feathered kisses down her neck, my hand moving up her exposed legs to where the hem of her nightdress had ridden dangerously high.

"Maybe I've always been waiting for you too," she whispered against my mouth so softly, I almost missed it.

I stilled as hope flooded me. And then I was kissing her more feverishly than before, her soft moan into my mouth unlocking something primal within me.

Estelle's fingers found the buttons on my shirt, tearing them open. I groaned aloud as they moved to the ties of my pants. Catching her fingers in mine, I brought them to my mouth to kiss them as I whispered, "Wait."

She jerked back, but my hold on her hand tightened.

Her legs slipped from my waist, her expression shuttering. "Do you want this or not, Princeling?"

I let out an incredulous breath. "First you don't want me, now I'm not getting naked fast enough?"

Her eyes flickered. "If you don't want me to—"

I was already shaking my head. "Of course I do. I just didn't want to go too quickly for you. We have a lifetime together…we don't have to rush into tonight. And I want this to be perfect for you." My mouth twitched. "We could even find somewhere more comfortable than a tree and the ground."

She gave me a slow smile that made my heart skip a beat. "And if I prefer it?"

Light glowed at her fingertips, and I felt my mouth drop open as tiny balls of it drifted upwards, resting against the willow's leaves. Estelle's face was illuminated in a soft, silver glow, the gold of her eyes gleaming like a crown around the dark dots of her pupils. Tiny flecks of light danced around us like fireflies, a few landing softly in her chestnut hair.

Her magic was Celestial—and with that kind of control, I knew it was a force to be reckoned with. My own magic itched to be released, to meet and match her own.

"Estelle—"

I let go of her hands. Instead of pulling away, she reached toward me, entwining her arms around my neck. When her lips met mine again, I lost all semblance of thought as she pressed herself fully against me, nearly climbing me in her insistence. I hoisted her up, and she wrapped her legs back around my waist, bringing her core against the straining bulge she had elicited.

She gasped as I brought us to the ground, still cradling her against me. Then she stilled as she realized her back didn't touch the mossy earth.

A blanket of darkness covered it, cushioning us as I brought my lips to her neck.

Estelle gasped. "You're—"

"Celestial too? Don't act so surprised, Princess."

She sighed as I hungrily worked my way down her chest. If the taste of her skin was this intoxicating…

I wanted to devour her. To taste every single inch of her. And to take my time doing so.

Her hips lifted, and I answered instinctually, moving against her. She let out a moan that rearranged something vital within me.

Suddenly I was desperate to get her to make that sound again.

"Tell me you want this," I rasped, grinding my almost-painful hardness against her. "Tell me you want me, *anima*."

Estelle's eyes met mine, something almost fearful behind that lust-fogged gaze.

"I—I want to believe you," she whispered.

I pulled down the neckline of her gown, drawing her peaked nipple into my mouth. She gasped and I grinned, before doing the same to the other.

"Not good enough," I murmured, hearing her sharp inhale as the warmth of my breath fanned across her breast. "If you accept the bond though, you know you'll be able to sense my intentions."

"And be bound to you for eternity," she added disdainfully, even as her fingers threaded into my hair.

Strands of darkness lifted her dress, baring her to me. The smallest scrap of lace covered her, and I worked my way down to it hungrily, kissing and tasting a path down her stomach. Finally, I reached my goal, placing an open mouth kiss against the warm lace that made her hips jerk.

"You say that like it's a bad thing," I drawled against her, delighting at the way she squirmed—her hips unconsciously moving toward my face.

"I'm just…not sure…what I—"

I moved back, looking up at her. "Do you want me to stop?"

Slowly, she shook her head. "No."

I hooked my fingers under the lace lining either side of her hips, then pulled it down, exposing her to me entirely. Our eyes met just before I slowly licked up her slit, groaning at her taste before doing it again. Her head fell back with a guttural moan.

"Tell me what you want," I said, as one finger slid inside her teasingly, then another as she clenched around me. Gods, she was so wet, so tight—

"I don't know...what I..."

"Yes, you do," I insisted. My tongue found her center, and her hips bucked as I lazily circled that sensitive bud.

"*Adrian*—"

I jolted at the sweet sound of my name on her lips—it was the first time she had deigned to say it. I resisted the urge to beg her to say it again, even though I knew I could spend the rest of my life trying to get her to say it *exactly* like that.

"Yes, Princess?"

"More...more of that."

I smiled, then obeyed. My fingers curled beckoningly as I pressed down harder with my tongue with each movement. She writhed against me, and I hardened further at the thought of that responsiveness once I was inside her.

My tongue pushed down, and she came apart, gasping as shudders ran through her body. I kept going, my fingers still moving inside of her as she clenched around me, drawing out every shiver of pleasure before she went limp and sated.

I pressed a kiss against her inner thigh. Estelle's eyes opened, and she gave me an almost shy smile before leaning toward me. Her lips brushed mine, then she deepened the kiss, her tongue chasing the taste of her pleasure.

Her hand pressed firmly on my chest, then she pushed me back against my darkness, impatiently yanking down my pants before straddling my thighs. I swore under my breath as her hand wrapped around my length, my hips involuntarily bucking against her grip.

She leaned forward, her bare sex tantalizingly close. But she hovered there, seemingly unsure as her wide eyes met mine.

My hands found her hips, bracing her. "You don't have to do anything you don't want to," I promised. "We can stop right now. And if you want to wait—for this, for the bond, for all of it—I'll be here when you're ready."

A small smile twisted her lips, the way her mouth curved heartbreakingly perfect.

"I don't want to wait."

She dropped her hips, sliding along my length. When she brought just the tip of me inside her, I let out an almost embarrassingly loud groan of need.

So tight, so hot, so...

She winced, and I stilled. "Are you...have you done this before?"

A blush spread across her cheeks, so inviting it was all I could do not to taste it. It was hardly an unusual thing for our kind to have sex before a bonding ceremony, the act of pleasure even encouraged after reaching maturity. But the innocence of her blush confirmed what I had already guessed.

"Not...exactly, no." She slowly worked me in another inch, and my fingers clenched against her hips, trying to keep myself still. "Puritanical, remember?"

She slid down further, and I struggled to form a coherent thought even as some primal part of me roared to bury myself inside her for eternity. "Estelle..."

"I might be new to this, but I'm pretty sure you're supposed to move," she said with a sinful smile.

I shrugged. "It's my first time too."

Her wide eyes met mine. I was hardly inexperienced, but this final boundary...maybe I had known somehow that there was only one person I wanted to be inside of for the rest of my life. As if she had read that thought behind my eyes, Estelle smiled. I lost my breath as she seated herself fully, biting the side of my cheek to keep this from ending far too soon at the rightness, the unimaginable urge to claim her and keep us joined like this forever. But her pained gasp brought me back, quieting the roar of my need. "I—I don't want to hurt you. Are you—"

"I'm sure," Estelle breathed. "Please?"

I rolled my hips against her, gently testing. She let out a small moan, but it wasn't one of pain. "You never, ever have to beg, Princess."

She leaned forward, kissing me as she lifted herself, then sank back down. Holding onto her hips, I pulled back slowly, then thrust all the way back in. She whimpered against my mouth, making hot, breathy sounds that I focused on drawing out again and again.

I flipped us over in one smooth motion, making her gasp at the new angle. Her eyelashes fluttered; her hair spread out like a dark corona, strands of my darkness playing with the curls of her hair. She was so, so beautiful, staring at me, entirely unguarded for once. Biting the inside of my cheek, I concentrated on going slow—on making this first time just as perfect as her.

Estelle yanked against the nape of my neck, her breathing ragged as she pulled my lips to hers. Then my hand slipped between us, my thumb pressing down, and her entire body shuddered.

"Adrian... *Adrian*—"

My control broke, and we came apart together.

I fell against her, barely having the wherewithal to keep my shadows in place as I panted against the curve of her neck. Leaving a soft kiss behind her ear, I carefully slid out of her, wrapping my arms around her as I tucked her against me.

My heart twinged at the way she was looking at me. Then her expression closed, and I fought the urge to wince as I watched that wall stack back up behind her eyes.

"You don't need to be afraid of this," I murmured. "I would never want you to regret me."

Estelle stiffened. "I'm not. I don't. I'm just..." She sighed heavily. "I feel like I don't have a choice in this. And even if it's something that's meant to be, it's—"

"Scary?"

She glared at me, and I tucked a strand of her hair behind the point of her ear. "Just because I want this doesn't mean I'm not scared too."

Estelle shook her head stubbornly. "There are ramifications of being with me that you aren't aware of yet."

"Something to do with the High Queen?"

She startled before that careful mask slid back into place.

"You did accidentally mention something about your birth." I grinned at her. "Or did you think I already forgot? Considering her gift, I'm guessing a prophecy is involved?"

Her lips tightened and the smile slid from my face.

"Whatever it is isn't going to change the way I feel about you," I promised. "Though I have to say I'm intrigued. No wonder she's taken an interest in your bonding ceremony."

Estelle started to move away. My arms instinctively tightened around her before I made myself let her go. Forcing the bond on her wouldn't help either of us. Not when there was obviously something more to it than just trepidation.

She swallowed hard as she pulled up her dress, awkwardly patting down her hair. "I just don't know you yet. Not really. Even if it feels like I do."

"I'd say we know each other pretty well, Princess."

A blush spread enticingly down her neck, and it was all I could do to stop myself from tasting it again.

I shrugged. "Fine then, keep your secrets."

She blinked in surprise, and I held out my hand. After a long second, she took it.

"You seem remarkably okay with this," Estelle murmured.

"With whatever you're hiding from me?" I led her from the willow, the balls of light winking out of existence one by one as we passed them. "I look forward to you trusting me enough to tell me everything. But I'm not in any rush."

"No rush, except the part where our bonding ceremony is in three days."

I came to a halt, tipping up her chin with one finger. "I told you already. If you don't want that, we don't have to do that either."

She was already shaking her head. "My father...the High Queen..."

"Have no say in our relationship."

"You have to know that's not true," Estelle said softly, even as her eyes flashed with a hint of her magic. "Half the realm is here on an extended stay to watch our bonding ceremony, whether or not that's what I want."

My jaw flexed as I tried to hide my own insecurity at her indecision, especially after what we had just shared. Even if she said she didn't regret it.

"If choice is what you're worried about, you should know I have no intention of bonding with anyone who doesn't consent to it," I said with forced lightness. "*Anima* or not, it's up to you. And if you say the word, I'll find a way to put a stop to this. Even if I don't want to."

Her mouth quirked. "Here I thought you were trying to convince me to go along with this."

"Oh, I have a feeling I'll grow on you despite whatever hang-ups you're attempting to wedge between us." I reached out my hand, inwardly sighing in relief as she took it. "But if three days isn't long enough to convince you, I'll take however long you need for you to realize what this was always meant to be."

Estelle blew out a breath. "You really want this, don't you?"

I laughed, and her lips curved upward before she could hide it. "Of course, I want this. Not only did I find my *anima*, but for my *anima* to be you? The brilliant, brave princess who enchanted me from the moment I met her? Not to mention a new, sandless kingdom to explore together." I smiled at her, my heart stuttering as she smiled back, albeit hesitantly. "The only thing I don't get is why you don't. But I'm happy to convince you."

"Fine."

"...fine?"

That smile lingered even as her gaze grew serious. "You have until the ceremony to convince me."

I raised a brow. "And if I don't?"

She tugged her hand out of my grip, her gown gleaming in the moonlight as she slowly walked away from me. Her hips swayed side to side mesmerizingly as she called over her shoulder, "Three days, Princeling."

CHAPTER 15
EVA

When we walked into a tall wooden home, there was a loud, recognizable squeal. My jaw dropped as Quinn Sagray rushed forward, my best friend I had last seen in another realm. She wore a scarlet dress that complemented her tawny-brown skin, silver threading crisscrossing up the bodice. Her normally wild curls were swept back in a tight bun, her mouth spread in a wide smile, those amber eyes alight with joy. Until her expression turned to horror, and I remembered I was still covered in a mix of Aviel's blood and my own.

"It's not all mine," I said weakly, unable to think of anything else to say in my shock.

Quinn lifted her hand to my face, her fingers hovering over my bruised cheek. "How hurt are you?"

"I'm—"

I let out a sharp gasp and then burst into tears, my eyes filling so alarmingly fast that my rapid blinking to clear them only caused more tears to roll down my cheeks.

Quinn pulled me against her, her hand rubbing my back in careful circles. Everything I had bottled up since the last time I had seen her seemed to burst out of me as I sunk into her familiar embrace, clinging to her so tightly my arms hurt. She nodded over my shoulder, and I heard the front door open and close as the others left us.

When my sobbing faded to wet-sounding hiccups, I pulled away, noting the matching tears staining Quinn's face. I rubbed my eyes with the heels of my hands, wincing as I pressed against a bruise there.

"Quinn—"

A blueish glow radiated from her outstretched fingertips as she reached for my cheek, gently smoothing my hair away before she rested her hand lightly above the wound.

I gaped at her, still too shocked at seeing her here to think clearly. While I had suspected she was fae, to see the proof of her here, pointed ears and all was staggering. And she was *healing* me. Though I had known what she was from her amulet alone, it was another thing entirely to watch her use magic.

Maybe I shouldn't have been surprised. After her parents died, *someone* had built the wards around my apartment.

I should've realized she would be a healer. In college, Quinn had been pre-med, though she had moved into research after we graduated. For her to have this ability was fitting in a way that anything else would have been unimaginable.

"First, you need to sit down and let me heal the worst of your injuries," Quinn said in a concerned yet no-nonsense tone so typical of her that it made me want to cry. "And then I owe you a *long* overdue explanation."

She ushered me into a well-appointed kitchen, the space warm and inviting. Pulling out a chair at a long, wooden dining table, she gestured for me to take a seat before bringing me a glass of water that I gulped down. She sat down next to me, her hands immediately coming to hover over my stomach, unerringly finding the spot where my side ached with each breath. Her magic ran over me like a cooling stream of water.

"You'll need to be careful with your ribs," Quinn murmured. Her brow furrowed as she placed her hands on my wrists, the torn skin fading into reddened lines, before moving to the matching marks on my ankles. "And you'll still have some bruising."

"Thank you," I said softly. But there was an edge to the words, despite their sincerity. As happy as I was to see her, I hadn't forgotten the fact that she had lied to me, at least by omission. Even if I hoped there was more to it—that her actions had been driven by some necessity rather than another betrayal.

Quinn took a deep breath, hesitating as though working up to the explanation I knew was coming.

I grabbed her still-glowing hand from where it had reached for the bite mark on my neck, suddenly impatient. "How long have you known? And why on earth didn't you tell me sooner?"

Those amber eyes flicked up to mine, their usual warmth tinged with guilt. "When did you guess that I knew?"

I snorted. "About two minutes after I realized what the amulets were for. Add that to how your parents were equally crazy about training you as mine were, plus the fact that there were wards on my new apartment *after* they died." I gave her a sympathetic look. "Not a plane crash, huh."

It wasn't a question.

Quinn let out a long breath, shaking her head. "When your family was killed, my parents told me everything." She spoke slowly, carefully, as if not wanting to miss anything important. "Who you were…well, *are*. They told me to stay with you, to keep you hidden and safe as they journeyed to Soleara to determine if it was finally time to bring us back." She swallowed hard. "But they never came back." Our gazes met and held, her eyes flickering with a mix of sadness and sincerity. "So I waited, wondering every day how to find a way to tell you. But they used the amulet to stop me from doing so—bound by my oath and my blood. Binding it so that the protection remained even if they died, unless you were in danger. So I practiced what magic I could figure out on my own— sparingly and carefully so as not to leave a trackable trace—and yes, created the wards on your apartment after you wouldn't move back in with me from the instructions I'd been left."

I didn't want to interrupt the explanation I had been waiting for, but I couldn't stop myself from asking, "Bound by your blood?"

Quinn grimaced. "Blood magic is powerful and can be very dangerous, especially when used for the wrong reason."

I nodded with a wince, thinking of the way Tobias's blood had been used to infiltrate my dreams. The thought of Quinn's parents using it on her, even if it was to keep us safe, made my stomach turn.

"I hated the position they put me in, but my parents were just trying to protect us. So I waited and scoured the books they left behind to learn about this realm, trying to find a way to tell you even as I wondered if it was better if you never knew…so you never had to return to this secret world still stuck in a secret war."

She gave another weary sigh, and I gripped her hand tightly, silently reassuring her that I didn't blame her, for which I was rewarded with a grateful smile, even as her eyes glimmered with unshed tears.

"I left one of the books out once, by accident. You sat down right next to it, and it felt like my tongue had stopped working. But you were too lost in your grief to notice, and the second you left, I felt that compulsion to hide it again. It made me realize there was a way around my bloodoath. But after my parents never returned, I knew it wouldn't be safe to bring you back. And you were finally starting to *live* again, and I told myself it could wait just a little longer. That it would give me more time to find a way to tell you besides blindsiding you and putting your life at risk should the crossing alert those looking for you. And to see if I could communicate with the Solearans here to determine when to bring you back. I didn't realize my attempts were being sent to an empty castle. But you were where I knew you'd be…safe." She let out a choked laugh. "So I practiced my magic in secret—though there was only so much I could learn on my own from the few books my parents left behind, especially when I was worried any large display might bring about the very danger I was trying to avoid. I was about to give in and take you through the mirror after your birthday, consequences be damned. I figured taking you to Agadot would put you in enough danger that I'd finally be able to tell you everything on our journey to Soleara."

She had been so close. Just as my parents had been the night of our Seventeenth. The stark reality of what might have been seemed to curdle with the bitter aftertaste of *almost*. If I had entered this realm more prepared…And yet, despite all that had happened, it was hard to fully regret the path that had brought me to Bash, and to the friends that felt like family.

But I couldn't change what had happened. Only forge a new path forward.

"When I realized the wards I'd placed to protect you had fallen, I knew someone must have found you," Quinn continued. "I came for you, but I was too late. When I saw your missive, I didn't realize that I *could* respond in kind after all my failed attempts to reach Soleara. So I traveled alone through the mirror to the Faewilds and made my way north as quickly as I could. I was able to buy some supplies and a horse in Imyr with the assets my parents left for me. But I didn't dare try to mirror here, nor could I risk asking too many questions on my journey. I spent the whole time hoping that it had been our own people who had taken you and not the False King's." Her eyes filled with tears, her lower lip trembling. "I'm sorry I didn't find a way to tell you. To keep you safe from him in the end. I'm so sorry, Eva."

I was already shaking my head, pulling my chosen sister into a long hug, my tears matching the ones now streaming down her cheeks.

"You have nothing to apologize for, my friend," I whispered. "I'm only glad I found you again."

"And I'm glad you came back to me," she hiccupped.

I held her close, waiting until her tremors had stopped before asking, "Your parents?"

"They were captured before they reached Soleara, betrayed by one of the False King's supporters." Her expression shuttered. "They were taken to Morehaven, and never heard from again."

I shuddered, remembering all too clearly that dank dungeon, and what Tobias had told me Aviel did to the prisoners there. The stealing of their power and magic to fuel his own youth. I closed my eyes, hoping Quinn had at least been spared that detail of their deaths.

Her hands found mine, her words choked as she asked, "Always forward?"

My gaze met hers. "Never back."

I took a quick shower to remove the blood and sweat before filling Quinn in on everything that had happened since we last saw each other. It was strange sharing my misadventures aloud. Quinn gasped on cue at each new reveal as I patted my hair dry with a towel. Her amber eyes filled as I stammered through the worst of Aviel's treatment—the magic-blocking collar, Tobias's imprisonment, and what he had done and almost done to me. As I explained that Bash was my *anima*—"*Obviously*," Quinn remarked —I shrugged on the long-sleeved gray dress and cozy woolen socks she had laid out for me. It felt strangely like old times as we sat on her bed, trading stories, Quinn braiding my hair to pull the still damp strands away from my face.

Until she gestured at a crate of leather-bound journals in the corner of the room.

My mouth went dry as Quinn carefully untwined the braided leather belt from around one, and the familiar writing stopped me in my tracks.

"Your mother's," Quinn whispered. "She has some interesting ideas on incorporating a more democratic form of rule on this realm. Many have already been implemented in Soleara, but she obviously had hopes to extend her plans further. Pari delivered them here for you. They're normally on display in the Solearan senate."

My fingers flew through the pages, greedily drinking in the words that felt like a lifeline—no, a roadmap—for the future my mother must have once thought would be hers, that, I realized with no small sense of awe, now would be mine. At least, if we succeeded in stopping Aviel.

I had just picked up the second journal when the air went static. My pulse quickened, my blood seemed to heat...and I abruptly lunged to my feet, nearly dropping the priceless book in my hands. I thrust it at Quinn, who opened her mouth to say something before stopping at the look on my face.

My heart leapt as frantic anticipation flooded down our bond, matching mine. I was halfway down the stairs before I heard a chorus of familiar, concerned voices, my heart hammering madly in my ears. Distantly, I heard Quinn calling my name as I practically flew down the remaining stairs, letting the tug in my chest lead me.

I didn't even try to slow down before I reached him, just launched myself into his waiting arms. Bash's name was a sigh of relief, a prayer answered as he hauled me tightly against him without hesitation, his shadows circling around me like they had missed me too. Instinctively, I wrapped my legs around his waist, my arms locking behind his head as I clung to him as tightly as possible. Breathing in the scent of petrichor—relishing that feeling of *home*. I could feel Bash shaking as he bent his head down to mine, holding me like any space left between us was unbearable.

When the tears started, I couldn't make them stop. A sob left me as I burrowed my face into his neck, feeling his pulse frantically beating through my trembling lips.

"Eva." My name was a broken whisper.

"You're here," I croaked. "You're *here*."

"I've got you," Bash breathed into my hair, his hand rubbing small circles on my back.

I pulled away, sucking in a shallow lungful of air as I stared at him for an endless moment, taking in the worry lining his face, the stubbled shadow of his auburn beard, the tears gleaming in his eyes. The crushing weight of his heartbreak across our bond as he wiped my tears away. Those turbulent two-toned eyes searched my face, and I knew I could forever fall into that stormy sea and willingly drown.

"Once again, you're just a hair too late to save me yourself," I said, my attempt at teasing lost to the hiccup in my voice.

Bash's mouth twitched like he almost wanted to smile. "I will *always* come for you. Even if you keep beating me to it."

But I could see the guilt in his gaze, multiplied across our bond, feel how much he blamed himself for not being able to save me back in Morehaven. How much it killed him that he hadn't.

"Hellion," Bash rasped, the rough caress of his voice making my heart skip a beat. "Are you hurt?"

"I'm okay," I whispered, my voice cracking. "Quinn healed the worst of it before you got here."

His gaze raked over me almost desperately, like he had to check for himself. Fury flashed across our bond, brackish and burning, as he caught sight of the ring of bruises I knew were still around my throat, dark against the white of the scars that circled around my neck.

"When I realized that I wouldn't get to you in time to stop him..." Bash swallowed, his eyes stormy. "I—I should have had faith that you would... that you will always have the strength to save yourself."

Vaguely, I was aware of Tobias standing beside me, Yael and Rivan grinning madly next to him, as Quinn looked on from the stairwell. My eyes met my twin's, colder than I remembered—the man standing in front of me startling in comparison to the jovial, gangly teenager that lived in my memory. "You're free."

His head dipped slightly. "Thanks to you. Though I'd like a word later about your methods."

Bash lowered me to the ground, his hand reaching to twine our fingers together as if unwilling to let me go entirely. I turned to Tobias and threw my other arm around him. He tensed slightly before relaxing into the hug. Then Rivan and Yael's arms were around me, and I smiled through my quickly blurring vision—no longer sure whose hands were whose as we held each other, almost giddy with the relief of being reunited.

"That was an incredibly reckless thing you did," Rivan grumbled as he pulled me closer.

"You would've died if I—"

"Thank you."

My mouth dropped open, then stretched into a smile.

Yael touched her forehead to mine, her eyes bright. "I'm furious with you, I hope you know that."

"You all would have done the same for me," I said quietly as we pulled back for air. Yael shrugged as if to say, fair enough.

Quinn now stood next to me, Tobias's arm still around her despite everyone else having let each other go. He stiffened as he noted the direction of my gaze, quickly lowering his arm to his side. But Quinn's eyes danced in delight as she looked at Bash's hand still firmly clutched in mine.

"Don't start," I begged her.

"FINALLY," Quinn squealed. "It's about time for you to be happy. I might have found a way to tell you the truth sooner if I realized you would finally be with someone longer than fourteen seconds, but here I thought—"

"*Quinn,*" I exclaimed, cutting into her diatribe. I felt my cheeks heat as Yael let out a muffled snort of laughter, Bash's lips pressing together as he tried to contain a smile. "This is Bash. And Yael," I said, gesturing at them both in turn. "And—"

"Rivan." He stepped forward, grasping Quinn's hand in his own larger ones. I saw her big amber eyes blink slowly as she stared up at the burly male, whose mouth twisted in a roguish grin before he let go. "And it's a pleasure to meet you."

Quinn fixed him with a look that I knew meant trouble.

"Oh, I'm sure it is," she said tartly, arching an eyebrow at him.

Tobias bristled, his shoulders squaring slightly though I was certain I was the only one who noticed. I could feel Bash's amusement across our bond, though it dissipated as his gaze lowered to where my sleeve had ridden up—the freshly healed red lines where my chains had dug into my wrists now clearly visible. Shadows swirled from his hand to mine, winding carefully around my arm in a slow caress.

"Interesting company you're keeping these days, Eva," Quinn murmured to me. "I didn't know you had fallen in with a whole faction of arrogant fae warriors." She gave me a pointed look as she turned away from Rivan, and Yael snickered loudly. "Though I suppose it's a little late now to warn you away." Her voice warmed as she looked at Bash.

Reluctantly, I let go of my *anima*, turning to Tobias and holding him at arms' length so I could really look at him. He was taller than I remembered, too pale and thin from his imprisonment, yet sculpted in a way that I knew he must have spent his time training in that damp cell. His eyes were still haunted as he took me in, darkening as he scanned the bruises visible on my face and neck.

Tobias's gaze dropped below my collar, and I realized my neckline had shifted enough to show off the bite marking the skin above my collarbone, still healing atop the scar below it. His eyes flashed with something that looked like lightning—nearly washing out the familiar crown of gold around his pupils. I stiffened at the memory of that power holding my friends, my *anima*, down as it choked the life from them, then shook my head. Though it was hardly Tobias's fault his power had been stolen from him.

He lifted a hand, smoothing my hair back from my face. "Hey, sis."

It was an effort to speak through the lump in my throat. "I thought I'd lost you, again."

"I thought I lost *you*, this time," Tobias murmured. "When I'd only just gotten you back."

"Never again," I said firmly, hoping it was true. I squeezed his hand, relishing the feeling of finally having him back with me as we nodded at each other in silent promise.

"Let's get everyone settled and fed, and then we can discuss what comes next in the morning," Quinn said in a light voice. "There are a few rooms down the hall from me, and more on the floor above that. I can show you the way."

I was still staring at Tobias as he turned to Quinn. And I wondered if he knew how much he gave away as he looked at her with his heart in his eyes. His mouth tightened...and I watched as his guard went up, shielding his true feelings from the world. Like after so long in that mask, he had forgotten what it was like to live without it.

It would take time for him to open up again, and I knew better than to push after the trauma he had endured. The years he had spent being tortured in that cell, guarding our secrets in order to keep me safely hidden, had no doubt taken a toll I couldn't begin to understand. Even if I hated the fact that he had carried that burden without me, I knew he had done it *for* me. A fact, I realized, that applied to Quinn as well.

Had he always had a thing for my best friend? Maybe that had been there all those years ago, and I simply never noticed until now. Though Quinn clearly hadn't either.

Perhaps I was reading too far into it. But as Quinn came forward to envelop us both in a hug, I grinned widely at my brother's too loud swallow.

My friend didn't seem to notice. "It's been too long since our trio has been together."

"I'm glad you were there for Eva when I couldn't be," Tobias said, his voice low and earnest.

Quinn's head cocked to the side, giving him a searching look before she looked away. "Me too."

My brother continued to watch her intently as Quinn gestured at the house around us. "This was where your parents lived when they weren't holding court below," she explained. "Your true home. It was built to accommodate visitors."

A thousand questions were on my tongue, but I was suddenly too tired to voice them. Quinn gestured at the main stairs and Tobias followed her lead, Yael and Rivan close behind. Before I could move, Bash gathered me up in his arms, sweeping me off my feet.

"How chivalrous," I murmured into his ear and his lips quirked. Of course he had felt my exhaustion.

I laughed as he took the steps two at a time until we reached the third floor, taking me into the first empty bedroom. It was decorated with mahogany furnishings and intricately embroidered curtains. The sage green linen bedding matched the stone inlay above the built in fireplace. It crackled merrily as if in greeting.

Yet Bash's brows were drawn as he set us on the bed, pulling me across his lap and holding me there. His renewed concern swept across our bond, swarming me in its intensity. My chest ached in response. I tried to quell my answering echo of fear and anguish that surged within me as it all came flooding back.

Bash's voice broke into the cacophony of my recollection. "What do you need?"

"Just you," I sighed. His arms wrapped more tightly around me, tugging me against him as he tucked my head under his chin. I used his steady heartbeat to count my breaths, letting my panic melt away with each exhale.

Bash pulled away slightly as I found some semblance of calm, then hooked a finger under my chin, lifting it gently. "What exactly happened, hellion? We were trying to find a way into Soleara when I could finally feel you again."

His face darkened, and I couldn't help my swallow. I knew exactly the moment he had felt me again—the volatile mix of fear and rage he would have sensed as Aviel took that collar off, knowing my *anima* would feel every second of my torment.

My voice broke as I said, "When I came to, I was back in his bed."

Slowly, I continued from the moment I woke without him, everything spilling out in fractured bits as I haphazardly strung them together. I told him about Alette's fire magic and how she had blasted a hole through Morehaven. He frowned, though I could feel his grudging admiration across our bond, even as he grumbled, "She could have *killed* you".

I shook my head. "I think she's more powerful than Aviel ever realized. That he underestimated her as much as I did."

Bash held me as I told him about the aftermath of the explosion, vibrating with fury even as he whispered reassurances into my hair when I faltered. Pure rage burned across our bond when I reached the iron box. He gently brought my hands up to kiss the still healing marks on my wrists, murmuring soft apologies against my skin. My lips quivered, then Bash tugged me back into his embrace. I hadn't realized how much I was shaking until he wrapped himself around me as if holding me together, careful to avoid the worst of my remaining injuries.

I sagged against his chest, listening to the furious beat of his heart. Clinging to him as he simply held me, his shadows flitting around us protectively.

My chin wobbled as I thought of how much I had yearned for this in that iron cage lurching through the darkness. For one horrible second, I could feel that icy metal leaching the heat from my skin as easily as Aviel had stolen my magic, that forever cold band tightening around my throat.

I closed my eyes, and his harsh, warm breath brushed against the hollow of my neck.

All my life I've had to take what I wanted. You, my darling, are no different.

Bash's expression turned wary. "Where did you just go?"

I shook my head, trying to banish that feeling along with his question, but I knew he wouldn't be dissuaded that easily.

As if reading my mind, Bash quietly added, "Are you okay?"

His hand found the dimples on my lower back, rubbing small circles between them with his thumb.

"Of course," I lied. Like he couldn't sense the sudden pressure in my chest. As if he didn't always see right through me, even before our bond became permanent. I counted my breath in, before letting it out to the same slow beat.

"Eva, look at me."

I closed my eyes, trying to steady myself but failing. Convinced the compassion in his gaze would destroy the flimsy dam holding my tears back.

"You don't have to prove anything to me," Bash whispered, his fingers tracing a tender path down my jawline. I gave in and looked at him at the silent plea in his voice, watching as his eyes filled with quiet shadows. "I know exactly how strong you are."

The tears I had been fighting spilled over, streaming down my cheeks in warm rivulets. His mouth pressed against one cheek then the other, catching my tears as they fell, before pulling me back into his embrace. One hand ran comfortingly through my hair, the other curled protectively around my waist.

How many times had I thought of being back in the safety of his arms while we were apart? Just as many as I had been certain I would never be again; not as I had been taken further and further away from him.

"Breathe, Eva," Bash said hoarsely. He held me as if he expected me to shatter in his arms, his fingers trailing up and down my spine. "Please, just breathe."

He kept talking to me in low, soothing murmurs as I counted each breath. Holding me until I could breathe again.

It took a minute to get myself under control, my trembling surrendering to the reassurance of him. Distantly, I recognized that talking about what happened was helping even as it hurt. Like sharing the burden had lessened its hold on me.

I cleared my throat. "When we reached Soleara, they used my blood to open the door. Seeing the castle…it triggered more memories from before my parents fled. Of when we were happy here."

Bash winced. "I wish you'd been able to return here under happier circumstances."

I nodded, sucking in my lips. Trying to find the words for what had happened next.

Bash seemed to sense my trepidation. "If you're not ready to talk about what happened, you don't have to."

"No, it's…cathartic to talk about." I took a deep inhale, breathing him in, that familiar scent grounding.

"Good," he said softly. "Then keep going."

In a broken whisper, I told him how I fought Aviel off, and why he had removed the band. What he had hoped Bash would feel through the very bond he sought to break.

Bash's mouth had set in a thin line. "Sensing your terror in that moment, knowing I couldn't do anything to stop it, was…" He swallowed, like he couldn't put words to it. "But I also felt your resolve. Your unimaginable bravery. And even if you hadn't been able to stop him, I'm glad I would've been able to be with you in at least that way. To be there through our bond when I should've been there to stop him from touching you in the first place."

My heart lurched painfully, the memory of his helplessness mixing with my own. "He didn't rape me." My voice broke as I envisioned what he *had* done, my hand reaching up to unthinkingly touch the bite mark on my shoulder.

"He did enough." Bash's eyes darkened with shadows as they formed a shield around us. His fingers trailed down the bruises marring my skin as if making note of each one to seek vengeance for, his icy rage seeping down our bond at what he hadn't been able to stop.

"I should've killed him," I said, my voice shaking. "Once again, if I'd only been faster, I could've stopped him, and this would all be over. I should've—"

"We'll stop him together, hellion," Bash murmured. "That's not your burden alone."

Shaking my head, I took his hand. A small tendril of darkness trailed between his fingers, looping around mine like they could bind him to me forever.

"I missed you," I said, my voice splintering. "Every second, I missed you."

His lips parted. Then he gently pressed them to mine, the kiss so heartfelt it stole my breath away.

"I've never felt more helpless." Bash's eyes grew haunted, a line forming between his brows. "Every second you were away from me, I just kept seeing my father's face when the False King killed him...when *Aviel* killed him. And then my mother, who I couldn't save either. I couldn't save either of them. And when it comes to you, Eva—" He sucked in a ragged breath. "If something happened to you too..."

His latent grief nearly cracked my heart in two.

Bash shook his head, the shadows in his eyes having nothing to do with his magic. "But this isn't about me. Not after what you went through."

"No, this goes both ways," I said firmly. "My ordeal doesn't diminish yours, nor are your feelings any less valid." My lips brushed his in a too brief kiss as the catching sensation in my chest faded away. "But I'm okay. I'm safe. And all I need is you."

His eyes guttered, swirling darkly as he stared at the bruises around my throat. "I wish I could swear to you that he would never take you from me again, but I've already failed you in that particular promise. And I won't make you another that I can't keep." He touched my cheek, then lowered his hand to my neck, hovering over the bite mark there. "You saved us—our friends, our family—and endured everything after that with unflinching courage."

"You wouldn't say that if you'd seen me in that iron—"

Bash was already shaking his head. "Especially then. Because even when you lost hope, you found a way back to it again. Then managed to survive him despite your lack of reinforcement...plus some rather impressive pickpocketing." He bent his head in the slightest of bows. "I am so very unworthy of you, but I'll spend the rest of my life trying to be."

"You are worthy, Bash," I said fiercely. "Don't you dare blame yourself. That's on him, and only him."

He pulled me closer, as if reminding himself I was still there. I could feel his guilt like acid as he buried his face into the crook of my neck. How much he blamed himself for not being able to protect me. How much it killed him that he hadn't.

"I hate that I couldn't save you," Bash said, his voice guttural. "I hate that I left you with him again."

Taking his face in my hands to make him look at me, I found his irises once again a slate gray. His shadows had trickled around us like they had also needed to hold me, their wispy strands twisting around me. With an exhale, I let my darkness join them, swirling together in dusky shades across our skin.

"You never left me." I brushed my lips against his, feeling a hint of his tension melting away. "Besides," I added with a grim smile, "you can be right alongside me when we finally end him."

Bash leaned back, tracing the dimple that had appeared on my cheek with his thumb. Stopping only as my smile faded at the undercurrent of self-reproach still coursing down our bond.

"Tell me something true," I said in a half-teasing whisper, determined to erase the bleakness from his face.

A hint of a smile curved his lips. "Something no one else knows? I have no more secrets from you. And I plan to keep it that way."

Slowly, I kissed a trail along his stubbled jaw, snaking my arms around his neck as I reached the corner of his mouth. His lips met mine far too fleetingly, his kiss both promise and apology.

I needed more. Needed him to erase the feeling of another's hands on me. To remember what it felt like to be safe and wanted. To hear him breathe my name against my skin as we lost ourselves in each other.

"*Eva*," he groaned, pulling away as his eyes flicked over me. I could feel his hesitancy, his need to make sure I was okay, warring with his desire to follow through with what we both wanted.

"Please," I whispered, knowing he wouldn't deny me this—wouldn't deny me anything. "I don't want you to be careful with me."

There was always something so intoxicating about the way Bash looked at me, like he would never be able to get enough of me. Like I was everything he ever wanted, and he was realizing all over again that I was his.

"You say the word, and we stop," Bash murmured. "No questions asked."

"Stop treating me like I'm made of glass. I'm not. I want this. I want *you*."

"I don't deserve you," Bash breathed, his eyes raking over the still healing marks that would no doubt leave fresh scars. But his gaze darkened as it lowered, the mix of lust and protective fury surging across our bond leaving me breathless.

"You've always been worthy of me," I said softly. "And I've always been yours."

Bash's eyes flashed, the last of his restraint escaping him in a breath. Then he kissed me, soft and slow, gathering me against him. And it felt like coming home.

I pressed my body into his, desperate to erase any space left between us until there were no boundaries between where he ended and I began. His tongue nudged inside my mouth, possessive and thorough. My back arched as his teeth found my earlobe, his hand tightening in my hair.

"Always," he whispered into my ear. "And forever. Promise me."

"Yes," I moaned, not caring about anything else but him as I curled my fingers into his back to pull him closer.

Bash captured my chin in his hand, his thumb tracing my lower lip— and when my tongue flitted out to lick it, his mouth replaced it with a growl. His kiss was starved, yet achingly tender, like despite my insistence, he was still holding himself back. I moaned into his mouth, and he tilted my head to the side, taking me deeper, kissing me as if he could fit everything he felt for me into it all at once.

There was too much clothing between us. I pulled away despite every cell in my body screaming to do the opposite, moving to stand between his legs as I tugged my dress over my head. Then watched Bash take in every last one of my remaining marks, every fading cut and bruise left over after Quinn's ministrations—the fact they still remained evidence enough of what I had endured. His eyes flashed murderously, a vortex of whirling gray that matched the shadows that reached out to me, carefully curling around my arms, my legs, my torso. They trailed lightly along each abrasion, as if creating their own list of all the ways that Aviel had harmed me so they might enact a precise form of vengeance when the time came.

"I'm okay," I said again. "And I need—"

I gasped, arching into that shadowy touch as they moved lower.

"I know exactly what you need, hellion."

Bash pulled me closer, his mouth tracing the same path as his shadows across my stomach, mapping out every bruise on my skin as I writhed under his touch. His tongue grazed my breast, and I sucked in a loud breath before letting it out in a moan as his hand slipped between my legs, lightly teasing me in a way that was almost unbearable. Those soft, deliberate brushes against that sensitive nub of nerves had my core clenching with need, an impatient whine leaving my throat as Bash took his time playing with me.

His eyes flicked up to mine as I reached for the ties on his pants, but he didn't object when I eased them down—as starved for him as I could plainly see he was for me. I trailed my hand over the impressive bulge straining to get free—and smirked at his ensuing groan.

"You're still wearing far too many clothes," I chided him.

I barely pulled up his shirt before he tore it off in one quick motion. When I yanked down his undershorts and curled my hand around his cock, he made a desperate noise in the back of his throat, his length twitching in my hand. Straddling him, I slowly pumped my fist up and down between us, twisting my wrist so my palm brushed against his sensitive head.

"Tease," he murmured.

"You started it," I said breathlessly.

He gently moved me onto my back, leaning over me before quickly moving to my side. My chest ached at the reason why.

"I'm okay," I whispered. "Don't stop."

He flashed me that crooked smile, then he kissed leisurely down my chest, humming appreciatively under his breath. I shivered at the ghost of his lips on my skin.

I needed more.

As if reading my mind, his shadows slid teasingly against my clit before wrapping around my thighs, spreading them wider—my low moan of need earning me another sinful half-grin.

"It's been far too long since I've tasted you, hellion," he whispered against my navel.

A spark of heat shot down our bond, an ache settling into my core as our desires merged into one.

"Is that so?" I managed to gasp as he nipped at my inner thigh.

"And that won't do."

A fog of lust clouded my mind as his hand trailed down my slick warmth, his fingers skillfully taunting and teasing, his lips and tongue following their path. By the time his mouth reached me, I could barely remember my own name, his tongue robbing me of every thought except my own need for him. More shadows drifted up my stomach, and I let out a gasp as they flitted across one nipple, then the other. His fingers busied themselves inside me in a steady, torturous rhythm.

When I came, my helpless cries of pleasure rang through the room, my fingers twisting in his hair as my back arched off the bed. Bash's name fell from my lips, and his answering groan vibrated up through my body as I splintered apart yet again. I couldn't tell where one climax ended and the next began as his tongue continued wreaking havoc on me until I was limp and shaking.

My head fell back against the pillow. When my eyes opened, a slow smirk had stretched across Bash's face—full of pure, male arrogance. I gazed up at him, still coming back to my body from whatever realm I had ascended to.

"What do you want, my queen? You're in charge here."

The velvety suggestion in his voice already had me panting for more. Sensing my need, he lowered himself over me. I wrapped my legs around him, tugging him closer.

"Please," I managed to say. "Please, Bash. I need you inside me."

"Hellion…" He groaned against my lips. "You have no idea what you do to me."

Bash's cock slid against me, and I whimpered. His hand moved up from my breast before it wrapped gently behind my neck, holding me there like he wanted to spend the rest of his life memorizing every inch of my mouth.

"*Eva,*" he rasped as I canted my hips against his, desperate for more. "You're too hurt for all the things I want to do to you."

"I don't care," I said, wrapping my fingers around the thick length of him, angling him at my entrance. "I won't break. And I need you not to be gentle with me."

I could feel my arousal slicken at the way he groaned my name and sense the way his control was fraying exactly the way I wanted it to, his need for me mirroring my own. He settled between my thighs, the head of his cock nudging against me.

His tongue slipped in between my parted lips at the same time he slid all the way in, his first thrust mind-meltingly slow. Everything inside me pulled taut as he filled me to the hilt, my core clenching around him as I adjusted to the sudden fullness.

Bash took his time, moving tantalizingly slowly as he rolled his hips in a leisurely thrust. His shadows made me gasp as they brushed teasingly down my body, making heat prickle through every part of me. I returned the favor as I bit on the lobe of his pointed ear, his gasp turning into a groan as I moved under him.

There was something about the way his eyes kept finding mine. The deliberate way his hands savored the curves of my body paired with the care in which he did so. The loving way his mouth, his shadows, brushed against every inch of me. The perfect way we fit together—this joining echoing the love streaming so freely down our bond I couldn't tell where his ended and mine began.

Bash panted against my lips, our breaths mingling as he sighed, "Gods, I love you."

He was buried so deeply inside me that for one precious moment, we felt like one. Then he kissed my neck exactly where Aviel had bitten me, his lips achingly gentle against the still healing wound.

"You're mine," Bash growled, as his lips tracked a trail down my chest, his teeth grazing my nipple. The tiny sting made me gasp, my head falling back as he sucked and teased me, each accompanying movement inside me bringing me closer to the brink.

"Yes," I panted, barely able to form words as I edged closer to that familiar tipping point. "*Bash.*"

"Say it," he demanded as he thrust back into me, his hands tilting my hips to somehow reach an even deeper angle.

"I'm yours," I gasped. "And you're mine."

A smile flirted with the corner of his lips. Then his shadows dipped between my thighs, sliding over my clit. And I lost myself—clenching around him as I came, pulling him right along with me.

He collapsed beside me, pressing kisses against my neck, my cheeks, my lips. One arm was draped around me, his fingers curling against my ribs. He gently traced the mottled bruises down my arm with his fingertips before his lips ghosted along the same path.

"I never want to be apart from you again," I said earnestly, willing it to be true from now on. "I needed—"

"I know," Bash said, his gaze half-lidded as his stormy eyes met mine, swirling leisurely in contentment. "I always need you."

His lips moved to my stomach, working his way up my midline. "I'm going to need verbal confirmation that you're never going to give yourself up for me ever again, hellion," he murmured between kisses, though his words held a bit of an edge to them.

"Whatever you say, freckles," I said, squirming as he kissed his way up between my breasts.

His lips formed a sly smile as he reached my face. "Or should I stick with 'my queen'?"

"Not unless you want me calling you 'my king'."

He made a face, and I couldn't help but laugh. He kissed me hungrily, as if to capture the sound.

"Your Majesty?" I asked, teasingly.

"It seems more appropriate for *you*, considering all I want to do in front of you is get on my knees."

I could feel a blush heating my cheeks despite everything we had just done. His eyes danced in delight, those blue and green swirls mesmerizing. But laughing about titles…

Bash raised an eyebrow in concern as my face fell.

"High Queen," I said with a swallow. "This is all because I'm supposedly fated to be High Queen. But why would the people of Agadot even accept me?" I shook my head, a strand of hair that had freed itself from my braid falling across my face. "I didn't even know this realm existed a month ago. And, somehow, I'm destined to lead it?"

"They'll accept you because of who you are *and* who you've proven yourself to be," Bash said, suddenly serious. His finger gently twirled into the curl of my hair, wrapping it around his finger before tucking it behind my ear. "Though most will accept whomever the Choosing decrees, since that's the will of the realm itself. Especially once they learn the truth behind their so-called savior's identity. But I don't doubt they'll fall in love with you as easily as I did. Not when you're fighting to create a world for them that's far better than what it is now."

"I don't want to fight forever though, Bash," I whispered, suddenly feeling exhausted at what lay before us and the battles I knew we would have to face. "I want to live to see this realm at peace again. To see what it was like before this endless war and explore it all together. I want to live in a world where people can laugh freely. Where they can play music and read and dance and fall in love."

Bash nodded solemnly. "One day, we'll make that world together."

And we could, I realized. If I lived to become High Queen.

As I pulled away, Bash tensed, sitting up as I got to my feet. I found myself momentarily distracted by the way his abs rippled as he did so. Shaking my head, I walked toward the bathroom, asking over my shoulder, "And if I follow my mother's footsteps in creating a more representative form of government?"

His eyes raised from where they had fixed on my ass, finding mine. Then the right side of his mouth tilted upwards, the left slowly following just after, as always, in that crooked smile that I would never get enough of. "Then I look forward to helping you establish the new world order."

When I returned, I barely yawned before Bash tucked me into his side, pulling the blankets over us. His arms wrapped around me, and I felt my eyelids droop as I relaxed into that feeling of safety. I was almost too warm as his body heat enveloped me, but I refused to move a single inch.

Pressing my face against his chest, I listened to his heartbeat under my ear—in sync with mine, beat for beat.

CHAPTER 16

BASH

I woke up from my nightmare with a start, my heart in my throat. Eva was still curled up beside me, fitted against me so perfectly it was like we were made for each other. Locks of her hair decorated my shoulder, dark eyelashes fanning across her cheeks. Our hands were still entwined—the last thing I remembered before sleep claimed me was her hand folding into mine.

But I could see the bruising around her throat, a sharp reminder of how close I was to losing her. The still-healing bite mark that set my blood boiling. I let out a shaky breath, clamping down on the bond between us so my shame and fury wouldn't wake her.

Eva's warm breath tickled against my neck as I fought to steady my breathing and settle back into her. She felt so fragile in my arms, even though I knew her to be entirely the opposite. Eva had always been a dichotomy, vacillating between breathtakingly powerful and yet heartbreakingly vulnerable from all she had been through, even if she was more than capable of taking care of herself.

Thankfully, I hadn't woken her from her obviously much needed sleep, her exhaustion pulling her too far under. Nuzzling into her hair, I breathed in an indulgent inhale as I carefully moved as close to her as I could, her warm body curled against mine almost managing to chase the worst of my thoughts away. Like how much I had failed her by leaving her in Aviel's clutches. How he had almost raped my soul bonded yet again while I fought, and failed, to reach her in time.

Eva was breathing softly, the sound that had lulled me to sleep so many nights in the Faewilds as the stars twinkled through the treetops. I had almost forgotten how much I loved that sound; the joy of it only secondary to having her safe in my arms at last.

Her full lips parted as she sighed, turning further into my body—needing me closer even in her dreams. My stomach swooped as her dark lashes fluttered, struggling against the lull of sleep as she tried to wake.

I couldn't resist reaching up and brushing my thumb against the smooth, tan skin of her cheeks, relishing how the color deepened at my attention. One eye cracked open, a hint of gold flashing in the morning light.

Her voice a sleepy rasp, she asked, "Why are you looking at me like that? Do we need to get up?"

"No, not yet," I whispered. "Go back to sleep, hellion. I'll be here when you wake up."

She needed to rest, to heal before what came next. Even if that indomitable fortitude was firmly intact.

But her eyelids fluttered open, though she hid a yawn against my shoulder, her lips grazing against my bare skin. Dark circles lay under her eyes as they suddenly filled with a worry I could feel like a twist in my gut. Her lower lip quivered before she bit down on it as if to hide it. But she couldn't hide the renewed hollowness in her gaze, the recollection of despair that echoed down our bond.

"What is it?"

She blinked at me like my question had brought her back from an unwelcome memory. Then she sighed, whispering, "I feel like this is going to fall apart somehow. Like I'm going to wake up back in that box, or in his bed."

I pressed a soft kiss on her forehead even as I tamped down on my rage that thought induced, the force of my hatred for the monster who had made her fear that. "This is real, Eva. You're safe. You're here."

A faint smile flickered across her lips. "I'm with you."

My stomach turned over at the trust in her voice. Like being with me somehow ensured her safety when I had so utterly failed her.

She was everything I didn't deserve. But I was going to keep her anyway.

"Do you want me to get you something to eat? Some tea?" I was suddenly desperate to do anything to erase that lingering despair. "Breakfast in bed?"

She gave me a little smile that never failed to make my heart pound, her one-sided dimple winking at me. "A little late for that, no?"

The sunlight streaming in from the window did seem to hint that morning had almost passed. I hadn't realized how long we slept.

"But I can think of something I'd like to eat," Eva said, her fingers trailing down my chest. That dimple deepened.

I let out a garbled noise at her lowering touch, utterly aware of the sinful curves wrapped around me. "We should really go downstairs and—" I nearly groaned aloud when her hand brushed against my rapidly hardening length. "—find the others."

Eva only shook her head, a small smile on her lips. "After."

It was less a want than a need, this endless longing for her. What we had already done should have taken the edge off, and yet it remained unquenchable, this thirst for her. The depth of my desire was a bottomless ocean in which I would happily be dragged beneath by her siren's song and drown.

"Sometimes I want you in a way that's almost too much to bear, hellion."

She smirked knowingly. "Sometimes?"

Pulling her on top of me, I kissed her, hard. She moaned into my mouth, squirming against me as I hardened, each unintentional movement quickly driving me insane.

I didn't think I could ever get enough of her. And I knew from the flush on her cheeks, the need burning across our bond, that she felt the same. She sighed as my lips moved down her neck, ghosting over the scar that encircled it and the new healing line to match. I pressed a kiss in the hollow between her collarbones, and she let out that breathless moan I was utterly obsessed with.

"Tell me you want this."

Eva made a small, inarticulate sound of pleasure as I gripped her ass, grinding her against me; cherishing the feel of her curves beneath my hands, the strength of her thighs as they gripped my hips, the way her pulse quickened under my tongue.

"*Bash.*"

There was that perfect little whimper again. "Is that a yes?"

"Yes," Eva breathed. "I need...*more*. More of you."

I smirked against her skin. "I want you to come on my fingers, my tongue, and at least twice once I'm inside you. Unless you have any objections..."

She made a desperate little noise deep in the back of her throat as I fisted my hand in her hair, bringing her mouth to mine like I could capture everything I felt for her into this one kiss.

Flinging the covers away, I spun her under me in one smooth motion, my fingers slipping inside that warm wet heat as she gasped. I grinned as she ground against my hand, even as I reached across our bond for any feelings of disquiet. But there was only that want, that *need*, that only served to intensify my own.

"So needy," I teased, feeling her clench around my fingers. My middle and ring fingers curled inside her as she rolled her hips against me.

"For you?" She let out a breathy laugh. "Always."

My shadows wrapped around her thighs, tugging her legs open wide to bare her entirely to me. When my mouth found her center, she was already shuddering, moaning so loudly I hoped our companions had the sense not to choose the adjacent rooms...or the ones next to those. I groaned as I tasted her, my tongue slipping inside her before licking up her slit, circling that bundle of nerves. My fingers moved in tandem, and I felt her thighs start to tremble as I sucked and nipped, my tongue moving in steady circles.

Eva's hips bucked as I lightly bit down, making her shatter with a cry, her hand fisting in my hair as her back bowed off the bed. My shadows held her in place as I felt her orgasm tear through her almost violently, my name a chorus, a plea, before her knees fell limply apart.

One hand tightened into my hair, dragged my mouth away from her as I licked my lips. Her eyes fluttered open, the gold at their center glinting.

"Bash," She whispered as I crawled over her. "I need all of you."

My tongue delved into her mouth, letting her taste herself as I plunged into her. I moaned as that tight, wet heat enveloped me, her nails pressing into my shoulder blades so hard I knew they would leave a mark.

She pushed against my chest, and I followed her lead, lying against the pillows as she straddled me. We both lost our breaths as I slowly pushed inside of her, letting her feel every hard inch. Her hips undulated, those inner muscles squeezing with every lift as her ass slapped loudly against my thighs.

"You take me so well," I murmured, watching as a flush crept down her chest. My shadows snaked between her thighs, teasing her before my thumb took their place.

Just when I was sure I was about to finish far too soon, I splayed my hands wide around her hips, dragging her up my body until she was straddling my face. Eva let out a surprised squeak that quickly turned into a moan as I breathed against her, "One more, hellion. Come on my tongue one more time before I lose myself inside you. I made you a promise, after all."

Then my mouth was moving on her, her greedy hips rocking against me with abandon. I circled her more roughly with my tongue, feeling her thighs start to quake on either side of my head. My shadows streamed up her stomach, circling around her breasts, nipping at her peaked nipples.

Her gaze met mine, her eyes wholly black—then they rolled back in her head, followed by a surge of familiar darkness as she came apart. Wispy tendrils trailed down my arms, lacing around my wrists as she sagged forward, my shadows surging to keep her upright as I wrung every last shudder from her body.

I pulled her astride me, watching her gaze meet mine with an entirely sex addled expression. Then her darkness tightened around my wrists, holding them above my head.

Her eyes met mine. "Can I..."

My answer was instantaneous. "I'm yours to command, my queen."

If she needed that sense of control, I would give it to her. Especially when the act in itself set my entire body aflame.

"Then it's my turn," Eva said as one of those wisps wrapped around my base. My hips jerked in surprise before she sank back onto me, the squeeze of her paired with that ring of darkness nearly making me finish right then. My shadows twisted around her calves as she moved on me, our magics twining together against her skin.

I couldn't get enough of the breathy little moans she made, the way her breath caught as she seated herself fully. The way her hands tightened against my chest as she moved against me, her breasts bouncing as she picked up her pace. How much I loved the way she used me, taking exactly what she needed.

She leaned down, kissing me hard, then drew in a little gasp at the new angle as I thrust up into her, my shadows bracketing her hips. Her eyes locked with mine, the raw pleasure I saw in them stealing my breath.

One hand pressed into my chest, holding me in place as she used the leverage to slam herself down again and again. Her pace grew frantic, her fingernails clawing into my skin as her inner walls tightened around me. She let out a desperate cry as one of my shadows slipped over her center, swirling exactly where I knew she needed it.

"That's it," I urged as my impending release coiled at the base of my spine. "Come for me. Come *with* me."

"*Bash.*"

My name on her lips was my undoing. Our pleasure peaked together, and I lost myself in her.

She collapsed against me, a mass of thick hair covering my face as we just breathed together, my arms wrapping around her as her magic receded. I nipped at her ear, if only to hear the hitch in her breath, as I rubbed a hand at the small of her back. "You're so beautiful."

Her muffled laugh against my throat was the most perfect sound in the world. "You can't even see anything."

She gave a sharp twist of her head, her hair whipping off my face.

"Doesn't change what I said," I mumbled.

She smiled, the sight of it making my heart clench at how much I had longed for it in our time apart. Then she moved to my side as I slipped from inside her, already missing that intimate connection.

I tugged her closer, listening to the familiar cadence of her breathing as I kissed her temple, her cheek, the space next to the barely scabbed-over mark on her neck that made a fresh wave of fury flood through me. Belatedly, I realized she had felt my reaction as her muscles tensed, then trembled, a wave of emotion spilling from her that mingled with my own devastation.

I braced myself on one arm, brushing her hair back from her face with the other.

When she finally looked up at me, there were tears in her eyes. "I wasn't sure if…if we'd ever have this again. If when I gave myself up to him, I'd ever see you again."

I pulled her closer, unable to stop the growl low in my throat at everything I hadn't been able to stop from happening—at everything she had willingly given up to save us. "What part of forever didn't you understand?"

Her watery laugh lasted for a second before it dissolved back into tears. But I would take even a moment of feeling that heaviness ease on the other side of our bond.

Eva's hand brushed my neck. It halted there, her other hand pressing against her heart. Her head cocked, then she nodded as if in confirmation.

"What is it?"

Her mouth twisted in a small smile. "Our heartbeats. They're in sync."

Our eyes locked together—the air between us crackling.

"My heart is your heart, Eva," I said, covering her hand with mine. Pressing down against the beating of our hearts, keeping time together. "Don't you know that by now?"

There was a flash of pure joy down our bond, her eyes bright with tears. "I love you, Bash. With all that I am. No matter what happens."

"Good," I murmured, kissing the flush on each of her cheeks. "Because I may not deserve you…but you're mine, and I'm yours. And I plan on creating a future where nothing and nobody will stand in the way of that ever again."

CHAPTER 17

EVA

By the time we made it out of our bedroom I could tell it was well past midday by the light streaming through the tan linen curtains. I found Quinn in the kitchen eating lunch with Rivan and Yael at the long, oak table, the smell wafting off the steaming bowls making me suddenly ravenous.

"About time," Yael said with a slow grin.

My lips quirked as I turned to Quinn. "I do hope they've been good guests."

Rivan laughed, low and rumbling. "We do happen to be housebroken."

"Debatable," Yael said with a shrug, and Quinn laughed. "We're already fast friends, don't worry. Even if she's been tightlipped on your most embarrassing stories despite our interrogation."

I raised a brow. "Knowing you, seeing if she'd give into your questioning was a test in itself."

Yael only smirked.

I nodded my thanks to Quinn as she set down a bowl in front of me, vegetable soup paired with a thick crusty bread that was slathered with salted butter. She sat next to me as I inhaled it, barely pausing between bites to breathe. Bash ate his own serving at a more leisurely pace on my other side. I noted the churning gray of his eyes before noticing the shadows that clung to my sleeves, seemingly unwilling to risk being separated from me.

Bash took my bowl as I finished mopping the remainder of the broth with my bread, rolling his eyes at my indignant noise in response before returning with a second helping. I gave him a sheepish look, and he brushed a kiss on the top of my head before going to help Yael and Rivan with the dishes.

Quinn sighed contentedly, leaning in so our arms rested against each other's. "While our parents were both bonded, I never really thought about the effect it must have, feeling another's emotions like your own."

"I'd say it took some getting used to," I said, swallowing a bite of soup-soaked bread. "But it didn't. With him, it felt as natural as breathing. Like it was always meant to be that way."

"You were empty for such a long time," Quinn said softly, watching the way Bash's eyes found mine across the room even as he responded in a low voice to whatever Rivan had asked him. "When I lost my parents, I at least knew *why*. Who and what they fought for. The reason they left me." She sighed. "I'm glad you finally got the answers you always deserved, along with someone who lights up your soul."

"My parents would have told us on our Seventeenth," I said, tensing at the memory of what happened instead. "I can't stop thinking about what it would have been like if they had. If we'd both made it back to Agadot with our families still intact."

Quinn gave me a sad smile, and I took her hand under the table. "It's easy to get lost in the would have's. I spent far too long wondering what would've happened if we'd gone with my parents when they left to see if it was safe to return. If somehow, I could've stopped what happened to them. Even if it's far more likely we would have all been captured or killed."

"I wish we had them with us," I whispered, a lump forming in my throat. "But I'm glad I at least have you here with me now."

Tobias walked into the room, his gaze immediately finding Quinn before he slowly walked over to the soup, ladling some into a bowl. His shoulders were stiff as he responded quietly to Bash, Yael, and Rivan's greetings, his face a cool mask. I frowned. My brother was a lot of things, but he had never been standoffish or shy. Though I knew he would be different after years apart and all he had endured.

I wondered if I seemed just as much of a stranger to him.

"What about you?" I asked Quinn. "Did anything eventful happen on your journey here that you left out?"

"You mean did I stumble into an *anima* bond with the fae warrior who brought me into this realm? Or did I fight off the False King himself more than once since getting here?"

Quinn laughed, and I noticed Tobias turn slightly at the sound, a smile teasing at the edges of his mouth before it slipped away.

I surprised myself by chuckling softly. "Just a few minor bumps along the way."

Quinn shrugged. "I ran into some trouble a few times, but it was nothing I couldn't handle."

She gave me a satisfied smile that I returned in kind. I was only too aware of how well-trained she was with the number of sparring sessions we had faced off against each other through the years.

Tobias silently sat down next to me, hesitancy radiating from every line of his hunched posture. I swallowed, trying not to think about how he had spent the last few years stuck in a cell, barely being able to talk while his magic was repeatedly stolen from him. Then winced as I remembered how painful that process had been for me just once. Now, my mental image of his time there was that much worse.

Yet I hadn't forgotten the fact that he had spent *years* not coming to find me after our parents' murders before his capture. Had made it all the way here to Soleara while letting me believe he was dead. I didn't care that he had done it to keep me safe. Quinn at least had the excuse of being magically bound not to speak about it. But my own brother? He had made me spend years missing him, *grieving* him. Even if the last few weren't his fault, he should've come back for me sooner.

And I was having a hard time getting over what could have been if he had.

Tobias turned to look at me, his mouth tightening at whatever he saw on my face. Even after all this time apart, he hadn't lost that twin intuition of knowing me so well he could practically read my mind. That sense of betrayal was only made worse by that. Because he should've known what I would've wanted.

And yet he had abandoned me.

Quinn's eyes narrowed as she looked back and forth between us, her brow furrowing. "Is everything okay?"

Neither Tobias nor I answered, still staring at each other in a silent standoff.

"We thought we might spend the afternoon training," Yael said as she walked toward us, Bash and Rivan close behind.

"Sure," I said, my voice tight despite my attempt at enthusiasm. Bash gave me a wary look, obviously aware of my change in mood. "I just need to go change."

Ignoring Bash's concerned expression, I dumped my empty bowl in the sink before rushing upstairs—my brother's gaze still boring into my back.

CHAPTER 18
EVA

I found Tobias in the courtyard, in an open-air garden surrounded by the giant house that had apparently once been my home. Plum trees surrounded us, their leaves a deep, blood red, the ground littered with them in a way that made me picture the aftermath of a battle.

Tobias was under a wooden overhang, partially hidden by a leafy branch. He was breathing deeply, his eyes closed, his feet shoulder-width apart, and his knees slightly bent. Slow and steady, he started to move, gracefully shifting his weight, flowing from one stance to the next. His muscles flexed against the simple white tunic he wore over black leather pants, seemingly unaffected by the chill in the air.

I recognized it immediately. A warm-up form our dad taught us in another realm...in another life. Balance and breathing, intention and movement all coming together to shape a calm I was sorely lacking in at the moment.

Sliding off my shoes, I came up next to my twin, seamlessly flowing into the familiar stances like putting on a second skin. Our breathing matched our movements, matched each other's even inhales and exhales as we moved purposefully together in an intricate series of footwork and poses.

It took longer than I thought to push away the thoughts trying to devour me. But whether it was the calisthenics, the breathing, or the company, I was able to force them down, burying them under a blanket of brief serenity.

I could feel curious eyes on us from where Bash, Rivan, Yael, and Quinn had silently paired up and started to spar. But neither Tobias nor I said a word to them, or to each other, up until our last breath out together.

We finished the form facing each other, open palms outstretched and reaching. Our eyes met, and we both dropped our hands to our sides. Tobias's gaze fastened around the familiar dagger I had kept safe for seven long years. His gaze dropped, then he stilled, shock clear on his face as he took in its mate at my side. "How—"

"Aviel had it," I said grimly. "He must have taken it the night of the fire."

I could feel Bash's eyes on me as I unsheathed it, holding it out so its black diamond gleamed darkly in the light. For a heartbeat, it seemed to emit a soft hum I faintly recognized before I flipped it in my hand with a flick of my wrist. My eyes locked with my brother's as I caught it.

Somehow, it felt unlike his in a way I couldn't entirely explain. Like this one was made to be mine.

It feels different than yours, I almost said. But it sounded even stupider on the tip of my tongue.

"So, no need to give yours back," I added nonchalantly, even as I anxiously continued flipping mine in my hand. "Not that I would have expected you to...though I thought I last saw it being thrown at a certain False King's head."

Shadows snaked around the hilt of my dagger, catching it midair before I could. *Ah.* Bash's mouth twisted in a small smirk, though he didn't miss a beat as his practice sword met Quinn's.

"I can't believe we're both back here," Tobias said in a low voice. "Even if it's without them. It's funny how it feels like forever ago our family was whole...and yet no time at all."

"I—" I stopped abruptly, as I couldn't seem to say the words without breaking. But his eyes seemed to reflect the words I couldn't say.

I still miss them so, so much.

"Me too, sis."

I looked away, blinking the sudden moisture from my eyes as I took in the orange-tinged sky. Tobias followed my gaze, faintly shuddering before seeming to steel himself.

"Eva, I owe you an—"

"Why didn't you come back for me sooner?" My voice shook faintly as that betrayal bled through. "Why—*why* didn't you tell me you were alive?"

Tobias tensed at the accusation in my voice, his lips tightening. My eyes narrowed. Then I raised my hands in a fighting stance, my elbows bent, one foot slightly forward. He copied me by habit, matching my sideways steps as we started circling each other.

The clash of metal from where Rivan and Yael had been sparring like their lives depended on it seemed to pause. Bash's eyes met mine over Tobias's shoulder where he and Quinn had been doing the same. He nodded at Quinn to keep going, but I could feel his gaze on me.

"I should have," Tobias said quietly, a hint of pleading in his voice.

I lunged forward, nimbly sweeping out a foot to knock him off balance. But he was ready, already spinning away, his arm reaching for my leg. I knocked it aside, before the blur of his kick nearly hit me in my stomach, his speed still impressive. Charging forward, I threw a fist at his face, my frustration breaking through. But Tobias deftly dodged, lashing out as he spun, moving with a lethal grace that made me hold my breath even as I deflected his attack.

As I punched toward his gut, he caught my wrist, the paleness of his skin against mine even more evident in the daylight. I stilled at the silvery scars on his wrists that mirrored mine, now visible with the way his tunic had ridden up his arm.

Tobias released me, then took a deliberate step back, breathing hard. "I thought I could stop him first. Make this realm safe for you before you even had to know about it. Keep you from the same fate as our—"

I launched myself at him, landing a strike to his chest that had him stumbling. He held up his hands, my blows glancing off his forearms as he backed away.

"And you just thought you'd let me think you were dead until then? Let me *grieve* for you, on top of Mom and Dad?"

"I thought—"

"You *left* me."

Tobias flinched worse than when I had hit him, looking stricken. I pressed my advantage, sweeping his legs out from under him in a quick twisting movement. Rivan let out a low whistle from somewhere behind us, but Tobias brought me down too, hooking his leg behind my knees. I rolled as he tried to pin me.

He winced as my elbow found his solar plexus but managed to pull me back against him. "By the time I made it here, to Soleara, it had been *months*. When I figured out how to return, you already thought I was dead. If you knew I wasn't, you would have wanted to know everything. And I wasn't about to break the wards keeping you safe, bring you here, and put you in danger. By the time I realized what a fool I'd been, I was trapped in his dungeon."

I struggled against Tobias's hold, but despite his captivity, he had noticeably spent his time honing his skills. Grunting, I kicked my legs back, using my momentum to fling my feet over my head, somersaulting backwards into a crouch. Tobias stood, eyeing me warily.

"You *were* a fool," I spat. "And look where it got us. With Aviel—"

What, precisely, do you think you can do against me, when all of you put together failed to stop me from getting exactly what I wanted?

A phantom pain swelled where my neck met my collarbone. Where that monster had marked me, as if saying his name had brought up what I had so carefully pushed down. Shakily, I brought my hand up, my fingers trailing under my shirt as I rubbed against the raised wound now scabbed over the old scar. Tobias's eyes flickered with light, his jaw clenching, and I knew he had put it together.

We would soon be forced to face him in order to end this. I sucked in a measured breath—the thought of seeking Aviel out made my skin crawl.

How could I be High Queen when I was a coward?

I glanced behind us. Bash had gone preternaturally still, like he could read my thoughts instead of just gods knew what I was sending across our bond. The rest of our group was no longer even attempting to pretend they were still training, having long since stopped pretending not to be listening.

Grimacing, I turned away. I couldn't stand the pity in their eyes. The way Bash's guilt swept down our bond in a flood of his own self-recrimination.

"I'm sorry," Tobias rasped. "I was trying to do the right thing and keep you safe from him. By the time I realized I was wrong to keep you in the dark, it was too late. But I did try to get back to you, sis. You don't know how many times in that cell I kicked myself for not trying to get home to you sooner so we could face this together."

I nodded stiffly. The light in his eyes flickered as I walked away to gather myself, still panting from our battle. Bash stepped toward me, but Yael got there first, a frown marring her beautiful face.

She tossed me a sword. "My turn."

I started to shake my head; my throat too tight to speak. But Yael had already raised her sword, her turquoise eyes narrowing. "You'll need more fight than that if you're going to survive this war."

My hands tightened around my sword, even as something inside me flinched at her finding me wanting. "I don't have to prove myself to you."

She feinted low. I evaded the swing of her sword, anger boiling in my stomach.

"Not to mention the wallowing."

My mouth twitched in annoyance. "I'm not—"

"Prove it."

Out of the corner of my eye, I saw Rivan hold out a sword to Tobias in invitation. He took it, still watching me closely.

Not wanting to think anymore, I lunged forward in an attack. Yael parried my wild blow, her agile movements and impeccable footwork quickly forcing me to go on the defensive. Her strikes were swift and unrelenting, obviously meant to engage rather than disarm. So quick that all I could focus on was anticipating her next move, the brutal pace giving me an outlet for the pressure still trapped in my chest.

She had baited me on purpose. Offering herself up as a target for my anger. She had known how much I needed to work out my frustration, my fear, before it could break me.

I found myself winded far too soon, my side aching. Holding up a hand, I then pressed it into the stitch in my side, wincing as I pushed against the remnants of a bruise while trying to catch my breath.

Yael stepped back, though her sword was still raised. "If you're going to be High Queen, the least I can do is help you stay in shape for the fight ahead."

Lazily lifting my sword, I snorted derisively before I could stop myself. "Some High Queen."

I felt too raw, too worked up from the hurt still shadowing Tobias's face to guard what was coming out of my mouth.

Yael shot forward, her sword sweeping low. "What is *that* supposed to mean?"

I leapt backwards, barely managing to defend myself.

"Exactly what it sounds like," I snapped, slashing downwards only for her to block me. "What is this, fight therapy day?"

Yael smirked as our swords clanged together once again. "Whatever works, Your Majesty."

I sighed at the title, lowering my voice along with my sword. "What if the people of Agadot don't want me? What if the Choosing rejects me, despite my magic?" My voice wavered as my fears tumbled out despite myself. "What if I'm just not good enough?"

Yael didn't hesitate. "You are. You will be. And the fact that you're worried about it instead of going straight to the overly entitled presumptiveness of most rulers speaks for itself about your worthiness." She dropped her blade to her side as she stepped closer. "You may not know this land, but you are kind and smart and brave. And we'll be here to teach you whatever you can't learn. Whoever isn't swayed by the magic of the land choosing you will learn to believe in you when you become the advocate I know you will be. The leader this realm deserves."

She grabbed my hand, looking over her shoulder to glare at the others, and I heard the clang of swords as they resumed their battling. "Besides, nobody in this bloody band has their lives together, let alone the rest of the realm. So take a breath. You can withstand anything. Including becoming High Queen. Especially with your family by your side." Her eyes narrowed. "And I'll fight anyone who says a bad word about you."

I cocked my head. "Including what I just said about myself?"

She raised her sword threateningly, an amused glint in her eye. "Square up then, let's go."

I chuckled quietly, somehow feeling better despite everything. With a smile, I raised my sword.

Yael lunged toward me with a sweeping strike that I barely managed to deflect. Sweat dripped down my back even as I felt a tingle of awareness on the nape of my neck. My blade met Yael's in a clash of metal as I blatantly ignored the searing weight of my brother's gaze, losing myself in the rhythm of our movements even as my arms started to shake. Refusing to look his way even as he waved Rivan off, wiping the sweat off his neck with his sleeve as he disappeared into what had once been our home.

CHAPTER 19
BASH

Quinn had yet to stop grinning at me as we settled in for dinner. I felt strangely proud to have gained Eva's best friend's immediate approval, especially after my disastrous start with her twin. Tucking a still-damp curl behind Eva's ear, freshly washed after our training session, I suppressed a laugh as Quinn beamed at me in response.

I wasn't sure whether to be happy that Eva had obviously never let anyone touch her like this or sad at how lonely she had been before we met. With the notable exception of her best friend. I caught Quinn's gaze and grinned back; grateful they at least always had each other.

Rivan's empty mug clunked down on the smooth planks of the cedar table, Thorin refilling it with ale before it even settled. He, Akeno, and Pari had joined us for dinner, dressed in formal clothes that reminded me once again of Eva's station here. She and Tobias were Solearan royalty even without her being the future High Queen.

"So," Pari drawled from where she sat by Yael. "I assume we're here to talk about a plan."

Rivan gave her a disgruntled look, and I raised an eyebrow. Had something happened between the two of them? It was strange to see him dislike anyone, let alone outwardly, when he tended to easily get along with everyone.

Eva nodded, her nails biting into the rose-shaped scar on her palm hard enough to leave a mark. "We know the False King's next step is to go through the Choosing. To trick it somehow with the blood and the magic he stole from me." She swallowed, looking faintly nauseous, and my fingers dug into the table. "But in order to stop him…"

"—we need to figure out where the Choosing takes place," I continued.

"And find a way to get there first," she finished.

"One impossible thing at a time, hellion," I murmured, reaching out to take her hand, my thumbs rubbing against the crescent-shaped red marks she had left behind.

Yael slowly shook her head. "Queen Amerie's old advisors have been systemically wiped out, taken by the False Prince to further his own agenda, then killed so they couldn't share that information with anyone else. Marin tried to locate the rest of them after the one staying in Imyr disappeared not too long ago. She found that they'd either been stationed in Morehaven, whether or not they went willingly, or vanished without a trace."

"So he likely already knows the location of the Choosing," Pari mused. "Which means he has the advantage."

"Right now, he's returned to Morehaven after the search for Her Majesty failed," Thorin said gravely, nodding at my *anima*.

Eva tensed. "Just Eva, please."

Thorin tilted his head. "But—"

"You three saved my life," Eva said simply, her gaze turning inward for a moment as if remembering the circumstances. She gave a quick shake of her head, then looked at Thorin, Akeno, and Pari each in turn. "So I'd like you to use my name." A smile quirked her lips. "I'd ask for you to do it anyway, but especially in light of that."

They all shared a solemn look before bowing their heads in unison.

"If he's back in Morehaven, then he's likely regenerating his power," Tobias said in a dark voice. "He'll need to before going wherever it is he needs to go after Eva's quick thinking with the collar. Unless the Choosing is held south of us?"

Yael shook her head. "Our remaining spies there say his army is preparing to leave, though no hint as to where except for the winter clothes. So we can count out the desert." Her lips twitched to the side, the only tell of her disdain for her homeland. "He's likely heading back north, with a larger contingent this time based on the number of troops he's recalled. But we still need to figure out where he's heading, unless we plan to just follow him."

Rivan smiled grimly, setting down his ale. "I have an idea, but you're not going to like it."

Yael groaned, taking a long swig of hers before asking, "What?"

"We need to find a sprite."

Eva and Quinn exchanged a wide-eyed look. Quinn leaned forward eagerly. "Like, *actual* faeries?"

Even Tobias had perked up, though whether that was from the talk of faeries or the excitement in Quinn's voice, it was hard to say. I hadn't missed the way his eyes softened when he looked at his sister's best friend. From the sideways look Eva gave her brother, neither had she.

Rivan nodded. "Though I doubt they'll be what you're expecting. Usually, they only deign to be seen as faerie lights—little blue lights in the forest that disappear the second you try to catch one."

Eva's fork clattered to her plate. Undiluted shock prickled down our bond, piercingly electrifying. "Little blue lights?" she choked out, her face pale.

Everyone turned to look at her. My grip on her hand tightened.

"I saw one," Eva whispered. "When I first escaped from Av—from Morehaven." My throat closed up as she looked past me with hollow eyes, lost in memory. "When I got to the forest, there was a blue light that led me to safety." She swallowed. "I forgot about it afterward with everything else going on...and even then, I thought I imagined it."

Rivan's face had turned deadly, as if remembering the moment he had found her half-dead in those woods. I suppressed a shudder as I remembered her bleeding and lifeless in his arms. But Rivan's voice was forcibly light as he said, "Well, that bodes well for my plan if one's already helped you once."

"You want to find a sprite," I repeated incredulously. "You realize that's asking for trouble if they decide they don't want to be found? And potentially more trouble if they do."

Rivan just nodded, taking a bite from his apple unconcernedly.

Yael was watching Eva closely. "Stands to reason they would make an appearance for their true High Queen."

Eva sighed with resignation, the flicker of unease disappearing as quickly as it appeared. She had gotten far too skilled at keeping me out, especially for the things that bothered her. While I appreciated that level of shielding, especially with Aviel's history of dreamwalking to her, I wished she didn't feel the need to do so with me even if I understood the impulse. Though we couldn't count on the lack of Tobias's bloodlink to keep her safe from Aviel's machinations...not when there was no telling what dark magic he had worked while she had been his prisoner.

Tobias raised a brow. "And why do we need a sprite in the first place?"

"Because they're seers by nature," Rivan said. "They'll know where we need to go. And the more we know about stopping Aviel, the more of an edge we have."

Yael snorted. "They're also notoriously given to twisting truths to suit their own whims."

Rivan sighed. "Does anyone else have a better idea?"

Eva looked at me imploringly, the trust in her gaze making my heart twist.

I shrugged, trying not to let my apprehension show. "One already helped you. Perhaps they'll do so again."

"Fine," Eva said, looking resolved even though I could feel her nerves. "It's worth a shot."

"That's the spirit," Quinn said merrily.

CHAPTER 20
ESTELLE

It began with flowers. Not the stuffy, perfect blooms that gilded my room already, but a bouquet of my favorite wildflowers—a veritable rainbow of color and life adorned with desert roses I knew must've come from Adrian's homeland. A quick trip through the mirror, and yet the thought behind it, the innate sense that he hadn't asked anyone else to acquire these for him but picked them himself made me pause, breathing them in.

But it was the note that made my breath catch in my chest...the love letter.

Princess,

I woke up dreaming of the taste of your lips, those sweet little sounds you make echoing in my ears. While I've heard the tales of the dreamwalking this bond entails, I'm concerned I won't be able to tell the difference as all my dreams now are of you.

You told me you don't feel like you have a choice in this...and yet, I feel that I'm the one who never had a choice in falling for you when, from the moment I met you, I had already fallen. Though choice is little match for fate, especially not when the two are aligned (at least for me. But I've never been afraid of a challenge, especially with you as its reward).

Yours,

—A

P.S. When can I see you?

There was a tiny sketch of a rose next to the swirling *A* of his signature, like Adrian had drawn it while staring at one of the partially unfurled buds now sitting on my bedside. I quickly found a piece of parchment, then sent my response in a flash of light before I lost my nerve.

Princeling,

You might have featured in my dreams too. Not in the night, but as a notion— a dream— that I might one day find someone to whom I might belong, and who would belong to me. Said person has always seemed fictious, nebulous, and entirely imaginary. An unattainable farce in a world not meant for happy endings.

But when I woke up today...for the first time, that figure had a face I recognized.

Cordially,

—E

P.S. I plan to spar after breakfast if you find yourself looking for another challenge.

I had barely gotten dressed when I jumped at a knock on my door. Before I even opened it, I knew who would be standing there.

Adrian leaned against the doorway in one long line. My letter was clutched in one hand, a steaming mug of what I could already smell was my favorite tea in the other. "Cordially?"

"Would you have preferred 'amiably'?" I kept my tone cool even as my heartrate skittered. "Or perhaps, 'best wishes'?"

He laughed and something inside my chest expanded almost unbearably at the sound. "I would've preferred 'yours', just as I am to you. But I suppose this is one more thing for me to work towards."

"You're unnervingly blunt," I said before I could stop myself, his earnestness once again knocking me a bit off-kilter.

"I don't much care for the games and false pleasantries of politics, just ask my brother." Adrian smirked unabashedly. "But there's no reason to be anything but honest with you."

I pursed my lips. "Then perhaps you'll tell me why you're here, Princeling."

"You mentioned breakfast," Adrian said, his eyes hopeful. "It occurred to me that you might need a companion for that too."

I took the mug from him, breathing in its rich, earthy scent before taking a sip. "I suppose I do. Though I had a book I meant to finish."

"Then I'll read it to you," he said, so sincerely I felt another piece of my resistance fall away. "I don't want to miss another minute with you."

As we left the room, Adrian wrapped his hand around mine the second he was close enough to do so. I found myself entirely unwilling to pull it away.

I promised Adrian I was wholly up to the task of changing for a ride in the woods by myself—an assertion I immediately wanted to take back as the heat in his gaze seared me to my core. His eyes had danced as though that *anima* bond was already in place, and he could sense my growing need for him. But he had merely lifted my hand, pressing his full lips against my knuckles as he promised to wait for me.

A ride in the cool air would be good for me. I couldn't get my mind off the way he had taken the book I had brought with me to breakfast—an autobiography I had found rather dry until his lilting accent made each syllable sound like an invitation. It was dangerous, the way he made me feel. Especially as I got to know him and couldn't blame my burgeoning feelings on a mix of loneliness and lust.

As I opened the door to my room, any lingering heat from breakfast was immediately doused in a bath of ice water as I saw my father waiting for me.

Thank the gods I hadn't brought Adrian with me.

I hadn't failed to notice that with my father being utterly preoccupied with planning for the ceremony, he had been far too busy to micromanage me for once. Nor that the lack of his watchful eye had left the way open for Adrian to spend every waking minute doing exactly what I had asked of him—convincing me we belonged together.

Velan Maris cut an imposing figure against the rising mist outside the window. Trim, and lightly muscled, he wore a high-necked waistcoat over his crisp white shirt—never one for adornments, though every stitch he had on was made of the finest of materials. The austere lines of his face tightened as he turned to me, no hint of a smile. Not that I had expected one.

"Estelle."

I dipped my head demurely. "Father."

"I thought it was past time we discussed what's expected of you."

He had never been much for pleasantries, though his courtly persona was another matter. I kept my face impassive, biting back my retort that what was expected of me seemed to be the only thing we had ever talked about. "Do you have an objection to this match?"

My eyes narrowed at the thought that he might try to keep me from Adrian, despite my own uncertainties. My father's head tilted as my jaw flexed, unable to entirely keep the suddenly braying beast inside me at bay.

"I'm not so foolish as to disobey the High Queen's wishes," my father said coolly. "But in this case, they appear to be aligned with my own aspirations for you. We can only be thankful that bond seems to have chosen wisely."

I inwardly winced at his clinical tone in comparison to Adrian's awe and excitement, though I knew better than to expect anything resembling affection from him.

My father cleared his throat. "While I've only been able to look into the boy so much in the short time I've had to do so, he's Celestial, royal, and well-bred. His parents seem to have raised him with the rigor needed to rule, and, despite Queen Amerie's age, she hasn't let it slip to them why this match is more fortuitous to them than they could ever imagine. Though—"

I hid a smile at the thought of the High Queen's reaction should my father ever share such a disrespectful assessment to her face.

"—it's far past time that she steps down and lets a new ruler take the throne, for the good of the realm. And with me to guide you, that's exactly what this match will accomplish—"

Tuning him out, I nodded along to the speech I had heard many times before. How only through his leadership and direction would I succeed. I should have known my father would be all too thrilled at the prospect of marrying me off to another Celestial, and a royal one at that—never mind that I was both. He must have been delighted that my *anima* was my age, and therefore someone he thought he could control. Because there had never been a concern about my happiness, only power—his, first and foremost.

"—you'll need someone like him at your side to go through the Choosing one day."

I hid my grimace, not bothering to ask if 'like him' referred to Adrian's pedigree, his magic, or simply the fact that he was born with a penis. Considering *I* had been born with everything but, I already knew the answer.

He stepped forward, taking my hands in a way I was sure was calculated, even as part of me wished it wasn't. "Your mother would have been pleased to see you find your *anima*."

I hid my bristle with another dip of my head as he quickly dropped my hands. It was all I could do not to clench them into fists. How *dare* he use her to sway me? As if I hadn't heard him lament my mother's 'weakness' that had led to her death during my birth, leaving my father with only me as his heir and not the male copy of himself he had always dreamed of—a fact he often shared whenever he found me lacking.

My magic crackled within me, and I knew if I raised my gaze, he would see the evidence of my fury.

I needed to calm down; to find some semblance of the control that was usually second nature to me. Yet, somehow, it evaded my grasp.

One day, I would be High Queen, and I would be free of the males who thought they knew better than me. It wouldn't be long until I no longer had to play this game.

But I couldn't help but add, "I haven't given Adrian my response yet."

"Well of course," he sniffed. "But now that I'm certain he'll be accommodating—"

He thought my decision hinged on *his* say so. I might have laughed if I didn't feel like I wanted to cry.

"Then I should tell him."

My father blinked in surprise. I realized too late that I had cut him off as his mouth tightened. "I think not. Perhaps after the bonding ceremony, and after we know his allegiances have shifted to our own ends. After all, we cannot simply trust an outsider—"

"An outsider who's meant to be my soul bonded."

My father's gaze narrowed. "It seems you have grown too used to your intended's kowtowing to remember your manners. I will forgive it, given the circumstances. But do not test my patience a third time."

I could feel my light demanding an outlet, my fingertips heating not at the insult to me, but at the slight to my *anima*—

There was a knock at the door. My light seemed to settle as I stepped toward it. I felt it practically *purr* as I opened the door to Adrian's dark eyes, that ever-present smile curving his lips. "I thought I'd check on you, Princess. After all, we have places to—"

Adrian cut off when he saw my father, then bent in a formal bow. "Your Highness." He straightened. "My apologies, if this isn't a good time—"

"Couldn't be better," I cut in before my father could say otherwise.

He shot me a look. "I believe we're done here. Unless you have any questions about our priorities."

Silently, I shook my head. I knew exactly what *his* priorities were.

Adrian frowned slightly as he took in the coldness in my father's tone. "I was planning to take your daughter to the stables. I hear she's quite the equestrian."

My father waved a hand dismissively. "Fine. Though don't stay away too long."

I straightened on impulse as he walked toward me, but he passed me without a second glance. Letting out a breath I hadn't realized I had been holding, I tried not to let my shoulders slump with the sudden heaviness that had descended upon me. When Adrian reached for me, I stepped away as though I hadn't noticed he had done so, moving swiftly to my dresser.

His swallow was audible. "Estelle…is everything okay?"

"Of course," I said woodenly. "I'll just be a minute."

I chanced a glance back at him as my fingers curled against the cool, curved metal of the drawer's handles. Adrian's brow was furrowed with concern, his hands flexing at his sides like he didn't know what to do with them. But his gaze softened as it met mine, and that creature that had awoken inside me seemed to settle as well.

"Take your time," he said earnestly. "I'll be here whenever you're ready. I'll always be there for you."

A faint blush tinged his cheeks before he turned around, shutting the door behind him before he could see the tears that sprang to my eyes at the casual declaration. The way he offered it so easily, and without expectation.

I furtively wiped my eyes as I bent down to put on my riding boots, wondering if I had ever been loved without conditions. Or if that even counted as love at all.

CHAPTER 21

EVA

The cool night air settled against my skin like it was waiting for me. A crisp wind whispered secrets through the branches of the towering pines above, casting swaying shadows as we wandered aimlessly through the mountain woods. I was thankful for the thick navy cloak Quinn had procured for me before we left as I wrapped it more tightly around myself.

Rivan had explained that we would know what we were looking for when we saw it—a fairy mound. The usually circular pile of earth where the Little Folk came to revel in the moonlight, and grant an audience to those seeking their council, should they find them worthy of their time. Quinn's jubilation at the prospect of meeting such a creature almost made me forget the stakes if we failed.

We split up, ambling through the moon bright forest, though my brother followed the same path as mine. The awkward silence between us seemed to deepen with every rustle of leaves. As we passed a desiccated section of earth, I winced at the thought of the curse so close to what was once again my home. Now that I understood the reason behind it, it was almost as though I could feel the absence of magic; the nothingness in its place making a shiver go down my spine.

When I looked Tobias's way, his shoulders were hunched, looking as though he was struggling to find his words. Like that iron mask was once again blocking what he wanted to say.

I had already forgiven him. I shouldn't have lashed out like I had in the first place. Not when we had been granted the chance to be together again, for gods knew how long. That ever-present anxious feeling in the back of my mind seemed to hum louder at that thought—knowing that our time together was as uncertain as whether we would survive what came next.

Quietly, I sat down on a moss-covered log, a curve in the wood serving as a seat. Beckoning my brother to join me with a jerk of my head, I took my canteen from my pack, taking a long sip as he did the same.

Night had deepened around us, though dappled moonlight still found a way in through the thick canopy above, the faint glow of fireflies lighting up the underbrush. On instinct, I sent a scattered wave of darkness up to meet it, letting it swirl around my twin and I like a dark current. I never wanted to know the feeling of not having my magic ever again.

Tobias looked up with awe, and I realized he had never had the chance to see what I could do beyond that final fateful battle with Aviel.

"I can't believe we went so long without knowing about this," I whispered into the beautiful, fractured darkness.

Tobias reached up a hand, and my magic swirled around it in response. A rare smile flitted across his mouth—then he sent a stream of sparks into the air, melding into my darkness like stars in the night sky. Together they left the somewhat startling impression that the sky had fallen down around us.

"You're right, you know," Tobias said, his voice scratchy. "I should have come back for you sooner."

"Toby—" I started, but he shook his head.

"Once I made it to Soleara and learned how to mirror back...I should have come back for you right away." Tobias hung his head, his chestnut hair falling around his face. "But I knew you were safer there. He was hunting for you and had been for so long, and everything I learned about him made keeping you in the dark sound like the only option." He blew out a long breath before looking me in the eyes. "Maybe it was hubris.

Maybe it was the grief of watching what happened to our parents and not wanting it to happen to you too. But I thought I could stop him…fix it, somehow, before you even found out about this realm and what awaited you here."

I leaned against his shoulder, watching his stars flicker above us.

"I wish you had too," I said simply. "But we can't rewrite the past. I'm just sorry I didn't know sooner so I could've been there to save *you*." I took a shuddering breath. "I don't know how you endured it. I was only trapped there for a few days, and I was going out of my mind being chained and magicless. And you endured *years* of that torture."

His eyes flickered, something cold and dark flashing across his face at whatever memory I had conjured.

"If you need to talk about it, I'm here," I said gently, remembering the look in Bash's eyes when he told me the same. "When you're ready. But I am sorry I didn't save you from him sooner, no matter the circumstances."

My fingers rested on his arm, lightly running up his forearm in an ascending arpeggio. An old habit, one he had once made fun of me for, of playing piano even when there wasn't one.

You know no one can hear it, right? he had once asked me as I ran scales along my desk, his tone full of wry amusement.

I had merely shrugged. *I can.*

His eyes flared in recognition, followed by a shadow of that familiar smile. "I guess we both need to work on our savior complexes."

I choked out a laugh. "After what happened in Morehaven, Bash would agree with you."

"I think we would all feel better if you listened to him," Tobias grumbled. "Your *anima*…who's growing on me despite my best efforts."

I couldn't help my smile. "I'm glad to hear you two are getting along. I knew you would like him."

Tobias's mouth twitched. "There's no need to look so smug about it."

I wrapped my arm around his waist, then leaned against him. His arm snaked around my shoulders, his breathing shaky as we sat and stared at the stars—those of our own creation fading into the ones far away.

"Come on," Tobias said in a low murmur, helping me to my feet. "We do have a job to do."

It felt like we had been circling the same spot in the forest for hours when we finally heard Rivan yell excitedly, "Found it!"

By the time we reached him, the others had already gathered. In the middle of an eerily perfect circle of trees stood a large mound of earth, covered in a thick layer of moss and glistening with dew in the moonlight. It was encircled by a ring of white mushrooms unlike any I had seen before, some as wide as dinner plates, each gleaming with an otherworldly light.

It felt unnervingly *alive*, pulsing with a strange energy I could feel in my bones.

Tobias and I swapped a glance, and I knew we were both thinking of the same bedtime story our father had read to us long ago. The one where the faeries had stolen the children away the second they were foolish enough to enter the circle. He frowned; his trepidation obvious.

Obviously, it was going to be me. I was the one the sprite had found once before when they led me through that forest. The one meant to rule this realm—and maybe the Little Folk knew that too.

I took a step forward, but Tobias grabbed my hand. I twisted back toward him, giving him an irritated look that he returned in kind.

His eyes narrowed, and I knew what he was thinking. *Like hell you will.*

My mouth pursed. *We both know I'm going to be the one to do this.*

The look he gave me was pure challenge. *Try it and see what happens.*

I rolled my eyes. If he was so afraid of what would happen when I stepped on the mound, he could go first, before my inevitable turn.

Crossing my arms, I said, "Go ahead, if you feel so strongly about it."

"*What?*" Rivan asked, and I realized we hadn't been speaking aloud. Yael looked faintly amused.

"Twins," Bash grumbled. "There couldn't be anything more fae."

Quinn looked curious. "What does *that* mean?"

Yael laughed; the soft sound quickly swallowed by the dense woods. "He means that twins, doppelgangers, spirit doubles...in our realm, they tend to be known for trouble and tricks."

"Well, that tracks," I said with a wicked grin.

Tobias merely rolled his eyes, the gesture so quintessentially like the old him, I couldn't help my small sigh of relief. Maybe Aviel hadn't stolen that from him entirely. With time, he might be able to regain some of what he had lost during those years, even if I knew that neither of us would ever be those carefree children again.

Muttering under his breath, he stepped over the ring of mushrooms, leaping gracefully into the middle of the mound. I held my breath for a long moment, waiting for something—anything—to happen. Despite the sudden, ominous hush of the forest creatures the moment he stepped foot into the faerie circle, no sprite appeared.

Tobias turned in a slow, expectant circle. Nothing happened.

"Told you," I said dryly.

Rivan threw up his hands in exasperation.

"At least we know it's not some form of gate," Tobias exclaimed as he jumped down.

"How kind of you to make sure," I said, walking past him. "But the children in those stories always seemed to find what they were looking for on the other side, didn't they?"

"Except for the ones who never returned," Tobias said darkly.

"What stories?" Quinn asked, her gaze amused as she looked between us.

I stopped at the edge of the mushrooms, the large lid of one nearly up to my knees. "A book my dad used to read to us about faerie circles and the children they stole away. Seems more accurate to the mirrors here, unless I'm about to fall through the veil to elsewhere and find my deepest desire, only to realize it was back where I started all along..."

Taking a large step over the mushrooms, I made it to the top of the mound feeling vaguely foolish. I stood there, looking at them all looking at me, for what felt like forever in the chilled night before I let out a loud huff of impatience.

Bash chuckled softly, though I knew he had already felt the emotion down our bond. Rivan gave us both an annoyed look.

"They're not going to come if you aren't quiet," Rivan muttered.

Quinn turned to him. "Did you also have a bedtime story about faerie mounds and sprites that has you so knowledgeable?"

Bash smirked. "I feel vaguely left out."

"They're not going to come at all with a crowd," I said, exasperated. "Just go wait back at the horses and give me some time on my own."

Bash looked like he wanted to argue but nodded. "We'll return in an hour to make sure everything's okay."

"Two," I replied pointedly.

"The woods here aren't necessarily safe," Bash said warily. "There's no telling what creatures reside here, and even if we're close by—"

"*Two*," I insisted. "I can take care of myself. You'll feel it if anything goes wrong, and I can hold my own long enough for you to return. With all the circling we did, we're not that far from where we started. Not to mention I can easily reach you."

Pointedly, I tapped my finger against my palm, the iridescent quill on my other hand shimmering as I wrote two words.

Stop worrying.

Bash shot me a baleful look as he read the message on his hand, before scribbling one back.

Don't count on it.

I could sense his anxiety at the thought of leaving me here, the bad memories it stirred. But he didn't argue as they all acquiesced to my demand.

"Remember," Rivan said, turning back to me at the edge of the clearing, "don't make any promises. Don't make any threats. And *don't* piss it off."

Bash paused, his eyes darting back to mine before he turned to leave, his shadows mixing with the dusk as they lingered behind him like they didn't want to go either. As the soft sounds of their footsteps were swallowed by the woods, I tried not to feel uneasy, even as I heard the rustle of wings from somewhere above me.

Perhaps it was just a bat. Perhaps it was something far more dangerous.

Carefully, I tightened my hold on my bond with Bash, unwilling to have him ruin my stakeout should some small creature surprise me.

I started to pace, then stopped, afraid I might trample upon something sacred. With a sigh, I sank into a seat, folding my legs beneath me as my hands balled nervously into fists. My fingers rubbed against my palm, tracing the rose whose ridges I had long since memorized. Struggling not to jump at each rustle of leaves or the occasional crack of branches as I tried not to worry this had all been for nothing.

"Hello friend," I whispered under my breath, trying not to feel silly for talking to the empty air. "I owe you a debt, one I'd like to thank you for in person. And I have a question or two…if you don't mind."

My nails bit into my palm as the forest didn't deign to answer. Closing my eyes, I thought back to the frantic terror of that night. Had I done anything inadvertent to summon it? I hadn't used my magic, not with that collar around my neck. Hadn't said anything of note, at least not that I could remember in my delirium. Only pure adrenaline and fear had kept me moving, the forest floor slicing my feet so badly I had left behind a trail of…

Blood.

Carefully, I removed my dagger from its sheath, the accompanying sound far too loud as the air seemed to thicken. Clenching my jaw, I sliced it against my opposite palm, wincing as I squeezed my fist so that my blood dripped upon the center of the circle. Wiping the remaining smear on my blade onto the moss, I returned it to my side as the dark drops sank into the mound.

The woods stayed silent, the night deepening as a cloud went over the moon. My breath caught as I realized the glow of the fireflies had disappeared, the sudden blackness reminding me far too much of a cold, iron box closing in around me, that once comforting darkness bent on smothering any last semblance of hope.

A blue light flickered through the leaves of one of the surrounding trees—one that I recognized immediately from that horrible night. That shimmer of sapphire that had led me straight to safety. To my friends.

Then the sprite was there before me, perched on a low branch so we were nearly eye to eye. She was barely the size of my hand, with elflike features and shimmering blue wings so oblong they reminded me of a dragonfly. And she was entirely nude, her skin so dark she almost blended into the night. Only the blue sheen on her skin allowed me to see the outline of her large, unblinking eyes, her deep blue lips, and the voluptuous curves of her body. Her hair was a wild, electric azure that matched her dragonfly wings, somehow still despite her continuous fluttering.

I didn't dare move an inch or take too deep a breath. She cocked her head, as if waiting for me to make the first move. Then she sunk into a deep bow, her wings tilting forward with a slow flap before she rose.

Hastily, I bowed back, though the hair on the back of my neck rose at leaving myself so exposed. While her features were human, they also *weren't*, in a beautiful yet terrible way I couldn't entirely comprehend.

"I remember you," I croaked, my throat suddenly dry. "It was you in the forest that night who led me to them...wasn't it?"

"And I remember you, girl," the sprite's voice was everywhere at once and louder than I expected, each word reverberating through the brisk night air. "Night with a soul of iron, forged in fire. The lost queen. Yes, I know who you are...and who you will be. Or I wouldn't have come."

I swallowed hard against my parched throat. "Thank you, for what you did that night. For saving me." The sprite nodded slightly in acknowledgement, her dark eyes never leaving mine. "But if you know all that, then you know why I'm here...and who I'm trying to stop. Can you help me?"

She nodded slowly, then flashed her sharp, black teeth in what I wasn't sure was a threatening look or a smile. Rivan's words echoed in my head. *Don't make any promises. Don't make any threats. And don't piss it off.*

"Seeing what lies ahead is a strange business," she mused. "We can see intent, and how it will shape what comes to pass. And we have seen the False One's attempt to circumvent the rules of this realm."

"I want to stop him for the good of the realm," I said firmly, hoping my sincerity showed. "But with the nature of his magic, he's too powerful for me to stop. I need to know where the Choosing takes place so I can get there first. And if he has a weakness that we can exploit to stop him if we don't. Something we've overlooked or can use to drain his stolen power or keep him from gaining more long enough to end him for good." I paused, belatedly adding, "Please."

Her head tilted from side to side, the motion almost birdlike. "It's not a matter of what to take from him. It's a matter of what he took from you."

She stared at me with those wide, unblinking eyes, wholly black and entirely disconcerting.

"He took my magic," I said, haltingly. "But that's—"

"And your blood," the sprite said, so matter-of-factly that my skin crawled.

"My…" I trailed off as I remembered the puncture marks down my arms after my initial imprisonment. I had assumed they were all from Aviel drugging me, or him making Alette do so. But in my unconsciousness, it would have been only too easy to take my blood as well. My insides twisted at yet another invasion.

"He would have to steal both from you to be crowned," she continued, those luminescent wings fluttering in mesmerizing rhythm. "Your magic at his command, and your blood in his veins, in order to complete the Choosing. But he took it one step further, creating a bloodbond not so easily broken." Those black teeth glinted in the moonlight in a vicious smile, her head tilting at an unnatural angle. "And so, you have the way to stop him."

"I'm sorry," I stammered, ignoring the sinking sensation in my stomach. "But I don't understand."

"He bound you to him, girl," she said, her voice harsh and all-encompassing. "Your blood binds your life to his…and his to yours. What happens to one will happen to the other."

The world seemed to narrow in on me as I finally made sense of what she meant. "You're saying…we're linked. That if I'm injured, it will slow him down—"

"He didn't link your bodies," the sprite sneered. "He bonded your *lives*. There is only one way to be certain. To stop him for good."

There was a dull, tearing sensation in my chest. A roaring in my ears as I realized what, exactly, her words implied. "The only way to stop him is to…kill myself?" The two words seemed to echo faintly in the thickening dark. I shook my head. "Absolutely not. There has to be another way."

"There is always another way," the sprite said placatingly. "And there is always another choice. But will you be able to make it?" Her laugh was high and shrill, echoing strangely in the night like it was coming from all around me. "Or will it be made for you?"

"Please," I begged, nausea roiling in my gut. "There must be something else you can tell me. Something to help me stop him before the curse, and the effects of his rule, destroys your home too. If you can tell me how to reach the Choosing first, if I can just stop him before he attempts to thwart it, then maybe I won't have to resort to that."

Those sharp black teeth flashed as she leered at me as though disappointed. "Changing destiny's a weighty business. Though there is something...strange. Perhaps it is not yet set in stone."

The sprite dipped her head down in consideration, her hypnotizing wings slowing. I realized I was holding my breath only when I was forced to take another.

"There is a mirror," she said deliberately. "The Seeing Mirror, deep in the heart of Adronix. It is there that you seek, there you must reach before the False One, for it is the gateway to the Choosing. Only those meant to rule may pass through." She darted forward, her wings a blur as she hovered only inches from my face. "Once he claims the crown with your power and your blood, you will lose your chance to stop him."

Adronix. I remembered the name—the frozen northern mountain the False King had supposedly been imprisoned beneath, though he had been safe in Morehaven posing as the savior prince. My heart beat unsteadily in my ears, hope forming against all probability. "And if I get there before he does...if I become High Queen. Will I be able to stop him?"

The sprite stared at me in a way that sent a shiver down my spine. "I met your mother once in these same woods. The Queen Who Might Have Been. I told her of the False One, and of the danger he would pose to her progeny. She was not afraid of her destiny. Of what would happen in the end."

She studied me, and for a second, I thought she almost looked sad. "My gift to you is the one left by her to my safekeeping. If only for her sacrifice, I hope you get to make another choice. Remember...the only way out is through."

An unbearable heaviness settled in my chest at the words that could have only come from my mother's lips. I opened my mouth, desperate to know more about their last meeting. About how much, exactly, my mother had known about her fate, and what awaited her—

But the sprite was already gone.

Something glinted on the moss of the mound below me, exactly where I had spilled my blood. I knelt down, feeling numb even as the word for what lay before me hazily surfaced from that long-forgotten fairytale.

A boon.

The silver ring's thin band split in four to hold an oval-shaped gray diamond the exact color of Bash's shadows. I pulled it onto my shaking finger, utterly unsurprised to find it a perfect fit. The diamond seemed to ripple in the moonlight as the clouds finally parted.

Gingerly, I stepped over the mushrooms now swaying mockingly in the breeze. Stumbling backwards the second I was free of the circle, I fell to my knees, struggling to breathe.

The night flickered strangely as a gust of icy wind tore through the trees. But it wasn't the source of my shivering as I slowly got to my feet, my steps far heavier than when I came here. I managed one, shuddering inhale, my exhale cut off in a sharp gasp that was quickly carried away with the wind.

CHAPTER 22

BASH

T he emotions Eva sent down our bond felt somewhat muted, though they were such a whirlwind that I knew she must have succeeded. I updated the others as we shivered by the horses. Yet there was something about what she was feeling that made me uneasy, the grimy taste of something like...dread.

My finger went to my palm, the impulse almost unconscious.

Any luck?

I stared at my empty palm, trying not to think about how much her lack of response reminded me of those days I had done nothing while she had been imprisoned, thinking she was safe with her prince. How I had watched that same crease-lined space during each insufferable hour after she had been taken from me the second time.

Just as I was about to head back to the faerie mound to check on her, consequences be damned, Eva stepped out from between the trees. Her face was too pale in the moonlight, looking lost even though she had easily found us. As her gaze met mine, her face twisted in something resembling a flinch before her expression shuttered.

My sudden nausea worsened when she didn't immediately speak once she reached us, as though carefully parsing through what she wanted to say. Her fingernails dug into the rose-shaped scar on her palm, a sign of her nerves I knew she wasn't conscious of making.

What could the sprite have told her that had her this shaken?

When she spoke, her voice was carefully devoid of emotion. "I found her. But I'm not sure if we can make it before he..."

"Make it where?" Yael asked impatiently.

"To Adronix," Eva said coolly. "The sprite said there's a secret mirror, the Seeing Mirror, that will bring those who enter to the Choosing. *That's* why Aviel brought me north. Why he was waiting to bring me with him before he stole my magic. If he makes it through first, he'll be able to be crowned High King."

Rivan swore. "And once that's bound in the magic of the land, he'll be truly unstoppable."

Eva nodded, but I noticed Quinn's brow furrow.

"The High King or Queen receives power from the land itself once they are coronated," I explained quietly.

"And with what Aviel can already do..." Yael grimaced. "Let's just say that magic is best left to you, Your Majesty." She gave Eva a short bow, frowning as she barely reacted. "Because if we can't stop him before that happens, it'll be infinitely harder after."

"I take it that we can't just mirror there?" Tobias asked dryly. But I noticed he, too, was watching his sister carefully, his usual detachment slipping due to his obvious concern. He and Quinn exchanged a worried look, the latter's fingertips glowing faintly as though her magic could fix whatever ailed my silent *anima*.

"It's a gateway to the Choosing, not a gateway to Adronix," Yael replied with a sigh. "And due to the prison below the mountain, there was never supposed to be a mirror there."

"We'll have to go the long way," Rivan said. "Besides, as we can assume that traveling there is the next step of Aviel's plan, we'll need to bring an army to match his."

Eva shifted on her feet and something in the set of her shoulders, her downturned mouth, gave me pause. There was something wild, something desperate sneaking down our bond that seemed out of place, even with the understandable anxiety of getting to Adronix before him.

There was more to it. I just couldn't put my finger on it.

"Is that all?" I asked, my unease building at the carefully blank expression on her face. Then the tumult of her emotions ceased as the wall she had built between us all too easily blocked me out.

Eva hesitated, looking anywhere but at me. I stared at her with panic building in my chest.

She gave me a nonchalant smile that didn't reach her eyes. "Isn't that enough?"

We rode back through the night, the journey tense. By the time we arrived, Eva had retreated even further into herself. By the time we reached our room, my hands were shaking.

Eva methodically undressed, reaching for a nightshirt. And suddenly I felt desperate to scramble for purchase. To grab her by the shoulders and keep her there with me.

After all, she should know by now—if she was descending into darkness, there was nothing that would stop me from going down with her.

My voice was gruff as I demanded, "Don't close me out, hellion. Whatever you're thinking, we'll deal with it together."

Eva's shoulders stiffened. Her lips parted, as if she were about to speak, then pressed tightly back together. A sick, anxious feeling coiled in my stomach. When I stepped toward her, her gaze darted away.

"I'm just tired," she said, her voice carefully flat. "It's been a long night."

I was sure it was something more. Was it the fear of facing Aviel yet again? Even though she had been able to get away from him, she had endured far too much during our time apart with barely any time to process it. Maybe this distance was due to the inevitability of confronting her tormentor. Especially after I had failed to stop him, despite my promises otherwise.

The thought was too heavy to carry.

"Last time we went after Aviel, I told you I'd never let him touch you again." I swallowed hard. "And I failed you, Eva." Her gaze shot to mine, an onslaught of emotions breaking through the damper she held on them in a dense current of fear, guilt, and anger. "You can be angry about what happened, be mad at me for leaving you again all you want, but please don't shut down on me."

Her eyes softened, something wistful twisting across her face. "That's not—I don't..." She stepped forward, grabbing both of my hands in hers. "I would never blame you for his actions. And you shouldn't blame yourself for mine. I made my own choices, and I stand by them."

Her hands were so cold. Her calluses scraped against my own as my thumbs moved up and down, attempting to warm them.

"You can talk to me though...you have to know that. Not that you need to if you don't feel ready."

Her face shuttered, those hazel eyes guarded. "Talk to you about what?"

"About what happened to you."

She hadn't gone into detail when she told me what occurred in that bedroom before her escape, and I hadn't pressed. The shadow that flickered behind her eyes sent a chill down my spine.

Her lips twisted to the side in a semblance of a smirk, though their slight quiver gave her away. "What else do you want me to say? That he chained me, that he held me down and..." She drew in a long, shuddering breath. "That I was sure my luck had finally run out when he had me magicless and trapped?"

The pure, primal rage I felt at those words had me shaking. She reached up, absently rubbing the scar at the base of her neck as she spoke, the other hand clenching into a fist as she pulled it from my hold.

"When he stripped my magic from me and took the collar off, I *knew* you could feel my terror about what was happening just like I could feel yours. And it only made things that much worse."

My heart snagged in my throat at the thought of how Aviel had used that bond against us, had weaponized my fear against her. I moved forward, aching to hold her, but stopped myself—letting her steer this, especially now.

"I fought and I failed, Bash." I flinched at the self-loathing in her voice, its echo viscous as it twisted down our bond. *"Again.* If he hadn't left the collar on the bed…"

"You didn't fail," I said vehemently. "Even if he'd raped you, you wouldn't have failed anything." I could feel my shadows erupt down my arms at the thought, betraying my need to reach for her. "And it wasn't luck that saved you. You had the wherewithal, even after days of captivity, even after that box they held you in, to find a way to save yourself. To keep fighting."

Even when I wasn't able to fight for you.

Her bleak eyes met mine. "How is this helping besides hurting you to hear it?"

"This isn't about me," I said gently. "This is about letting it out. Voicing it to come to terms with what happened."

I could see her trembling as her eyes closed in defeat. "I know. I *know.* And I know I can talk to you, Bash…It's not even about—" She cut herself off, swallowing hard. When she reached toward me I had her in my arms in a second, breathing in the scent of her hair.

"I hate feeling helpless," Eva said hoarsely, her words muffled against my chest. "I hate that he made me feel that way again. And I *hate* how much he scares me." She let out a wild, choked sound. "I don't know if I even *can* stop him when the time comes. All I've been able to do so far is barely get away."

I had never heard her sound like this. Even during those tremulous early days at the cabin, she had never sounded quite so defeated.

"I would never be so foolish as to doubt you," I whispered into her hair. "But we'll be ready this time."

She opened her mouth like she was going to say more, then pulled away instead. And I had no idea how to hold on to her—to keep her here with me. Not when my promises lacked the conviction of her own experience.

"I'm going to go get ready for bed," Eva said softly, a yawn escaping her as she disappeared into the bathroom.

I stripped down to my undershorts, seeing to my own needs when she had finished, only to find Eva sitting on our bed when I was done, her knees pulled to her chest as she stared at nothing.

Something hollow crept across our bond as she slowly lay down on the bed. I could sense the words she didn't say hovering just out of reach as I settled in next to her, silently waiting. Watching as a hint of her darkness spread across the hazel of her irises.

Her magic swirled around us, hovering like a shield, but it didn't keep me out. Instead, it reached toward me as if to tug me closer. I wrapped my arms around her, and she nestled into my chest, her heart beating like the wings of a trapped bird.

After a long moment, she pulled away slightly, her eyes searching mine. When she spoke, it seemed to resonate in the deepening darkness of the room.

"I'll do anything it takes to stop him."

I could hear the iron will in her voice—and knew without a doubt she meant it. Just as I knew she was still keeping something from me.

Then I watched her eyes dim, the fire in them dying before being replaced with an emptiness I had hoped I would never see again. She turned away, curling into herself...the distance between us widening as she closed herself off even more than before.

CHAPTER 23
EVA

The morning mist clung to the kitchen window, blanketing the courtyard in a hazy fog that felt as if I was still in a dream. Like I was alone in the world, or perhaps at its very beginning. The soft, diffused light of sunrise cast a gentle glow on the sprawling plum trees—their dark leaves sparkling with dew as the world gently woke.

I wasn't sure how long I sat here until the air around me changed, suddenly charged like it did whenever Bash was near. My heart pounded as I turned around to see him leaning against the doorway, his jaw flexing as my attempt at a smile fell flat.

Even this early he looked effortlessly handsome—the only hint of the apprehension I could feel down our bond visible in the way he was nervously rolling up the sleeves of his shirt, exposing his strong, freckled forearms.

"I didn't think you were awake," I muttered, turning back to my untouched breakfast. It had long since gone cold.

"Something important was missing from our bed," Bash said simply. There was a sad sort of smile on his face as I raised my eyes to his, trying to ignore the roiling in my gut.

His stare tore right through me, exactly the way I knew it would—

exactly the way I wished it wouldn't. From the very beginning, he had always seen every part of me.

Quickly, I tamped down on our bond, even though I had been doing so since last night. But Bash could always read me like a book, even before our bond fell in place. His eyes narrowed almost imperceptibly, as if squinting at the words written behind my gaze.

I should've known he would find me already, even though it was only just dawn. I had barely made it out of our bed with the way his shadows had wrapped around me after slipping away from the warmth of his arms, like they hadn't been ready for me to leave just yet. Perhaps they had taken it upon themselves to alert their master of how I had woken straining against invisible chains, unable to scream.

Bash's hand had curled against the warm sheets I had just vacated as I silently snuck out of our room, unable to quiet the buzzing in my head after the way I had ended our conversation last night. I hadn't wanted to see anyone at the breakfast table and have them notice the war going on inside me—needing to find some control before I had it in me to look them in the eye.

Because the guilt felt like it might shatter me. I couldn't get over the nauseating thought that I could end this all right now. That I was allowing the people of this realm to suffer, that soon everyone I loved would be forced to fight a war when one sacrifice would solve everything. I almost laughed at being faced with the ultimate utilitarian quandary that had come up during my mother's many strategy lessons—what *was* one life worth when surrendering it would save so, so many?

But to actually go through with it felt like the worst sort of betrayal, both to myself and those who cared for me. It was one thing to forfeit my life in the heat of battle, to actively give myself up for my friends, my family—to die in response to an immediate threat. It was another thing entirely to consider killing myself in a void, the act passively heartless. And especially not when there were still other options. When there was still another way, one that wouldn't require me to give up everything in order to win.

It had been a close thing, yesterday, and my decision not to tell Bash—

not the tell them all—was already wavering. Yet I knew that if Bash learned what it would cost to stop Aviel, he would talk me out of a choice that was already too difficult to make. Impossibly so when I wanted to cling to my life, cling to him, cling to all of it.

A dozen questions flickered in Bash's expression, but he didn't voice any of them. Instead, he said, "Let's go on a walk."

"I'm..." I glanced down at my untouched plate of food. "Eating."

That muscle in his jaw flexed again before he said, dryly, "Are you?"

I opened my mouth to respond, then closed it. Bash just arched an eyebrow at me, then turned to walk out the door.

"It's freezing," I muttered as I followed him into the misty morning, pulling my cloak around me. I slid my hands into its pockets, if only to hide their shaking.

Bash's hand slid into my pocket a second later, his fingers curling around mine. His thumb circled absently against the scar on my palm as he traced each petal.

I glanced at my *anima* to find his gaze already on me. A brisk wind ruffled through his auburn hair—tousled, like he had been tugging at it—those two-toned eyes swirling in concern. He hadn't put on a cloak, seemingly indifferent to the chill.

We came to a stop beneath one of the plum trees, its blood-red leaves vivid against the fog. Bash's hand caught my chin, calluses grazing against my skin as he gently turned my face back to his. His eyes were soft but expectant. I fought the urge to close mine, as if that could stop him from seeing everything.

Why had I ever thought I could keep this from him?

"Eva," he said gruffly, my name cadenced like a demand.

My traitorous lips wobbled, but I pressed them together in a thin line. Bash's eyes narrowed when I didn't respond, a storm building around his pupils. I wondered if he could feel my unrest over the bond or if it was just written across my face. Because I knew what I should do.

And I had never been more terrified.

Bash's hand moved to brush a strand of hair blowing across my face behind my ear, his fingers trailing down my cheek. My chest tightened as I remembered the way he had done so in that lake, long before we had acknowledged what we were to each other. He was studying me so intently, I was suddenly grateful he could only feel my emotions, not read my thoughts. That he couldn't uncover exactly what I was trying to hide.

"Sometimes I worry that you don't know that you don't have to do any of this alone," Bash murmured. "That there's no burden I wouldn't take on with you."

Guilt flared within me. My mouth opened, but I found myself unable to say the words to deflect his concern. Not when they would've been a lie.

His features turned stark, his eyes flickering with something like hurt. "Talk to me. Please."

It was the plea that almost broke me. "About what, exactly?"

Bash let out a low, humorless laugh. "You may have been raised in the mortal realm, but you're pure fae. Would it kill you to just give me an honest answer?"

I took a half-step backward, attempting to put some distance between us. Bash pulled me right back, one arm looping around my waist. His other hand caught my face, shadows swirling in his eyes, the touch grounding me despite myself. I closed mine, unable to look at him as I tried to find the right lie.

"What is it?" His whole body was thrumming with tension now, shadows licking up his wrists. "What's wrong?"

There was something crumbling in me. The urge to let him in warring with the knowledge that if I did, there would be no way I could go through with it.

"It's nothing," I hedged, the lie twisting in my chest. "It doesn't matter."

"It matters because you're shaking, Eva," Bash said, panic creeping into his voice. "It matters because something is upsetting you, no matter what it is." His grip tightened protectively. "It matters because you're mine."

My heart broke a little, as I desperately tried to hold on to my resolve.

"Hellion, you should know by now that I want your good and your bad," Bash murmured. "Your nothings, your anythings, and absolutely everything in between."

"It's just..." My voice trembled. "I'm having a more difficult time than I thought with the idea of what we have to do next. What I need to do. And it's hard not to…be back there, with him, when I let my thoughts wander. Especially now that we're about to seek him out."

I hated lying to him, even if it was only a half-truth. The unwanted shadow of Aviel's presence—the feeling of his hands on me, the fear those pale blue eyes instilled—still haunted me like a wraith I couldn't exorcise. But I knew the guilt Bash harbored over what he hadn't been able to stop, just as I knew I had succeeded in derailing his too-pointed questions by using it against him. I winced at the mix of rage and devastation mingling on his face, his remorse streaming across our bond with renewed force.

Taking a measured breath, I held it before exhaling to the same, slow four-count, trying to slow my racing heart. "I appreciate you talking it out with me though."

"And you're sure that's all?" Bash swept his hair back with a hand. "Is there anything I can—"

"Bash," I said imploringly.

"*Eva*," he shot right back, clearly unwilling to let this go. "Just tell me what you need…please."

My unfocused gaze zeroed in on his face. "You."

I pushed him back against the tree trunk, its leaves shuddering at the impact. The morning light disappeared as I wrapped us in a cocoon of my magic that mingled with the mist—a flurry of blood-red leaves decorating the dark as they fell all around us. His breath hitched as I lowered myself onto my knees, my hands already fumbling with the laces of his pants. My hand wrapped around his hardening cock, Bash's groan rumbling through me as I took him into my mouth.

Maybe it was cowardice to want this distraction rather than face my supposed fate head on. But I didn't want to think about what could very well be my death. And if I did have to die to stop Aviel, then I didn't want to waste another second with my *anima*. I refused to live another minute without his hands on me, his body entwined so deeply with mine that we could never be taken from each other ever again.

I wanted to lose myself in him—in the taste of him down my throat, in the feel of him filling me so completely I couldn't focus on anything else. Needed the respite from the thoughts that had chased me from his arms once already this morning.

"Eva..." Bash's moan as I sucked him deeper traveled through me. "Gods, you're perfect."

Bash pulled me to my feet. I let out a soft whine at the interruption before his mouth found mine. His fingers flew to unbutton my pants, and I blocked it all out—so completely that I could almost pretend to fool myself along with my *anima* as I let myself feel nothing but pleasure and lust and that endless *need* for him.

Winding my arms around his neck, he lifted me against the tree trunk, my bare thighs wrapping around his waist. And when our bodies joined, all I could think about, all I knew, was him. How right he felt inside me, how much I needed him—how forever wouldn't be long enough.

I kissed him hungrily, moans building in the back of my throat as he thrust into me faster, the roll of my hips urging him on.

"Harder," I begged. "I need you."

Because someday not too far in the future, I could very well be gone and wouldn't ever be able to get enough of him.

Bash's gaze never left my face, even as he found his own pleasure amid my own shuddering climax, as if he knew there was something ephemeral between us, something frighteningly perilous.

Something that could be taken away.

When we broke apart, still wrapped in our own dusky world, we were both panting.

A dark smile graced Bash's mouth. "You know, it's a bit of an inconvenience having a world to save when I just want to spend the rest of my life making you moan."

"Promises, promises," I said under my breath as I pulled on my pants, brushing bits of bark from the back of my cloak.

But there was worry in the crease of his brow that belied his words, coalescing into something tangible across our bond. A hint of fear still swirling in those ever-changing eyes. The feeling like he knew more than he was letting on...but was willing to give me the space I needed until I was ready.

I almost laughed as a fit of hysteria hit me. Because of course he noticed my disquiet, even as he tried to explain it away. He had always seen right through me.

As that familiar panic leaked back in, I told myself to breathe—that I didn't need to do anything now. That it would all seem less petrifying if I could only manage one deep inhale.

But I couldn't do anything except stare into my darkness as it dissipated into the day, and wish my fears were as easy to eradicate.

CHAPTER 24
BASH

The future High Queen still had a shadow behind her hazel eyes, each ringed with a crown of gold around her pupils like they had known exactly what she was destined for all along.

Carefully, Eva pulled off her leathers, the fabric sticking to her skin from the sweat of our training session this morning. She had thrown herself into it with almost reckless abandon, especially when she and Quinn went hand-to-hand. When she had laughed for the first time in far too long as they had fought—the sound far too rare to begin with—I had to stop myself from granting her best friend my kingdom in gratitude.

Eva's eyes met mine across our room. Her mouth hitched in a forced, unconvincing smile as she caught me watching her, but I couldn't match it. As I stepped forward, she turned away, that smile fracturing. I hid my wince.

Obviously, whatever was consuming her had returned to haunt her.

It was an effort not to howl at the weight that was slowly crushing her. To demand answers about the dread leaking across our bond like she couldn't hold it back. But after our discussion this morning and what I had only belatedly realized was her successful distraction, I had resolved to let Eva talk about the rest of whatever was worrying her in her own time—even if I desperately wished I could help carry her burden.

This war was already wearing on her, and the worst of it hadn't even begun. I needed to find a way to help her before it did, though I found myself at a loss as to how to do so beyond giving her the reassurance I was there for her, and the time and space to process. Though time, as usual, wasn't on our side, a thought that had me breathing through my own anxieties.

She disappeared into the bathroom without a word. I wasn't sure if it hurt more that she still couldn't bring herself to talk to me, or that she kept pretending everything was fine.

Was she really this haunted at the thought of facing Aviel again? Or was it memories of her imprisonment that wouldn't let her out of their grasp?

After the way our last encounter with him ended, it should have come as no surprise that she clearly had little faith in our ability to win this. But I couldn't entirely account for the fear behind her gaze when she didn't think I was looking.

Steam wafted from the bathroom as she opened the door. When she walked past me to the wardrobe, I placed my finger on my palm, drawing a tiny heart in shimmering ink.

She stopped in surprise, and I couldn't help my smile at the sight of her mouth curling up to form that perfect dimple as she looked down, then back at me.

"Just a reminder," I said, grinning as she blinked at me.

"I hardly need a reminder of how much you love me," Eva said, a smile still playing on her lips. "The whole *anima* bond and all."

"Agree to disagree."

The buzzing feeling under my skin settled a little as I clung to the brief reprieve of lightness between us, like it might chase some of the darkness away.

But that wasn't quite right. Not when Eva *was* darkness, its velvet dim ever beckoning. Her considerable power had never scared me, that Celestial night the mirror to my own shadows.

She rolled her eyes, pulling on a cheeky lace thong that nearly made me groan aloud. "What now? To Adronix?"

"Not yet," I said, holding up a thick piece of parchment. "It will take time for my rangers to mirror here en masse. And this came from the eastern kingdom." I lightly slapped her ass as she bent down to pull up her pants, grinning as she yelped before being rewarded again with another brief smile, albeit paired with the roll of her eyes. "Come on, I'll explain when we're with the others. After you've eaten something."

She hadn't been eating well, the dip in her weight from her captivity all the more pronounced because of it. I silently resolved to make sure she didn't miss another meal, even if I had to hand feed her all the way to Adronix.

Eva tugged on a dark green shirt and black leggings Quinn must have brought with her from the mortal realm. I watched as she deftly wove her chestnut curls into a braid before carefully sliding an oddly glimmering ring onto her right hand.

A tendril of her hair had already escaped from her braid, its loose curl framing her face. I arched an eyebrow as I tucked it behind her ear. "Should I be concerned about who's giving you gifts?"

Eva rolled her eyes, splaying out her fingers to give me a better look. I caught her hand with my own, lifting it closer. A strangely familiar feeling emanated from the shadowy stone, one I couldn't quite place.

"It was my mother's," Eva whispered. "Apparently, she left it with the sprite."

My thumb brushed along the top of her hand in a soothing stroke. "Did the sprite say why?"

Eva sighed. "She wasn't exactly forthcoming. But she seemed fond of her."

The ring's surface glinted, its gray stone almost seeming to ripple in the light. I frowned, trying to figure out what about it made me hesitate.

Eva's mouth quirked as she pulled her hand away. "If the sprite had ulterior motives, there were easier ways she could've killed me."

I arched an eyebrow. "Don't get too comfortable. It could be playing a long game."

She laughed softly, though something about it felt hollow. "I have no doubt about that."

CHAPTER 25
EVA

T followed Bash down the strangely familiar wooden staircase, déjà vu ingrained in each step. He didn't turn around, but his hand reached behind him, a curl of worry flashing across our bond. I didn't hesitate before taking it, letting my fingers intertwine with his, Bash's larger hand nearly swallowing mine. A flicker of shadows wisped across the top of my hand, like they too needed to hold onto me.

Bash had hardly stopped finding ways to touch me since last night—like he knew better than to let me go. As usual, his instincts weren't far off.

He gave me a tentative smile as we reached the main floor, and I returned it, letting my resolution flow down our bond. I almost winced at the intensity of his relief.

Because I knew what I had to do.

I had to unlearn what the sprite had told me. Bury it so deep that Bash wouldn't suspect anything was amiss more than he already did…and so he wouldn't know to stop me if it came down to it. Keep the secret until I was certain there was no other choice. Because I *would* find a way to defeat Aviel without resorting to that awful option—even if, deep down, I feared that fate wouldn't be so easily outmaneuvered.

There was time, after all, before this war began in earnest. Before others died because I was too much of a coward to give up my life for the greater good.

I wasn't ready to lose this life. I couldn't, especially not with the way Bash was looking at me, his love an endless current down our bond.

But I also wasn't going to rule it out as a last resort, a fallback if all else failed. I knew that Bash would only try to dissuade me if he knew and telling him would only make it harder to go through with it if the time came. And I couldn't bear the thought of speaking it aloud. Of triggering the same helplessness and rage I had felt from him ever since our bond had reanimated only magnified.

There was no point in telling him. In worrying him. Because I *would* find another way.

I had to.

My heart pounded against my ribcage as if in agreement. Bash lifted our joined hands, pressing a kiss against the back of mine before he let it go to pull back my chair, our friends and family already eating. I tried to tell myself their inquiring eyes were just my imagination as I softly said hello while loading my plate from the food set on large platters along the table. Each was covered with fresh baked rolls, sliced meats and cheeses, tiny quiches, yogurts, fruit, and a tray of circular buns that I immediately reached for as the smell of cinnamon tickled my nose.

A kettle sang from the stovetop and Bash jumped up, returning with two mugs of black tea sweetened with honey. I shot him a grateful look, and he raised his cup in response.

I took a careful sip before toying with a piece of apple. Bash's hand cupped mine, bringing it and the apple to my lips. I took a bite before he moved my hand to his mouth, finishing the rest. Something inside me went molten as I felt his tongue flick over my fingertips, his gaze never leaving mine.

Yael set down her mug with a thunk. But she was smiling when I looked her way, a blush rising to my cheeks as I remembered we had an audience. "Are we still flirting or are we going to get to it?"

Bash rolled his eyes, opening his mouth to respond, but I cut him off. "Shouldn't we head north? Reach Adronix first so we can get through the

Seeing Mirror before..." Aviel's name died on my tongue, as I added lamely, "...before anyone else?"

When I break you, when you learn you are mine...we will remake this world together.

Bash's eyes filled with shadow, and I realized my hand had gone to my throat, my fingertips brushing the bite mark now fully scarred. I deliberately placed my hand back on the table, letting it flatten slowly along its wooden grains. Bash's hand immediately came on top of mine, wisps of shadow lacing around our fingers.

Yael looked at Rivan. "Has there been any word of the False King?"

"Aviel's still in Morehaven," Rivan replied before turning to me. "Putting that band on him was ingenious. It seems it took some time to remove."

Good. I hoped he had suffered in the process.

"Though his return to the Source will mean he's drained more power," Tobias added quietly.

"His army could begin their journey to Adronix any day now," Rivan said grimly. "Our rangers are readying to travel through the mirror to Soleara as we speak, so we should be able to head them off. And Queen Sariyah sent word that she and her forces have begun their journey east."

I caught my brother's gaze, my nails digging into my scarred palm as I asked, "How often did Aviel have to draw from you?"

A flicker of a wince crossed Tobias's face, and I cringed at my bluntness.

"I just mean...he needs my magic to trick the Seeing Mirror. Will it fade if he doesn't use it?"

Tobias's light sparked in his eyes as if he were reliving all the times the same had been done to him, though his expression remained carefully blank. "I can't be sure, but from what I gathered, I think it has to do with if, and how much, he uses it—expenditure, not time." A muscle tensed in his jaw, the only sign of his discomfort as he added grimly, "There was never a rhythm to how often he drained me."

"He used some against me," I said, my voice hollow as I was transported back to that bed, that room. My own darkness holding me down in a cruel mockery of my magic. "So between that and the band, he might not have enough?"

"Not something we can put to chance." Tobias grimaced. "But if he does need you...well, he knows where you're heading, right?"

I swallowed. "Another reason we need to beat him to that mountain."

We shared the slightest of nods.

My breathing quickened, a slight buzzing in my ears as I thought of the danger of him making it to the mirror before me. "And if we rode ahead? Just us, and have our forces follow?"

Yael pursed her lips. "It would be safer not to. There are creatures in those woods that would be scared away by an army but would happily go after a smaller group. It will only delay us a day to wait. Besides, we have a head start from Soleara, and Aviel's forces won't be able to travel any faster than ours."

I could feel Bash's reluctance to let go of my hand as he pulled out the scroll from his jacket. "We also have one last task before we can leave."

Right. Esterra.

My gaze immediately found Yael's, who was glaring at the broken seal on the parchment. It had formed an ornately twirling *E*, I realized—thus her response.

"What does the Eastern King want?" Rivan asked through a mouthful of eggs.

Bash's voice was carefully controlled, though I could feel his flicker of impatience. "King Eliav would like an audience before committing to another war."

Yael's mouth pursed. "Confirmation before committing his troops? Likely. Someone to make him feel like his contribution's worth it? Most definitely."

Tobias, Quinn, and I shared an equally confounded look.

"Can someone please explain the politics for those of us not brought up with maps that move?" Quinn asked tartly.

I blinked. "Maps that...what?"

Yael bounded down the hall to what I assumed was a study, coming back with a large, rolled-up map she opened with a flourish. It almost covered the entire table, nearly rolling over Rivan's plate before he pulled it onto his lap, grumbling low obscenities.

Bash, who had gracefully snatched our mugs out of the way, handed me mine before leaning over the map. "We're here," he said, pointing to Soleara. The map was indeed moving: lines of wind whipping around the mountains, the seas choppy with waves. At Bash's light touch, a glowing dot appeared where we were in the mountain top, a bronze castle gleaming below it.

"Nice to see it on the map again," my brother said wryly.

It *was* nice seeing a glimpse of joy across Tobias's face again, however fleeting. He had always loved the part of our lessons that involved poring over maps for our war games, each topographical curve shaping his strategies of attack.

Rivan set his plate on his chair, placing both hands on the map as he stood. "And in the west is Mayim. Queen Sariyah already committed her troops wherever they're needed after Bash's letters...no boot licking required. Though with the unrest there due to the King's supporters, I have no doubt their forces will be as divided as they were in the last war." He tapped a finger next to Mayim, and I watched as an enormous eel-like monster leapt from the water surrounding the castle. Then he smirked at the look of surprise on my face.

"That's Imyr and the Faewilds," Yael said, pointing to the swaying treetops in the south. For a second, I thought I saw a tiny shadowbeast slinking through the forest. "And Esterra to the east." Her finger flicked dismissively toward the kingdom she was born in, the one she had long since stopped calling home. She looked away, and I knew returning there, with the memories it held, was likely the last thing she wanted to do.

"We don't all have to go," I said quickly. "Surely Bash and I should be enough to talk them into helping us."

Yael was already shaking her head, but I caught her brief, grateful look at me. "They'll expect a full entourage. The east is far too obsessed with propriety. Besides, if they'll trust anyone, it'll be someone who looks like one of their own."

"King Eliav is vain, but he'll listen to reason," Rivan added. "Even if he'll likely put us through the song and dance first."

"A quick trip," Bash said. "To gather the last of our allies."

Tobias cocked his head thoughtfully at me. "And maybe learn a bit more about where Dad came from."

So he hadn't missed the familiar lilt of Yael's accent.

I smiled softly. "Alright then. All of us."

One last journey together before our adventure to Adronix. To face Aviel…unless I used what I knew to end him first.

I shuddered, all too aware of Bash's eyes on me. Seeing far too much, as always. Carefully, I pushed the thought from my mind.

Quinn shook her head. "Someone needs to stay to help Pari coordinate mirroring the Imyrian forces here. Besides, the Esterran King won't be expecting me."

"I'll stay too," Tobias said quickly. "They're my people. And I'd like to help the Solearan forces with preparations to make sure they're ready to head north once you return."

Quinn smiled warmly at my brother. A hint of a blush reddened his cheeks before he ducked his head.

Rivan nodded. "Good. We won't need all of us anyway. My mother has returned from her travels and is keeping an eye on the Keep, so Marin should be here to join us shortly."

"We have a day at most to convince the Eastern King that the time has come to return to war," Bash said gravely. "The same players in the same war that began a hundred and one years ago. The war that was never truly finished." He looked around the room, meeting each gaze before his eyes found mine. "We'll end it together, once and for all."

My dress had been my mother's. Something about the way it smelled seemed faintly familiar, as though this house had magically preserved that too, along with the contents of her closet. The silky, golden fabric looped around my neck before twisting across my breasts, leaving a triangle of skin exposed on each side where it crisscrossed around the small of my waist. Its skirts flared out from there in fluttering folds, shimmering like liquid gold in the light. The long slit up the side allowed easy access to my dagger.

Bash had insisted I bring my sword, potential alliance or no. I strapped it to my back, the black jarring against the dress's bright shine.

The gold brought out the crown around my pupils, the color itself an obvious statement. Not to mention that Quinn had braided my long tresses into a less than subtle crown on the top of my head, though half of it cascaded down my back. It would have also matched my mother's eyes, I realized, as I tried to picture her in my place.

I wondered what she had worn this to...some stately function alongside my father? It felt strange in a good way to slip it on, like I was trying to fit into what used to be her place in this world.

Bash's eyes darkened as I walked down the stairway to meet him. My cheeks heated as exactly what he thought of the dress flowed down our bond.

"My queen," he murmured, bending to brush his lips against my knuckles.

"We talked about this," I grumbled, a smile lifting my lips despite myself.

"As if anything else is appropriate to call you when you're wearing *that*."

Bash's fighting leathers were gone. He looked every inch the Imyrian King—elegance stitched into each seam of his ensemble. His linen pants and matching tunic were an almost metallic dark gray and made up of simple but sophisticated lines. Silver threading at the neckline and cuffs swirled in intricate patterns. His sword hung at his side.

My mouth went dry. Bash gave me a devious smirk as he looked up from where his mouth still hovered over my outstretched hand, then turned my wrist to kiss my pulse point. I knew he could feel my heart hammering as his lips worked their way up my arm, his other hand curling against the bare skin of my waist to drag me closer.

"I swear we weren't this bad," Marin muttered to Yael as they walked in from the kitchen.

"Marin!" I yelped, running over to her. She grinned widely, in a way that was so much like her brother. Her dress was the same green as her eyes, with capped sleeves and a flowing, tiered skirt. Eyelet details patterned the edge of each tier, fluttering with every movement.

"King Eliav will expect the full contingent," Marin explained to me. "As much as I've enjoyed holding down the fort in Imyr for its king, I wasn't about to miss out on the fun."

Bash merely shrugged. "Seems only fitting for its future queen."

Marin let out a garbled sound, her eyes widening as she slowly turned to her brother. "What?"

Yael had stilled at her lover's side, her flowing violet jumpsuit slightly swaying at her sudden inertia.

Bash smirked. "My *anima* is the future High Queen. Though I'm tempted to knock the whole castle down, I have a feeling that with some serious redecorating, we'll be able to call Morehaven home when she takes her rightful place on the throne."

Now I was the one staring at him with wide eyes.

Bash smiled at me; his gaze soft. "I do have plans for after we win this war, you know."

After. I didn't want to think about why I hadn't let myself consider what came next. Refusing to let my mind go there, I plastered a smile on my face as I turned to Marin and Yael. "I have no doubt you two will be exactly what Imyr needs."

Marin nodded solemnly, though Yael still looked flustered.

"Oh, before I forget…" Marin reached into a hidden pocket in her skirt, pulling a familiar necklace from it. My breath caught as I took in the silver star amulet I had left behind in Imyr what felt like a lifetime ago. Taking it, I gave her a grateful smile.

"Thank you for bringing it back to me," I said in a heartfelt whisper.

Marin smiled. "I'm just happy you're here to claim it."

I started to lift it to my neck, but Bash held out a hand, motioning for me to turn around as he unclasped the lock. He moved closer than was strictly necessary, his warm breath grazing my ear as I lifted the hair from my nape, carefully placing it around my neck.

The cool metal brushed against the white scar encircling my throat, and I recoiled as the memory of being collared and helpless crashed over me. Bash immediately froze, and I knew he had felt that momentary terror across our bond.

Pressing my hand against the familiar six-pointed star, I forced some levity into my voice as I managed to say, "I remember when you two were more intent on taking this off of me than putting it back on."

Carefully, Bash finished clasping the amulet, pressing a swift kiss against where the chain lay against my skin. I leaned back against him, and his arm circled around my waist in silent comfort, his breath rustling my hair as his chin rested atop my head.

Rivan walked down the stairs, wearing an embroidered cobalt blue tunic, his lavender eyes twinkling as he took in the looks on our faces. "What did I miss?"

"Just Marin being the Imyrian heir now that Eva's the future High Queen," Bash said with a hint of amusement.

Rivan gave us all a strange look. "That seemed obvious, no?"

Marin let out a choked sound, and Yael reached over to grab her hand.

"Besides, you've already been doing the job since this all started," Bash said. "Seems only fitting you get the title too."

"Queen Marin does have a nice ring to it," Yael added quietly, a familiar devious gleam in her eyes.

Marin sighed, her mouth twisting in resignation. "So does having you as my consort." She tugged Yael closer before brushing a soft kiss to her lips that quickly deepened into more.

"And you gave *us* a hard time," Bash said with a smile that belied his tone.

Quinn and Tobias walked down the stairs together. She was softly laughing at something he said, the look in his eyes in response making my chest ache.

Then his gaze fixed on me, taking a careful step away from Quinn as if he had just realized their proximity. "We're here to see you off."

Quinn winked at me. "Try not to get into too much trouble without me."

"It's just a day trip," I said with false outrage.

Bash nodded. "I won't risk staying longer than it takes our forces to ready. But I appreciate both of your help in doing so."

Tobias looked at him. "Keep her safe, would you?"

Bash gave him a slight bow, and I saw Tobias's mouth curve up just slightly. Perhaps there was hope they might be friends someday. Not that I was going to give them a choice.

"I can keep myself safe," I protested.

Bash and Tobias exchanged a look.

"Your precedent of martyrdom notwithstanding," Tobias said dryly. "So, my request stands."

I felt a squeeze in my chest as that insight hit a little too close to the truth I was trying to hide. Tobias's eyes narrowed slightly, and I belatedly rolled my eyes.

Quinn led us toward the living room, where a prominent bronze mirror made me stop short, that old fear clenching my stomach. It was almost the twin to my family's mirror in the mortal realm, though instead of roses, its sides were lined with a flowering vine. My eyes fixed on the identical filigree pattern at its top, and the acrid smell of smoke filled my nose.

Bash took hold of my hand, squeezing it, and I realized my nails had been digging into the rose scarred there. He brought it to his mouth before placing a chaste kiss on the raised ridges of its petals. I gave him a weak smile, swallowing against my dry mouth as I looked back at that too familiar mirror.

But I didn't hear those screams as I walked toward it, chanting our destination in my head. Not with Bash's hand still holding mine. My other hand clenched in a fist, that shadow-colored stone I now wore on my ring finger seeming to undulate as if with its own magic.

"Good luck," Quinn called out.

Turning over my shoulder to where she stood by my brother, I raised my hand in a small wave goodbye. Then winked, adding wryly, "You say it like we'll need it."

Before I could think about it, Bash and I stepped through.

CHAPTER 26
ESTELLE

I hadn't wanted to admit to Adrian that he might have already won with almost a full day to spare. Whether it was the bond pushing me toward him, or that all those seemingly innocuous ways to show me how much he cared had softened my heart along with my guard, I could no longer deny that his intentions seemed pure.

Nor could I deny how much I wanted him, our first tryst only leaving me wanting more. Though I had heard whispers of the effects of an *anima* bond, I hadn't realized the intensity of it before even accepting the tie between us. I found myself pressing my thighs together beneath my skirts at the mere sound of his voice and watched as his eyes darkened at the way my skin flushed in response.

He hadn't hidden how much he wanted me in return, though each night he had only given me the barest of kisses before leaving me at my door. As if he knew it would only make me yearn for him more, along with everything else we could be together.

The second I opened my bedroom door, Adrian was waiting there with a steaming mug in hand, as had become our tradition. "Come on."

I took a sip and let out a contented sigh at the taste as his hand slipped into mine. That initial charge between us at his touch, the undercurrent of some ancient magic, made my heart quicken. "Where?"

A saccharine smile. "We have places to be, Princess."

"Oh?" I raised one eyebrow. "Here I thought the bonding ceremony preparations were being handled by basically everybody *but* us."

Adrian laughed, and I inwardly swooned at its deep rumble. "Well, we'd better disappear before they remember to come find us then."

I smiled and let him lead me away.

Whether it was the *anima* bond or just him, my last semblance of restraint faded far faster than I had imagined. Adrian seemed to sense my concerns before I could voice them, eradicating my every fear about any ulterior motives, even as I came to realize they were all echoes of my father's voice urging me to distrust outsiders for how they might use me. It had been simpler than I thought to let down the walls I had built around myself in the name of duty and let myself trust him.

My worries about controlling my own destiny seemed to fade just as easily as Adrian made it more and more clear that it would always be my choice with him. I hadn't even realized that he stood to inherit the Esterran throne until he had introduced me to his older brother, Eliav, last night at dinner. He shared the same golden-brown eyes and flirty grins, though his mannerisms were far more calculated.

But his brother wasn't Celestial. Which meant Adrian hadn't even considered his own ambition before letting me choose where I wished us to spend our lives together.

"Your brother seems happy about his change in station."

I winced at my lack of tact, but Adrian's pace didn't falter as he led me up a staircase I didn't recognize. "He'll be a good king."

"And you don't wish you were in his place?"

Adrian stopped so suddenly I ran into him. He caught me effortlessly in his arms, then tilted my chin up so I looked him in the eyes. "My place is with you."

Something indefinable danced between us, something that felt like forever. And I realized the last of my reticence had somehow disappeared without my realizing it, Adrian's earnestness having chipped it away piece by piece. He led me down a bright, open hallway, his hand in mine as he tugged me into a library I had never seen before, the stacks of books towering all around us on glossy, white shelves. A lovely, cushioned window seat overlooked the misty forest below, and I brought Adrian over to it, setting down my mug. Then laughed as he immediately pulled me onto his lap.

His lips were on mine before I could protest...not that I wanted to. Everything about him felt like home, like belonging. Even the sinful stroke of his tongue as it demanded entrance reminded me that being together somehow made me feel utterly whole.

Adrian drew back, and I blushed as his gaze remained fixed on my mouth. But he didn't lean back in. Instead, he looked into my eyes so deeply, it felt like he was staring into my soul.

"I've never seen eyes like yours. They're beautiful."

I winced, just slightly, thinking about the prophecy the High Queen had told my parents before my birth. The reason I had been so carefully sequestered since that moment—the northern princess no one was allowed to visit, awaiting her secret crown like some silent specter to her own future empire.

Adrian's brow furrowed at whatever he saw on my face. Like he could sense my displeasure across the bond I still hadn't accepted.

Except now...maybe I wanted to. Maybe I didn't want to live that lonely existence anymore. And maybe, despite my former misgivings about trusting some foreign prince with everything to gain...maybe he was actually as lonely as I was, with nothing up his sleeve but his love for me.

His heart beat steadily beneath the hand I braced on his chest, its rhythm soothing my racing heart.

Adrian raised an eyebrow. "So?"

I blinked. "So..."

"Have I convinced you? Or am I to spend the rest of my days trying?" He leaned forward, his mouth brushing against the exposed skin between my neck and shoulder. "Because I could spend the rest of my life happily doing so if it means getting to hold you like this."

I sucked in a shaky breath. "You have been...convincing. More than I imagined you could be in so short a time. But if we are indeed doing this, there are a few things you might need to know."

Adrian had the nerve to smile at me, that godsdamned dimple peeking through to taunt me too. "Indeed."

I bit my lip, letting it slide out from between my teeth. "That is to say... something important that I've been keeping from you."

"I gathered," Adrian deadpanned, with an utterly annoying lack of concern. That dimple deepened.

"It's not something...bad, per se. It's simply that I'm...well..."

"You don't have to tell me. I'm not expecting you to open up all at once—"

"I want to," I snapped and was surprised to realize it was true.

We stared at each other for a too long moment; everything I wanted to say on the tip of my tongue. But this was my *anima*, and as much as I tried to tell myself that he was a virtual stranger, that telling him would change things, that I couldn't trust anyone besides my family with the secret I had kept since my birth...wasn't that what he was about to become?

"It's fascinating seeing you at a loss for words for once." Adrian pressed his lips together like he was holding back a laugh. "I must admit, it's quite endearing. You realize there's nothing you could say that could make me not want you?"

"I'm going to be High Queen."

There was a beat of distended silence, then Adrian let out a relieved breath. "Here I thought you were going to tell me you were cursed or dying. If you want to go through the Choosing one day, I have absolutely no objection." He frowned. "Did you think I would stop you?"

I sighed, shaking my head. "It's not really a choice. The Choosing...it's predetermined, its outcome inevitable. Or at least it is when there's a seer involved. Queen Amerie herself foresaw that the golden crown in my eyes would be worn by her true successor."

Adrian blinked slowly, then his brow furrowed. "That's why your father was so concerned about another heir. Because he knew you would one day leave your station to rule the realm, leaving Soleara to whoever's magic was strongest, and not necessarily someone of his bloodline." He swallowed hard. "And that whoever ruled by your side would be..."

"Yes," I whispered. "Though based on the myriad of insipid suitors he's flung at me over the years, he was hoping for someone he could easily control. And through them, me."

His jaw flexed, anger darkening his face. But his voice was gentle when he asked, "Do you *want* to be High Queen?"

I looked at him askance. My mouth opened then closed again before I managed to respond. "No one's ever asked me that."

He frowned. "We'll get back to that. Why were you so afraid to tell me?"

"I've always been told that if I were to tell someone, they would use that information to their advantage," I explained as his fingers stroked up and down my back. "To *use* me. I was already set apart as the only heir to Soleara, my friends handpicked, my movements guarded. *Everything* in my life has been chosen for me, down to who I would one day be."

"I'm sorry," Adrian said softly.

I shook my head. "You don't have anything to be sorry for."

"Not sorry for. Sorry that. I'm sorry *that* anyone ever made you believe that you were only worth the crown on your head. That this honor has been anything but that for you."

I swallowed against the lump in my throat, adding wryly, "In that case, I have a lot of sorry that's, and extraordinarily few sorry for's. But thank you all the same."

Adrian pulled me closer, those golden-brown eyes seeming to stare right into my soul. "No wonder you weren't interested in another thing preordained. Or did you think I also wanted to…" His jaw clenched. "…*use* you?"

I winced. "I'm sorry if I made you feel unwanted."

"No apologies necessary, Princess," Adrian murmured. "As long as you understand that the only thing that I've ever wanted is you. I don't care whether you're High Queen or the court jester. I just want you to be mine."

My lips were on his before I even realized I had leaned in. Something slid into place, some final piece of the answer I had been waiting for. Something I might've known since this whirlwind began but had been too scared to allow myself to believe in.

Because maybe I could trust in someone—and let myself belong to him just as he belonged to me. Maybe I didn't have to do this alone.

Something fluttered wildly in my stomach as we breathlessly broke apart. "Let's do the bonding ceremony right now."

Adrian barked a laugh that quickly quieted at the look on my face, his smile turning more than just a little wobbly. "And here I thought tomorrow's grand event was still tentative."

"I don't care about that one," I insisted, wrapping my arms around his neck. "I'll show up and wear the dress and smile and do whatever it is our parents planned and we had no say in. But I want one that's for *us*. Just us."

"Are you sure?"

The slightest of smiles curved my lips at the hope on his face. And I knew that if I were to say no, Adrian wouldn't hesitate to face down the whole realm to stop the proceedings tomorrow, even if it was the opposite of what he wanted.

Maybe that was why it was so easy to say, "Yes. Are you?"

"As if I'd ever say no to you, Princess."

We snuck into the garden, under the willow tree that had become ours. The full moon's light trickled through its leaves as we circled each other the traditional seven times, one after another. Adrian's gaze only dipped once—as he slipped the ring that had once been his grandmother's on my finger, its gray diamond seeming to ripple in the dappled light. I placed a matching silver band on his finger, stolen by a sneaking tendril of darkness from the jeweled box marked for tomorrow's proceedings, as we whispered the words that would bind us eternally.

"You are my beloved."

"And I am yours."

His hands tightened on mine. And then there was magic, mine and his, surrounding us unbidden in an explosion of light and dark. As we glowed like two stars—my light surrounding us with its warmth as his darkness wove throughout it, the willow's leaves fluttering wildly as our magics whirled around us.

And I felt it then. The bond indelibly linking us, our souls forever joined. His love for me was so pure, I felt embarrassed to have ever questioned his intentions. A belonging so definite, I knew I would never feel lonely again.

When we came together this time, it was with one heart. Mapping each other's bodies in a way that was far more intimate now that I could feel his every emotion, and I knew he could feel mine. Adrian's darkness wrapped us in a sanctuary as tiny balls of my light flew around us like fallen stars—a realm for just the two of us, an eternity in which time itself seemed to stand still.

"*Estelle.*" Adrian breathed my name like a promise, as sacred as any wedding vow.

He is mine. And I am his, was my last thought before I came apart—my release taking him over the edge right along with me.

Adrian's lips brushed against my brow as we lay there, sated and still entwined. Watching as our magics gave way to the beams of moonlight streaming through the tangled leaves, mottling our naked bodies in light and shadow. He picked a leaf from my hair as we found our clothes, laughing softly before I stole the sound from his mouth with a kiss I never wanted to end.

With his hand in mine, we snuck past the still unsuspecting guards, tiptoeing through the silent castle. Muffling our breathless laughter as our eyes met in the darkness, the dizzying current of his delight infectious.

I laughed aloud as he picked me up, spinning me around before carrying me past the threshold. "You know it's bad luck to see me the day of the ceremony, right?"

Was it possible to be drunk on joy?

As I looked into his eyes, it occurred to me that this was what happiness must feel like.

His answering amusement across our bond only added to it as he shut the door behind us. "I'm willing to risk it if it means I get to stay with you."

CHAPTER 27

BASH

The first thing I felt was the heat. My eyes closed automatically against the harshness of the midday sun, my shadows shifting uncomfortably under my skin like they felt unwelcome here. One brave strand circled around my arm before hiding under my shirt sleeve, as though it didn't dare venture farther. Even with winter quickly approaching, the Esterran desert was still uncomfortably warm, the sweat already forming a trickle down my back under the cool linen of my tunic.

I had been here before though it had been years. The outdoor courtyard in the center of the palace was covered by a kaleidoscope of colorful tiles, which matched the border of the enormous, arched mirror behind us. Lush gardens surrounded it, bursting with fragrant desert blooms. Flowering vines snaked up the towering archways leading into the palace, where intricately carved stone doorways bookended either side of the enclosed space.

Our hosts sat underneath a colorful canopy opposite us before an enormous fountain. The water sparkled in the sunlight as it arched from hundreds of tiny holes carved into a central chamber in an interlocking design. King Eliav looked exactly as I remembered him, with darkly tanned, handsome features, and a neatly trimmed beard. He wore a burnt orange caftan over fitted silk black pants and braided leather sandals, his jet-black hair pulled back in a sleek bun. Eliav's sharp, golden-brown eyes narrowed probingly as he got to his feet. His husband Noam stood next to him, tall and slender in comparison, with light brown skin and eyes that gleamed an unnatural emerald that matched the bright color of his tunic.

Placing a hand on the small of Eva's back, I drew her forward as Marin, Yael, and Rivan came through the mirror behind us, squinting in the bright sunlight. Before acknowledging the awaiting monarchs, I turned to her, lifting her chin with my thumb and forefinger. Though the tightening sense of anxiety that had permeated our bond the moment we had neared the mirror had ebbed, I whispered, "Are you okay?"

Her eyes crinkled. "Worrywart."

It was hard not to remember the last time I had brought Eva to a castle, to another royal...and abandoned her there. Left her to be tortured in my ignorance and folly.

Eva took my hand and squeezed.

"Evangeline, I presume," Eliav said, breaking me out of my thoughts as he walked toward us. "Lovely to see you again, Bastian."

If he was expecting me to bristle at the lack of titles, he would be disappointed. "Eliav," I said with a casual nod of acknowledgement. "Noam. Good to see you both."

"Eva is fine," she said with a small tilt of her head—an acknowledgement from one ruler to another. I didn't miss Eliav's look of slight surprise before his mouth spread in a practiced smile.

"A pleasure," Noam said with a noticeably deeper bow than necessary to my *anima*. He straightened, his eyes twinkling with delight. "We've heard so much about you, my dear."

"This is my sister Marin, and her *anima* Yael," I said, gesturing at them both in turn. Eliav's eyes tightened ever so slightly as he took in Yael before his bland smile resumed. "And—"

"Rivan," Eliav finished as they both bowed. "Of course I remember. The war wasn't so long ago, no?"

"And not quite as finished as we thought." I matched his courtier's smile, keeping a tight leash on the disdain I felt for this song and dance. "Or did I fail to convey the urgency of the situation in my letters?"

Eliav frowned. "As I said, I prefer some assurances before I commit myself to another war. After all, I must do my rightful diligence before offering the support of my people at the cost of their lives and our tentative peace. Or did you forget that our city was nearly decimated by the civil war of the last battles?"

I hadn't forgotten. Esterra had been nearly torn asunder by their divided loyalties, some of their people taking it upon themselves to set their cities' defenses aflame before the False King's army had arrived to conquer it. There had been far too many here who had believed in his vision for bringing both realms under his ultimate power, and the resources it would yield. That they were *owed* servitude from the mortals currently unaware of their existence. Eliav and his army had retreated south to Imyr where they had fought in the final battle before the King's apparent downfall at his son's hands.

Adjusting my tunic, I asked evenly, "Do you forget who took you in when you needed it? Who you once fought beside?"

"Your parents were magnanimous rulers," Eliav said placatingly. "I mourn their loss to the realm. But it doesn't change the fact that you are asking me to put my people, this kingdom, at risk yet again. To trust that what you say is true about the False King, who you say was never truly defeated, just biding his time as our beloved Prince Aviel until he found *her.*" He looked at Eva, who had stiffened at my side, as a flurry of emotions whirled down our bond that left no doubt what Aviel's mention evoked.

Shadows gathered at my fingertips, my jaw clenching. I took a deep breath, letting them dissipate into the sunlight.

She's safe now, I told them, and myself. *She's safe.*

For now, a taunting voice answered me.

"And what did your spies in Morehaven tell you about everything that occurred?" My voice stayed miraculously calm when inside I felt anything but. "Or am I to believe you think the False King is still imprisoned in the northern ice?"

Eliav's brow knitted. "We've received mixed reports about your so-called *anima's* stay in Morehaven. Though some confirm your story, Prince Aviel told another tale in the missive that arrived not long after yours. He wrote that this war is about whose *anima* Evangeline truly is, and who she belongs to. I will not deny our scouts have seen the prince readying his army. But he says it is to retrieve his *anima* after you stole her away. That you've taken her twice now after growing to covet her on your journey from the other realm while bringing her to him. He suspects you used an old, dark magic to supersede their bond. And so you're to blame for the continuation of the curse."

Eva let out a shocked sound of protest. "The only one obsessed and dabbling in dark magic is *him*. Shouldn't the fact that I'm here with Bash of my own free will tell you that's not the case? That he's my soul bonded, and the prince a liar?" Her eyes flashed. "He took me and tried to keep me against my will when I found out who he really was. Tried to do far worse than that…" Her voice wavered, and I wasn't sure if the diving sensation in my stomach was hers or mine. "We're telling you the truth."

I forced myself to unclench my fists, noting that Noam's stare followed the movement. Rivan met my gaze, the fury on his face quickly cooling at the slight shake of my head. Yael's jaw clenched, likely holding back a stream of expletives I wholeheartedly agreed with. My sister's gaze remained impassive, her royal training the same as mine, even if I didn't miss the way her mouth had tightened.

"Thus, why I made you come all this way," Eliav said genially. "To determine the truth from the lies before I pledge my support. It's no small thing to commit my people to a war that I'm unsure we can win again, especially as you say, we never truly won it in the first place. Even if it is in support of my niece."

Shock hit me like a wave down our bond, mingling with my own surprise.

Eva's mouth fell open. "Your…I'm your…"

"My brother, despite his Celestial magic guaranteeing his rule here, chose to live and rule with his *anima* in that oh so secretive kingdom in the north. The one that no one in my kingdom but me seemed to remember thanks to an ingenious bit of magic until very, very recently. But we are indeed blood." Eliav arched an imposing eyebrow, and I saw Eva's eyes narrow in recognition. "Do not think that bloodlink will sway me should the rest of your reasoning for this war not be sound."

Noam made a tutting sound. "Refreshments first before we start talking business, my love."

He took his *anima*'s arm, gesturing for us to follow as he led us inside the desert palace.

CHAPTER 28
EVA

We sat at a long ashwood table in front of enormous open windows that overlooked Esterra—a city of domed spires and stained-glass windows, rising from the swirling sand. The heady scent of the hanging gardens on a balcony below wafted toward us in the breeze, the greenery a stark contrast against the white sand dunes in the distance.

Despite the view, I hadn't been able to stop staring at my uncle. The resemblance was obvious now that I knew to look for it—the color of his eyes and raven-black hair, the slant of his brow, even the way he held himself. Something inside me ached at the living reminder of my dad, a pang going through my chest at the small mannerisms I had forgotten about so easily.

Eliav had brushed away any further talk of what we had come here for until after the meal. The heaping trays of grilled meats and eggplant, olive oil doused dips accompanied by warm flatbreads and crudité, eggs baked in tomato sauce, and artfully arranged fruits had kept our hands and mouths far too occupied to hold more than the most basic conversation.

But I could feel him watching me too, those familiar eyes seeming to catalogue my features as diligently as I had his.

My stomach stuffed to bursting, I pushed back my chair, walking to the windows to take in this new city. What I assumed were palace guards were training in a lower courtyard, flames shooting in carefully controlled bursts down the line of similarly leather clad soldiers. The way the elemental fire users wielded their magic seemed more like a dance than anything else as they twisted and swerved, their movement flowing yet precise. Unable to help myself, I copied some of their motions with my fingers, my darkness flowing around them like black flame.

A particularly wild blast from below made the hair on my neck rise as, for a second, I saw the fire that had consumed my home around me, felt it licking at my heels as I ran—

"Impressive, aren't they?" Eliav said from behind me, making me startle enough that he raised a brow.

"That they are," I agreed, noting Bash's eyes on me...along with a protective surge of concern in response to whatever old terror I had sent down our bond. I sucked in a carefully counted breath through my nose, hearing my father's voice as I let it out slowly. Grounding myself back in reality as I pretended to still be watching the training below.

"My Kingsguard are the best in the realm," Eliav continued. "Though your *anima* and his coterie might disagree."

I shrugged with feigned nonchalance. "I haven't met a lot of fire users."

Though Alette's fireball tearing through Morehaven had certainly shown me what they could do.

His gaze fell to my hands, then back to my eyes, where I belatedly realized my darkness must still linger. "Your father wielded darkness too."

I hadn't known that. While I knew about my mother's light, the bittersweet realization that I shared my magic with my father but could never talk to him about it, learn from him...It was yet another injustice of his murder, another thing that had been taken from me.

The declaration took me so off guard that I blurted out, "You look so much like him."

Eliav flinched, almost imperceptibly. "When my brother disappeared in the night with his children, I never expected them to return without him. I had hoped we would one day be reunited here."

"Then you should be willing to fight against the king who killed him," I said firmly. "To ally with your family, before it's too late to stop him."

"What I know is that the False King is buried beneath rock and stone and ice," Eliav said with a condescension that made my blood boil. "That my brother fled because of him, and never came back."

"But *I* did," I whispered. "As did my brother. And we need your help."

"You're far too revealing to play the game of kings," Eliav said, his voice sincere for once. "Though your father was never one for politics either, despite his station and Celestial ability."

"Lucky the game I play is for High Queen," I said, matching his tone while trying my best to share a confidence I didn't feel. Though my parents' stringent strategy lessons had prepared me more than I realized, it was another thing entirely to take on the role that was needed of me without feeling like an imposter.

His mouth quirked, just a hint of a dimple forming on the right side of his mouth. "Then I look forward to seeing if more than just his darkness was passed on through you."

I tried and failed not to tense as a blast of fire so hot I could feel it rose from the Kingsguard in a fiery inferno, more than one of them adding to its fury. They were putting on a performance for me, I belatedly realized. A way to show off their might, no doubt ordered by the king beside me.

Did he know the exact circumstances of how his brother died? The fire wielders that had terrorized us on the False King's orders?

If he didn't, I wasn't about to offer to tell him.

I tilted my head as I realized that no one had told me something important. "Do you wield fire too?"

In response, Eliav let out of burst of blue flame so hot, I could feel it prickle against the skin of my face despite the space between us. It swirled upwards in a tight spiral before dissipating into falling embers.

"Not Celestial," he said, so casually I knew it must bother him. "But powerful enough to rule this part of the realm."

Everyone was watching us now.

"I wouldn't be so foolish as to discount any display of power like that," I said with a shrug. "Nor expect magic to have anything to do with what it truly takes to rule."

Eliav stilled, as if shocked, before quickly recovering. The first crack in that careful mask of his I had seen yet. "Your mother told me something similar once. Perhaps you haven't been taken over by dark magic after all."

I tried not to let the longing that overcame me show on my face, even as I knew I had failed by the way his eyes softened, just slightly.

"Happy to hear I've passed your test," I said coolly, still not over the affront to my *anima*.

Spinning on my heel, I walked back to the table and sat next to Bash, leaning back into the arm he had draped over my chair.

Noam offered me a tiny porcelain cup he filled with coffee from a brass pot. He smiled as I gave him a nod of thanks before taking a sip. "If it makes you feel better, we hoped the son of our Imyrian friends hadn't become what was claimed." He turned to Bash. "Especially after you fought so bravely in the last war."

Bash lifted his own cup in acknowledgement. "I understand that there's much at stake here. But rest assured that we're not the ones trying to trick you with false narratives."

Noam nodded politely, though I doubted we had yet convinced him.

I turned to him. "If you don't mind me asking, what is your magic?"

"Air and wind and open sky," Noam replied with an easy smile, a swift breeze whipping around the table. "Though I'm sure you know all about that form of elemental magic," he added, lifting his chin at Yael in acknowledgement.

Yael was chasing some hummus around on her plate with a piece of grilled carrot, her expression slightly pinched—as it had been since the moment we had arrived. The concern in Marin's eyes had me wondering what exactly she was sending down their bond.

"How did an Esterran end up in the court of the Southern King, so far from home?" Eliav sat across from me, gesturing with a hummus-covered piece of flatbread. "I always meant to ask you during the war, though it never seemed the right time."

Yael bristled almost imperceptibly. "I've considered myself Imyrian since I was adopted by one." Her fingers twitched toward her opposite arm—towards the faded scars I knew lay there, the reminder of the monsters that were her Esterran parents. She stabbed another piece of carrot a little too violently. "Esterra is not my home."

Noam's eyebrows flew up in surprise, but Eliav merely smiled, if insincerely. "Strange how war can displace so many. I take it you have no family here then?"

Yael scowled slightly as she shook her head, picking up a goblet full of green-tinged wine and taking a large gulp.

"We're her family," Marin said a little too sharply, as Rivan let out a low sound of agreement. Bash nodded definitively, even as I saw him shoot them a warning look, as if gently chiding, *We're here to make allies.*

I cleared my throat. "In any case…perhaps it's time to discuss why we're here."

"Ah yes," Eliav said, sitting back in his chair. "Another war."

Bash mimicked his stance, his voice casual in a way that I knew was calculated. "We wouldn't be here asking for your assistance if the fate of our realm didn't hang in the balance."

My blood heated at seeing this side of him—the king he was, even if he would always be just 'freckles' to me. From the ghost of a smirk that crossed his face, I knew he had felt my response.

Eliav sniffed. "And you're certain the savior prince is indeed the same old enemy that started it all?"

"Very." Bash's tone was light, only the thin streak of shadow working its way protectively around my calf under the table betraying his displeasure.

"Then it seems even fate picks its favorites," Eliav said darkly.

Bash said nothing, though his ire rumbled down our bond.

"I would need some assurances, of course," Eliav continued. "Something more binding than just your word. A blood oath, perhaps, that what you say is indeed true."

Rivan lurched forward slightly, a snarl curling his lip. Yael let out a scoff like she should have expected this. I might have thought the quirk of Bash's lips was teasing if I didn't know better; his annoyance acerbic down our bond.

"Is that all?" Bash's voice was dry though I could see his eyes flash, swirling faster.

"Did you expect me to go to war for you on just your word?" Eliav's tone was more clinical than cruel. "To put my people at risk when they've barely put themselves back together from the last one? To believe the False King is truly behind all of this without assurances?"

Bash simply drew the dagger from his side, slicing it into his palm right below where he would receive a silvery message from me. I pressed my lips together, wanting to argue, to cry out at the very sight of his blood. But I trusted him to know how to respond.

Squeezing his hand into a fist, Bash let three drops spill onto the table in front of him before breaking the palpable silence. "The False King is back. Or, rather, he never left. He manipulated our world to his benefit, including stealing my *anima* from me after posing as the Crown Prince. I swear it on my magic and my life's blood."

He raised an eyebrow, as if daring anyone to disagree. I looked over at Eliav's shocked face. He obviously hadn't expected Bash to acquiesce to his demand, even if I didn't understand the meaning of it. But the fact that Bash had seemed to have changed something significant, Eliav's reserved calm gone in place of grim acceptance.

Bash's blood glowed with a faint blue light, then disappeared in a wisp of shadow. I looked at him with wide eyes, but it was Noam who answered the question on the tip of my tongue. "To lie under a blood oath is to risk your magic returning to the Source from which it came. We do not take such a thing lightly in this realm, not when one misspoken word could cost the giver so much."

My eyes shot to Bash, who simply shrugged. "We don't have any time to waste."

I placed my hands palm up on the table in a silent plea as I looked at my uncle. "We have to stop him. The fate of both realms hangs in the balance. And your help could make all the difference."

Eliav stared at where Bash's blood had disappeared, then around the circle, pausing at Yael before his gaze finally rested on Noam.

"Peace was nice while it lasted," Noam said softly. "But we both know the price to keep it."

Eliav nodded slowly, moving to briefly press his forehead against his husband's before turning back to me. Whether it was Bash's show of deference or the ugly truth he had shared, Eliav's face was solemn as he looked at me.

"You look so much like her."

I froze, the statement catching me entirely off guard.

A sad smile ghosted across Eliav's lips. "It's strange the things that are passed down from your parents. The hair, the eyes...they're mostly hers. But my brother is present in the most innocuous things about you, like I'm seeing into the past. And if what you say is true, the bastard that took him from me was never truly punished."

"He fought...the night Aviel came for us. It bought my brother and I the time to escape as he took the False King on." My voice was hoarse as I asked, "Will you continue his fight?"

Eliav reached toward me, handing me a wine-filled goblet before lifting his own. His eyes softened in a way that felt familiar, and I knew I already had his answer.

"To vengeance," Eliav intoned, raising his glass to me. "To continuing the fight. And for the realm."

"For the realm," came a chorus of responses.

But I stared straight into my uncle's familiar golden-brown eyes as I echoed, "To vengeance."

The taste of the wine on my tongue felt like a covenant. A promise bound by blood.

Bash's hand lightly trailed down my back, breaking the spell. There was pride in his gaze as I turned to him, as something like hope flurried across our bond.

"Noam will begin the arrangements," Eliav said. Seeing my surprise, he gave me a wry smile. "My *anima* was my general long before he was my lover. While our path to each other may not have been as complicated as your own, it took a war together before I accepted what he was to me."

Noam's smile was dazzling. "Even though I knew it all along."

"And will never let me hear the end of it," Eliav added with a long-suffering sigh.

Noam turned to Bash. "I assume you have thoughts about where our people should be positioned?"

Yael stood, looking around with a frown. "I brought some maps with us, if you know where they went. We have limited time to strategize before we need to depart."

The guard by the door cleared his throat. "They must have been moved by mistake. I can take you to them to make sure you retrieve the right ones."

Eliav nodded, looking distracted. "Escort her to my study when she has what she needs."

Yael brushed a chaste kiss on the top of Marin's hair before walking quickly to the door.

CHAPTER 29

BASH

My fingers tapped the edge of the round, mosaic-covered table, the blood red tiles cool under my fingertips. The pattern faded into orange then yellow, then white, then an electric blue in the center like the essence of flame.

Eliav's study clearly doubled as his war room. Ancient maps covered one wall; newer ones plastered atop the old. A large mahogany desk faced a fancifully arched window that looked over a narrow balcony.

I had a feeling that balcony had mostly been used for pacing.

"Our forces are gathering in Soleara as we speak," Eva said. "After this, we'll return to join them, then head north to Adronix to cut off the False King."

Her fingers were playing piano scales on her leg, each run through slightly faster. I took her hand as if I could calm her anxiety with my touch. "According to our last correspondence, Queen Sariyah is readying to join us as well. Though her army will likely be split with the upheaval in her own territory." Though the queen was on our side, the False King's supporters had done their best to destabilize her reign, many of her people having supported him in the last war. They had laid low all these years, hiding in plain sight while waiting for their chance, and the queen shared my worries that they wouldn't waste their opportunity now. "The real question is where your troops will be best utilized—reclaiming Morehaven or at the more pivotal battle at Adronix?"

"From what our intelligence has gathered, Aviel's army plans to split," Rivan added. "The numbers heading to Adronix should outweigh those remaining behind, but with Soleara in between Morehaven and Adronix, we risk an ambush."

Noam frowned. "And with that large of a contingent of Aviel's soldiers left at Morehaven, I would argue our forces would be best used to deny him any chance that army can provide him assistance, or they'll trap you between them."

Rivan nodded. "Between the Imyrian and Solearan forces we have, and those we can expect from Mayim, we should be well matched for the contingent readying to journey northward."

"But you're right," I said to Noam. "We can't simply leave a second army at our backs. Especially with the majority of the Solearan forces heading north."

I glanced at the ashy wooden doors again, wondering what was taking Yael so long...and wanting to make sure she was okay after her obvious discomfort at dinner. It hadn't escaped my notice that my sister's gaze hadn't strayed from those same doors since we arrived.

"He's attempting to beat us to Adronix to circumvent the Choosing," Eva said, and Eliav stiffened. "I assume Bash told you in his letters about the False King's abilities. He stole my magic, my..." Her voice faltered, her face paling slightly. "...everything he needs to become High King. Though I won't pretend I have any understanding of what the Choosing entails beyond where the Seeing Mirror is located."

The thought of it—of the pain he had put her through—made something feral inside me unsheathe its claws. A wisp of shadow threaded between our fingers, twirling lightly against the circular scars on her wrist. Eva barely blinked, but her eyes darkened as a tendril of darkness joined it.

"Not like we can put it to chance that he might fail." Rivan's tone was light, though his gaze was worried as he watched Eva. "Though it would be nice if that mirror spat him right back out."

"We can't let him get that far," I said grimly.

Eliav sat forward in his chair, one long finger twisting his dark beard. "My grandfather was the High King before dearly departed Queen Amerie. He told me a bedtime story long ago about the mirror that led to his destiny."

Eva sat up straighter, the jolt of her excitement echoing down my spine.

"From what he told me, the Choosing does not take place in Adronix," Eliav continued. "The mirror is only the gateway to where the real test takes place."

"What test?" I demanded.

Eliav shrugged. "Only the ones who have gone through it know where the mirror takes them and the test they must face. Which is to say, no one left alive."

"Though if the High Queen's advisors knew anything, they would have told him, whether they wanted to or not," Marin said with a grimace, glancing at me before frowning at the still-empty doorway.

Noam looked thoughtful. "I heard that her inner circle has been going missing."

Marin nodded, though her gaze remained fixed on the door. "The one that lived in Soleara went missing right before Eva showed up."

Eva's expression tightened. "He knew I was on my way to him. And if that advisor told him exactly how to succeed in the Choosing..."

A sense of dread was settling in my gut, the feeling not only my own. "Did your grandfather tell you anything else?"

Eliav shook his head. "He only said the true heir has it within them to be chosen."

I fought the urge to shake him. "So if the False King gets through the Seeing Mirror with Eva's magic...will that be enough?"

Eliav let out a breath before his face relaxed into its usual aloof façade. "That's the question, now isn't it?"

My sister gasped, doubling over before leaping to her feet. "Yael..."

Marin's double blades were at Eliav's throat before anyone could move.

CHAPTER 30

EVA

"Where. *Is*. She." Marin's voice held none of its usual kindness, each word forced out from between gritted teeth. "Where is my *anima?*"

Bash stepped to my side, shifting so he was shielding me. White-hot rage flashed across our bond.

"I don't know," Eliav gritted out as Noam's fingers inched toward his blade. "This wasn't me. I swear it."

A shout echoed down the tan stone hallway, then the familiar clang of clashing swords. I drew my dagger on instinct as a guard burst into the room, the black diamond gleaming.

The guard stopped short at the scene before him. "Your Majesty—"

"Just tell us what's happening," Eliav ordered calmly, like he didn't have two blades at his jugular.

"It's our own people," the guard said hurriedly. "The Kingsguard. They're...it's a coup."

Bash swore under his breath, shadows swirling up his arms.

"A coup." Eliav was nearly expressionless, his voice flat and disbelieving. "Abrahim, are you sure?"

"They are the False King's," Abrahim said, glancing behind him as if he expected them to appear at any moment. "And they know *she's* here." He nodded meaningfully at me.

Rivan swore. "Of course the False King's supporters found a hold here again."

Marin's eyes flashed. "If *they* have Yael—"

"Then I know where they would've taken her. If you'll remove your blades," Eliav added silkily. "This appears to be an attack on *my* rule."

Marin's blades didn't move an inch. "One that was timed for the visit that *you* demanded."

"Something they must have taken advantage of since the False King's supporters appear to have infiltrated our own Kingsguard," Noam argued, a hint of shock coloring his tone. "*They* must have taken her."

Marin's features were deadly with rage. "And we're to believe you had no idea that your personal guard was behind this? This was *your* people."

"Not on my orders," Eliav retorted. "We're wasting time. If my Kingsguard are truly among the False King's supporters, they would have known where to lie in wait. We've both been betrayed."

Bash glanced at his sister. "Marin."

Her blades were sheathed at her sides as quickly as they had appeared. I remembered Yael telling me once that her *anima* was the more dangerous of the two of them. The silent way Marin moved, the way those blades had found their mark before I could so much as blink, was more than enough to confirm why.

"I'm going to trust you," Marin said, eying the Eastern King with utter distaste. "For now. Even after you lured us here into a trap. But if you're lying—if you had *anything* to do with her capture—I will flay you alive."

Eliav merely raised a reproachful eyebrow at her, entirely unruffled as he drew his sword.

"Those still loyal to you are gathering in the throne room, Your Highnesses," Abrahim said. "Though it appears our way back is blocked, if you wish to use the alternative route."

"Of course," Eliav said cryptically.

Quickly, I retrieved my sword from where it had been stowed by the door, feeling its pommel sing under my grip as I reattached its sheath to my back—wishing I had decided to dress in my leathers rather than the thin fabric of this dress.

"If our Kingsguard are indeed with the False King, we must move quickly," Noam said, his brow furrowing. "They'll likely move any prisoners to the dungeons...and if Yael is as powerful as I remember, they'll need the iron down there to bind her."

"Then we need a way down there, and quickly," Marin snapped. "If they targeted her before Eva and Bash, they're likely looking for someone to torture for information that they deemed expendable."

Eliav nodded. "Especially if they see her as a traitor to Esterra for siding with the Southerners."

Bash's shadows curled around his sword as if getting ready to strike.

"I will attempt to discourage anyone who decides to come down this hallway," Abrahim said, bowing to Eliav, then to me.

My eyes widened, but Eliav held up a hand. "Absolutely not. You're coming with us."

Abrahim opened his mouth as if to argue, then bowed slightly, closing the double doors behind him. "As you wish, my liege."

I tensed as flame flickered in his palm before he pressed it against the lock, effectively melting the two doors together.

Rivan let out a low, threatening sound, stepping toward the door, but Eliav held up a hand.

"Unless you think it wise to waste time fighting our way down to the lower levels," Eliav drawled. "I suggest you follow me."

He walked briskly to a brightly colored, ornate rug in the middle of the room. Pulling it back with a flourish, he revealed a round red mosaic on the tiled floor, patterned like a radiating swirl of fire. Carefully, he pressed on three of the inner tiles. They sank down with a heavy clunk before the entire circle of the mosaic lowered, slowly exposing a spiral staircase.

"Do all the castles in this realm have secret passageways?" I asked, unable to help myself.

Eliav shrugged. "Whether for escape routes in times of need, for eavesdropping, or for carrying on elicit affairs—"

"Historically, of course," Noam cut in.

"Many of the rulers who built these ancient palaces included them, though their existence is a highly kept secret."

"Count yourselves lucky they did." Noam nodded at the door where, from the clash of swords in the hallway, it seemed the fight was getting closer.

"Hurry now," Eliav said almost cheerily as he led the way, a ball of blue flame bouncing ahead of him.

We hastily followed, our footsteps resounding on the dark metal of the stairwell as we rushed downward. The air was thick with the mineral scent of rust and particles of dust glittered around us as the light scattered into the darkness below. Noam pressed a tile underneath the mosaic as he ducked underneath it. It slid seamlessly back into place over his head.

Without the daylight, the tunnel reminded me unnervingly of the secret passageway I used to escape Aviel back in Morehaven, its stone walls lit with a bright blue glow. And not all of it from Eliav's fire, I realized, as a familiar rock shone from within the stone. Sensing my trepidation, Bash reached down from behind me to hold my hand.

I didn't let go as we continued downward.

Rivan's low voice echoed as he asked, "Will the Kingsguard know about these tunnels?"

"Most don't," Noam replied. "They're known to the royal family and only our most loyal guards," he nodded at Abrahim. "Though we can't count it out."

"They won't have expected us to escape the way we did," Eliav said firmly. "They'll be looking for us in the wrong place. But if the thick of the fighting is in the throne room, then that's where we'll go."

He came to a sudden stop as the pathway split, a metal stairwell leading upward to the left, a narrow corridor veering to the right.

"This is where we must leave you," Eliav said softly. "Abrahim will take you the rest of the way. We'll reconvene in the throne room when you have retrieved Esterra's lost daughter."

"Please feel free to leave none alive for their treachery," Noam added, looking at Marin. She gave him a sharp nod before they quickly clambered upward.

"Quiet now," Abrahim warned us as he ducked into the smaller passageway.

The only sound was the dripping of water as we hurried through the narrow tunnel. Bash ducked down behind me so not to hit his head on the low, rocky ceiling. The glowing blue rocks were few and far between here, and the cramped, dark space was getting to me more than I wanted to admit. My breath came in shallow pants as I felt the walls start to close in around me, the cold iron of the box seeping into me like I might never again find warmth or safety—

I stopped short as I heard a cry of pain. Blinding wrath burned through me in the next moment—so strongly I couldn't tell if it was Bash's or my own. Abrahim motioned to us to follow him into a cramped alcove where he pointed at a barely visible outline in the stone. He held up a hand in warning, looking through what appeared to be a peephole.

"Tell us what you know, traitor, and your death will come more quickly," said a deep, rough voice on the other side of the door.

Yael's laugh didn't hold a trace of fear. "Yours won't."

Abrahim held up four fingers. Four adversaries then.

Easy.

There was a yelp of pain, then the unmistakable, acrid smell of burnt flesh. Marin's knuckles went white against her blades.

"Then we'll *make* you talk, traitor," a second voice sneered.

"How exactly am I a traitor for not following the False King in his new face?" Yael panted. "Or am I simply a traitor for leaving this sandy piece of earth and never feeling the need to look back?"

Abrahim gave us a nod, mouthing a countdown, then pressed his hand against a notch on the doorway.

It was hard to say whose magic incapacitated Yael's torturers first. One second, they had turned in surprise, a ball of fire sputtering in the hands of the one directly next to Yael. The next, they were all mangled on the ground—their features barely discernible from the force of our collective fury. Marin's blades had sunk into the head of one, the heart of another.

But that was Yael's blood spattered on the ground, running from her nose, her lip. The unmistakable signs of a struggle in her dishevelment, the marks of her mistreatment all over her bruising face and the red, blistering skin of her chest and arms.

They hadn't deserved the quick deaths they had been granted.

I removed the keys hanging from what remained of one of their belts and tossed them to Marin. She was already at Yael's side.

Yael grinned as her chains fell to the floor. "What took you so long?"

We hurried back the way we came after ascertaining that Yael was healed enough to continue. Marin's magic soothed away the worst of her burns, as well as her thankfully bruised and not broken ribs. She still held herself stiffly, flashing me an exasperated smile at the concern I was sure showed all over my face.

I could practically feel Abrahim's anxiety to find Eliav and Noam as we followed him up the dark metal stairwell after them. Marin walked ahead of me, her arm around Yael even in the narrowest sections. As we reached the end of the passage, Abrahim pressed his ear against the wall, then raised his sword before tapping on a glowing blue stone. A bright, rectangular outline appeared in the rock that Abrahim carefully pulled inward.

We emerged into a nondescript, empty corridor. I blinked owlishly at the sunset shining through a small half-moon window, even the dim rays blinding after so long underground. There was no need for Abrahim to gesture around the corner—the cacophony of noise that preceded the ongoing battle left little doubt of how close we were. He bowed deeply to me. As I bent to return it, he disappeared around the corner, no doubt to find his kings.

Bash's shadows crisscrossed up his sword as his eyes became the same color gray. He smiled devilishly at me as he admitted, "I've been aching for a good fight."

Rivan grinned as he came up next to him. "Let's go then. Before we miss all the fun."

"Yael..." Bash's gaze dropped to the pinkish burns still visible on her bronzed skin.

"I'm fine," Yael said, her mouth twitching with annoyance. "I can help. And I'm not sitting on my ass while the rest of you keep a kingdom from falling."

Marin inclined her head. "And I have no plans to ever leave your side again."

Yael laughed as she raised her sword, the long, thin blade glinting in the dying light. She limped slightly as she started toward the sounds of battle, Marin at her side. We followed them around the corner to an enormous, domed room, a great golden throne shining in the center of the chaos. The two sides were all in the same uniform, as those who had remained loyal were forced to fight against their former brethren.

Noam was standing in front of Eliav, a shield of wind whirling around them like a tornado. Fire pelted them from all sides. Their own Kingsguard surrounded them, far too many of them adding to the assault.

A burst of wind blew my hair forward as Yael's magic joined Eliav's shield, strengthening it against the onslaught. Then a guard moved toward us, a flare of his fire heading straight for me. For a split second, my darkness seemed to cower before it, then Bash's shadows engulfed him. The fire disappeared, and the guard was lifted off his feet by the smoky tendrils that snapped his neck before he slumped lifelessly to the floor. Bash glanced at me quickly, concern permeating our bond as he stepped over the body, already ready for the next of them.

I nodded slightly in thanks as I breathed in for a familiar four-count, letting my exhale strengthen my resolve—finding that calm even as fire lashed out at us from all sides. But now wasn't the time to falter.

A flame arced toward my *anima*, and my magic flooded into the room without a second thought. Like it had been waiting to be freed from the shackles of my own fear, eager to extinguish the fire that threatened me once again, and those I loved. Darkness streamed from my hands, forming a shield in front of me. Ready, this time, to smother anyone and anything that might threaten me or my family.

Yael and Marin fought side by side, and those who faced them didn't get any farther. Rivan raised walls of stone, bursting from the castle floor to shield him from the flames before they hurled forward, crushing the oncoming guards who weren't quick enough to jump from their path. Bash's sword and shadows sliced through the room in deadly tandem.

Enough, I thought, as I watched a flame whip far too close to Bash for comfort. There was a slice along his forearm I hadn't seen him receive, the sight of his blood illuminated by the encroaching fire filling me with a primal sort of fear.

Magic rattled my bones, then my darkness pulled me under.

My back arched as it flooded down my spine, my head thrown back, my lips parting with an inhuman cry as the power became more than I could bear.

ENOUGH.

I erupted. Night flew out of me just as it had in Morehaven—pure blackness blasting outward in a shockwave from my eyes, my feet, my hands. Whipping around me in a hurricane of inky tendrils, wrapping around my enemies who had foolishly raised their swords against me. Bending to my will as it hurtled toward the traitors surrounding their former king and his *anima*, the very people they had sworn to protect.

Unyielding, solid darkness attacked soldier after soldier, their magics flaring and dying as they did. I caught a glimpse of teeth and claws as my magic tore apart my enemies—the flickering shapes of my nightmares come to life.

And I let myself hate them—for what they would've done to Yael, for what they wanted to do to my family. For whom they had chosen to side with, and what he had done to me.

No, I would not mourn these deaths.

Rivan opened his mouth, then shut it soundlessly, lowering his sword.

Bash let out a low laugh as an entire swath of bodies slumped to the floor. "What happened to leaving some for the rest of us, hellion?"

I stared at him through my night darkened eyes. There was heat in his shadow-filled gaze as he came up next to me. His thumb stroked my cheek until I could feel the darkness slip away.

Rivan's wide eyes met mine. "You're kind of terrifying now, you know that, right?"

My smile was a bit shaky. "Thank you."

"An absolute menace," Bash said, with that crooked half-grin that never failed to make my heart flutter. "But I've known that from the moment I met you."

I rolled my eyes. "I gathered that from the nickname."

There was a yell from the doorway as more guards rushed in, fire igniting from their outstretched hands as they came at us. More traitors, both against their kingdom and their realm if they believed in the sort of future Aviel promised.

With a smirk, Bash raised his sword, running toward the wall of flame rushing to meet him. His shadows streamed out of him, more pulling from the corners of the room before slamming into the flame with a sizzle, extinguishing it with half a thought. Then his sword met that of an oncoming guard, Rivan engaging another.

I couldn't look away from Bash as he fought. That easy, vicious grace, the power behind each movement. His muscles bulged against the finery he was wearing—the thin tunic clinging to his frame as sweat plastered it to the defined muscles of his back. A warrior incarnate, the sight of him heating my blood in a way that was entirely inappropriate.

His blade went straight through a guard's heart, before he spun around, his voice gravelly as he said, "If you keep thinking those thoughts, I'm not going to be able to focus."

I winked, then ran forward to where Yael and Marin had joined Eliav and Noam and the remaining traitors closing in. Marin's dual blades moved so quickly, I paused for a moment to admire her speed and skill as she dispatched one opponent, then another. Yael shot me a knowing look, the circle of guards around her clutching at their throats in unison before they fell to the floor.

Noam had an arm wrapped around Eliav's waist. Holding him up, I realized, as I rushed to his other side.

Eliav waved me off. "Take one of them alive. I want answers."

Indeed, the remaining traitors seemed to realize there was no hope for anything other than their own escape. My remaining darkness wrapped around the feet of one who had turned to run, and his flames lashed out blindly. Darkness engulfed his hands, his feet, smothering them as they held him tight.

For one brief moment I saw those shackles that had once bound me.

Then those tendrils dragged him forward, his eyes narrowing in hatred as my magic held his own power in check.

"*Why?*" Eliav demanded.

The traitor let out a cold laugh, then winced as my darkness bit into his skin. "You chose wrong when you didn't ally with the True King the first time. And now you would have us back some untried girl? We weren't about to wait for you to make the right choice."

Eliav sighed. "How unoriginal."

"He will not be stopped," the traitor laughed, staring directly at me. "The King will not be—"

Blue flame consumed him, my darkness dissipating as his screams quickly cut off, leaving only charged silence.

Eliav sagged, and Marin rushed forward. Healing light spread from her fingertips to treat the burn across his thigh, so deep I could see flayed muscle and charred white bone.

The Eastern King's eyes met mine, barely a hint of the pain that I knew must be unbearable reflected in his gaze. "Return to Soleara and begin your trek north. I'll see to securing your castle."

"My…"

Eliav smiled, the first one I had seen from him that felt real, before dropping his chin in the slightest of bows. "Morehaven, Your Majesty. Stop that bastard from claiming your crown, and you have my word your throne will be waiting for you."

CHAPTER 31
ADRIAN

"There's something I need to tell you."

We both said it at the same time. Estelle's face broke into a smile I couldn't tear my eyes away from, even with the gravity of my news. She looked worn out, drawn despite her beauty—the face of too many sleepless nights as we faced a realm at war. But her smile faded too soon as she sensed my trepidation.

Her throat bobbed. "Bad news first then."

A distant bout of thunder rumbled as if on cue, the clouds in the distance dark with impending rain. I often found my *anima* seeking solace among the plum trees that lined the courtyard of our home, though her meditations had given way to pacing more often of late. The blood-red leaves rustled in the wind, a few of them whipping into the air. One fell upon the neckline of Estelle's black dress, catching in the intricate beading above her heart.

I hated how much it looked like blood. Like her own heart had been ripped right open.

But I didn't waste time with platitudes, not when I knew she would want me to be direct. "The battle was lost. The first of the survivors are just now returning."

She reeled back slightly, then straightened, obviously about to run to help—to give aid wherever she could. I took both her hands in mine, softly adding, "Your father is dead."

My *anima* sucked in a sharp breath, her gaze going distant. Her lower lip quivered then her entire body started to tremble. Shock and anger and grief streamed across our bond in waves, each larger than the last. Taking her into my arms, I tried my best to buoy her.

"Big breath in," I murmured, rubbing her back in slow circles. "Count each second. Breath out. And count the same."

I breathed with her, needing the release of my own uneasy thoughts, trying to let go of the automatic, primal urge to seek vengeance at her pain. Matching her slow, shuddering exhale before her eyes met mine, those golden crowns shining with her tears.

"The False King."

It wasn't a question. Velan had joined Morehaven's forces in the High Queen's attempt to stop her would-be usurper. But the False King's might had only grown, his supporters stirring dissent in our ancient hierarchies, promising change with poisoned words, even as it was clear that the False King would only ever serve himself. This war was for his own gain, his own greed and lust for power. His aims for the human realm were evidence enough of that, even as his supporters cheered the promise of finally revealing themselves so the mortals would kneel in servitude.

"He was killed during the battle," I said, wishing I could assuage the pain on her face. The choking sense of sorrow down our bond.

She seemed far away as she whispered, "At least he wasn't captured."

I winced. It was no secret how prisoners of the False King fared.

Then, in a hoarse whisper, "I should have gone with him."

I was already shaking my head. "Your father wanted you here, leading our people in his stead. He wouldn't have wanted you in danger."

Estelle let out a choked laugh. "The whole realm is in danger, whether we hide in Soleara or not." She slowly shook her head side to side as if attempting to clear it. "I didn't think losing him would affect me like this. Not with our disagreements over the years as he ruled down below. But we were finally finding some common ground. And now I've lost both of them, and I never even got to tell him..."

She dissolved into sobs. I pulled her back into my arms, needing to hold her. Needing to fix what couldn't be as her arms tightened almost painfully around me.

"I don't need to tell you what else this means," I whispered into her hair.

Estelle blew out a breath, stepping out of my embrace. "That I'm now the Queen of Soleara, and you're my king?" Her mouth twisted to the side, almost dismissively. "Or that, should the False King succeed in murdering Queen Amerie as we all know he intends to, then it will be time to battle for my birthright?"

"We'll deal with that if it comes. Until then, I take it you aren't interested in a coronation?"

Her eyes snapped to mine, the fire in them liable to consume me whole.

Finally.

"How can you joke about this?"

I reached for her hand, but she jerked away. "It's not humor, it's hope. Because no matter the circumstance of how your reign began, I know exactly how lucky this kingdom is to have you."

Her eyes softened, then her mouth twisted to the side as she said, wryly, "He would hate how I plan to rule."

I smiled as I thought of the stacks of leather-bound notebooks piled in our room, each filled with plans for how to turn our aristocracy into a more democratic society. Most had been modeled after some of the more successful approaches from the human realm. We had spent months there, undercover as foreign dignitaries, despite her father's strenuous objections, getting to know the ways of their world and learning from many of their brightest minds. We had even built a home there, in a quiet town we hoped to return to visit one day.

But Estelle's aspirations for what we had learned didn't stop at just Soleara. Not with the future we knew awaited her when this war was won.

"They were able to retrieve Duskbane for you. He would have wanted you to wield it."

Estelle blinked, the only confirmation she heard me.

"Princess…"

She gave me a watery smile. "It seems that title no longer fits."

"Fair enough," I said softly. "What can I do?"

"Nothing," Estelle sighed. "There's nothing we can do to change what already happened. All we can do is deal with the aftermath." Her eyes hardened. "And plan for the day we make him pay for what he took from me."

"There you are." My knuckles brushed lightly against her jaw, and she leaned into my touch. "I was starting to get worried."

A ghost of a smile crossed her lips before she let out a weary sigh. "I need to go help."

"*We* need to," I affirmed, reaching out my hand. Her hand slid reflexively into mine. "But...you had news?"

Estelle's bright eyes met mine just as the clouds broke. One raindrop, then another fell around us, mingling with the tears on her cheeks. She looked up, staring into the storm as the world wept with her, unmoving even as lightning streaked across the sky.

A glimmer of joy flashed across our bond before her grief swallowed it. "I'm pregnant."

CHAPTER 32
EVA

I barely had the energy to bathe the battle from my skin before collapsing into bed, unable to muster the strength to even find a nightgown. My magic was almost entirely spent, the little that remained curling up inside me like a cat. We had stumbled through the mirror back to my Solearan childhood home, though Bash had immediately mirrored down to the bronze castle below, checking in on his people now setting up camp inside it despite the late hour. From the message that appeared on my palm, a steady surge of them was still passing through its towering, rose-adorned mirror, readying to leave come morning.

Rivan had assured me before he left that there was still no word of movement from Morehaven. That Aviel was still gathering his forces, just as we were—even as the thought of him beating us to that ancient mountain made my blood run cold. We were still closer, despite today's delay, though his words did little to abate the anxiety thrumming in my veins.

But despite the voice inside me that whispered there was no time to waste, my display of power had weakened me far more than I realized. I was asleep before my head hit the pillow.

I awoke to Bash's hands roving my naked body, his lips working their way up between my breasts, his teeth nipping at my neck to wake me. One hand palmed my ass, the evidence of his arousal pressing into my thigh as he yanked the bedding completely off me. I arched into him with a sigh.

My voice was still clogged with sleep as I asked, "Is it time to wake up already?"

I arduously forced my eyes open. It was still dark. Too dark to be morning, the room lit only by the hazy light of the full moon. My brain felt sluggish, my body heavy and sore in the aftermath of battle.

Bash didn't answer beyond a low growl—instead kissing me firmly, his tongue plunging inside my mouth with forceful purpose. I wrapped my arms around his waist, trailing my nails down his naked back. One hand found my nipple, pinching it so hard it made me gasp. His knee slid between my legs, pushing them apart as he positioned himself between them. Then his weight pressed me into the bed as his hand tightened almost painfully on my hip.

Something made me pause. Something in his touch that had me jerking my head back against the pillow to break our kiss. Something muted across our bond that felt faintly like terror.

"Bash?"

His husky laughter floated through our bedroom. An involuntary shiver skittered up my spine, goosebumps rising on my flesh.

There was something *wrong*.

Suddenly, I was fully awake, fully alert, detecting a threat I couldn't make sense of yet. Tensing even as I reached for him, my hands splaying across his cheeks to make him look me in the eyes. "Are you—"

Bash gripped my wrists so suddenly I cried out, forcing them above my head with one hand. The other found my throat possessively, his thumb pressing into a pulse point on my neck where a band had lived, not long ago. Where another's hand had wrapped around it.

And I *knew*.

My voice cracked as I whispered, "*Aviel*."

Terror froze the blood in my veins. I couldn't breathe, couldn't think straight as I stared into the glacial depths of those pale blue eyes, startlingly still in place of Bash's ever-moving gaze. Like that magic, too, had been silenced.

His head tilted questioningly, a slow, sinister smile spreading across his face as he asked, "How did you know, darling?"

I flinched at the smug malice in Bash's voice, the tone one I had never once heard from him, each syllable warped with that aristocratic intonation. And at the pet name I couldn't help but cringe away from despite myself.

The upward curve of his lips told me he had seen it.

A memory flared—a pale-eyed coyote staring at me from the tree line. But *this*. How was this even possible?

"Your beloved left plenty of blood behind the last time I saw him," Aviel said, laughing quietly at my shock as Bash's face twisted cruelly. "A simple sort of blood tie, albeit fleeting. But enough to remind you to whom you belong."

No.

I struggled, bucking against him—but he had me pinned, my *anima*'s face smiling at my panic. Stolen shadows blocked the door, and I knew my screams would go unanswered even if I could be heard over the muffled din of the preparations below. My darkness sputtered at my fingertips, a few weak tendrils trying desperately to come to my aid, before disappearing entirely.

"Push him out," I pleaded over the sound of my own thundering heart. Remembering Rivan's words and how I had fought Aviel in my dreams. "It's your mind, your body. Don't let him win."

I saw the storm. The slight, familiar swirl of his eyes that told me he was still in there, still fighting. The loosening of the hand at my throat raised my hopes as I redoubled my efforts to get free—

My stomach dropped as those eyes went still and cold.

"You should hear him screaming," Aviel whispered into my ear, teeth biting down on the lobe so hard I cried out. "Begging you to stop him. To kill him before he can hurt you."

Bile burned my throat. "Bash—" My voice broke as I battled against the body I knew so well. "Fight this. *Please.*"

A flicker of anguish and something like loathing crossed his face. I could see it as he fought, throwing himself against the cage of his own mind, his body trembling from the battle within it. Fought…and lost, his irises freezing over once more.

A cruel, wicked grin spread his lips wide, and my skin crawled.

"You were foolish to think she could ever be yours," Aviel sneered, pure hatred burning in his ice-cold gaze. "Not when I claimed her first."

With a curse, I threw myself against Aviel's hold. But his hands held firm, his grip bruising as he pushed me down into the bed with Bash's superior strength. He let out a dark laugh, then his teeth found my neck— that same scarred spot—drawing blood as he bit down. I couldn't help my cry of pain.

Instinctually, I bit down in response, my teeth sinking into his shoulder. Aviel's grip on my wrists slackened. I shoved as hard as I could into the center of Bash's chest, pushing him off me before launching myself off the side of the bed. Aviel moved toward me, but I had already palmed Bash's dagger from the bedside table, pointing it at him.

I was shaking so badly the tip trembled.

"Here I thought to keep you somewhat dressed while in my bed," Aviel's gaze lowered, and I had never felt so exposed. "I prefer this for next time."

He moved closer, his sneering smile widening as he did. So close now that Bash's chest touched the tip of the blade—

I froze. With a sickening grin, he leaned into it.

I pulled the blade back with a low cry, unable to look away from Bash's blood as it welled from the shallow wound on his chest. But his eyes flickered from solely blue to their normal split shade, just for a moment. So quickly I might have imagined it.

Aviel's vicious laugh had no trace of Bash in it as his hand gripped my arm with bruising force, pulling me back against him. "What exactly are you going to do, darling? Stab your *anima*? Somehow, I don't think he'll appreciate it."

I didn't let myself second guess what I was about to do.

"Then you don't know him very well."

I sliced downward, watching Aviel's eyes flare in shock.

The blade embedded into Bash's thigh, and Aviel let out a startled shout. Not too deep—nothing that would slow him down for long. Just something jolting and painful enough to break Aviel's link to him, as it briefly had already. To interrupt that bastard's concentration long enough to give Bash a chance to—

"*Eva,*" Bash choked out, his body crumpling.

I sucked in a breath that sounded more like a sob as I threw myself at him, dropping the dagger to the floor. My relief was so potent I felt lightheaded.

"*Bash.*"

I wasn't sure which one of us was shaking harder as he held me, and held me, and held me.

CHAPTER 33
BASH

That feeling of being caged in my own mind would haunt me forever. Of silently, futilely screaming against the intruder using my body like a marionette. Begging Eva to stop me, fight me, *kill* me, before I could so much as bruise her.

But gods damn me, I had done worse than that. And I would sell my soul to never have her look like that again—helpless and completely terrified—not for herself, but for *me*.

Possession magic was so dark and dangerous it had been forbidden long ago, though evidently not forgotten. That bastard had gotten in tonight because I had been drained from the fight, distracted, and unprepared for the surprise assault on my mind. But even though I had finally pushed him out with her help, I wanted to rage at what I had been forced to do to her. At what I had been so powerless to stop; the utter betrayal of my body, my mind, and my very soul.

Eva sucked in a broken breath that cracked something in me. Her fingers were ice cold and shaking as I took her hand in mine, trying in vain to let go of the wild, feral feeling I knew she could sense.

"I hurt you," I whispered brokenly. "Eva, I'm so—"

"I *stabbed* you," Eva gasped out.

"Thank the gods."

Eva looked at me askance, then let out a choking sound that was almost a laugh. "And here I thought I already knew all your kinks."

But her eyes were haunted, searching mine as if to be sure any trace of her tormentor was gone. I reached out, gently caressing the bruises blooming on her wrists. Where his—where *my* hands held her down.

A faint tremor coursed down my arm.

I could barely look at the bite mark, where he had claimed her yet again, her blood dripping down her chest.

"You need a healer," I said hoarsely, moving to extract myself from her embrace. "I can wake someone…"

But her focus was on my leg—at the blood steadily leaking down to stain the cream-colored sheets.

"You're the one who needs a healer," Eva said, her voice trembling.

"Eva…"

She was already tearing a page from a notebook by her bedside, writing a quick note that disappeared in a dark swirl of her magic. Her lips were tightly pressed together as she hurried to the bathroom, coming back with two robes, a wet washcloth, and a steaming bowl of water. She threw a fleece robe at me before wrapping herself in her own.

"You don't need to—" Firmly, she pressed the washcloth to my wound, cutting off my protests. "It's fine." Her hand trembled as she kept pressure on it, ignoring me entirely. "Eva, please stop and talk to me."

I reached out to touch her. My hand stilled over the red marks on her arm—the *handprint* that perfectly matched my grip. I yanked my hand away, unable to tear my gaze from the darkening mark, the outline of my fingertips marring her skin.

A knock on the door snapped me out of my spiraling thoughts.

"Come in," Eva called out, her voice pitched low.

The door opened a crack, then Rivan slipped inside. "I leave you two alone for…" He stopped still as his eyes fixed on Eva's bleeding neck, now dripping down onto her robe, then the stab wound on my leg. "What the hell happened?"

"Av—Aviel used Bash's blood to try to attack me." Eva gestured at my leg with a still-trembling hand. "I was able to snap him out of it."

Rivan let out a low growl, coming up to the bedside. He reached out a hand, already aglow with the healing green of his magic, but I shook my head. "Her first."

Eva rolled her eyes. "You're the one who's bleeding."

"So are you," I gritted out. And immediately regretted it at the stricken look on her face. She reached up to touch the reopened wound on her neck like she had forgotten it was there, wincing as she felt it. Slowly, she lowered her hand, her face carefully blank as she took in the blood on her fingertips. Then she lifted her eyes to mine, her fingers curling in to form a fist—smearing her blood against her scar.

I looked away first. "Start with—"

But Rivan's magic was already flowing into my leg, the pain of the knife-wound already dulling. I glared at him, snapping, "Since when don't you know how to follow orders?"

"Since it was a stupid one." Rivan scowled at me, then heaved a sigh. "But considering the rate at which you were losing blood, you already knew that. And I'm not in the business of enabling suffering, especially when it isn't deserved."

"You don't even know what happened."

"I know enough."

The silence thickened as I watched my skin knit back together, an angry red scab forming over the injury.

"Your turn." Rivan held his hand out to Eva, waiting for her nod before he placed it over her neck. "Though Quinn may do a better job getting rid of it entirely, especially since it's fresh."

Eva shrugged slightly. "It won't change what's already there."

Another layer to the scar Aviel had marked her with, the inherent claiming of it making me see red. My shadows flitted angrily up my arms, though they didn't try to reach for her—like they were just as unsure if they could trust themselves as I was.

"It's not your fault," Eva said in a quiet rasp, her voice still unsteady. Those hazel eyes met mine, the golden crown around her irises seeming to shimmer as her gaze flickered with concern.

"Please don't do that," I choked out. "Don't comfort me when I'm the reason you're bleeding right now. I can't stand it."

She grabbed my arm, pulling herself up to her knees on the bed so we were nearly nose to nose. Rivan took a step back, his gaze heavy.

"It's *not* your fault," Eva repeated more firmly. "*You* didn't do anything."

"*Exactly*," I gritted out through clenched teeth. "Once again, I couldn't stop him. Couldn't even get him out of my own mind while he—"

I thrust a hand into my hair and turned away, unable to look at her. At the bruises forming where that monster had used my hands to hurt her, to hold her down. My body was vibrating like I was about to combust.

"He would have used me to—" I choked, unable to voice the thought to its conclusion. "And I don't know if I would've been able to stop it."

Rivan's face had tightened in rage with the confirmation of what had almost occurred.

"But you did," Eva whispered. "You stopped him."

"No," I said hoarsely, closing my eyes so I didn't have to see the pain in hers, even though I could feel it in my own heart. "I didn't. I couldn't save you, Eva. From *everything* he's done to you. To have him use my own body to show me how much I can't protect you from him is just my latest failure."

Eva pulled me toward her so our foreheads nearly touched, her eyes searching my face. "Blaming yourself for his actions won't change anything. You *fought* for me, even before we knew what he was, even when he was too powerful to defeat. That's all I could ever ask from you. That's all that matters in the end." She swallowed hard, as something like self-recrimination flashed across our bond. "Besides, giving myself over to him was my plan…and it worked. So I can't let you hold on to the guilt for my own actions, especially when they were what saved you. Saved our family." Her gazed darted to Rivan before returning to me. "You don't get to monopolize the need to save the other in this relationship."

Her eyes crinkled slightly, and I was struck at how few and far between her smiles had been of late. I reached out and traced that one-sided dimple with my thumb. Her mouth trembled, just slightly, that dimple slipping away.

"I've been telling him that for years," Rivan grumbled. He smirked as I looked at him, slightly startled to find him still there—like in the moment she smiled at me, everything else had ceased to exist.

"Thank you," I said quietly to him. "I'm sorry that I snapped at you."

He waved me off, frowning at the bruises still marring my *anima*'s neck. "I can heal that too."

"Get some sleep," Eva said firmly. "We have quite the journey tomorrow, and you need your strength."

Rivan looked like he was about to argue, but nodded, smothering a yawn with the back of his hand. "*Do* try not to find any more trouble before the dawn if you two can manage it."

He slipped out the door, shutting it behind him.

Eva took my hand, giving me a tremulous smile. "So about that whole monopolization of who gets to save—"

"Okay," I interrupted, reaching for the damp towel she had used on me. I pressed a clean edge against the blood drying on her neck, working my way down the track dried onto her chest as I pressed a kiss against her temple.

"Okay?" Eva repeated, immediately suspicious of my quick switch to acquiescence.

"You're right," I said. "The False King has taken far too much from both of us. To hold on to the blame for that would be letting him win in a different way. Because he has no power here."

As if saying it aloud might make it true.

Eva's eyes danced. "Telling me 'you're right' will get you everywhere though…just so you know."

"Is that so?"

I dropped the towel, my hand stroking almost lazily down her side, taking my time as I slipped through the part in her robe. I heard her breath catch as my thumb traced a path up her inner thigh.

Mine. She was mine. *And I, hers.*

But I paused there, wincing at the memory of his hands on her. *My* hands, pushing her down, about to—

"Bash?"

She took my hand from where it had frozen against her before I could move away, her eyes searching my face.

I forced myself to meet her gaze, if only to show her it was still me.

"What if this is only a temporary reprieve? If he regains control of me and…I should have told Rivan to stay."

Eva was already shaking her head. "He caught us off guard. You'll be ready if it happens again. *We'll* be ready. But if you don't want to—"

"It's not that." In fact, it was entirely the opposite; the primal need to claim her after what had happened practically redirecting the blood from my head. She started to undo her robe, but I caught her hand in mine, then smiled at her impatient huff. "Are you sure? Are you even…okay?"

The question sounded stupid just coming out of my mouth. Of course she wasn't. Not when I knew exactly what had been done to her.

"No," Eva said simply. "But I don't want to think about *him* anymore. Not tonight. And if we aren't getting back to sleep anyways, I want…" The deep, lush feeling of her arousal across our bond left no questions about what, exactly, she wanted.

And maybe I also needed the reminder, the comfort of how right we were together. A chance to chase away the nightmares that would surely haunt me should sleep not elude me entirely.

I knelt before her on the bed, dragging her hips to the edge. "Then let me make sure you can't think about anyone else but me."

My shadows spooled from my hands, gently tugging her thighs open. Eva let out a gasp as my mouth found her, rolling my tongue against her wetness. Her head fell back as she tilted her hips up toward me, my hands obligingly sliding beneath her.

I licked her hungrily, greedily, feeling her fingers tighten where she had laced them into my hair. Letting her moans drown out the blame of my thoughts as her thighs began to quiver, tightening around my ears.

"Wait."

I stopped immediately, starting to back away.

Her fingers fastened around my wrist, yanking me back to her. "I didn't mean for you to stop. I just wanted to see you when I…"

"Tell me what you want, hellion," I demanded. "Tell me exactly what you want me to do to you."

Heat burned across our bond, like a fire in my blood. "Lie down."

Untying my robe, I let it fall to the floor. Then I crawled onto the bed, leisurely following her orders. Impatiently, she pushed me back against the pillows, her fingers digging into my pecs as she straddled me. Casually, I folded my arms behind my head. "Any more orders, Your Majesty?"

Eva bit her lip, slowly releasing it between her teeth. "I want to look into your eyes when you make me come." I could feel myself harden even further, but I stayed carefully still, though my shadows coiled around her. "But first…"

She traced a finger down the lines of my abdomen, tantalizingly slowly. Carefully avoiding my injured thigh as she shifted lower, her hand wrapped around the base of my hard length, twisting her wrist as she stroked me. Then she leaned forward, teasingly licking the glistening bead of moisture at the tip before wrapping her lips around me. I let out a full body groan as she took me all the way inside her mouth.

Every thought slid from my mind as I bumped against the back of her throat. She hummed before moving back on my shaft, the vibrations deliciously torturous.

"*Eva.*"

My balls tightened as she moaned around me, her gaze fixing on mine as she picked up the pace. The sight nearly broke my control.

"Gods, Eva…" I said her name like a prayer. "If you keep doing that, neither of us are going to get what we want."

Grabbing her, I pulled her up my body so she sat astride me. My shadows ran down her hips, looping lightly around her thighs, my hands sliding down the curve of her waist as she gazed down at me with a hunger that mirrored my own.

"I need you," Eva whispered.

Entwining our fingers, I slowly pushed inside of her, ignoring the pain in my thigh.

Her head fell back, a cry of pleasure breaking from her lips. I sunk into her until she was seated against my hips, my shadows obediently sliding between her legs.

"Eyes on me, hellion," I ordered. "And don't you dare look away."

Her eyes snapped to mine. I stilled as she pressed her hand against my chest. Then she rolled her hips, lifting herself up and down to encompass me inside that wet warmth again and again—each cant of her hips driving me to the edge.

Wrapping my fingers into her hair, I pulled her head to mine. She kissed me eagerly, her tongue tangling with mine as I thrust up into her.

"You *are* injured you know," Eva said, a flicker of concern crossing her face.

"And yet, I've never been happier about it."

I kissed at the dimple that appeared by the side of her mouth, relishing her exasperated smile.

"In retrospect, I'm surprised it took you this long to stab me considering the way we met." I raised an eyebrow. "Just try not to make a habit of it."

She let out a breathy whimper as I reached down to replace my shadows, two fingers teasing her in tight, careful circles. The intoxicating feel of her tightening around every inch of me almost took me over the edge.

"*Bash...*"

"What do you need, hellion?" I held her hips in place with the shadows that now crisscrossed around her waist. "Use your words."

"More," Eva begged, almost senselessly. "More of you. All of—"

My shadows obeyed her, pushing her back down onto me as I thrust inside her. I could feel that searing need, that hunger I would never get enough of across our bond. The satisfying crest and break as her body shuddered, clenching around me as she came.

Moaning her name, I spilled inside her.

Eva collapsed against me; her chestnut hair strewn across my face as she panted for breath. Gathering her into my arms, I stood up despite her gasped, "Don't you dare."

"If I'm fixed enough to fu—"

Her lips met mine even as she extricated herself from my grasp. She gave me a pointed look at the shadows now bracketing my leg.

"It'll be fine by morning," I said with a shrug. "Or at least enough to ride."

I wish I hadn't added that afterthought as Eva's face sobered with thoughts of what the dawn would bring. Forcing a smile on my face, I nodded toward the bathroom. "Let's get you cleaned up."

When we made it back to bed, I tucked her against my chest, shifting us away from the spot where her blood stained the sheets even though they had been magically cleaned during our brief absence. The memory of that moment had my arms wrapping around her...as though that would do anything to protect her.

Eva's breathing evened out almost immediately, her exhaustion from the battle and the night's events all too obvious. But I didn't dare close my eyes again as I worked to fortify my mind against the bloodlink. I doubted Aviel had enough of my blood left to repossess me. But I wouldn't let him catch me unaware again.

Yet sleep eluded me, like to give into it would invite another intrusion...another attack I might not be able to stop this time.

Tightening my arms around my *anima*, I listened for any change in her breathing—the hint of shallowness, the soft whining before it could turn into the choked screams of a nightmare that was all too real.

CHAPTER 34

EVA

I jerked awake in Bash's arms, his gaze already on me. I hated that I felt relieved to see the swirling blue and green of his eyes, even as the way they had turned ice blue last night flashed in my memory.

Whether he saw the look on my face or felt my recollection across our bond, Bash's face went bleak. "Eva—"

I didn't let him get another word out before I kissed him, swallowing whatever he was about to say. Muffling the apologies for something he had no control over as he tugged me even closer.

Pulling back, I traced the side of his jaw, his stubble scratching against my fingertips. "I hope you know better than to apologize again."

His face was pale, his eyes dark with the rage that he was just barely keeping in check. Shadows twisted around the edges of him, wrapping around my arms and my wrists in an unusually unchecked claiming. But their soft caress could never feel like the bonds that had caused the white scars they now covered.

Bash blew out a breath. "If he does that again..."

"He won't," I said with more confidence than I felt. "We were unprepared and exhausted. And he took advantage." My mouth spread in a slow smile. "Though is there somewhere you prefer I stab you if there *is* a next time?"

He let out a low laugh, those swirling eyes slowing as I felt his amusement break past that wall of self-reproach.

"Speaking of which," Bash said, wincing as he stood. "I should probably have Marin look at my leg after I shower. And also, you." His eyes flicked to the bruising on my neck, a shadow crossing his face. "I'm going to kill him slowly."

"I'll ask Quinn to take a look if it makes you feel better," I said softly. "Besides, we should probably fill them in on what happened before we get going." Stretching, I asked, "Do we need to hurry?"

He shook his head. "We won't leave until after breakfast, so we have some time to get ready."

Bash peeled back the sheet covering me, scooping me up in his arms. "I could use some company in the shower though, hellion…just in case."

He carried me into the shower despite my protests, not setting me down even as he turned on the water, which streamed down like rain falling from the ceiling. Drops clung to his lashes as he kissed me, and we lost ourselves to each other amidst the steam and suds.

My anxiety had turned into a frenetic hum by the time I got downstairs—the need to get going, get moving, that we had delayed too long, blaring through me like an alarm. There had been no word of Aviel's movements during our time in Esterra, but I knew Bash's network of spies had been mostly depleted; recalled for their own safety as Aviel cracked down. Yet he had to know we were racing him to the mirror that would decide the very fate of this realm.

Our visit to Esterra had been necessary. But I couldn't shake off the feeling that we were already behind.

Marin immediately zeroed in on Bash's limp as we walked down the stairwell. I ducked from beneath his arm, walking over to where Quinn and Tobias sat at the breakfast table, dressed in similar fighting leathers to mine, swords strapped to their sides. My own adamant sword peeked over my shoulder, my dagger at my hip. Their eyes widened almost comically as I unzipped the front of my jacket to expose the bruising on my neck and the mostly healed bite mark on my shoulder.

Tobias's eyes flashed with pure white light. Quinn immediately reached for me; her voice full of rage. "What happened?"

I told them a condensed version as her hand hovered over my skin, the soothing sensation of her magic immediately clearing the remaining aches of my injuries. With a sigh of relief, I pressed my hand against the now healed wound atop the raised scar—the embodiment of my terror, Aviel's casual cruelty, and my nightmares all carved into my skin in one permanent mark.

My brother's jaw flexed as he started peeling a clementine in one long spiral, just like he used to when we were kids. I smiled at him despite the look on his face.

It fell away, replaced with a frown as I took him in.

Tobias's eyes narrowed. "What is it?"

"Where's your dagger?"

The faintest hint of pink dusted his cheeks. "Quinn needed one. I let her borrow mine, since apparently these," he gestured at the sword on his hip, its hilt matching the ornate looking dagger on the opposite side, "are family heirlooms."

"I offered to find another," Quinn said airily. "There's plenty to choose from in the armory."

Tobias stared at her intently. "I'd rather you keep mine safe for me."

Their eyes met, and a flush darkened Quinn's cheekbones. Her lips parted slightly as neither looked away.

I cleared my throat, trying not to smile. "Does the sword have a name?"

Quinn jumped slightly, turning to me. Tobias still watched her as he said quietly, "Duskbane."

"Seems fitting for you then," I said as I stared at the clear stone on its hilt. "I wonder if mom ever used it."

Quinn nodded at the basket-hilt of my sword. "Did you name yours?"

"I haven't yet," I admitted. "Though that feels like bad luck going into battle."

I jumped slightly as Bash set a loaded plate of food in front of me—

poached eggs on fresh bread with crumbled cheese on top, a medley of sliced fruits, and a few thick slices of bacon on the side. Everything I would have picked had I been the one choosing. Bash kissed the now hidden mark on my shoulder before nodding his thanks to Quinn. His hand rested on my collarbone, one finger gently grazing against her handiwork.

"If only someone hadn't already taken Shadesong," I said teasingly. A smile quirked Bash's lips, and I knew he was remembering our first nights together as we journeyed through the Faewilds, the name of his dark sword one of a million whispered topics.

"Darkbringer," Marin called out.

Yael looked thoughtful. "Nightreaver?"

"Nightshade would be a good match," Quinn said thoughtfully. "Both for your magic, and because you're just as deadly."

"They grow around here," Tobias murmured. "In Soleara."

For a split second, I saw a small, star-shaped flower I had once tried to pick. My mother smiled down at me as she told me it was both beautiful and deadly.

"A dangerous mix, and one that is not to be trifled with, Evangeline."

"I like it," Bash murmured.

I smiled up at him. "I do too."

"If that's settled…" Bash placed my fork in my hand. "Rivan's readying our horses, but it'll be time to leave soon. Once you've eaten, we'll—"

"I can eat on the road," I cut in, even as Bash's hands pressed into my shoulders before I could stand. "I'm not making a literal army wait for me, not when we've taken too long to—"

There was a loud crash in the hallway from the mirror. Rivan burst into the kitchen, his chest heaving. A ripped piece of parchment dangled from one hand.

Bash rushed over to him. "What happened?"

"The False King," Rivan panted, and my stomach plummeted. "His army's already on the move. They crossed the Nahar confluence to reach the Mountainborn river."

The air itself seemed to freeze as we stared at each other in shock.

"Then we've lost our lead," Yael said bleakly. "Though with the time it'll take them to cross the western pass…"

Marin came up next to her, looking pale. "It'll be close."

"How did this happen?" My voice sounded foreign, removed, like the question had come from somebody else even though I felt my lips move. "I thought…"

"Queen Sariyah's troops should've been there by now," Bash said, looking stricken. "How could she not warn us?"

Rivan held up the stained parchment. "They were ambushed. By the time someone was able to alert us, the battle was already lost. The False King did something to keep messages from escaping. The same reason we weren't told when he left Morehaven."

"A spyfinder," Bash spat, though his self-condemnation lay heavy across our bond. "He used it once during the last war. All communication under the area of his spell first goes to him. But the price for that magic is in lives willingly given. To stretch across that radius…"

"His supporters have waited a long time for this moment," Yael said quietly. "And desperate people lead to desperate acts."

Tobias gestured to the parchment still clutched tightly in Rivan's hand. "And Mayim's forces?"

Rivan slowly shook his head. "The survivors are few, but the queen is among them."

My voice broke as I asked, "How few?"

"Hundreds," he whispered, his eyes lowering. "Out of thousands."

Blood pounded in my ears. The room seemed to go out of focus as my stomach heaved, like I might throw up the few bites of breakfast I had managed to get down.

Thousands dead.

And it was all my fault.

The back of my throat burned. I hadn't realized how much I was holding on to the hope of beating Aviel to Adronix—to gain the power to stop him before anyone had to die because of me—until it was torn away. That the real battles wouldn't start until *after* I was ready. I hadn't realized I had been clinging to the thought that I didn't have to make this choice yet; that there was still time left to make it to that mirror and fix my fate. After all, the sprite had told me my future wasn't yet set in stone.

But it felt like that destiny had shifted, had solidified like a spear of my darkness before finding its way into a heart. I had a way to end this, no matter how much I wanted it all to be different. A future that seemed more certain with the added weight of each life I had been too selfish to save.

If I hadn't been so naïve as to think we stood a chance of everything going to plan, Aviel would be dead in their place. Instead, he had slaughtered thousands while I had been basking in my *anima's* arms this morning. While I had been *happy*.

Dread devoured me, eating at my insides until there was nothing left but a hollow pit where hope once lived. I knew what I needed to do—I just wasn't ready to do it. But if I waited until I knew for sure, waited until it was the only choice left...I could no longer fool myself about what the price would be: more innocent lives, when so many already weighed heavy on my conscience.

And what if I was only delaying the inevitable? Clinging to one more day, then another as we chased Aviel on parallel paths north?

Unless I stopped him now, once and for all.

Bash's eyes snapped to mine, and I knew he had felt whatever maelstrom I had sent across our bond. Sucking in a breath, I tried my best to tamp down on it. Hiding away any further hint at what now felt inevitable even as I prayed he attributed my reaction to what had happened.

"This is a setback, *not* a defeat," Bash said firmly, and I felt my blood thrum at the power in his tone. "We still have two armies. One to take Morehaven. The other to destroy the force heading to Adronix. Aviel's route is more treacherous, not to mention his forces are recuperating from battle. We still have a chance of heading him off." His eyes swirled violently, like a storm about to strike. "So we do what we do best. Fight. Get into that mountain and take down an empire."

Yael released a subdued sigh. "One impossible thing at a time, huh?"

Bash's face was solemn as he nodded. Then he reached out a hand, his fingers entwining with mine as he helped me to my feet, his worry coursing across our bond.

I forced myself to relax, forced myself to nod even as I felt something inside me go cold and still. Trying my best to seem fine when I just felt fractured.

There was a slight stickiness where Bash's palm touched mine. I looked down to see four half-moon marks where my nails had bitten into the rose scarred there, painting it with my blood.

CHAPTER 35
EVA

We journeyed north until long after day turned to night, only stopping to make camp when the moon peeked from behind the dusky clouds littering the starless sky. Despite Aviel's head start, it wasn't enough to warrant us riding through the night and risk injuring the horses, though we had only scant hours until daybreak and our journey began again.

There would be no more updates from within Aviel's ranks. I hadn't needed to ask to know that Aviel's spyfinder had done its work.

Bash caught me as I dismounted Nisa, his face haggard with concern. His thumb skated over the pulse in my throat, its rhythm traitorously giving away my nerves.

I had spent most of our ride trying to block my feelings from him, hoping he wouldn't read too far into whatever I wasn't successful in suppressing. And yet that worry swallowed me like a shroud—the thought of what I could have done differently wrapping inescapably around me.

"I'll take care of them," Bash said, nodding at our mounts. "Rest while you can. I'll find you back at our tent."

I lifted onto my toes, my hands coming up to frame either side of Bash's face as I looked him in the eyes for perhaps the first time since breakfast. "I love you."

His head tilted slightly, the only hint of his concern as he replied, "I love you too."

Yael came up beside me, hooking her arm in mine. Her other side was already taken by Marin who was holding a small lantern, the light inside crackling with some form of suspended fire. "Figured you could use an escort."

"Tents are being set up this way," Marin said as Yael led us through the trees. Indeed, the tents had sprung up as if by magic. I blinked, not having it in me to smile at that entirely apt description. Because of course they had.

Yael led us to a few tents near the edge of a lake, no larger or grander than any of the others—just gray fabric and four walls brought to a peak. She let out a yawn, muttering, "Don't worry, they're more soundproof than they look."

I pulled them both into a silent hug before I ducked under the tent flap, unable to manage another word. As I walked inside, I barely took in the plush sleeping mat in the center of it, the space far too large and the amenities far too nice to match what I had seen from the exterior.

Instead, I stared blankly forward. All I could think about were the consequences of my own selfishness, about each and every life that could've been spared today. Picturing the sprite's endless dark eyes staring me down as she said the words that might doom me.

There is only one way to be certain. To stop him for good.

Looking down, I curled my fingers in, one at a time...and a blade of darkness, short and sharp, appeared in my hand, slowly solidifying as I clenched my fist around it. I could stop this all right now. I could end him —if only I had the courage to end myself. Or, perhaps, the lack of it. The lack of faith that we could pull this off without my sacrifice.

I had never been suicidal. Not even after losing my family in that fire, though it felt like my heart had torn asunder. To choose to die now without even a fight, except with my own soul and will to survive...

Would it be worth it to stop the battle ahead from taking even more lives? To save both realms? I wondered if my mother had any idea that the philosophical scenario she had once posed would one day become my own personal trolley problem.

I couldn't shake the foreboding sensation that it still felt utterly wrong. Not only for myself, but what my death would mean for those I loved. I could barely think about what it would do to Bash. To Tobias, who I had just gotten back from the dead, especially when I knew exactly how his death had nearly destroyed me. To Quinn, my lone family for so long, who had already been through so much loss. To Rivan, Yael, and Marin— the family I had found here who had welcomed me with open arms. To the Solearans who had finally gotten me back after years of sacrifice and struggle.

After all, death was only felt by the people left behind.

The sprite's shrill laughter filled my ears, and I fought the urge to cover them.

There is always another way. And there is always another choice. But will you be able to make it? Or will it be made for you?

I knew that if it came down to a choice between my family and myself, I would swallow my damnation without a murmur. But to premeditate my own murder? Yet I couldn't deny the lives I was putting at risk by not taking my own.

Taking my own life. *Taking it.* From myself, from my future, from everyone who loved me. Even if doing so was *for* them, along with everybody else.

Bash would never forgive me for this. I could barely think his name, knowing what my loss would do to him. Would he waste away like his mother had after his father's death? Or would his sense of duty, his resilience, and the help of our family keep him among the living, even if I took his heart with me?

But even if I added his life to my death toll, our happy ending didn't outweigh the greater good.

I should have known I couldn't escape my fate. That even though I may have been able to delay the inevitable, I wouldn't be able to run from it forever.

Slowly, I brought the obsidian knife an inch from my face. I stared, mesmerized, as its black edge glinted ominously in the dim light, the tinier twin to the blade on my back. The walls of the tent pressed in, the edges of my vision blurring. But I only felt cold, paralyzed, as if all feeling had seeped from my bones into the magic blade before me, taunting me with its deadly choice.

A voice in the back of my head screamed at me to stop as I tilted its tip toward my heart. A voice that was far too easy to silence.

The tent flap swung forward. Bash stormed in before I could let the magic go. His face was ashen, his stormy eyes whirling with alarm as the tent darkened with shadow.

"What—what's happening? What's wrong?"

The blade disappeared into nothing, but it was far too late. I knew he had felt my turmoil through the bond, that creeping sense of emptiness.

I opened my mouth, but nothing came out.

Why had I been so foolish as to think I could keep this from him?

Bash had gone utterly still as he stared at the space my blade had been, his freckles stark against the pallor of his skin. He reached for me, but I shrank back, stepping away from him. His broad hand engulfed mine before I could get any further.

"Why are you pushing me away?" Bash's voice was frantic, pleading. "What the hell is going on, Eva?"

I sucked in a shallow inhale. It did nothing to clear the buzzing in my head.

"Please, just forget it," I said in a last-ditch, futile effort to keep him from this. "I was upset, that's all."

But I knew he could feel the maelstrom of emotions I was failing to keep a hold on anymore—the despair deep inside my heart—just as I could feel his growing outrage.

A lump formed in my throat that I tried to swallow down to no avail. I realized too late that his thumb pressed against the frantic pulse of my inner wrist, feeling the frenetic beat of my foolish heart.

Bash's eyes were dark with shadow as he said in a dangerous tone, "*What* exactly were you about to do with that?"

"Nothing," I lied sharply, wound so tight I might snap.

The bond between us went taut as I felt his terror at my feigned nonchalance. And I knew he had understood my intent, if not the reason behind it.

My eyes burned; the cracks in my resolve spreading.

I backed away, needing the distance between us again to think straight. To attempt to find a way out of this trap I had set for myself.

Bash took a moment to examine my expression, his anger palpable. Then he slowly came toward me, matching me step for step until my back touched the fabric of the tent—no space left to run. But his touch was infinitely gentle as he took my chin between his thumb and forefinger, bringing my eyes to his.

"Let's try that again. And this time, tell me the truth."

His eyes were a storm as they fixed on mine. As he searched them for answers, reading me like the words on a page. I knew from his expression he wouldn't let it go. Nor would he let me get away without telling him the whole story this time.

And it was too hard to pull myself together now that I had started to break.

A traitorous part of me let out a sigh of relief as I breathed, "Whatever it takes."

His eyes narrowed. I could sense the rolling current of his building anger, the powerful pang of hurt intwined within it.

"Explain."

I hesitated for a heartbeat, but I knew it was too late to hide any longer. "He took my blood, along with my magic. I don't remember it… but it would have been easy to do, especially when I was drugged. There were plenty of needle marks."

Bash's shadows escaped his hold, roiling around him—betraying the sharp, molten wrath I felt down our bond. But he stayed silent, waiting for me to voice the rest, even as his jaw hardened.

"He used it to link us," I added miserably. "More than just a link. A powerful sort of bloodbond, to fool the Choosing itself. *That's* what the sprite told me. So…I know exactly how to stop him." Bash's eyes narrowed. "And I'm guessing you do too."

He was too smart not to figure out that if I was bloodbonded to Aviel, then the easiest way to stop him would be to end my own life. To use the link between our lives to kill him before he could hurt anyone else.

I saw the moment the realization hit him. The way his breath hitched as something fractured behind his eyes. He reeled backward, fear flashing across his features before it gave way to outright horror. The blood drained from his face, a visible swallow working its way down his throat before he let out a low, wounded sound.

I had expected anger. Might have managed to steel myself against it if it had been. Instead, I was overwhelmed by the heartbreak curdling across our bond—like I had shoved a blade into his chest and sliced his heart in two.

When he finally spoke, it was barely above a whisper, his voice achingly raw. "I can't lose you."

The desperation in his tone crashed into my soul. "I don't want to lose you either."

"Why didn't you tell me?"

"What good would it do to tell you when—"

"What good would it do for you to tell me the *truth?*"

I winced at the betrayal in his voice. "I didn't lie."

He let out a low, bitter laugh. "Don't you dare tell me that carefully concealing this from me is any different. That distraction and omission aren't the same godsdamned thing."

"I didn't want you to—"

"To *worry?* Do you think I haven't felt the vise around your heart, the cold fear that wakes you in the night despite your attempts to shield it from me? Do you think I haven't been going out of my mind trying to figure out what's been haunting you? If something happened when he captured you that you hadn't told me, or if it was simply the resentment that I couldn't stop it in the first place? But *this...*"

"Bash—"

"You should have told me," he growled. "Why the *hell* didn't you?"

I had never seen him so angry, not at me. Never felt the soul-flaying level of distrust emanating down our bond, its icy heat searing into my heart.

"Because you would have talked me out of it," I shouted, the words ripped from my lips. "Don't you understand? I already couldn't bear to go through with it. And telling you...it would have made it even more impossible to do what I should have done already."

"*Good,*" Bash yelled, the hurt in his tone immediately dulling my indignation. "Do you think what we have is so ephemeral?" His throat worked as he swallowed, shadows winding down my arms as if to keep me with him. "Our love does not bend to death. Nor will it bow to it."

I could feel myself shaking. Not wanting him to give me hope while trying desperately not to crumble.

"And if it's the only way to stop him?"

"We aren't there yet, hellion." His voice sharpened. "But even if we were, what good is giving yourself up again, dying for the people you love instead of living for us instead? How can you be so *selfish*?"

"How can *you*?" My voice broke. "It's not about us, it's about everyone. No single person matters more than what's at stake. If we fail, what then? And how many more lives will be sacrificed while I wait?"

I yelped as he picked me up, then pulled me onto his lap, positioning both of us on our makeshift bed.

His throat bobbed. "I am *done* with blind duty—with putting the realm in front of what truly matters. Eva...I won't lose you. It won't come to that because there *will* be another way."

This was exactly why I hadn't told him. Because I knew I couldn't hold out against the anguish flooding over our bond, the reality of leaving him. Not when I needed to think about this clinically. I was meant to be the ruler of this realm, and that meant I needed to do what was best for it. Even if that meant never claiming my throne.

"And what if there isn't one?" My voice splintered apart, a tremor going through me. I was being torn in half—everything I had been trying to hide now spilling into plain view. "This isn't a godsdamned fairytale. Good doesn't always conquer evil. What if there was never a happily ever after for us, and *that's* the price of stopping him?"

"I don't *care*," Bash rasped, his voice cracking as my heart echoed it. "Don't you dare pretend we aren't forever. Whatever comes next, we'll face it together—consequences be damned. And if the choice is between the world and you...I choose *you*, always."

I was already shaking my head. "You don't mean that. Not with your kingdom and mine on the line. Not with the entire realm at risk."

His eyes flashed. "Don't tell me what I do and do not mean. Not when the choice was made the moment I fell in love with you."

"I could finish this right now," I whispered. "And instead, we lost *thousands* of people today, Bash, before the main battle has even begun. I can't live if it means others will die."

"Their deaths aren't on you. They're on him."

Slowly, I shook my head. "The longer I wait, the more our people will be killed because I'm too much of a coward to give up what I have in order to save everyone else. Too much of a coward to tell you and let you talk me out of how we both know this is going to end."

Bash flinched back like I had hit him, heartbreak etched on every feature. "Is that really what you think? Do you have so little faith in me after what happened to you that you think that's truly the only way we'll defeat him? Because we don't know that…or rather, I don't, and you shouldn't either."

"Bash…" My eyes burned. "Even if I'm not the one to do it, this bloodbond…won't defeating him take me with him?"

"No, *killing* him would, and those two aren't the same." A muscle feathered in Bash's jaw. "You're not dying, Eva. It's not an option. And if you think I'm just going to let you, you're very much mistaken." He sucked in a shuddering breath. "Are you so willing to sacrifice yourself? Sacrifice our lives together?"

I knew the answer. Had known it since the day that sprite had told me what would happen, and I hadn't acted immediately. Instead, I had waited as the knowledge burrowed deep inside me, digging under my skin like the thorns of a vine as it ensnared me further. Because I hadn't wanted to end my life—now or ever. Especially not now that, for the first time in a long time, I was finally, miraculously whole.

"No, Bash, or I would have done it already," I confessed. "Even though every moment I don't adds to the blood on my hands, I can't bear the thought of leaving you. Of leaving my brother, who I *just* got back. Leaving our friends, our family, this world, and what we're trying to rebuild." My darkness wrapped around me like it might hold me together. "When I met you, you showed me what living was like again. I'd forgotten." A tear slipped down my face, then another. "But if it comes to it, I need to be prepared to do what I must. And I knew telling you would only make it that much harder if I was forced to make that choice."

And there it was, finally laid bare. The weight that had been slowly crushing me.

The tension that had been in my chest since that ill-fated meeting with the sprite lightened, like I should have known it would at sharing the truth with him. The tears in my eyes were overflowing, but I didn't bother wiping them away.

"Please, hellion," Bash said in a low, desperate voice. "This isn't the end, not by a long shot. You can't give up. Not after all you've survived." His shadows enveloped me, twisting with my darkness. "I can't watch you die. You're the one who made me want to *live*."

My heart ached. I could hear the silent *too* that followed the word 'die', the reminder of all that he had lost.

Bash tilted my head up with the crook of his finger, kissing one tear-streaked cheek, then the other. "You want me to tell you something true? Something real? I would rather lose this war than lose you. None of this is worth it without you." His hand trembled as he stroked it against my cheek. "Don't ask me to watch you die. I won't allow it. We'll find another way."

"And if there isn't one?"

Bash's jaw flexed. "Not an option. Especially since there *is* another way: go through the Choosing and then we'll defeat him as we planned. But even if it defies all logic, I can't—I *won't*—lose you."

I wished I had his confidence. His courage. I was lacking in both right now—and had been ever since that dark forest and the destiny that had been revealed atop that fairy mound.

And so, you have the way to stop him.

So I nodded, unable to say the lie aloud. Because I knew that if it came down to it, I couldn't forget what I had learned. Not if it meant ending Aviel. A last resort—even as the guilt for those I would put in peril in the meantime risked consuming me.

Bash pulled me closer, his hands bracing my hips. And maybe he could sense that fleeting feeling of residual stubbornness. That he hadn't ultimately changed my decision, only delayed it until there was no other way. That I *wouldn't* let Aviel win, even if the cost was myself.

I didn't let myself say any of that as I brought my mouth to his, kissing him so deeply, both of us were panting when he whispered against my lips, "If you won't live for yourself, then live for *us*, Eva."

My lower lip trembled. Then he tugged me back against him, his kisses hungry and frantic, his tongue stroking my own in a way that left me shaking. I fervently hoped he didn't realize the distraction it was, for both of us, from the act something in the back of my mind whispered was still inevitable. But the stark dread that thought summoned was quickly banished by the warmth of his mouth moving down my neck, my back arching as his fingers adeptly found that spot that made my breathing turn shallow.

His shadows pulled at my clothes, stripping them away from my body until I was fully naked. They stayed against my skin, stroking and caressing me until I was writhing. As if he could also sense the ticking of the clock, he tore off his own attire, those dark tendrils tugging my legs apart for him as he settled between my thighs.

"Bash," I begged. "I want you to fuck me until I scream."

"Then you'd better hold on tight, hellion."

I obeyed, my nails digging into the corded muscles of his back, feeling every hard inch of him as I rocked against him, silently demanding more. White-hot need speared through me, so powerful I couldn't tell which one of us it originated from.

But Bash went still. "Promise me..." He lowered his face a breath away from my lips. "Promise me this is forever, hellion. Tell me that you're mine."

I attempted a smile, but I could feel my mouth quiver. "No matter what happens, I'll always be yours, Bash." His fingers flexed on my hips, digging in as he ground me against him, just barely stopping before pushing inside me. "But as much as I want forever with you, it's not that *simple*."

I gasped as his hand closed over my breast, rolling my hard nipple between his fingers.

"It is," Bash growled, nudging at my entrance. "It's as simple as *you*—" He punctuated the word with a sharp thrust that rubbed against my clit, "—and me."

My eyelashes slowly fluttered. "Bash, please—"

"Say it," he demanded, his gaze hardening at whatever he saw on my face. "Say you believe in that happy ending. Say you'll always be mine."

I could feel his desperation—almost painful in its intensity, like it had wrapped around my own heart.

"Promise me because you want it to be true. Promise me because I know you'll think twice before breaking it, and I want to make sure you try absolutely everything before you take everything from the both of us. Promise me because you love me."

Tears filled my eyes. Bash was unmoving, every muscle in his body trembling as he waited for my answer.

"I promise," I breathed.

Bash thrust inside me so sharply I gasped at the delicious stretch. My legs wrapped around his waist, urging him on as his hips moved at a punishing pace.

His shadows wrapped around me, trailing down my arms, nipping at my breasts, sliding down the curve of my stomach. I gasped as they reached between my thighs, those tendrils circling against me until I saw stars. Bash pulled my knees over his shoulders, bearing down in an even deeper angle, and I lost myself, shattering around him. He didn't let up until I was done shaking, riding me through one orgasm straight into another.

"You don't play fair, freckles," I grumbled breathlessly.

A smirk tugged at his lips. "Never said I did."

Bash's eyes swirled almost violently as he looked down at me, drinking me in as his chest heaved. Pressing my foot into the hard lines of his abdominals, I pushed him away with the point of my toes. He sat back on his heels, his gaze predatory as I moved onto my hands and knees. Arching my back, I bared myself to him. One of his hands gripped my hip a second later, the other one fisting himself.

"Tell me you need me, hellion."

I whined in the back of my throat as he rubbed the head of his cock up and down my wetness, my inner muscles clenching around nothing.

"I need you. I always need—"

Bash slipped inside me with one hard thrust, burying himself so deeply I gasped. Robbing me of every thought except him.

He pulled back teasingly, leaving me teetering on the edge of desperation. I moved back onto his cock, taking him back inside of me. It was his turn to gasp, groaning as I squeezed around him.

"*Fuck.*"

"That's the idea," I said dryly.

His hand came down on my ass, and I let out a sound between a yelp and a moan. "I'll never get tired of that mouth of yours."

"More," I breathed, my gaze half-lidded as I looked over my shoulder at him. "I need more."

I whimpered as his hand came down again, riding that exquisite line between pleasure and pain. His fingers dug into my waist as he pushed into me again and again. When his shadows found my clit just as his cock pressed against something inside me that made my eyes roll back in my head, I wondered fleetingly if we were testing the limits of the soundproofing before my release tore through me again.

I was still quivering when Bash flipped me over, pushing back inside me as his thumb circled my still sensitive clit.

"Bash..."

"You can give me one more."

His mouth closed around my nipple. I moaned as his tongue lavished it in maddening whorls. That perfect pressure was already building inside me, and I rocked my hips, our movements deliciously in sync. Joined so deeply, I couldn't tell where I ended and he began.

Bash's hand gripped my chin, and my eyes opened to a swirling storm.

"Touch yourself," he ordered, his voice a little ragged. "And let me tell you how this is going to be, since it seems that you've somehow forgotten." His shadows wrapped lightly around my wrist, tugging it between us. His growl was downright feral as he watched me follow his command. "This is forever, Eva. I need you to remember that, even if things start looking bleak. That we can win this if we don't give up." He thrust into me slowly, every sensation almost excruciatingly magnified. "And as long as you don't give up on *us*."

"I won't," I promised.

He buried himself to the hilt before he unleashed himself. My legs were already shaking as our eyes met. Then that pressure broke, his length twitching as my climax clenched around it.

"Good girl," he breathed. A smile curved my lips, my body too blissful to even open my eyes.

Bash moved us onto our sides, and I relaxed into the safety of him surrounding me. I didn't want to ever leave this moment together, as if doing so would tempt fate to break us apart once again.

"I don't want to ever leave you, Bash," I whispered.

"Tell me you aren't about to sacrifice yourself if something goes wrong," Bash whispered, touching our foreheads together. "That you know we can stop him."

"I already told you—"

"I need to hear it one more time, hellion."

"I promise this won't happen again," I whispered. "That we'll fight him, together."

Unless there's no other way, I silently added. I would give myself a fighting chance. Even if I couldn't shake that sense of looming inevitability.

But it was impossible to forget that glimmer of hope in his eyes. The one that promised a future I hadn't let myself dream about anymore.

Bash got up, shushing my drowsy sound of dissent. He returned a minute later with a damp towel he used to tenderly clean me. Then he pulled me back into his arms. His gentle caress found my stomach, my thighs, fingers tracing patterns the entire journey.

His touch was a love letter and a plea all at once.

I could feel it in the possessive way his hands stroked my face. In each brush of his lips against my cheek, my hair—begging me for the same thing over and over until I finally fell asleep.

Stay with me.

CHAPTER 36

ESTELLE

Queen Amerie was dead. Perhaps still alive for now, captured and imprisoned in her own castle as the False King and his supporters took up residence there like an unstoppable, invasive weed. But I couldn't imagine her usurper would allow her to live long. Not when he was obviously after her crown.

Or was it now *my* crown? It was my birthright. The future I had always been told would one day be mine—even as the words rang somewhat hollow, like a promise that wouldn't be kept. Yet how was I meant to take on the False King when, after our crushing defeat at Morehaven, I knew that to do so was madness?

He had been able to catch Morehaven unprepared, the queen's forces already spread too thin defending the other territories. The battle was already over, the feather-gilded gate blocked from our reach by the time their pleas for aid reached us. I shuddered to think of the lives taken to fuel the dark magic needed for such a barrier that it had lasted the entirety of the battle.

Was I meant to go through the Choosing against him? Normally, a conclave would be called to Morehaven, the most powerful Celestial representatives from each region then sent on a secret journey for a test I knew little about, despite my supposed destiny. I had once practiced my serene smile in the mirror, to be given to those faceless contenders who didn't yet know the crown's choice was predetermined. But these were not normal times, and I knew the False King's supporters would be on guard to prevent any from participating in the test before he did.

If that mantle was truly meant to be mine, was I to rally our exhausted armies under one banner to oppose his forced rule and likely decimate Soleara in the process? Or—

My foot caught on a raised tree root I could have sworn hadn't been there a moment before, and I went sprawling. The night was unusually dark, even beneath the canopy of trees I found myself often visiting when my mind wouldn't stop whirring. I cursed under my breath as pain twinged up the arm that had taken the brunt of my fall. My fingers flew to my elbow as I pushed myself up, their tips coming away dark with a mix of blood and dirt.

There was something missing. Everything inside me went on alert as I realized the forest had gone strangely quiet, devoid of the usual chatter of its denizens, its absence eerie. Even the gnarled branches of the trees around me seemed to stop their swaying, the stars above dimming like the realm itself was holding its breath.

A faerie circle.

In my haste to flee the castle, to run away from the constraints of a destiny that felt more like a curse, I hadn't noticed I had stepped directly into a large mound of earth surrounded by a perfect circle of trees. My blood glistened on the moss covering it before it disappeared like just another drop of dew. I winced as I realized I had trampled a few of the enormous white mushrooms that surrounded me. As I reached toward a headless stem like I might be able to undo the damage, I realized I wasn't alone.

A sprite was perched on the mushroom top, her enormous, pitch-black eyes devouring me.

She was nude, an electric blue sheen coating her dark skin, its hue matching her hair. I froze, my hand barely an inch away from her, then slowly dipped my head in deference. She cocked her head in response, her blue lips parting to reveal sharp, black teeth. Then sunk into a low bow, her iridescent wings fluttering mesmerizingly as she rose.

"The Queen Who Might Have Been." Her voice reverberated through the glen, like each word danced around my brain. "Some things still remain to be seen. But some things cannot be changed, not now that they have been put in motion. The False One will come for you. For your progeny. He seeks the girl for his own ends, and to the end of all. So you must flee, now, or all will be lost before it has even begun."

It felt like the forest mist had invaded my mind, each word adding to my shock and confusion. My mouth opened, closed, then opened once more. "He seeks...*what?*"

The sprite seemed to grimace; a baring of teeth that made the hair stand up on the back of my neck. "Surely the one who would have been queen can understand something so simple as the need for flight. To protect one's own. To evade the fight until the time is right."

"I only meant..." My words caught in my throat as what she said came back to me in full clarity. "The False King wants *Eva?*"

My daughter. Precious, precocious little Evangeline whose little bursts of darkness would float around her like a lively second shadow. And if the False King wanted her...

"*Why?*"

The sprite tilted her head at me, then nodded as if glad I had finally gathered my wits about me. "The False One will take you all if he can. But the former queen ensured the child's fate, and his obsession, when she told him who the next High Queen will be." Those black teeth glinted in the night. "And she will tell him how to *take* it. Or perhaps she has already for this path to be so clear."

His obsession with *her*. Because she would be...

"No," I blurted out. "*I'm the—*"

The words shriveled on my tongue. Had Queen Amerie ever said it would be me? My mind flashed through snippets of memory, scouring for any hint this could be a lie. But all I could hear was my departed father's voice crowing about what the High Queen had foretold: that the crown of gold in my eyes marked the next true queen.

Both of my children had my eyes, almost exactly. Down to the speckled flecks of gold that converged around their pupils.

I sucked in a harsh breath as everything I thought I knew came apart. Slowly, I let it out, giving myself a moment to mourn not what might have been, but the burden I couldn't take on myself. Taking the fear for my daughter, the imminent danger she now faced, and honing it into the very blade of fury I would use to protect her.

Because I was the Queen of Soleara. The mother of the true heir of Agadot. And I wouldn't let her down.

"Tell me what I need to do."

The answer, apparently, lay in the hands of another queen: the Queen of Imyr. I had once visited the Southlands shortly after I had been coronated; their forests reminded me of home. Trisanne had been quiet then. Not shy, but introspective, a daze to her expression like her mind was moving too fast to focus on what was immediately in front of her. She was also a mother, both children old enough to take part in this war. I had heard the stories of her son's Celestial magic turning the tide in battle, not to mention the whispers about how the strength of it might one day lead him to become High King.

Once, I had felt thankful that Tobias and Evangeline were too young to know the brutalities of war. I no longer felt that way anymore.

The powers of the sprites lay in intent—in how one action would affect the next. So I trusted her when she told me to write to the southern queen for a weapon she had created. One that could defeat the False King when the time was right.

I had asked her for two.

No sooner had my message disappeared in a burst of white light than another had taken its place in a flash of green.

But how did you know? The stone I created...it can remove the magic from those cursed by it. I thought to use it as a cure, not a weapon.

My reply had been quick, and to the point.

I hope it can be. But I need you to make two more for my twins—I was told by a sprite that they'll need it one day. I'm afraid I cannot tell you more than I already have, nor can anyone ever know of our correspondence. But I'm begging you, one mother to another.

Your doing this might very well save the realm. But there are two, too young lives your invention will protect most of all.

I remembered her children from my visit. Her son, her daughter, both too young to live in a world at war.

Her response was immediate.

I'll need two stones.

I ran to my mother's old jewelry box, its hinges squeaking in protest as I threw the top open. Two diamonds sat there, waiting for me as if for this exact moment. One light like Tobias's burgeoning magic that was all mine, one gleaming darkly with the night Eva had gotten from her father—her ability already frighteningly effortless.

Though I hadn't planned to give them to my children for years yet, I had commissioned two daggers, one for each. A gift for my little warriors to strive for as they learned to wield their strength—the stones yet to be placed.

My hands shook as I tucked the diamonds into my next missive, then watched as it all disappeared.

CHAPTER 37
EVA

Rivan was watching me too closely as I walked into the woods after we made camp, tired yet too restless to turn in for the night. He had been silently doing so all day as we rode through the frosty countryside, Adronix looming over the clouds far ahead. My legs ached, my thighs and calves sore from gripping Nisa's sides, my lower back tight from absorbing her movements in the increasingly rough terrain. Sometimes I missed the simplicity of car rides, though I couldn't muster the energy to laugh at the concept of magically powered dirt bikes or ATVs.

Then winced at the thought of machines encroaching upon this realm —though I imagined the forest would swallow up any attempts at paving a road. Perhaps that was part of why Aviel wanted to rule both realms. While his desire for power was obviously the driving factor in his plans to subjugate the human world, the thought of him gaining access to its resources—including its more deadly creations—was truly terrifying.

I looked behind me to see Rivan following. His eyes narrowed as ours locked. And I knew he knew. Bash must have already told him of my ill-fated plan. Of the bloodbond and what it meant.

Ignoring him, I stretched out the stiffness from the long ride before I finally looked where he casually leaned against a tree trunk. It was foolish for us not to take advantage of the few hours of sleep we would be afforded. And yet, I might prefer this confrontation to failing to fall asleep while Bash's concern seeped down our bond, coagulating with mine.

Raising an eyebrow, I held up my hand, palm up, bending my fingers toward me twice in outright challenge. A ghost of a smile crossed my lips as I remembered all those training sessions together in the Faewilds. Rivan's mouth twitched like he was thinking the same. Wordlessly, he swaggered toward me, raising his hands to match my fighting stance.

Rivan's first swing nearly took my head off. I ducked just in time, thrown off balance, and his elbow jabbed into my side. Twisting away from the blow, I swung out the opposite foot. Rivan was too fast, too ready as he leapt back. He lunged forward, our hands meeting in a furious series of blocks and strikes, his moves so quick, I could barely keep up.

I could practically feel the admonishment behind them, his usual style sharpened with something like outrage. But I didn't want him to take it easy on me. No sooner had I thought it than he caught my fist, twisting my arm behind my back until I went to my knees. Tumbling forward, I broke his hold. When he followed, I kicked behind me to sweep his legs out from under him.

Catlike, he rolled as if he had meant to fall all along before tackling me to the dirt.

Breathing hard, I nodded in defeat. Rivan rolled off me, his face twisting in barely concealed judgement. I stood up, groaning.

At least my muscles would be sore in a different way tomorrow.

Ignoring him, I walked over to a fallen log, panting as I sat with my back to him.

The silence stretched in the space between us as Rivan gracefully sat down next to me. I waited for him to speak first, but he simply sat there as if we didn't have anywhere to be, those lavender eyes full of reproach. The muffled sounds of those in camp hurrying to sleep for the few hours we had before daybreak had faded into mere murmurs, only intensifying the quiet. I wondered fleetingly if this was an approach he had used to break prisoners during the last war.

Sighing, I gave in. "Was there something you wanted to discuss, Rivan?"

One eyebrow twitched, his voice dry as he asked, "Was there something you wanted to tell me?"

I gave him a baleful look that he returned in kind.

He folded his arms, muscles flexing. "I suppose it's my turn."

I looked at him askance. "Your turn for what?"

"For my heart-to-heart with you." Rivan's reluctant smile still managed to light up his entire face. "Everyone else got at least one. I should be hurt that all we've done is spar."

I laughed in spite of myself, the sound almost too loud in the cool night air.

"Is that so?" I asked wryly. "So, who goes first?"

Rivan gave me a long look, and my humor faded as a muscle ticked in his jaw, the accusation renewing in his glare.

"Did Bash tell you?"

Of course he had.

"Of course he did," Rivan said, the anger in his tone giving way to hurt. "You should've told us the second you returned from the faerie mound. Though I had a feeling something was going on ever since you came back from that meeting like the world was on fire."

He shook his head, his long braids falling over one shoulder.

"Have I been that obvious?"

"You've been off," Rivan said with a frown. "Distant. And it only started after your visit with the sprite, not before, so I knew it couldn't just be the False Prince." He snorted at my scowl. "Besides, self-sacrifice? You? How entirely unexpected."

For a second, I saw a flash of him unconscious, blood seeping from where Aviel's stolen light had cut into his mouth as it suffocated him. Hanging limply from his bindings after the False Prince had nearly killed him.

"You almost died, Rivan," I whispered, taking his hand. He swallowed hard as if remembering the light that had tightened around his throat, but his hand squeezed mine back. "You would have, if I hadn't done what I did."

"So did you." His voice caught. "And just because I'm grateful for what you did back there to save me, to save our family, it doesn't change the fact that you sacrificed yourself for us then, just like you're trying to do now." I opened my mouth in protest, but he shook his head, glowering at me. "You can't go through with this, Eva. No matter what. And don't insult me by pretending you've given up on it entirely."

"You say that like it isn't a concession to even wait," I hissed. "Like it's okay that people are dying because of me."

"No one is dying because of *you*," Rivan countered. "They're dying because of *him*."

I wet my lips, wishing I could believe that. "I told Bash that I wouldn't."

"I know what you told Bash," Rivan said derisively. "And what you didn't. I'm not saying I don't understand. Nor am I going to pretend I believe you've entirely dropped it. And don't think for a second that Bash believes you did either."

"Rivan—"

"Don't bullshit a bullshitter, Eva. And don't you dare try to lie to me."

"And what if it's the only way?" I whispered, suddenly unable to keep up the façade that I wasn't terrified. "What if we get under the mountain and it's too late, and I have to go through with it anyways? Because if it comes down to losing this war..."

"You don't know that it would even work," Rivan said adamantly, his grip on my hand tightening almost painfully. "I wish I'd never brought you to that forest. You can't take any seer's vision as straight fact, let alone a sprite. For all we know, she led you astray somehow and your death would mean *nothing*."

I opened my mouth, then closed it again. I hadn't considered that, not when the sprite had sounded so certain. Rivan gave me a grim smile, apparently satisfied with the seed of doubt he had managed to sow within me.

"Eva...I would've died that day in Morehaven. Had you not done what you did." Rivan suddenly sounded tired, spent, like all the days of ceaseless travel and sleepless nights were catching up to him too. I opened my mouth again, but he held up a hand to silence me. "I owe you a lot more than a thank you for that. And for a lot more than only that." He turned to me, his eyes softening. "You should know that Bash was a shell of himself after his parents died. He pretended he wasn't, but he was...joyless. The young Southern King: brave and strong and so very broken. And you brought him back from that." He sighed heavily. "So please give us the chance to take Aviel down together before you do something so unselfishly selfish as to take your own life. Especially when we both know it'll mean more than just *your* death."

I gave him a weak smile, hastily wiping my eyes with the back of my hand. "I already promised Bash the same. But…"

"But what?"

"I'm scared, Rivan."

It seemed easier to admit it to him, even though I knew Bash could feel it.

"So am I," Rivan said almost flippantly. "Courage isn't the lack of fear, it's acting in spite of it. Bravery is in not allowing that fear to consume you."

"I'm not scared for myself," I whispered. "I'm scared that by *not* acting I'm making the wrong choice, and I'm dooming the realm I'm meant to rule because of it."

Rivan slowly shook his head. "When we get to the end of this, with you wearing your crown and your *anima* beaming by your side, I'm going to remind you of this moment. Of how close you came to losing everything when there was everything to be gained."

We sat together for a long beat, watching the shadows dance through the trees as I desperately tried to believe him. Rivan didn't let go of my hand.

"Don't think I'm going to go easy on you during training just because I owe you one though," Rivan muttered with a hint of his usual joviality.

I winced as I touched the sore side that would no doubt be bruised by morning, making a face at him. "Wouldn't dream of it."

Leaning into him, I rested my head on his shoulder. When my eyes started closing despite myself, he helped me to my feet, wrapping his arm around me as we silently walked back to camp.

CHAPTER 38
EVA

When I woke, it was still dark, though our tent was lit in the dim glow of the lantern that Bash now kept on through the night. Like he had realized how little I liked the feeling of waking up in total darkness, along with the suffocating sensation that came with it. Or perhaps simply so I could see the color of his eyes.

My eyelids felt heavy, like I had merely blinked rather than caught a fleeting moment of sleep. I was in dire need of more rest, the combined days of disjointed slumber wearing on my mind, my mood, and my magic. But that anxious hum in my bones already had me on edge enough to know that closing my eyes again would be futile. A yawn escaped me despite my efforts to hold it in.

Bash's body was hot and hard against mine, his fingers tightening where they were tangled in my hair as his eyes slowly opened. My heart stumbled a beat as his face buried into my hair, planting a kiss behind my ear.

"I missed this," Bash mumbled, his voice still heavy with sleep. His lips pressed against my neck, and I let out a happy sigh that had him turning my face, his mouth finding mine like he wanted to capture the sound. His wolfish grin as he pulled back told me that he knew exactly what he was doing.

Bash's gaze fixed on the right side of my mouth as I smiled back, asking, "Missed what, exactly?"

"Being with you. Without anything between us."

A lump lodged itself in my throat. "Me too."

"Is that so?" He kissed his way down my neck, his lips lingering where I knew that pale line encircled my throat.

"Just a little bit," I managed as he nibbled along my collarbone.

"I'll have to remind you how much then." Bash smiled against my skin as his fingers ventured down my sternum, tracing a path to my stomach. He deftly unbuttoned my nightdress as he went.

"You could try." I gasped as his teeth nipped my bare breast. "Don't we need to get going soon?"

"Yes, we do," he said in a low murmur, his words brushing over my taut nipple. "So be a good girl and come for me first, hellion."

He moved behind me on the sleep mat, letting my nightdress fall to the floor before he sank into me from behind. One hand splayed against my stomach, the other moving between my legs. His breath was warm against my ear, growing more and more labored as I reached behind me, my fingers digging into his hipbones as I moaned his name.

We came together frantically, desperately—our bodies acknowledging the reality that our time left together could be limited, even if neither of us would admit it.

For a few heartbeats, the world fell away and there was only the two of us. Smothering a shaky breath, I kissed him until my fear and trepidation faded to the background. Until there was nothing except him, and me, and the growing need I could feel echoed across our bond in whirls of heat, the ache of desire. Where nothing else mattered except the feel of his mouth against mine, and the rapidly disappearing space left between us.

His hands trailed languidly over my thighs; firm yet gentle—like we had all the time in the world. Even as I could feel it racing forward, its inevitable passage somehow more present with every second ticking away.

I love you, I could feel him say with each kiss. With each press of his lips against mine. With the way his shadows tugged me closer.

I love you, I thought as I tasted the freckles dotting his skin. Saying it in the way I dug my fingers into his hips to keep him against me, my darkness entwining with his.

Our magics wrapped around us, our moans blended together, and I lost myself to that building pleasure while gasping his name, feeling his shudder as he joined me.

When I came back to myself, Bash's hand had pressed against my cheek, turning my face to his as we panted against each other's lips.

"I love you," I whispered, needing to say it out loud in case it was the last time. "No matter what happens, I'm yours until we're both just a whisper of darkness between the stars."

"Until even those stars have faded from the sky, Eva," Bash breathed. "And forever after that."

He kissed a path down my spine before handing me my nightdress, helping me up before nipping at my backside—rewarding my yelp with a devious smirk. Regretfully, I pushed myself out of bed, wrapping a robe around myself as we stumbled in the waning dark to the magically heated camp showers. Bash had told me they were an invention from Mayim, where water magic was most prevalent. I was just grateful to have the escape of warm water flowing around me, like it might wash my tension away.

As if he could hear my thoughts, Bash's thumbs pressed into my shoulders, and I let out an inordinately loud moan. He chuckled, low and rough. "I suppose it's about time the rest of camp woke up."

I couldn't help but watch Bash as he got dressed, the distraction welcome. The towel dry had his hair even more tousled than usual, glowing a fiery orange in the candlelight. His arms flexed as he put on his fighting leathers, fitted enough to show off the long, powerful lines of his legs, the firm, rippling muscles of his shoulders and back.

"If you keep looking at me like that, we're never getting out of here on time." Bash said, a sad sort of smile on his face like he wished he could give in to that desire.

With a sigh loud enough that it brought a smile to his lips, I reached out to grab my cloak before walking out into the early rays of dawn.

The camp was already bustling to beat the sunrise, some soldiers busily packing up, others scarfing down a quick breakfast. Scanning to see where I could help, my eyes caught on a group of Solearans already gathered.

My breath snagged. They were all moving in unison in a form my muscles strained to join them in. I hurried forward before I could second-guess the impulse.

A few looked up at my approach, wobbling slightly in their single-footed stance. Akeno gave me a brazen wink, though his position didn't so much as quiver. Pari smiled slightly as she shifted onto her other foot in time with the others.

With a long breath out, I took my place in the middle of them. Thorin grinned at me as I raised both hands, moving into the next stance in a sustained, fluid movement that I could feel echoed all around me.

Tobias and Quinn, both dressed in their leathers, silently came over to join in. Beside me, Quinn's amber eyes were alight with joy, even Tobias's lips curving in a smile, though it felt slightly out of practice.

I closed my eyes as I pushed into the next stance, then another, feeling my magic humming under my skin in response. Strands of darkness wrapped up my arms and down my legs, as if they, too, wanted to join in.

Drawing in a full breath, I settled into the final stance as I slowly let it out, my eyes burning. When I opened them, Bash was staring directly at me, his mouth slightly parted. Rivan and Yael stood at his side, wearing similar looks of awe.

The Solearans broke apart as if nothing special had happened, though I saw a few glances at me and my brother. Part of me wanted to shy away from their attention, their undeserved looks of worship, but I forced a serene smile to my face, nodding to those who acknowledged me.

As we headed towards our horses, Quinn elbowed me in the side. I grinned, hooking my elbow with hers.

"That felt like home," she sighed. "Though I missed the way your mom would lead it."

"I miss the way yours would test if our form was off with a broomstick," I said wryly. "Even if I was usually the one to tip over."

Tobias came up beside us, his shoulders hunched. Taking a deep breath, he drew the hood of his cloak back over his head, muttering, "When this is all over, I want to figure out what else we thought was just our crazy parents' idea that's actually Solearan tradition."

Quinn snorted. "Looking forward to it."

As we reached where the rest of our group stood next to the already saddled horses, Bash held out a mug of nut-laden oatmeal to me. "You need breakfast if you want to have the energy to ride," he admonished, though a smile belied the sternness of his words.

As I took it, Bash wrapped an arm around my waist, effortlessly lifting me onto Nisa's saddle. His hands lingered on my thighs, his thumb circling almost absently.

Gingerly, I settled in, my inner thighs already sore. I winced, grumbling, "You'll be lucky if I have the energy to ride you after."

Bash laughed, a deep, delighted chuckle that I hadn't heard in far too long. "What if I promise to make it worth your while?"

Rivan groaned as he rode up beside me. "We do have a war to win if you two didn't notice?"

Yael smirked from where she sat atop Indra. "Oh really? I thought we were just here for fun. Maybe a little bit of life-threatening chaos."

"So nothing too out of the ordinary?" I asked around a mouthful of oatmeal.

"You forget we've attempted to control the chaos of this realm long before you fell into our laps," Rivan said, plucking a protruding walnut from my breakfast.

I scowled at him. His violet eyes twinkled as he took his time chewing.

The hoofbeats and whinnies of impatient horses topped by impatient masters brought me back to reality. The bustling camp had transformed back into a barren patch of land, the only sign of our stay the indentations in the earth.

We had lingered here for too long. That sensation like a ticking clock bore down on me, the ceaseless anxiety that every second not moving toward Adronix was one wasted. That we were ahead of schedule hadn't shaken the feeling, especially when I tried to calm my mind enough to sleep at night. Like even that delay might doom us.

My stomach felt tight and not from the hasty meal now turning leaden in my stomach. Bash leaned over, plucking the empty mug from my hand, then wrapped it in a cloth before stowing it in his saddlebag. "One day, we'll get to see this realm at peace."

A knot lodged in my throat at the promise in his words. I nodded, unable to look him in the eye as I urged Nisa down the path.

CHAPTER 39

BASH

The air had grown colder the higher we rode. We had taken extra time to blanket the horses in addition to upping their feed to maintain their energy levels for the uphill ride, but the more frequent stops had me anxious to get going. I knew I was pushing them too hard—the horses and our people—in my haste to beat Aviel to Adronix. But with only two days left to ride, barring anything unexpected, even these quick stops and scarce hours of rest at night felt like a risk when our maps couldn't be trusted, and we had no way to know if our lead held.

"So, what are we going to do about Eva?"

Yael rode up next to me, Indra nickering softly as Arion came beside her, extending his neck to brush their noses together. Though Rivan's dusky steed hated most other horses, Indra was one of the few he tolerated, let alone allowed that close. Yael lifted her chin toward my *anima*, who was passing out rations and a few extra blankets to a group of Solearans she had fallen back to ride with today. While tonight the tents would magically compensate for the colder weather, I knew that the gesture would be appreciated with the long, cold hours left in our journey as twilight turned to dusk. She knew each of them by name, I realized, as she exchanged a few words with one, then another. I could see the hero worship in a young Solearan's eyes as she leaned forward, taking their hand with a quick smile of encouragement.

She was already a natural leader, more fit to be the High Queen of this realm than she realized. I only hoped she would get that chance.

Not for the first time, I wondered exactly what the Choosing entailed. If all went to plan, Eva would face whatever trial awaited her the day after next. And while I had no doubt she would be more than up to the task; I couldn't help but wonder what else she would have to endure.

"Since she still seems determined to die for the rest of us?" Rivan asked, knocking me from my thoughts.

I gritted my teeth. "We've discussed it."

Rivan let out a humorless laugh. "As have we. But I know when I'm being mollified."

I knew Eva hadn't let her original plan go, not entirely. I was still terrified that she saw herself as disposable when she was anything but.

Yael shook her head, her gaze still on my *anima*. "I think we all know that if it comes down to it, she'll sacrifice herself anyway."

Eva had been steadily drawing into herself the closer we got to Adronix. Not shutting me out like she had before but…I could feel something stagnant across our bond, wearing away at her. It was like she was slowly going into shock. It scared me to see her so lost; her dead-eyed stare at the ceiling of our tent when she thought I had fallen asleep. And I hated myself for it—that I couldn't seem to help her.

Instead, I waited, struggling to keep my breathing even as I wrapped my arms around her. Feeling her apprehension deepening across our bond with each day, like a storm looming on the horizon. Straining to keep my own impotent anger in check as it raged against a threat I couldn't fight.

I wondered if she realized that taking her own life would be tantamount to taking mine along with it.

For a second, I thought of my mother, wasting away before our eyes after my father's death. How much I hated her for it then. It seemed a strange form of cruelty that I now understood the reason she hadn't been able to go on without him, even for us.

Because even if I didn't let myself wither away like she had, there was no doubt in my mind that I would no longer be whole if Eva was taken from me.

"I know," I admitted hoarsely, flexing my hands from where they had formed into fists.

Rivan sighed. "She doesn't get that option if we defeat him first."

Yael let out a mirthless laugh. "I'll add that to the list of impossible things."

I closed my eyes, careful not to let my worries leak down our bond. They would only add to Eva's.

"She's one of us." Rivan took my hand, then Yael's, his lavender eyes narrowing in stubborn surety. "We won't let anything happen to her."

I watched Eva laugh softly at something one of my rangers said, wishing I could hear the fleeting sound of it over the din. "In the meantime, it can't hurt to remind her exactly how much she has to lose."

The clouds had lifted, the night vast and startlingly clear. A thousand stars glistened in the sky, peeking through the snow-dusted treetops in a glittering cosmic display.

It seemed foolish to even try to sleep with what lay ahead. To toss and turn in the few hours we had to do so, or pretend we weren't both separately spiraling—Eva's carefully even inhales and exhales a far cry from the soft breathing of slumber.

She held my hand as I led her down the dark path past camp. I frowned as we reached a patch of gray, a desiccated stump sticking through the thin layer of snow, carefully leading her around it so her boots didn't touch the curse's erosion.

A ribbon of shadow wrapped around Eva's eyes, blindfolding her, though she had promised me she wouldn't look. She shivered as a gust of wind brushed snow from the trees, bespeckling her chestnut hair. I pulled her cloak tighter around her, using it to tug her closer to my side. The moon lit her face in an otherworldly mosaic of light and shadow, and I couldn't help but run my thumb along her jaw, tracing her lower lip as her mouth curved upward at my attention.

"Just a little further," I promised.

In a clearing of the forest, a fire crackled merrily, blankets already laid out on the logs my shadows had pulled into a circle around it. A paltry version of our first nights in the Faewilds together, but a passable one.

"You can look now," I whispered low in her ear, smiling at the way her breath caught. A tremble traveled through her that had nothing to do with the cold.

Eva's lips parted as I let my shadows fall, her eyes gleaming in the firelight. That perfect dimple formed as a slow smile crossed her face, the stress of our journey banished for one single moment. I gave her an easy, lazy grin in return like everything was as simple as I wished it could be. My fingers spanned the side of her face, my focus wholly centered on her lips as I leaned in and kissed her, feeling her melt into me in response.

She let out a soft sigh as she pulled away, sitting down heavily in front of the fire like the weight of the world had crashed back down on her shoulders.

"I thought we could both use a moment," I explained as I sat beside her, slinging an arm around her waist and dragging her legs across my lap.

Her smile was a little sad. "More than one, but I'll take what I can get."

I pressed a kiss into her hair. The fire crackled, the embers flying upward before they faded into the snowy trees.

Despite the circumstances, traveling through the woods with Eva brought back a flood of perfect memories. Even if this time, our bed was shared rather than two bedrolls carefully positioned head-to-head, our hands reaching for each other in our sleep.

A hint of melancholy crossed our bond, and I realized Eva's eyes were closed as if memorizing this moment. But I could sense the instant her thoughts darkened, her exhaustion a sharp contrast to the way her apprehension thrummed, could hear the careful cadence of her breathing I knew was instinctual. It killed me to see her so scared, so hunted. I was suddenly afraid of what I might see when she opened her eyes.

When she did, her irises had darkened into pools of obsidian. My shadows wrapped around the wisps of night that darted from her fingertips almost uncontrollably, my heart lodging in my throat.

"Tell me what you're thinking."

Eva let out a bone-weary sigh. "The same thing I've been focused on since we began this adventure. When we get inside that mountain, I need to find that mirror."

"*We* need to find that mirror," I corrected her sharply. "Do you think you have to do this alone? To face him by yourself?"

"*If* the mirror lets you pass," Eva countered. "Even with your Celestial eligibility, it's not like there's a rulebook. If this is my destiny, then what if it only lets my magic through?"

I glared at her, and she glowered right back. "Then Tobias will come with you to help. Your bloodlink should be enough even if I can't—"

"What exactly are you worried about? That Aviel will kill me, or that I'll do it for him?"

My reply stuck in my throat.

She slammed her hand down on the log and darkness shot from her fingertips, careening into the night. "Do you think I *want* to die? Do you think that every time I look around me, I'm not reminded of what I have to lose? That when I look at you, I don't know *exactly* what I'd be giving up?" Her voice wavered. "Do you think I don't want another way? A different world?"

It broke something in me to hear the vulnerability in her voice, the fear of what was to come. The pang of her grief that resonated in my own chest. Wordlessly, I held her more tightly.

"Of course, I'm afraid it might come to that," Eva whispered. The flecks of gold in her eyes seemed to come alive in the flickering firelight. "But what I have to do is more important than fear."

"We can do this without your sacrifice," I said staunchly. "We *can* stop him."

"I do *want* to believe you." She pressed her forehead to mine. "But even if I don't..." Her voice broke off, and she swallowed. "Do you really think we can stop Aviel without killing him?"

"Way ahead of you, hellion," I said, grimacing at his name on her lips even though I was happy to see she wasn't avoiding it any longer. "After you've gone through the Choosing, we'll fight him together, wearing him down until he's drained of his stolen power. Then secure him in iron to keep him from touching anyone else to gain more." Eva shuddered, and I knew she was thinking about the iron box I knew still haunted her nightmares. A ruthless part of me hoped we could track down that same box after this war was over and let Aviel live in it for the rest of his life. "And then we'll finally trap him under the mountain he was supposed to be in all along. Or at least until we can figure out a way to undo what he did."

If that was even possible.

She nodded slowly, consideringly, even if something about it felt placating.

He deserved to die. For the curse, for the wars, for all of it. For my father's death at his hand, and my mother's death because of it. For the murder of Eva's parents, for her brother's imprisonment, and for everything he did and tried to do to her. For the nightmares still lurking in her mind and for the ones that turned out to be real. And for all the years she spent sad and suffering and lonely.

But not at the cost of her life.

Eva absentmindedly rubbed her hand against the scar by her neck and rage coiled in my stomach. She looked tired as she quietly said, "But if it doesn't work...it's not such a terrible thing, to die for what you believe in and for the people you love. To leave this world to make it a better place."

I could feel that combination of terror and resolve across our bond, the same as I had felt from her before she had given herself up for the rest of us. For a heartbeat, I could even feel those bands of light cutting into me as they dragged me away from her.

Despite my best effort, my voice wavered as I said, "It won't be a better world without you."

Her teeth skated over her bottom lip. "Bash..."

"Don't even try to argue against that," I said warningly.

"Every time I stop to think, I remember that I could stop this all now," Eva whispered, her voice hesitant. "I know that there's another way. But I can't help but feel horribly selfish. Our people's lives, our friends' lives, *your* life...they're all depending on me. And I feel like I'm failing."

My hand curled into a fist at my side. "What if I were to ride out tonight alone?" Eva's eyes shot to mine, suddenly wide with alarm. "Use my shadows to shield me. Find a way into Aviel's camp and see if I could take him down like the assassin I was trained to be in the last war?"

"And why exactly should I let you risk your life instead of mine?" Eva's words were clipped despite her pressing panic across our bond.

"Because we're more expendable than you are," Yael said from behind us. "All of us."

Eva went still. Yael, Marin, Rivan, Quinn, and Tobias stepped out from the tree line, coming to sit on the logs beside us.

Quinn's lips were pressed into a hard line, not a hint of her usual smile to be found. Tobias folded his arms across his chest, though his face remained an impassive mask. Yael simply smirked, tugging Marin to her side and wrapping a blanket around them both.

Eva's hands were so tightly fisted, I knew her nails bit into her scarred palm. "No. Never. Not to me."

"Hypocrite," Quinn coughed.

Eva stiffened, a strange mix of shame and determination shining in her eyes.

Rivan sat down on Eva's other side with a sigh. "Blood and magic are a strange, fickle thing, in some ways more so than Seeing. Even if you were to sacrifice yourself now, it doesn't mean it would stop the war that's coming. The battle that was always meant to happen, so long delayed. Some of our people will die fighting to stop the False King from once again taking over this realm. And it will be worth it, to die fighting for what we believe in. But to lose you now before the fight has even begun? If that sprite wasn't right, we lose our best chance to stop him, and our future High Queen all at once."

Eva's lips were trembling. She squeezed her eyes shut, and I reached out to take her hand. "I don't want to fight about this. Not when our time together might be limited."

"Then believe in us," I said softly. "In all of us. Because none of us can fight a war while being distracted that you might suddenly decide to end yourself. You need to believe we can win this without your sacrifice."

Tobias nodded from where he sat across from his sister, his eyes sparking with light too bright to be a reflection of the flames. "You and I haven't survived what we have and made it this far to fail now."

Eva bit her lip, her eyes darting between us before she whispered, "Okay."

Yael raised an eyebrow. "Okay?"

Eva's mouth twitched. "I believe that we can win. Even if Aviel does beat us to Adronix. I won't use what I know, even then, unless I'm absolutely sure there's no other way to stop him."

It was a careless truce. But one I could live with.

"Though don't expect us to entirely let this go either, or to take our eyes off you until this is over," Rivan added with a dangerous smile.

Eva let out an exasperated sigh. "I don't suppose there's any way I can convince you otherwise?"

Rivan's smile widened. "Not a chance in hell, sweetheart."

Yael chuckled grimly. "Now that that's out of the way, I suppose it's time to talk about what comes next."

"When we get to Adronix, we need to get Eva to the Seeing Mirror so she can complete the Choosing," I said, having run through these steps in my head as we rode so often it felt strange hearing them aloud. "Then defeat Aviel's army, isolate him and drain his magic while doing so, and imprison him underneath Adronix where he belongs."

"One impossible thing at a time," Eva added with a slow smile.

I grinned at her.

"I've been thinking about how to better drain his magic," Marin murmured. She reached into her pocket, withdrawing a familiar oval stone. "The way our mother's invention works is to draw power from that which shouldn't possess it, such as the magic-blocking bands you two wore." Tobias and Eva let out an identical wince as she gestured at them both. "But she originally made it to be used on those cursed with unwanted magic. It should be able to drain Aviel of the magic he's stolen."

"Hopefully, it will protect whoever uses it on him if he tries to steal more magic from them," Yael added. "Or at least long enough to incapacitate him."

Marin held it out to Eva, who shook her head. "Keep it for now. If he finds us while I'm off wherever the Seeing Mirror takes me for the Choosing, I won't leave you all unprotected."

"And if Aviel beats us to the mountain after all?" Quinn asked pointedly.

A muscle flickered in Rivan's jaw. "Then our first priority is to keep him from reaching the Seeing Mirror."

"But if he does, Eva isn't the only one who can make it through the gate," I said. Tobias nodded gravely, obviously following my train of thought. "So Tobias and I will do whatever we can to keep him from going through the Choosing long enough that Eva can claim her birthright."

I refused to think of the alternative—the one where he already succeeded in stealing my *anima*'s crown.

"And take him down any way we can, short of killing him," Tobias added grimly to a chorus of nods.

There was a restless sort of hope in having a way forward, despite the many ways it could go wrong.

Eva's mouth twitched as she looked around the circle. "As much as I'm enjoying our late night gathering, I didn't realize my fallback plan merited an intervention."

"You're our High Queen," Yael said. "But more importantly, you're our family."

"And we're not letting you go without a fight," Quinn murmured, shivering slightly as a cold breeze tore through the trees, a shimmer of snow falling from their branches. Tobias shifted closer to her, as if he might shield her from the chill.

"Come on," I said, reaching out a hand to pull Eva to her feet. "We should all try to get some rest before tomorrow's trek."

Eva let out a long breath as we ducked into our tent, her shoulders slumping. She had been silent as we walked back to camp, looking into the night as though it might look back. I cupped her face, coaxing her gaze back to mine.

I half expected an argument, but she simply lifted up onto her tiptoes, her teeth grazing my earlobe.

"Are you trying to distract me?" I managed as her mouth worked its way downward.

She laughed softly, her breath caressing my neck. "Is it working?"

"Yes," I admitted.

Gods, I wanted her—*needed* her. Wanted to make her feel anything but the looming dread trickling into a suffocating stream down our bond. Needed to lose myself inside her for the same reason, the primal urge to feel her around me outweighing even the ceaseless building exhaustion from so many days of travel, worry, and limited sleep.

And somehow, I let myself be distracted. Somehow, I found myself distracting her in return from the horrible truth of what we would soon have to face, losing ourselves in each other's bodies until she was all there was.

Our bond was free of worry, hers and mine, as we finished. Sleepily, her eyes drank me in, her fingers tightening against my chest like she was as afraid as I was that she would slip away.

"Stay," I whispered, my voice thick. "Right here, with me. Whatever happens, we'll fight it together."

Please don't make me watch you die.

Eva looked at me, eyes more golden than hazel in the lantern light. "Always."

She settled against me, and I held her against my heart, the love shining across our bond warming me from the inside out.

"I'm yours," Eva whispered, that dimple deepening. "And you're mine."

"Always," I repeated, my fingers trailing down her side in leisurely strokes.

Her breathing evened out as I traced our names against her skin with my fingertips. As if the act itself was as magical as writing words upon our palms; a silent plea to forever keep us as entwined as the invisible looped letters I continued drawing until I went to find her in my dreams.

CHAPTER 40
EVA

There was a strange music in the air, its dissonance ringing in my head. A tug in my gut that felt like it was leading me toward Adronix. Pulling at me, whether I wanted to go or not.

It had been there ever since I woke, unable to sleep without Bash there anyway. Like it was calling to something inside my soul, whatever magic it held within beckoning me closer. The nearer we got, the tighter my anxiety coiled. Yet my limbs felt leaden even as my mind buzzed, my eyes squeezed tightly shut like I could avoid the day that was already underway.

Bash had woken, if he had slept at all, while it was still dark, brushing a kiss on my forehead before retreating somewhere to ready for the day while I fitfully tried to rest. He seemed calmer, more focused after our gathering last night. Despite his trust in me, I knew exactly why he had done it—to show me one last time everything I would lose should I embrace my supposed fate.

The sounds of the birds welcoming the dawn finally urged me to pull on my leathers. I found them neatly laid out for me next to my sword, cloak, and boots. A smile came to my lips at Bash's thoughtfulness, the small, casual reminder of his love for me.

I was thankful for my leathers' fleece lining as I was hit by a gust of wind immediately upon leaving the tent, its icy chill spurring me to wrap my cloak tightly around me. The frosted ground was hard beneath my feet. I knew more snow wouldn't be far behind.

The camp was quieter this morning as I helped pack up, thankful for the magic that made the process easy as tents simply disappeared into bags too small to hold them. It was as if the looming mountain had cast a shadow over us all, any hint of merriment gone.

There were circles under Bash's eyes that hadn't been so pronounced the day before when he lifted me onto Nisa's back in our now daily ritual, his hands lingering on my hips before he finally backed away. A brisk wind shuddered through the trees as we started onward, the casual chatter of the army at our back a pale imitation of the previous day's banter. Our pace felt hurried for our last full day's ride, like the rest of them felt that tug too. Or perhaps it was just the uncertainty and the cumulative lack of sleep taking its toll.

The route abruptly began to climb, the ascent anything but gentle as the terrain grew rougher. I found myself focusing on every breath, suddenly more precious now that they felt numbered, welcoming the mist of each exhale like a barometer of time even as it was quickly stolen away by the wind; savoring each inhale as proof I was still alive.

Thorin and Akeno rode together, looking more comfortable with each other than I had realized during our time together. When we took a quick break to water the horses, and eat some rations ourselves, Akeno casually took Thorin's hand, pulling him against him in a swift kiss that confirmed my suspicions. I looked away, smiling.

Bash caught my eye, dragging me to him in a similar fashion before claiming my lips with his. I relaxed into his hold, feeling the tension ease from my body as he held me close, his stubble rough against my chilled cheeks.

"They had the right idea," he murmured against my mouth before kissing me again.

I walked through the Solearan section of the camp as Tobias lit the way, offering help where I could despite my trembling legs. Many accepted before doing a double take, gazes lingering as I felt a flush creep under the collar of my cloak, thankful the redness of my cheeks could be explained by the cold. I tried not to feel unworthy of the adulation in their eyes. As if the circumstances of my birth had any bearing on a character yet untested by the people that claimed me as their own.

When I walked into our tent, Bash was kneeling in front of a gigantic map, a hint of foreboding flowing icily down our bond.

"Hi there," I said, my attempt at playfulness mostly lost to my exhaustion. I knew we should sleep with the scant hours we had left to do so. We had traveled late into the night, and I desperately needed the rest. But the thought of laying down while my mind whirred, and I pictured every worst-case scenario, sounded entirely unbearable.

A smirk played at the corner of Bash's mouth, his eyes swirling faster as he looked at me. "Hi yourself."

Yet there was an edge in his tone, something that slithered across our bond that made me pause.

"What's wrong?"

Bash's forehead creased, worry lines forming between his brows. "We're making good time. We'll reach Adronix tomorrow as planned, and the Esterran forces are nearly in place for their attack on Morehaven, but I...I just can't shake the feeling I'm not getting the whole picture." He let out a deep sigh. "I suppose I know I'm not, since we can't track their movements."

My nails dug into the scar on my palm. "Should we risk traveling through the night? It's not too late to pack back up..."

Bash shook his head. "The wards around camp keep us safe from the worst of the forest's denizens. We're already pushing into their hunting hours. And rest, however brief, will help strengthen our collective magic ahead of tomorrow's battle. Not to mention the horses need some respite." He rubbed his eyes wearily. "I'm probably overthinking things. But after everything...I just want to be sure I'm not taking you into another trap."

I walked behind him, kneading out the tension in his shoulders as I looked at the map spread before us. Then jolted as a creature moved in the forest not far from our camp, repressing a shudder as I remembered the feeling of a furry tentacle wrapping around my ankle. I didn't even want to imagine the beasts that might be passing us in the night.

Bash looked at me, smiling as I took in the realm laid at my feet. And I realized that was exactly what it could be if we won this war, and I became High Queen.

When I looked up, Bash's expression held a hint of melancholy before it smoothed into a wan smile. I tilted my head to the side. "Are you okay?"

He shrugged. "Objectively."

I gave him a look, and his lips quirked in response.

"That's not a real answer," I pressed. "Is there anything I can do? Did you need something?"

Those stormy eyes slowed. "Just you, hellion."

I squealed as he pulled me down and we fell against the bedding, cushioning my fall with his body. His greedy kiss left me breathless. I nipped at his lip in response, drawing a shameless groan.

Then my eyes narrowed. "Now tell me what else is wrong."

The corner of his mouth twitched. "Why do I feel like my own methods of interrogation are being used against me?"

I just raised an eyebrow, waiting. Bash sighed.

"War is a crucible. And I wonder if any of us will come out of it the same as we were before it. If all of us will live through it this time. Even if we beat Aviel to the mountain, there will still be a battle. The final one in far too long a conflict."

My hand balled against his chest at the thought, before slowly flattening as I forced that fear away. "Sometimes I forget you've lived this all before. I'm sorry that you have to go through this again."

"If we achieve what we should have during the first war, I won't be," Bash said grimly.

"Still, I wish I could save you the stress of it," I murmured, kissing the line between his brows.

He arched an eyebrow. "Said the cause of the majority of it."

I laughed, the sound of it almost startling. Bash pulled my head down, capturing the sound with his lips.

"When this war is over, my main priority is going to be making you laugh," Bash murmured, a wisp of his longing seeming to curl around my heart.

"Here I thought your plan was to make me moan," I said teasingly.

A smirk played at the corner of his mouth. "That too."

"Along with a few minor endeavors like ruling the faerie realm," I added flippantly. I was rewarded with a real, full smile this time that made my stomach flip.

We sat there, entwined with each other for a long moment. I knew we should at least try to rest, but despite my fatigue, the act felt impossible even as dawn steadily ticked closer.

Bash's thumb ghosted over my cheek, his fingers winding into my hair. "What's that look, Eva?"

I let out a sigh, my fingers lazily tracing the freckles on his neck. Gently, I connected the constellation hidden on his skin. His heart beat beneath my fingertips as I drew the bound shape of Andromeda, awaiting her death by the sea before someone unexpected saved her. Slowly, I worked my way down to where his freckles disappeared under his shirt— to where her outstretched arms were chained even amongst the stars. "I was just thinking about what I have left to do. What I'd like to do before my life is over."

He stilled slightly. "And what is that?"

"I'd like the chance to explore this world," I said longingly. "There's so much of this realm I haven't seen. So much left to visit together if we get the chance."

"*When*," Bash corrected quietly.

"And I always thought I'd have kids," I said, watching as his eyes heated. I elbowed him, and he smiled shamelessly. We had talked about this once before, so long ago it seemed a lifetime ago. "One day."

"When this war is over, we'll have as many as you want."

I laughed, throwing a pillow at him. "And what if I want ten?"

He looked far too delighted at the prospect. "*Whatever* you want, hellion."

I rolled my eyes. "Maybe not that many. But I'd like them to have siblings. A friend for them to grow up with, like we had."

Bash nodded. "Someone to get into trouble with. And hopefully out again."

I rolled over and propped my chin up on my hand.

"I'd like to accomplish more," Bash said thoughtfully. "Before my time comes."

"Oh?" I asked, still wrapped in him. "And what would you be remembered for?"

Bash's mouth curved in a wistful smile. "For something more than just who I am, but what I did with my time. As someone who was there for my people, and the people who needed me. For a strong arm, a steady heart… and an occasional moment of divine madness."

He flashed me a quick, impish grin that left me breathless. The King of the Southlands and the Faewilds, far more concerned about his mark on those around him than his own mark on history.

"If I die tomorrow, I hope they remember what we tried to do," I said hoarsely. "What we all risked, in the hopes for something better."

Bash's throat dipped in a telltale swallow. "I was hoping to have a few hundred years with you, hellion. But if tomorrow…If we—"

I quieted him with a finger to his lips.

"It'll break my heart if you stop believing that we can somehow defy the inevitable together," I whispered. "Maybe it's selfish, but I need you to believe for the both of us."

The look he gave me made my heart stutter. "I'll always believe in us."

I laid my head against his chest, listening to the steady beat of his heart as I whispered, "Can you just hold me, please?"

Bash's arms wrapped around me protectively, and I let myself feel safe, pretending tomorrow wouldn't change the very destiny of the realm as my eyes fluttered closed.

My last thought before I succumbed to the lure of sleep was that I wished I could make this moment last forever.

CHAPTER 41
EVA

The weight of memory was so heavy it felt suffocating. The fire crackled around me, threading up the walls in the corners of the room, the smoke stifling. Yet I couldn't feel its heat, even as I heard its roaring in my ears.

I stood mere feet from the rose-covered mirror, feeling like I was already falling. Yet my mother wasn't where she should have been, nor was my brother.

The hooded figure stalked forward, but there wasn't anyone to stop him this time.

That blinding, stolen light flashed toward me, far too familiar now. My gaze locked with Aviel's across the haze of the heat, his pale eyes flashing with the light of his stolen magic. My skin prickled, a shiver running down my spine as his lips curved in that terrifying, soulless smile.

"What's the purpose of this?" I gritted out the question between clenched teeth, willing them not to chatter. "I already know you're the one responsible for my nightmares."

I struggled against the cage of his hold on my mind, trying to calm my racing heart. But even if it wasn't real...it was, at least to some degree. And I was trapped in the illusion as surely as any nightmare.

"Because you could stop this." Aviel smirked. "Not their deaths, of course." He waved an irreverent hand at the burning room. "But you could stop the deaths of *everyone else you love before you lose them too. So I thought I would give you one last chance to give up. To give in to me at last."*

My mother wasn't here, but suddenly, I could still hear her screams ringing through the room. The pain he had put her through before he killed her.

"Fuck. You."

"Soon, darling."

My darkness shot out like a spear, aiming for his heart—but Aviel blocked it with a blinding shield of light. Before I could stop him, he was in front of me, one hand wrapped around my throat, burning into my skin as bands of light secured my wrists. He yanked me forward, then his lips violently crashed into mine, swallowing my cry of rage and pain.

"EVA!"

Bash. The panic in his voice made me want to scream his name, but I could barely think, barely tell the difference between what was real and what wasn't in this dream that felt far too much like reality.

Something cold pressed into my hand. My dagger. The reassuring weight of it ripped me from the past before it could keep me here, its pommel humming beneath my palm.

With all my remaining strength, I threw myself backwards, breaking out of Aviel's hold. His eyes were black as they met mine, a cruel smile curling his lips that made something inside me tremble.

The flames twisted around me as I stumbled away from him—just as before— and fell through the mirror.

Bash was repeating my name like a litany. He sucked in a breath as my eyes opened, his own dark with shadow.

"Eva. *Eva.* Are you okay?"

"I'm…" I trailed off, unable to voice the lie that I was anything close to fine. Fear-laced adrenaline hit me like a shockwave, lighting up every single one of my nerve endings with the need to fight something that was no longer there. My hand clenched around my dagger, its pommel still in my grip, Bash's large hand covering mine.

He followed the direction of my gaze. "I thought it might ground you."

"It did," I managed to say, my breathing still short and shallow. I sucked in a sharp breath, holding it even as I rushed through my four-count, blowing it out too quickly before trying again.

"Are you hurt?" His shadows ran down my arms, flitting down my body as if checking me for injuries.

"I'm okay," I said hoarsely, my throat dry from the imagined smoke that somehow, wasn't.

His eyes were blazing. "Nothing about what just happened was okay."

I saw the moment he took in the handprint blistering the skin of my neck, just as his shadows raised the sleeves of my nightdress, exposing the burns on my wrists. His expression turned murderous.

"I'm okay," I repeated softly. "Please don't wake anyone up to heal me. Not when everyone needs their strength today."

Bash looked ready to argue, then let out a shaky breath, obviously trying to settle the turbulent mix of fear and hate careening down our bond—his rage reflecting in those beautiful shadow-filled eyes. Then I was enveloped by the safety of his arms, his shadows as they wound tenderly around me.

The pressure in my throat tightened unbearably.

"What did he want?" Bash asked, quiet fury lining each word.

"My surrender." The attempt at nonchalance was lost to the quaver in my voice.

His jaw flexed. "Unconditionally, I'm sure."

I let out an empty-sounding laugh. "He must know we're close, somehow. Either through the bloodbond, or..." I didn't want to even think about the possibility of spies within our ranks, though I knew it was naïve not to.

"He probably wanted to be sure you hadn't already beat him there," Bash said tightly.

I winced, knowing the rancor in his tone wasn't meant for me but despising it all the same. Silently, I berated myself for letting Aviel get so close, for not having the wherewithal to push him out of my mind sooner. A shudder ran through me at yet another violation. Bash pulled me closer, as if his arms alone could shield me from further threats.

When he spoke again, his voice was a broken whisper. "I'm sorry I couldn't protect you. I hate the thought of you near him without me."

From the guilt across our bond, I knew he didn't just mean now.

"You never left me, Bash," I whispered, burrowing my face into the crook of his neck, breathing him in. Letting his scent wrap around me as surely as his arms—of petrichor and safety. "Not even then."

"Eva..."

"I know," I whispered.

And I did. Because everything he felt, I felt too—no more walls left between us now. His fear, not for himself, but for me, born from that unrelenting love that lined the bond between us.

"If he knows where you are, then we need to get moving right away."

I heard what he had left unsaid. The fear that despite our best efforts, we would be too late.

Bash's lips pressed into my hair as I listened to his heartbeat beneath my ear, even our breaths synchronized. Holding each other for one more moment before we went to face our fates.

CHAPTER 42
EVA

A maelstrom had opened above Adronix like it sensed us nearing it, lightning flashing across the stormy skies in an endless flurry of light and shadow. Icy rain poured down in a torrent and even the circular pockets of magic Yael conjured around us were unable to keep the chill from my bones. My heavy cloak stayed tightly wrapped around me as the sleet turned into snow. Yet the cold ran deeper than that, like the frost had invaded my very blood.

The closer we got to the icy mountain, the more I felt like I was losing my mind. This close, its presence felt like a constant thrum inside my head, growing more demanding with every step. Perhaps that was the mirror that waited within, luring me like a moth to a flame.

Or, if fate was to be believed, a fish already on the hook.

My nerves skittered as we came to a halt. I turned to see Bash striding toward me, the hilt of his sword rising above his shoulder from where he had it strapped to his back, the two daggers on either side of his narrow hips exposed as his cloak streamed behind him. His storm-filled eyes studied me, his snow-speckled lashes brushing against his freckled cheeks as his eyes narrowed at whatever he saw.

I dismounted Nisa, my boots hitting the frozen ground hard. "What are we waiting for?"

Bash closed the gap between us in two long strides. "The next section of the route is prone to avalanche. A few Elemental water users are riding ahead to make sure it's safe. They'll report back as soon as we can proceed."

I wondered if he realized he ruled so easily. Effortlessly commanded the trust of his people, their respect freely given because it had been earned, not because of his titles, but through years of serving alongside them in this war.

Not for the first time, I wondered why he hadn't been chosen to lead this realm. He was eligible for the Choosing, after all. And yet, he hadn't once mentioned the desire ever crossing his mind. Perhaps I should simply be glad of the fact that he was my *anima* and would lend a level of credibility to my own claim through his devotion to me.

Part of me hoped that if I were to fail, Bash might take my place as the leader this realm deserved. Another part of me knew without a doubt that if I were to die in the attempt, Bash wouldn't be far behind.

Bash's eyes shot to mine, a muscle feathering in his cheek. I belatedly tried to calm my thoughts, knowing he could sense the full weight of my unease now that I was no longer holding him at bay.

"Talk to me," Bash said, almost too quietly to be heard amongst the bustle around us. "Please."

It was the plea in his eyes that unraveled the words on my tongue. "I can feel it. Like it's calling me."

"The mirror in the mountain?"

I shrugged slightly, something snagging in my throat. "Either that or destiny itself."

His eyes flared slightly at that, his head tilting to the side as if appraising me.

"Perhaps we'll make our own destiny today," Bash murmured, reaching out to cup my cheek. His thumb moved against it in lazy strokes.

I leaned into that touch, retreating into the comfort it offered. Trying and failing not to notice the raw worry that streaked across our bond.

My hand reached down to rest on the hilt of my dagger, feeling it almost hum beneath my hand as I steadied my resolve. "Today, we stop him. Or at least gain the power to do so."

Bash's gaze darkened, his irises swirling madly as he leaned in. "There you are, hellion." He stopped with his lips a breath from mine. "Do you know how hard it is not to kiss you when you get that look on your face? Determined, cocky, deadly...the one that promises vengeance."

My mouth quirked, relishing the way his gaze dropped to the dimple I knew had appeared. "What's stopping you?"

Bash let out a sound somewhere between a huff and a groan. Then his mouth was on mine, his fingers twisting in my hair. Kissing me like there was no tomorrow as I desperately pushed away the thought that it could be true.

I stopped feeling the chill as I clung to him, losing myself to the warmth of his mouth and lips and tongue, tangling and unraveling me. Knowing we had only minutes before we would begin our journey again, but unable to let him go for the life of me.

He pulled back, panting against my now swollen lips. My hand tightened behind his neck as I drowned in the endless feeling of his love—letting it banish my desperation and dread, if only for a moment.

"I was lonely and broken, and you helped put me back together piece by piece," I whispered, watching as wet flakes of snow settled on his auburn lashes. "I might have loved you, if for nothing else but that. And for taking me home where I belonged."

"Don't you dare say goodbye to me," Bash growled, sensing what lay behind my words. Understanding too much, as always. "Not now, not ever. Stop talking like you're going to die."

I swallowed against the lump in my throat. "I'm just being practical. This is war, after all."

"Well, stop it," he snapped. "You're not allowed to die today."

I raised a brow. "Is that so?"

"Yes," Bash said staunchly, glaring at me as if I was being the stubborn one. His arms wrapped around me protectively as his shadows formed a hazy shield around us. "I won't let that happen."

"And if the universe has other ideas?"

"Then I'll let the universe know exactly where it can put them."

He kissed me again, almost lazily. Like there wasn't a doubt in his mind about how this would end.

Maybe he knew I needed that reassurance. Or maybe he just felt the need to show me exactly what we could have together when this was all over—if we won. A future that felt utterly out of reach, as much as I wanted it. Like the outcome of today had a chokehold on it, even in my dreams.

Or perhaps it was the feeling that my life would still be the price of winning.

When he looked at me, I didn't miss that glimmer of hope that promised a future I didn't dare yearn for. Unable to control my wince, I tried to turn away, but his hands held me in place against him, no doubt sensing my shift.

Bash's irises swirled with agitation, his jaw hardening. "Stop thinking that this realm would be better off without you. Not when we're so close."

I tried desperately to make the lump in my throat go away, but I wouldn't lie to him. Couldn't—not when he saw right through me. "And if we've exhausted all our options?"

He growled in frustration, lifting a hand to cradle my face. "We're not done yet. Not when there are other ways to stop him."

"If he goes through the Choosing, he'll be unstoppable," I said dully.

"Then we'll stop him first. I'll do anything to rid him from this world."

My throat tightened. "Except give me up."

Bash's jaw flexed. "Except that."

It was getting harder to breathe. Carefully, I counted my breath in, then out.

"We've been over this, Eva. I won't lose you," Bash said firmly. "I'm yours, and you're mine."

"Bash..."

"You promised me forever," he growled. "And I intend to collect."

I opened my mouth, then closed it, trying not to let myself hope.

"And I'll be right there with you, whatever happens in the end." His voice faltered. "You don't have to face him alone. Not again."

"Then trust me, Bash. Trust me to do what needs to be done. Trust that you'll be with me, even if you aren't at my side. Trust that if I have any choice in the matter, I'll come back to you."

His lower lip trembled. "I do trust you. But that doesn't mean I've forgotten—"

"I know I scared you that night." My voice wavered as I thought back to the blade of darkness I had come so close to turning upon myself. "But I made you a promise, one that I intent to do my best to keep."

"Unless there's no other way," Bash countered.

"Trust me," I repeated, more firmly this time. "That I'll do everything I can to avoid that last resort. That I'll find a way. That I can handle myself."

"I know you can," Bash said hoarsely. "It's me who can't handle it. I can't—I *can't* lose you. It's more than I can bear. But that's my problem, not yours. Not when you've more than proven how capable you are."

"Then trust in us." I leaned my forehead against his as we breathed together in that slow four-count he needed as much as I did. Our exhales melded together, visible in the chilled air, and I saw some of the tightness in his body melt away.

"I will. I *do*," he whispered, those last two words more heartfelt than a wedding vow.

He kissed me then, almost frantically, a strange sort of desperation spreading across our bond. Love and fear and longing all wrapped up in the press of his lips against mine—as if he was trying to fit everything he felt for me into it all at once. As my arms wound behind his head, I was struck by the need to stop time and forever relive this moment. To memorize every part of it should this kiss be our last.

His teeth dragged along my lower lip as we broke apart, his lips hovering there as if reluctant to pull away before his mouth barely brushed mine in a brief echo of before. Like he, too, was committing every nuance to memory before what was to come.

And it was that kiss that almost broke me.

There was a possessive sort of terror in his eyes, like he had finally given in to the fear he could lose me. I wished there was something, *anything* I could say to assure him that he wouldn't...

But I was done lying to him.

He looked at me, seeing entirely too much as usual. His throat bobbed in a telltale swallow that made my heart ache.

I should tell him how much I wanted that future, that happily ever after—for myself, yes, but also for *us*. But I couldn't find it in me to offer him false hope, not with so little time left before this final reckoning. Not when he already knew my heart.

And there was a part of me that felt like I might somehow doom us if I let myself acknowledge that future. That, just maybe, if there was something left unsaid, then tomorrow would still come.

So all I did was twine my fingers through his, squeezing far too tightly until it was time to depart. Even then, the feeling of his hand holding mine felt branded on to my palm as surely as my scar.

CHAPTER 43
ESTELLE

I left Adrian by the enormous castle doors of Soleara, my own blood shining next to his and the two pinpricks of our children's. It dripped ominously down the gleaming writing that would spell its entrance closed, casting away even the memory of our kingdom until our bloodline's return—an ancient bit of magic only a ruler of Soleara could wield. As much as I hated using blood magic, it was the only way to ensure the safety of our people in the mountains high above, their existence hidden away as more and more territories fell to the False King's insurmountable advance across this land.

I tried not to feel the ever-present guilt that I was abandoning my people along with this realm. But the war had escalated to the point that I knew remaining here would put our kingdom in even more danger as the False King searched for my daughter—for all of us. Just as I knew that fleeing was our only hope, trusting the sprite's words that to stay would mean our doom.

But to actually put it into practice still rankled.

"I'll just be a minute," I promised, kissing Tobias's and Eva's sleepy faces on both chubby cheeks. They wore their traveling cloaks as they waited for us by Quinn next to the mirror. Eva's eyes drooped closed as she leaned into her best friend who was already fast asleep on the divan beside her, Tobias yawning widely as he determinedly kept guard beside them.

My eyes locked with Amirah's, noting the crease in her brow that betrayed her apprehension. "I'll be right back. There's something I need to do."

"Strange how history repeats itself."

The sprite's words seemed to echo through me, as they had before. She had been waiting for me, the circle of trees seeming to appear the second I stepped into the forest in a place I knew for sure hadn't existed before. Her wings fluttered wildly as those black eyes drank me in.

"More death. More war." Her head cocked at an unnatural angle. "A shame even fae haven't learned from their pasts."

I hated that I was leaving, even if we would be free of that war. There was an intrinsic part of me that balked at the idea of running away, of hiding from a threat. But if it meant our children's futures, the future of this realm...

"I wish we had."

Perhaps the next generation would finally learn from our mistakes. But that wasn't why I was here.

"Plenty will pay the ultimate price for the failures of a few."

"Thank you," I whispered, even that too loud in the muted forest. "For saving us."

Those unblinking eyes seemed to widen, her head tilting to the other side. "It was *them* that was promised. Your young ones, *their* future. The future queen and the king who will save her. Not..."

When I closed my eyes, it was Adrian's face that greeted me. The quirk of his smile, the dimple that accompanied it, the love in his gaze. My legs gave out from under me, and I suddenly found my fingers curling into the mossy knoll. I couldn't stop the tears welling in my eyes as I opened them with a slow, defeated exhale. "Not us. Adrian...*we* aren't going to survive this."

It wasn't a question. The sprite landed in front of me atop a giant white mushroom. Her large black eyes filled with something that almost looked like regret, her wings drooping forward as if weighed down by something heavy.

"But my children...they'll live?"

"You will not return to this realm. But if you do not hide your young ones—take them away until they fully come into their power—it is the entire realm that will suffer your fate. Because the False One will win."

Fate.

The word seemed to echo, reverberating out into the mist shrouding the trees before fully fading away.

"Can you help them? If I'm not going to be..." I choked, the words dying in my throat. "If they need someone after I'm gone..."

My gaze fell to my hands, my knuckles white where they curled into themselves. To the ring Adrian had given me long ago, its shadowy gray diamond shimmering in a familiar way as if to hint at what it truly contained. My plan to leave it here with her had been a contingency. Now the need to do so felt horribly prophetic.

Pulling it off my finger, I held it out to the sprite. "When my daughter returns...I can't bring this with me, or I risk its magic being tracked. I was going to leave it in the castle but..." A tear ran down my cheek. "Give her this when the time is right. An escape, should she need it. Tell her to remember that 'the only way out is through'." My voice trembled as I added, "Please."

The sprite's eyes narrowed at the ring in recognition. Then she nodded. My hand shook as I placed it at her feet.

"Be safe," I whispered as I turned away, rushing back to my children. To my *anima* whose days were numbered right along with mine.

Our time together hadn't been enough. Though if we had been granted an eternity, I doubt it would have been sufficient either. But to leave our children behind with the weight of the world on their shoulders...

My tears fell silently down my cheeks as I ran back toward the castle, pausing by the tree line to take in the home I would likely never see again. By the time I reached its gates, there was nothing left but their dried tracks on my skin.

CHAPTER 44
EVA

The looming battle felt like the air a heartbeat before a lightning strike. Our horses galloped as quickly as they could through the snowy trail, their ears pricked with anticipation as if they, too, could sense what was coming. Even the snowfall seemed to pause mid-flight, thick, pillowy flakes hovering around us as if forever suspended.

There was a palpable energy in the air as we stopped one last time to feed and water the horses and ourselves. I shoveled down a few handfuls of food I barely registered, even as I ate it, listening to the clink and clatter of metal as soldiers adjusted their armor—strategically placed metal plates, their matte black matching their leathers. Bash had helped me with my own battle gear this morning, the new adornments so magically light and perfectly conformed to my chest and back that I barely noticed the difference in wear. Or perhaps that was because I could hardly focus with what came next.

Our next stop would be the mountain. The only question was who would get there first.

The forest was too still. Too quiet as I returned to Nisa, offering her the apple that I had been unable to stomach. She snorted softly, nuzzling against me in comfort, and I rubbed a gloved hand against her mane. As I swung my leg over her, my hood fell back. A few snowflakes landed on my braid; its pleats so intricate, they felt like armor.

I felt more than heard Bash approach, Smoke's steps muffled by the sounds of our armies and the fallen snow. When he came up next to me, our thighs almost touching with how close our horses stood, his gaze had already filled with swirling shadow.

"I don't like this."

I knew what he meant. Every part of me was coiled with tension, my instincts screaming that something was wrong.

"A little late to turn back now," I half-heartedly quipped.

Bash's attempt at a smile barely managed to curve his lips upward. "I sent a few of my rangers ahead to report back. While I expect we'll have to defend the mountain against Aviel's forces, especially depending on how long it takes to locate the Seeing Mirror and for you to go through the Choosing, I can't help but wish we had a way to track him. Especially when the same likely isn't true for us."

I shuddered in a way that had nothing to do with the cold, the memory of Aviel breaking into my mind all too fresh.

A ripple of worry snaked down our bond. Then Bash pulled me off my mount and into his lap atop Smoke's back, so I sat between his armored thighs. Nisa nickered softly, almost as if she was chiding us. Bash's hands cupped my cheeks, and I couldn't stop myself from leaning into his warmth. Savoring this last moment of contact before what was to come.

He brushed a wind-loosened strand of my hair behind my ear, his knuckles trailing down the side of my neck. "Tell me something true. Something real, hellion."

I burrowed my face under his jaw, closing my eyes as I breathed in his scent—that musk of impending rain I knew better than my own. Wishing we already knew the outcome of today while simultaneously hoping the looming battle never came.

"I love you, Bash. No matter how this ends."

That constant, steady love seeped from his soul to mine, warming me to the core.

"I think more than one person knows that, hellion."

"Then you should have been more specific." I smiled, the feeling of it almost strange as I leaned in, brushing a kiss against his lips. As I started to pull away, his fingers threaded through my hair to keep me there for an extra, selfish second.

It took me a second to remember how to breathe by the time he let me go. "Try not to die, freckles."

Bash's eyes narrowed, and a protective sort of helplessness drifted across our bond. "Right back at you."

The crunching sounds of hoofs on the frozen ground came closer, but I didn't open my eyes as our friends surrounded us. Just let myself stay in the comfort of Bash's arms for one moment longer.

"Eliav's forces are nearly at Morehaven," Yael said, and I resignedly opened one eye. She held a piece of parchment, looking startled that the missive had been delivered to her. "He'll reach them right before we begin our own attack."

Marin rode next to her, her mount keeping a healthy distance from where Arion had thrown back his head, shaking the snow from his dusky mane. Tobias and Quinn rode side by side behind them. My brother looked tense; his face wan as his eyes darted from us to the dark clouds overhead. Then Quinn said something in a low voice that brought his attention to her, that hint of fear melting into something more controlled. I shot her a grateful look.

"About time," Rivan grunted. "A battle on two fronts."

"Don't sound too excited," Marin said impishly.

Rivan's grin was vicious. "Oh, believe me, I am. I'm looking forward to finally finishing the war that was never won."

I shrugged. "Or die trying."

"Please save the inspiring speeches for later, Your Majesty," Quinn quipped, her voice droll.

My lips curved up into a smirk, and I saw Bash's eyes fix on the dimple that appeared there, looking for all the world like he was memorizing it one last time.

I shifted back toward Nisa, but his arms held me in place.

"This isn't the end, hellion," he said in a low murmur, his lips brushing against the shell of my ear. "Not by a long shot."

His hand turned my face back to him, then his mouth met mine, devouring me. I was breathless by the time he returned me to Nisa's back as easily as he had taken me from her. He brushed the snow from my leathers before wrapping my cloak more firmly around me. With a grateful smile, I pulled up my hood, tucking my braid inside to keep it dry.

Reaching down to give Nisa a comforting pat, I rubbed my gloved hand up and down the side of her neck as we started forward.

"It won't be long now, girl."

We broke through the tree line only for my heart to slam into my stomach as two rangers I recognized rode at breakneck speed back toward us. Bash's shadows immediately raced before us, shielding us from view as we retreated into the safety of the forest, while simultaneously warning the expanse of soldiers behind us to do the same in a silent signal.

Something solidified in my stomach as they came to a stop in front of me. "The False King..." The hair rose on the back of my neck as I realized I already knew what they were going to say. "His forces are just ahead. They're attempting to breach Adronix's gates."

Rivan swore loudly, though Yael's string of curses was far more colorful. Pari swung her mount around from where she had been riding beside me, immediately rushing to tell the others what lay ahead.

Bash's silence seemed to feed into mine as I dragged my eyes to his, my own fear reflecting in their whirling depths. Adrenaline raced through me, but I forced my panic down even as its accompanying despair almost overwhelmed me.

"We won't be able to stay undetected for long," Marin said, her tone unusually grim. "They'll no doubt have scouts watching for our arrival."

Slowly, I lowered my hand from where it had unconsciously clasped around my throat. "He hasn't beaten us to the Seeing Mirror yet. Which means we still have a chance."

My brother nodded, his face pale. "Then we take this time to make a plan."

Bash's gaze turned to his rangers. "Can we fight our way through in time to make it into the mountain first?"

One licked her lips nervously. "Not with their numbers. You should see for yourself."

Bash's shadows wrapped around the seven of us before I could ask what she meant, motioning for us to follow. We halted just before the crest of the ridge, the dissonant symphony of clanking metal and whinnying horses that had been hidden by our approach preceding the size of the force ahead. I silently slipped from Nisa's back, following Bash's footsteps through the snow as his shadows hid our growing horror.

Aviel had indeed beaten us here, though just barely from the look of it. But his army stretched too far and was too vast for us to have any hope of winning this. They spread across the snow-covered plain below us, reaching all the way to the bottom of a mountain so great its peak was shrouded by the ominous storm clouds that surrounded it. Adronix was an ancient, malevolent giant, its slopes stretching endlessly upward in jagged lines, its black rock jutting through the snow like spears. A blast of wind howled through the trees, blowing an icy gust of snow directly at me as if in welcome.

A colossal iron gate was built into its base, standing sentinel as blasts of fire melted the snow encasing it. The massive chains attached to each side of the doorway were pulled taut, like the mountain itself was resisting the intrusion.

Impending death hovered in the air like a specter seeking its next victim. I could feel it waiting in the eves—its darkness more eternal than anything I could produce.

There was a buzzing in my ears as I numbly looked around me. Yael, Rivan, and Bash exchanged a glance, some silent communication passing between them born of fighting side by side for so long. Marin simply palmed her dual blades as if she was picturing the battle ahead. Quinn's hand trembled against the hilt of her sword. Before I could reach for her, my brother beat me to it, his gaze fierce as her eyes shot to his.

You cannot have them, I silently swore. *Any of them.*

Bash's hand in mind tugged me back from my thoughts, and away from the army between us and the mountain, even as that vow rang in my head. As soon as we reached the horses, he lifted me onto Nisa's back, his gaze steely.

"How?" Rivan asked hoarsely.

As if in answer, a flash of parchment appeared in front of Yael. She snagged it from the air before it could flutter to the ground. A breeze whirred around her as she read aloud, "Morehaven is abandoned. We will ride north as quickly as we can."

The parchment crumbled to ash in a flicker of shadow.

A muscle feathered in Bash's jaw. "A trick. They must have left only enough to fool our scouts if they got too close. He knew we would split our forces and wouldn't risk being pincered in between two armies. And without Queen Sariyah's people..."

We're outnumbered. He didn't have to say it for me to realize how hopelessly we were outmatched.

I swore under my breath, feeling Bash's mix of rage, fear, and heady determination across our bond. We couldn't wait for Eliav's forces to arrive. And they wouldn't get here in time anyway. Not to stop Aviel.

"If anyone has a brilliant plan, now's the time," Yael muttered under her breath.

Bash's eyes shot to mine, the warning in them clear. *Don't even think about it.*

But I wasn't ready to give up yet. Without looking away, I pulled up my glove enough to expose my palm, then wrote one word.

Worrywart.

Bash shot me an exasperated look, though a hint of airy amusement floated across our bond.

A whirl of white lifted from the snowy ground, blowing clear over the heads of the army ahead. It flew up and over Adronix until it disappeared into the cloudy peak where I could sense the Seeing Mirror, its call like a siren coaxing me to my death.

"We don't need to win the battle," I said slowly, chewing on my bottom lip. "Just the war. Which means *we* need to get inside that mountain."

A horn sounded that seemed to echo across the clearing, another adding to it. And I knew that our limited time was up. That we had been spotted.

"There's the small issue of the False King's army in the way," Rivan said offhandedly, gesturing with his sword at the mass of soldiers in front of us now raising their weapons. A wall of them formed against the mountain, guarding its entrance from our approach, their efforts to open the gates renewed. But a group of warriors split off from the throng, running toward the ledge with their swords raised.

"Then we'll have to find a way through."

I lifted Nightshade into the air, my darkness winding around the blade as I stared down the oncoming death.

CHAPTER 45

BASH

The sky had darkened, the very air crackling with electricity. The hair on the back of my neck stood up as lightning flashed across the sky, illuminating Adronix's sharp peak high above us. Snow blanketed the battlefield before us, huge white flurries momentarily shielding the opposing army. The imposing mountain loomed behind them, its icy white glowing strangely in the reflection of the yellowing sky.

"STAY IN THE TREES," I bellowed, knowing my rangers would belay my orders. "Let them come to us."

With the tree cover, we at least had a chance against their numbers. Especially as their forces split between those coming after us and those staying to guard our path to the mountain.

A soldier came at me, sword raised. I didn't bother using my shadows, nudging Smoke forward to cut him down where he stood in one swift blow. The one behind him hesitated before lifting his blade. It cost him as I flung my dagger, blood spurting from his neck as he fell to his knees. My shadows retrieved it before he hit the forest floor, my sword already plunging into another.

I didn't care about their lives. I only cared that they were on the wrong side of this fight—the side that wanted everyone I loved dead, and my *anima* enslaved to their king.

"We need to find a way in," Eva yelled. "When he gets inside...we're running out of time."

Her sword clashed against her opponent, easily dispatching him even as her darkness wrapped around the throat of another. Utterly, almost effortlessly deadly. An entirely inappropriate reaction surged through me, and Eva's mouth twitched as she caught my eye, the heat of my desire clearly having not gone unnoticed.

I winked, then raised my sword, blocking an oncoming blow just as my shadows rushed past me, eviscerating the soldier about to kill one of my rangers. She spun around, giving me a hasty two-fingered salute in thanks, before a branch from the tree above her pierced the heart of her next opponent.

Eva's darkness reached for a soldier behind me. My blade beat her to it.

"Save your magic for *him*," I ordered.

Eva nodded, her darkness receding until only a thin strand of it latticed around her sword.

"We need a distraction," Yael yelled. "Something that won't drain either of you before we get inside."

Tobias leapt from his horse, landing protectively in front of Quinn. A blow meant for her glanced off his sword as he swept it low. I saw the dagger in his other hand before his opponent did, just as he plunged it into their chest. Quinn's eyes narrowed at him, then she threw her own dagger over his shoulder. Tobias turned around as the soldier behind him slumped off his mount, falling to the ground as the horse cantered away.

His surprised expression turned into a devilish smile. From the look in her eyes, Quinn's flush wasn't entirely due to the exertion.

"We should all go," Tobias gritted out as he retrieved her blade, hastily wiping the blood from it on the snow in a slashing red line. "We don't know how many we'll have to face inside. And Bash and I need to make it to the Seeing Mirror with Eva before that bastard beats us there."

"Oy!"

I spun around in my saddle to see Pari, Akeno, and Thorin following quickly behind, their swords raised.

"You lot just figure out how you're going to get past them," Pari shouted. "We'll provide the distraction."

Yael released arrow after arrow, buying us a brief respite without my even having to ask. Bodies fell from the ridge before they could even breach the tree line as her magic sent the bloodied arrows straight back to her quiver.

"Once we're inside, pull back," I ordered. Pari looked ready to argue, but Eva nodded in agreement. "There's too many of them to win this battle outright."

It was a risk to send them running with Aviel's army at their heels, but better than the alternative. And I was willing to bet that the majority of his forces would continue to guard the mountain, and their leader within, rather than follow immediately.

"And if you don't succeed?"

I swallowed, wishing I could refute that outcome. "Regroup with the Esterran forces. They're headed this way, and if you hurry, you should be able to meet them in Soleara. With a united front, and the castle's defenses, you might stand a chance."

My gaze darted to Eva. "Between the two of us, we can blanket this place in enough shadow and darkness to keep us covered. But if that's the only entrance..." I gestured with my sword at the main gate where the two massive steel doors were currently being wedged open, an entire army in our way, "...then we need a better way through than just brute force."

"Cover me," Rivan demanded, and Marin immediately rode in between him and the oncoming forces. Yael drew back her bow, an arrow finding its target. Another arrow was locked in her quiver faster than I could process.

Rivan dropped from Arion's back to come to his knees in the snow, digging his bare hands into the frozen soil as his eyelids fluttered closed. Then his eyes shot open, gleaming with greenish light.

"There's a tunnel." Rivan pointed to the right. "Small. Likely used for drainage. About a hundred yards that way, built into the stone. We can take it to the side of the mountain, but it stops there. I'll use my power to redirect it to those doors."

Marin put a hand on Yael's shoulder. "I'm staying here. Someone needs to help Pari rally our forces without you lot in charge." She straightened. "And I'm Imyr's queen."

Yael turned to her, leaning across Indra's back to catch Marin's lips in a quick, chaste kiss that promised more. Her eyes stayed on my sister, even as she reached for another arrow—striking true despite her gaze never straying. "Stay alive, Your Highness."

"You too," Marin replied, raising both her blades threateningly. "That goes for all of you."

I bowed my head solemnly.

My sister reached into her pocket, retrieving our mother's stone. "But if Aviel's at the mountain…"

"I'll take it," Tobias said. "I'm looking forward to a rematch with that bastard, especially if he can't steal my magic this round." Light crackled from his fingertips as Marin tossed the stone into his waiting hand.

Rivan swore, and I realized his power still spread through the earth. "They opened the doors."

He didn't need to say we needed to hurry, not when we all already knew. Rivan leapt onto Arion's back, galloping through the trees without a backward glance.

My gaze automatically found Eva's, our eyes meeting for only a moment before she kicked Nisa into a gallop, tearing after Rivan. The snow streaming through the trees nearly blinded me as I followed.

You can't have her, I swore to the False King that waited for her and the so-called fate that I refused to bow to. *She's mine, and I'm hers, and we deserve the happily ever after she thinks is the price of winning this.*

I idly wondered if willing it into being would somehow make it true.

We reached the edge of the stone tunnel, the entirety of it hidden beneath the snow, a swath of bodies in our wake. My shadows had covered us as we ran from the battle, streaking behind us to silence any soldiers so foolish as to try and stop us.

Smoke whinnied his dissent as I dismounted. I gave him a sharp pat on the rump, and a whispered, "Find Marin", before he galloped back to the forest, the others' horses behind him. We were far enough from the battle not to raise attention, especially not under the cover of my magic, but we couldn't risk anyone finding this tunnel and raising the alarm.

My shadows flew from my grasp as I sidled closer to Eva, spinning in agitated circles around her. A blast of air cleared the snow in a split second, leaving only a frozen bramble of thorns and leaves atop a metal grate. I nodded at Yael in thanks. Rivan's magic made short work of it, the metal curling in on itself, peeling away the grate like he was brushing away a curtain.

He looked up just as the first explosion went off.

I spun around, watching as a giant orb of spinning magic rose above Pari. Air rushed from her palm, somehow containing Akeno's fire as she launched it across the battlefield, one after another sailing through the air. Where they hit, they burst apart, exploding outward in a blast of fiery gas and scarlet-tinged snow. Thorin stood in front of them, entirely in his element as he fended off those foolish enough to try to stop them by freezing them solid.

Eva's mouth had dropped open. Tobias only smirked.

"That's one way to do it," Rivan said admiringly before lowering himself into the tunnel.

I took Eva's hand as we followed. Tobias nimbly leapt down behind us, turning to catch Quinn as she slipped on the iced-over ground, before quickly letting her go. Yael slid down the small slope, using her power to steady herself.

The tunnel was indeed a drain, though it must have been built centuries ago. My shadows kept me from slipping on the frozen muck within as I bent over to keep from hitting my head on the icicle-covered ceiling. Eva ducked down beside me; the tunnel so small that she had to crouch. There was a tremor of fear across our bond, and I focused on the steady count of Eva's breathing.

It was the dark, I realized as fury nearly consumed me. *The confined space. The cold.*

My hand found Eva's instinctually before gritting out, "Tobias?"

A second later, three bobbing balls of light appeared, just enough to illuminate the tunnel in front of us. Tobias stared at the largest one sitting in his outstretched palm. I wondered if I just imagined how pale he had gone until I saw Quinn reach over to squeeze his free hand.

"I'll go first," Rivan said as though one of us might try to push past him in the narrow space.

Tobias gave Rivan a slight nod in a voiceless *'go on'* as one of the orbs floated in front of him.

We rushed forward as quickly as we could on the frozen ground, our hands bracing against the icy sides of the tunnels. Not daring to slow our pace when Aviel was already inside and hunting for the mirror. Maybe he had already thwarted the Choosing with my *anima*'s blood and magic. Perhaps we were racing toward our own destruction.

What if all of this was for nothing?

Rivan came to an abrupt halt. I caught Eva around the waist as she skidded forward on a patch of ice. The tunnel narrowed in front of us where ancient copper piping dripped down into it.

Rivan grinned, pressing his hands against the solid stone wall. "Now for the fun part."

The ground split in front of him, and I frowned, knowing how much effort it must be taking for this level of precision. It was necessary, yes, but the drain on his magic so early in the battle...

His eyes met mine as if he could sense the worry behind them. "It's not far."

A series of explosions went off, sounding distant from underground.

Yael smirked. "And I take it they're too distracted up there to notice us bursting from the ground."

"They'd better be," Rivan muttered. "The magic is different inside the castle walls. This leads right up to it...but not in. So we'd better get the doors to the mountain shut fast, or we'll have a whole army to contend with."

Quinn's brow furrowed. "And once they're shut?"

Rivan and I exchanged a look.

"We'll assess when we get there…" Rivan said slowly.

"But we need to find a way to keep that door closed," I finished.

"If it's metal, Rivan can warp it to the stone," Yael murmured. "If it's pure iron…"

Then one of us would likely need to stay behind to hold the door as long as they could, while the others sought out Aviel.

"It all depends on what we find inside," I said firmly, unwilling to entertain the consequences of the alternative just yet, even if I was already planning for either outcome. "Maybe we can just block the right passageway off. Find a way to delay them long enough to get to the Seeing Mirror."

"You say this like we have any idea where the mirror is," Yael said, crossing her arms over her chest.

Eva cleared her throat, her voice hoarse as she said, "The top of the mountain."

Five sets of eyes all snapped to her in surprise.

She audibly cleared her throat. "You can't all feel that?"

"There's a power emanating from the mountain," I said carefully. "But no, hellion. Nothing that specific."

I could feel her buzz of apprehension, though it lacked any real surprise.

She grimaced. "Lucky you then. My headache gets worse the closer we get."

Quinn reached out a hand, already alight with her magic. She set two fingers on Eva's temples, who let out a small sigh of relief.

Then Eva's lips tightened. "Hopefully he doesn't know the mirror's location either."

I hated the way she once again skirted around saying Aviel's name— like to do so would give him power.

"Or already through it," Tobias grumbled.

That fear of losing her was getting worse by the second, but I had given my fears enough of myself. They couldn't have her too.

I stepped forward, taking Eva's face between my palms. "We can still stop him. We *will*—"

She surged forward, kissing me so deeply it caught me by surprise—kissing me like it might be the last time—before breaking away far too soon.

Rivan cleared his throat as a cloud of dust appeared from the newly formed hole in front of him. "Shall we?"

He ducked into the self-made tunnel, and I saw the rock form into handholds in his wake. I followed closely behind, lacing my fingers through Eva's as I led her onward. My shadows moved from my forearm to hers. If we were together, somehow, it felt like everything would be okay. I was determined to keep her close to me for as long as I could, like holding her hand could possibly stop the worst from happening. That if I could only keep her from being taken from me this time, we could win this.

The makeshift tunnel narrowed. I ducked my head against the falling silt, each far off explosion and the thunderous stampede of booted feet now above us shaking it loose. The smell of earth and metal hung in the air as the tunnel tilted sharply upward, our destination evidently approaching. Reluctantly, I let go of Eva's hand to find Rivan's handholds, copying his path as we climbed higher.

Rivan stopped abruptly, his hand splayed onto the frozen soil above him.

"We should be shielded by the left side of the door." His voice was barely discernable over the shouts of the battle above. "Not a lot of space between it and the mountain, but we'll fit."

I clasped a hand on his calf. "Then we just have to get around a door."

Rivan snorted. "How hard can it be?"

I reached out with my shadows. "There's enough of them inside that even if we get those doors closed, we'll have to fight."

"How many?"

I smirked up at him. "Not enough to stop us."

Rivan looked down at me, violet eyes gleaming in the reflection of Tobias's light, his answering smile just as deadly. His tone was almost polite as he asked, "Ready?"

"Do you even have to ask?"

Wrapping my shadows around us, I tensed as Rivan pushed the last of the tunnel to the side. A gust of Yael's magic kept a pile of snow from falling on top of us, pushing it back as Rivan pulled himself over the edge.

The storm had grown markedly worse during our brief stint underground, the temperature dropping drastically as we emerged. I drew my sword as soon as I was able, but no one saw us behind the enormous iron door swung wide, the only thing between us and the massive force in front of it.

Rivan swore under his breath as he caught my gaze. Because of course it was iron.

I reached down, silently pulling Eva over the lip of the hole. Snowflakes clung to the twists of her braid, the length of her lashes. I reached up to brush a few from her cheeks, feeling them melt under my thumb. Tobias climbed up next, Quinn behind him as they squeezed further behind the door and the snowy mountainside. Yael nimbly sprang upward, her boots sinking into the packed snow beside me.

I reached out with my shadows, closing my eyes as they dispersed around the door into the mountain itself, rustling over booted feet. It wouldn't be an easy fight—especially when the more magic I used now meant the less I had to fight Aviel. But if we didn't get the doors closed, and the False King's entire army came after us…

Leaning over, I spoke directly into Yael's ear. "Do you think you can get these shut if I create enough of a shield to hold them off until you do?"

She tilted her head down in the smallest of nods, then reached for the bow resting on her shoulder. An arrow, I knew, could be notched and ready to fire before I had a chance to blink.

I signaled over my shoulder, knowing Rivan would take up the rear without looking back to check. We had trained and fought together for too long not to sense what the other would do.

Raising my hand, I jerked my fingers forward in a silent *Go, go, go.*

My shadows wrapped around us as we came around the corner, even though I knew they couldn't shield us entirely in plain sight. But the army in front of us was too distracted by the battle raging in the forest before them to notice the creeping shadow against the dark door behind them. Their forces were still busy raising magical shields against the continued barrage of earth-shaking explosions. Grimly, I wondered how long Pari and Akeno could keep that up before utterly burning themselves out.

We skidded into the threshold. A shout of alarm rang out from inside the mountain just as I ordered, "*Now!*"

Yael's hands were already up, spread wide apart as she tried to bring them together. Her magic whipped the falling snow into a cyclone as it pushed against the open doors. We might not be able to manipulate the iron door itself, but we could close it with enough force.

Soldiers rushed toward us, their swords raised, moving in from both sides of the entrance.

I quickly erected a wall of solidifying shadows, forcing the soldiers outside back. Magics collided against mine, swords clashing behind me as my friends fought their counterparts.

"*Yael.*"

She gritted her teeth, snow swirling from the ground and the sky as her power barreled against the doors. They barely inched forward. Despite the warning in my head to save my power for the final fight against Aviel, we didn't have *time*.

Shadows rippled down my arms, gathering from the corners of the room as they entwined with the current of air attempting to force those doors closed. With a groan of metal, our combined forces slammed them shut with an echoing crash, immediately dampening the magic outside it. My shadows wrapped around the two enormous door handles, chaining them together as the army outside turned its full attention on getting back in.

A myriad of magic bore down upon me, attempting to open what had been closed. Yael gasped in pain.

"I've got this," I grunted, sparing a glance at the battle behind me in a plaintive gesture that she was needed there. While I knew she could handle herself, I could hear Eva's pants of effort as her blade cut through the air, clearly taking my order to conserve her magic seriously.

Dimly, I realized our bond felt muted somehow, like the magic of this mountain was running interference. A chill ran down my spine, even as I forced my focus back to the task at hand.

Yael's eyes narrowed for a fraction of a second. Then her arrows flew. I didn't have to look behind me to know each struck true before she rushed forward, her sword raised.

My hands shook from the effort of keeping the door closed, and I clenched my jaw, my teeth grinding against the strain, barely able to hold out against the various powers trying to break my shadows' dark embrace.

The clamber of the battle behind me grew somewhat quieter. I didn't have to look to know my friends, my family, and my *anima* were making short work of our greeting party.

I grimaced as a renewed onslaught of magic turned my attention from that battle to the one that I had to control. My shadows seemed to shrivel against the sheer force of so many magics used against me, yanking at the door to try to muscle their way in—my power draining far too fast.

But without it...

Iron or not, I knew the door wouldn't hold for long.

CHAPTER 46

EVA

I couldn't feel Bash. Our bond felt muted the second we crossed the threshold of the mountain, as if I was still wearing that collar around my throat. The buzzing in my head had grown louder, like this cursed place had thrown a damper over everything except for the blaring call of the mirror I had no choice but to follow.

Gritting my teeth, I held up my sword as a fresh wave of Aviel's soldiers rushed from a side passage. My darkness leaked from my hands as I struggled to keep it in check. To reserve that death blow, or something close to it, for the one who deserved it.

Yet there was something within that well of power, something volatile. A vicious undertow deep beneath that called for pain, for vengeance by any means necessary. One I might get swept away in if I wasn't careful.

One soldier saw my expression and took a step back.

Smart. But not enough to save him.

"Surrender now," another demanded, flame bursting from his fingertips in fiery whips. "Or we'll be forced to kill you all before we bring *her* to our king."

I didn't bother replying, just inclined my head in mock invitation.

They could certainly *try*.

Before he could take another step toward me, Yael's power shot forward, the fire extinguished in the same vacuum that tore the breath from their throats. Stones moved up from the ground in jagged bursts, impaling more soldiers not quick enough to get away. Tobias and Quinn moved in tandem to my right, Duskbane glowing in the dim light.

I glanced behind me, where Bash still held those towering iron doors closed. His arms were shaking from the strain of his magic, his shadows firmly wound around the long handles of the doorway like a rope made of dark iron. I didn't need to feel him across our bond to know that wielding that much power was draining him. Sweat formed on his brow as more and more shadows whipped from him, joining their brethren.

We don't have time for this.

My darkness shot forward as if it couldn't be contained any longer, forming into spears that impaled the remaining soldiers, skewering them where they stood. I lifted my sword, waiting for more to appear...but there were only bodies left in front of me.

"Our forces need to retreat now that we're in," I whispered, thinking of the mix of Solearan and Imyrian forces fighting for their lives where we had left them in the forest. "To regroup with the Esterrans as planned. Especially with the storm."

Rivan grinned, admirably nonplussed. "Retreat? Hell, we just got here."

I glared at him. *"Rivan."*

Those violet eyes danced, a warrior obviously in his element despite the danger. Or, more likely, because of it. "Way ahead of you. I sent a missive the second that door closed. But I'll send another just in case."

He pulled a piece of paper from an inner pocket, writing a quick note that read, *Thanks for the distraction. Let me know when you're far enough away.* It disappeared with a flare of his magic.

Bash swayed on his feet, still facing the iron door. Despite the cold, his pale face shone with sweat, his jaw tightly set from the effort.

"Bash."

"I can't let go of this," Bash gritted out, his teeth chattering. "It's not going to hold without me."

And then we would have the entirety of Aviel's army to contend with.

"You can't hold the door forever," Yael exclaimed.

"Leave that to me," Rivan said grimly, then turned to me. "You do what you need to do, my queen."

"*No*," I insisted, my voice sharpening. "I'm not leaving either of you behind."

Every fiber of my being protested at the thought of leaving them. Leaving *him*.

"Bold of you to assume you have any choice in the matter," Rivan said with forced flippancy. "Not when you know this is what needs to be done. We're running out of time."

Bash bared his teeth, snarling against whatever was trying to force its way in from the other side of the door.

Yael stepped forward. "I can help—"

"We don't have *time* for this," Rivan growled. "And unless any of you have a previously undisclosed affinity with rock and stone, then I'm the best person for the job. We need as many people as we can to get Eva to that mirror. You all need to hurry up and stop the False King or all of this is for *nothing*."

"You idiots will burn yourselves out trying to hold off an entire army by yourself," Yael snapped, stepping toward him. "There has to be a better way."

"We can stop them." Bash's voice shook. Something stung on my palm, and I realized my fingernails had drawn blood. "But you'll need all the help you can get to stop Aviel." Bash's eyes met mine. His fear seemed to permeate the air between us, fighting through the static of our bond—not fear for himself, but for me.

"You should go with her," Yael said to Bash. "You're the one who can go through that mirror with her."

Bash shook his head, just slightly, like even that effort cost him. "If I let go of this now, they'll open this door, and I'm not going to let that happen. But if he's already through the mirror..." Bash swallowed, shadows violently swirling in his irises as his eyes met mine. "Just keep fighting until I get there."

"I won't let her face him alone," Tobias promised, light flickering at his fingertips. His shoulders set as he subtly inched closer to me. "You're not the only ones with a score to settle. And I know all of that bastard's tricks."

Rivan caught my gaze, his voice solemn as he vowed, "I'll make sure Bash returns to you."

Bash winced, his eyes closing as the doorway shuddered. His shadows wrapped around his arms as if to steady him as he gasped, "*Rivan.*"

"On it." Rivan grimaced as he pressed his hands against the stone floor. A layer of rock began to climb upon itself, bracing the iron door as the stone closed in around it.

"You can do this, Eva. I trust you. But you have to go." Bash's eyes were wholly black as his shadows streamed from his hands against the endless onslaught that I knew must be close to breaking him. "*Now.*"

The edge of panic lacing his tone lodged a knot of fear in my throat, which only grew as I stepped away from him. Like my heart was begging me not to leave him, even as something above us urged me forward. Like the mountain itself was whispering, *Run, run, run.*

"Promise me..." I swallowed roughly as I looked at him for a long second, my eyes searching his. "Promise me that you'll come back to me."

"I promise," he said, his voice thick. "I'll be there as soon as I can."

I started to turn, but his voice stopped me in my tracks.

"Eva?" He sucked in a deep, gasping breath. "This isn't the end. I love you."

Perhaps he also remembered how heartbroken I was that I didn't get the chance to say those three words back to my mother before it was too late. All I could think was that if this was the last time, I wouldn't miss my chance.

My voice broke slightly as I said, "I love you too."

An expression of despairing resignation flickered in his eyes, a few tendrils of shadows reaching back toward me like they could keep me at his side. As I turned away, I tried to shake off the uneasy feeling that those might be the last words we would ever say to each other, even though he had promised to come back to me.

He hadn't asked me to promise the same. Maybe we both knew it would have been a lie.

CHAPTER 47
BASH

Eva disappeared down the long stone tunnel, Yael, Tobias, and Quinn at her heels. I hated that I couldn't fully feel her across our bond with the mountain's interference.

Would I even know if she was in trouble? If she...

I shoved that thought away. One impossible thing at a time. And I wasn't about to lose faith in her—not now, not ever.

"I'm not going to be able to hold that army off much longer, even with your help."

The onslaught of magic bearing down on my own was rapidly becoming too much to bear.

"You don't have to," Rivan said calmly. "It shouldn't be too much longer for them to be far enough away. To retreat before it's too late."

My head was too bleary to understand what he was saying. "What are you..."

"Just keep those doors closed as long as you can," Rivan said calmly. "When I'm sure our people are safe, I'll take care of everything."

It was getting harder and harder to do so, the iron repelling the very magic I was using to reinforce it, the onslaught of my adversaries only increasing in strength on the other side. Sweat dripped down my neck, down my back. Rivan's eyes shot to mine in alarm.

"New plan," he said, kneeling in front of me—and it was only then that I realized I had fallen to my knees. "Let them come."

I shook my head stubbornly from side to side.

"Bash—"

"Not yet," I rasped. "I can hold them."

"It won't be long now," Rivan said sternly. "We can hold them off the old-fashioned way until then." He raised his sword with one hand, pulling me to my feet with the other as I begrudgingly nodded.

Releasing the breath I had been holding, I let my magic drop, unable to wield it a moment longer. My shadows streamed back from the door, hovering around me. Gathering my strength, I focused on my breathing, counting each second just as Eva had taught me.

It felt like a mere moment before the iron doors burst open. Fire whipped through it, but that stone wall still stood, and it redirected harmlessly to the sides. The stone turned a deep red, but Rivan looked entirely unconcerned at the unceasing fiery onslaught, even as the wall split down the middle, thousands of tiny pebbles tumbling toward us. Soldiers rushed forward, forced to enter through a narrow crack in the middle of the stone. But Rivan was ready for them, cutting them down one by one, the pile of bodies building a wall in itself.

I belatedly realized that the rest of the stone wall was thickening, more and more pebbles melding together to create a veritable copy of its iron brethren. A piece of paper appeared right in front of Rivan's outstretched hand. He snatched it from the air, a pained groan slipping from his lips before he slashed his sword across his adversary's exposed throat.

"Cover me," Rivan roared.

With a blast of shadow that was far weaker than it should be, I knocked the next round of opponents back through the narrowing split in the stone. My shadows slipped from my grasp just as solid rock took its place, the rubble strewn around us, uncaring as those trying to force their way through found themselves embedded inside it, their screams suddenly silenced. The rock turned a dull red as it heated once more, but the glow was fainter this time, the wall now a monument as it spread to close any remaining gaps, its barrier not so easily broken. My eyes fixed on where a hand still reached from the center of where the opening had been, its owner now an eternal piece of the mountain itself.

Rivan dug his fingers into the stone floor. It melted around his touch like oil. His hands were raw and bleeding, but he didn't seem to notice; his face serene as he closed his eyes. The very mountain seemed to shudder as his magic took hold.

My mouth went dry. "Rivan..."

Sweat beaded on his brow, a dark trail of blood dripping from one nostril, then the other. The ground lurched beneath me, and Adronix started to shake like it was about to collapse on top of us. The shouts of the soldiers trying to get to us turned into panicked screams.

"What did you—"

Rivan's eyes flew open just as I heard the roaring from far away. *"Run."*

My eyes shot to his. "What did you do? They—"

"—won't survive. Now get down that damn passageway and help her, Bash."

I didn't move. Wisps of shadow flurried around me in a panic, barely managing to catch Rivan as he slumped forward with a groan. I knelt beside him, my arms replacing my shadows, even as his hand curled stubbornly into his homemade handhold.

"That sound you hear?" He drew in an unsteady breath, and my grip on him tightened. "That's an entire mountain's worth of snow about to bury Aviel's army alive. And it's attempting to come through those doors."

My mouth dropped. That roaring sound was now deafening, drowning out the screams from the other side. It was already far too late for them.

Rivan's hand stayed firmly on the rock, the other hand pressed to his side.

Where blood was leaking through his fingers.

"RIVAN."

My scream was lost in the cacophony, so loud it felt as if Adronix was coming down on itself. I could feel the very mountain shudder, vibrating with the rage of what Rivan had done. My shadows flew forward, pressing up against his wall. Trying my best to reinforce it against the power of nature itself as frozen death swept away the army on the other side of it, even as the avalanche of rock and ice tried to force its way in. Attempting to ensnare us in its icy grasp and take us with it too.

Rivan bared his teeth, grunting against the battle of magic against the mountain, the tide of the latter nearly pulling me under.

And then it stopped. The sudden silence rang in my ears. Rivan slumped to the ground.

"How did you…"

"Avalanche," he panted, as though that part wasn't obvious. "You move the right piece of rock and…The whole side of the mountain will be keeping that door firmly closed against whatever's left of Aviel's forces, *if* they manage to dig themselves out." He let out a short laugh. "We'd better hope our people have enough fire and water wielders to find us at the end of this."

He'd taken out the army outside the mountain in one fell swoop. It was a small miracle he hadn't managed to kill himself right along with them. I gaped at him, unable to find the words to express my astonishment.

"Now go," Rivan demanded weakly. "Go help her. There's nothing else you can do here."

"I'm not leaving you," I said even as I knew I needed to. But there was so much blood on his hands, still dribbling between his fingers. Too much blood. And with his magic this drained, I knew he didn't have it in him to heal himself.

"There's nothing else you can do here," he said grimly. "I'll be right behind you. But I'll only slow you down."

He gave me an echo of a smile. Like it might convince me he was okay, even as his blood dribbled from the corner of his mouth.

To leave him was unfathomable. But the alternative…

My *anima* needed me. And the entire realm needed her to succeed.

"Make sure they survive this," Rivan ordered.

My grip tightened on my sword like it might stop my fingers from trembling. "I will. Stay alive, or I'll kill you myself."

With one last glance behind me, I ran into the passageway my *anima* had taken, praying to any god who would listen that I wasn't too late.

And that I wasn't leaving my brother behind to bleed out in an icy tomb.

CHAPTER 48
EVA

Dread curdled in my stomach as we squeezed through the narrow tunnels, stone pressing in on all sides. The darkness felt unnatural, insidious, my own magic cowering away from it like it was an ancient monster about to swallow me alive. I could barely see a few feet in front of me despite the dim sconces that flared every few meters as we passed, each one extinguishing a moment before we reached the next. My heart seemed to stop each time we were plunged into total darkness, then raced as I prayed for the light to return.

I tried to take a breath, but my lungs wouldn't function, an aching, weighted sensation pressing in on my chest. My throat felt like something was closing around it—a phantom collar that constricted ever tighter.

Trembling, I tried in vain not to picture the dark box I had been trapped in. Tried not to feel like this place, with the walls pressing in, wasn't another coffin. That these dark tunnels weren't leading me to my doom.

I sucked in a loud, gasping breath, then another, struggling to get the knot in my chest to loosen. But I couldn't take a deep enough breath, couldn't *breathe*—

"Hey." Tobias wrapped his arm around me. "Big breath in. Count each second. Breath out. And count the same."

Tears sprung to my eyes as he repeated the words our father had said so many times. I took an unsteady breath in before exhaling to the same slow beat even as I forced my feet to keep walking. We didn't have time for this. Especially when the thought of being afraid of the dark when it was the source of my Celestial power felt both absurd and shameful.

Tobias's arm stayed securely around me, holding me upright.

"Again," he said firmly.

I followed his command, clinging onto the semblance of calm each breath brought. "I know it's not the time to—"

"You don't have to excuse yourself to me," Tobias said quietly.

"The box…" I whispered anyway, barely loud enough to be heard over the sound of our footsteps.

"The cell," he whispered back. "And that godsdamned mask. I'm not exactly the biggest fan of dark, confined spaces either. Though I have to admit, after so long in that cell, being out in the open…" His swallow was audible. "The sky feels too large."

My heart squeezed like it might break apart. We had been traveling for *how* long through the forests, making camp in open fields under the endless sky? I hadn't even realized his daily discomfort. And I had been so focused on my own fears that I hadn't thought to check in on my brother, whose trauma had obviously left a lasting mark, despite his stoicism.

I could commiserate when I whispered, "You must be so tired."

Tobias's reply was cold, his tone laced with a bitter malice I had never once heard from him. "We'll rest when he pays for it."

The light went out again, and I flinched. Tobias swore under his breath as if in realization, coming to a stop. Then his light flared from his fingertips, floating upwards like tiny stars.

Yael let out an appreciative sound. Quinn's concerned look melted into a smile.

Tobias let out a rough laugh. "Sometimes, I still forget I can."

I squeezed his hand, my heartbeat slowing slightly as we continued onward. Tobias's magic hovered closely around us, lighting the way.

∝

The crooked stone steps seemed never ending, our footsteps and panting the only sounds as we travelled upward. Quinn came up beside me as the tunnels widened slightly, her sword glinting in Tobias's light. Our eyes met as we heard the clamor of metal and hushed voices in the same instant, raising our swords in unison.

The staircase led to an arched, open hallway. We turned the corner to find a horde of Aviel's soldiers. The one in front opened his mouth to shout the alarm when one of Yael's arrows appeared through his head as if by magic, more clutching at their throats as she stole the air from their lungs. Light leapt from my brother's outstretched hand, and I flinched as I watched it wrap itself around his opponent's neck, pulling him onto Tobias's sword.

Banishing my nausea as I remembered the feeling of that same light reaching around my own throat, I raised a hand to summon my darkness. Before I could, Quinn dragged my arm back down.

"It won't help if we win this battle only to lose the war."

Letting my darkness dissipate, I nodded. Then I jumped into the fray, almost grateful for the opportunity to shove the thought of what we were heading for aside as I focused on the next right move—the deadly dance of steel against steel.

Quinn fought by my side. The way we moved together felt effortless after a lifetime of learning to cover each other's backs. We made short work of the rest of them, running past their bodies to reach a narrow flight of ancient, worn stairs carved into the stone. Each sloped in the center, a testament to the number of feet that had treaded this path before us.

Blood trickled down the black steel of my sword. I didn't bother wiping it away.

My thighs burned as we raced up the steps, the buzzing in my head growing louder. When we reached a crossroads, I didn't question how I knew the passage to the right would bring us where we needed to go.

"This way," I gasped, unable to spare the breath for an explanation I didn't have after so many steps uphill.

Not down to the prison where the False King had never been held, but up to the very top of the mountain. To where I knew the Seeing Mirror waited, likely rippling in anticipation.

I could feel it drawing me ever closer. Like the power inside this mountain was calling to me, its melody just out of reach. Its pull was no longer painful, but a beckoning now that I was heeding its call—taking me toward my destiny. I couldn't resist even if I wanted to, my urgency impeding my fear.

The rock around me now gleamed with a familiar, faint blue light. One that momentarily took me back to another night, running in the other direction in a stone stairwell. But at least I no longer felt trapped as we ran up the illuminated steps two at a time.

The tunnel was widening, and Quinn hooked her arm through mine as I stumbled on another age-worn, slanted step.

"We're close," I panted. "I can feel it."

I nearly fell when the next step wasn't there, the flat landing strange beneath my feet after so long running upward. My throat closed as we turned a corner to find two massive doors built into the stone on the opposite side of a cavernous hallway. They looked like they were made of the same silver quill embedded into my palm—its iridescence as beautiful as it was ominous.

"They'll be ready for us," Yael added grimly. "And if Aviel has already found a way into that mirror…" She cursed under her breath. "I should have stayed with Rivan, not Bash."

I shook my head, even as I reached for the faint feeling that was Bash through our bond. Alive at least, but after the way the mountain had shaken when we left them…

But I couldn't stop to think about that now.

"I'll go with her through the gate," Tobias assured her. "Eva won't be alone, even if they don't follow us here in time. I'll hold Aviel off while Eva does what she needs to do."

"And if he finished the Choosing, we'd know," Quinn said stoutly, as if reading the apprehension on my face. "Which means we can still win."

Yael's chin dipped. "We'll hold off whoever's with him." She looked to Quinn, who gave an answering nod—far too coolly with the odds currently stacked against us—before turning to Tobias and me. "You two focus on stopping Aviel from getting through that mirror or getting into it if he has already. Divide and conquer."

Quinn smiled. "That easy, huh?"

Yael's lips curved. "Let's hope so."

"Yael—" My voice cracked, and I saw her turquoise eyes soften in understanding. "If anything happens, tell Bash...Tell him that I—" I cleared my throat, shaking my head. "Never mind. I imagine he knows by now."

"He'll never forgive himself for this," Yael said, her mouth quirking in a sad sort of smile, "if you go through that mirror without him. So do me a favor and don't you dare die on my watch."

A shudder ran down my spine, but I managed a shaky grin. "Only since you asked so nicely."

As I turned to my brother, the gold of his eyes glinted in the dim light. But his focus wasn't on me. He was staring longingly at the smile fading from my best friend's lips.

I took his hand. "If I die...don't let them burn me."

To his credit, he didn't try to argue. "Only if you promise me the same."

I nodded once, holding his gaze. Then looked at my best friend, my sister in every way but biological. "Always forward."

"Never back," she breathed.

We raised our blades in unison, my trembling determination turning into pure steel.

A torrent of air rushed forward, the doorway violently slamming inwards.

The soldier-filled cavern stilled as the two sides took each other in, its vaulted ceiling soaring into darkness. Then the very mountain seemed to rumble as the silence broke.

There were too many of them, all moving toward us at once. But I could see it—the Seeing Mirror. It was smaller than I had expected. Ancient, yet untarnished, despite how long it must have lived in this cavern. The glass was embedded into the stone wall of the mountain itself, its gilded filigree frame cutting into the dark rock like golden vines. Each swirl and point glimmered in the light of the blue glints hovering around it like shards of sapphire dust. Its six points refracted with the familiar light as if they couldn't contain the magic within. The glass's rippling surface gleamed with the same silver iridescence as the doorway...the same silver as the words that found their way to my palm, like that simple heart Bash had once sent that somehow encompassed everything.

We had made it to the mirror we had come so far to find.

Only to be just barely too late.

Aviel stood right next to it, my stolen darkness flaring from his fingertips in a show of Celestial power.

"*NO.*"

Aviel turned at my cry just as his soldiers reached us. A funnel of flame barreled toward us that Yael countered with an airless void, extinguishing the flame as well as its creators. But my gaze was trapped in Aviel's. Darkness streaked from his fingertips, the air between us stagnating as his mouth curled in the slightest of smirks.

He broke our gaze first. Twisting bands of night darted forward from each of my fingers like dark vines, my knuckles locking into place as they ensnared a swath of soldiers in my way. My darkness tore them apart without a second thought. It was far too easy to appease my anger, my magic aching to reach out and destroy the one who deserved it.

But I wouldn't survive this by giving into it now.

My stolen darkness arched across the room. I raised Nightshade, its dark twin twisting around the blade. But Aviel's magic wasn't aimed at me. It speared directly at my brother, who was too focused on the fire wielder fighting Quinn to react.

I screamed. Then Yael was there faster than I could see, pushing him out of the way. The darkness slammed into her, throwing her into the air. Her arms crossed over her chest as her magic tried to keep its point from impaling her, a thin barrier of air the only thing saving her from annihilation.

She slammed into the iridescent door with a sharp crack. Then slumped to the floor, sprawled against the stone.

Tobias yelled something I could no longer understand as fury coursed through me, too vast to be contained. I ran forward, wrapping my darkness around me in an impenetrable shield. Dark spikes flew from me in bursts, running through any who tried to stop my progress. Refusing to slow down when Aviel was so close to everything he wanted.

"Eva, *wait!*"

Tobias was fighting off half a dozen soldiers, Duskbane shining with his pure, bright light. More took their place as his light flared, eviscerating those closest to him. Quinn stood beside him, her amber eyes flashing a deep, blood red—

But I couldn't wait for them.

Not with Aviel a step away from the mirror.

It rippled in invitation, sending a shiver down my spine despite everything. It was almost ironic that I was racing toward the very thing I had feared for so long, desperate this time for it to let me through.

Quinn's yell mixed with Tobias's from too far behind me. But for them —for my family both by blood and by choice—the idea of facing Aviel no longer seemed quite so frightening.

And it was time for me to face what lay before me.

Aviel's pale eyes had turned black from the darkness streaming from him. Then his hand pressed against the mirror.

The glass shuddered, and for one elongated heartbeat, hope surged in my chest that all his planning had been for naught. It shattered as he fell through.

I blindly sent a wave of power behind me, even as I realized the soldiers following me were no longer fighting back—just herding me onwards as they blocked my retreat.

You'll regret that, I thought, hoping it would prove to be true.

It occurred to me far too late that they were *letting* me through. They had likely been ordered to do so by their master, especially with my companions facing so much more resistance. That in following Aviel here, I was doing exactly what he wanted—providing him with the very magic he needed to steal should something go wrong.

My steps faltered. Then my heart leapt into my throat as I realized the edges of the Seeing Mirror were evening out, like a pond starting to freeze in winter. I watched them harden, darken, still—

The gateway was closing.

Summoning my darkness, I leapt forward just as a wave of pure, gut-wrenching fear broke through our strangled bond.

I heard Bash's roar of helpless rage.

But it was too late to stop, even if I wanted to.

I twisted to look over my shoulder as I tumbled forward in what felt like slow motion—the old terror of the last time I had fallen through a mirror into the unknown almost overwhelming. The last thing I saw was Bash, our eyes meeting across the room like mine knew exactly where to find him.

There was so much blood covering him.

He yanked his sword from what was now a corpse as he ran for me, his fear palpable in those ever-swirling eyes. I wondered if he could sense my regret, or if it had been eclipsed by pure determination.

"*EVA!*"

With his anguished cry still ringing in my ears, I fell through.

CHAPTER 49
ESTELLE

I knew this moment had been coming, but it was somehow worse now that it was here.

My eyes locked with my *anima's*, his horror mingling with my own as I heard the voices outside our home. They were surrounding it, shouting orders to *"smoke them out"* even as I started to smell the stirrings of our fiery future. My eyes flitted over Adrian's face, desperately cataloguing each detail for what I knew in my bones was the last time, even as my heart railed against that certainty. The strength of his gaze, the heartbreak in it, told me he was doing the same.

We had planned for this. Because of course we had, when we had known who and what was coming for us, for our children. Even as something inside me was screaming now that our fate had finally found us.

I could feel the ache of sorrow mixing with the grit of resilience as Adrian took me in his arms. There would be no time for prolonged goodbyes, not when destiny had come to tear us asunder. Though perhaps the knowledge of our limited years had the bittersweet silver lining of letting us say those lengthy goodbyes every day, in each kiss and in every heartbeat spent together.

If this was indeed the end, we had used our time—each moment all the more precious in knowing our minutes were numbered.

It didn't mean that I was ready. Only that I didn't regret the time I had been given.

"The only thing that I've ever wanted was this life with you," Adrian murmured, an echo of the words he told me long ago in another realm. "If we were allowed an eternity together, it still wouldn't have been enough."

Then he kissed me, his fingers twisting in my hair. It was over before it had begun, his lips replaced with the bitter taste of goodbye.

"I love you," I whispered so my voice wouldn't break. "More than life itself."

Those golden-brown eyes met mine one last time. "I love you. In this life and the next. Wherever we end up, we go together."

He is mine. And I am his.

Adrian kissed the top of Eva's head, then Tobias's, drawing them both into a brief hug before backing away.

"Dad?"

Tobias's voice was high and frightened, even as he moved protectively toward his twin. They were just turning into the people they would be, and my heart ached that we wouldn't be there to see who they would become. Just as, if my suspicions were correct, we wouldn't be able to protect them any longer from what was coming.

"Go with your mother," Adrian said calmly, his eyes narrowing in determination as he turned toward the front door. "I'll hold them off."

I grabbed Eva's arm as she started toward him. *"Dad!"*

"Come with me," I said firmly. "Now."

The fire was moving fast—too fast—magic moving through the flames. Abject dread flooded through me, seeping into my bones. My children had already started to cough, and I stifled my own as smoke scorched down my throat. Eva started down the smoke-filled hallway, but I pulled her back, taking Tobias's hand as I half dragged them toward the living room.

We didn't have time to escape another way, not with those fire wielding Elementals at our door. Nor with whom I suspected was with them.

Adrian would hold them off for as long as he could, but he was outnumbered. And Celestial or not, even he wasn't invincible.

Something in my gut twisted. I stifled the primal urge to run to him as I felt his pain ricocheting across our bond, knowing what he would want me to do even as his stalwart acceptance nearly brought me to my knees. Because that pain was that of a canary in a mine, its death buying time so that others might live.

Flames licked up the walls of the living room. Tobias yanked on my arm, pulling his hand away. "We need to help Dad—"

"No," I barked. "This way."

Eva struggled, trying to reach what she thought was the nearest exit. "There's no way out from here, we need to—"

"Trust me," I gasped. "This is the only way out. You need to get to Quinn's…"

A cough wracked my body, just as pain flared down my bond from Adrian.

"Mom, you need to tell us what's going on," Eva croaked. "Who are those—"

I felt the moment my *anima* was torn from the world like a scream from my soul. My heart felt like it was being split in two as it attempted to leave this earth right along with him, the death that claimed him reaching for me across our bond. Blood welled in my mouth, and I realized I had bitten through my tongue while attempting to stifle my cry.

To keep the truth from our children.

"*Go,*" I gasped, my ears ringing. The crowns around Eva's pupils gleamed ruthlessly at me, as if reminding me exactly why this had all come to pass.

Placing my hand on her chest, I pushed as hard as I could.

She threw her arm out reflexively, catching the edge of the mirror—stubborn to a fault and too well-trained for me to catch her off guard, even in her state of shock. Her scream as the hot metal burned into her palm wrenched through me, adding to the cacophony of pain that was now my serrated heart.

"You need to go, *now,*" I choked out, my voice breaking as I lied, "Your dad and I will hold him off." I grabbed them both, wishing I had the time to tell them everything but knowing I didn't. "Eyes up, stout hearts. Remember, the only way out is through."

It was the only goodbye I could manage. The last piece of safety I could give her, repeated so often it had become habitual. As much as I wanted to tell her, tell both of them everything, I would have to trust they would figure it out on their own when it came down to it. That the pieces I had put into place would reveal themselves in due course; that the same destiny that would take me from them would yield to its true and future queen.

"Come with us, Mom," Tobias pleaded, his eyes flicking over to the rippling mirror in alarm. "Don't...you don't have to leave us."

I took one last look at them both. "I love you."

The door on the other side of the room crashed open. A hooded figure stalked forward, barely visible through the smoke. I knew exactly who he was, and who he wanted. With a yell, I ran at him, my magic flaring at my fingertips.

My light tore out of me, a manifestation of the silent scream I hadn't allowed myself, seeking vengeance. But he was faster. His own Celestial light burned around me, and I cried out as it seared into my skin.

Tobias and Eva had frozen in place behind me.

I wouldn't let him hurt them too.

My light speared toward Eva. She stumbled back; her burned hand reaching toward me, the shape of a partially unfurled rose that lined the gate now forever marking her flesh. But this time, her attempt to stay with me was in vain. Her mouth parted as if she were about to speak—

Then she was nothing but another ripple.

The False King let out a bellow. My light surged forward, forming a wall of pure power in between us.

Tobias's face went slack as he took in the space where his twin had disappeared. "How did...Mom—"

My light reached for him, but it sputtered before I used it against him as I had to his twin, my magic draining far too rapidly. Dimly, I wondered if it was the force of the False King's magic, or the repercussions of losing my *anima*. Either way, far too much of my power was being spent at once, at a rate I knew I couldn't sustain.

"I can't hold him back much longer," I rasped. "You need to go."

"I won't leave you here," Tobias insisted, taking a step toward me. "I can help."

I shook my head again. "You need to live to fight another day. He's too powerful, it's why we ran in the first place—"

As if in response, the wall of light wavered, so close to bleeding out entirely even as I kept pouring more and more of myself into it. Like trying to fill a bath without a plug, it flowed endlessly out of me in a painful torrent.

Except I knew there would be an end to it, and to me.

I didn't have time to argue. So I tried another tactic, a pale substitute of the explanation I owed them both, even as my voice shook with the strain.

"He's after both of you," I said urgently. "But he's mostly after *her*. You have to keep her safe. You need to get her far away from here. Your magic…" Tobias's eyes widened almost comically. "It's contained in the amulet you wear. Make sure you keep it on, or he'll be able to track you. One day soon, when it's safe, when it's time, the Solearans will find you. And help you defeat him."

Tobias's mouth had dropped open. From the horror in his gaze, I knew he had heard me. Perhaps he had even realized the fact that I hadn't included myself in the future I was hastily trying to prepare him for, nor his father. "Mom…"

The ceiling shuddered, smoke curling dangerously around the beams above us. Tobias looked up just as a band of my light wrapped around his chest, redirected from the wavering wall. His expression changed to one of betrayal as it dragged him backward.

"I'm sorry," I whispered. "I love you."

The barrier holding the False King collapsed, my light fizzling into sparks. His magic danced from his fingertips as if in mockery of the light I had been unable to maintain. I gaped at him as he stepped through, the last of my light disappearing before a jolt of pure energy slammed into me. I screamed, even as I fought to keep my hold on my son, to get him out—

"No. *Mom*—" Tobias's last shout seemed to reverberate through me as I forced him through the mirror.

Then he, too, was gone.

I raised both hands in a fighting stance, hoping I didn't look as on the edge of collapse as I felt. But this bastard had taken my *anima* from me, and was hunting our children. He might very well kill me too.

But not before I tried to take him with me, fate be damned.

The False King's lip curved as he pulled down the hood obscuring his face. "You can't keep me from her forever."

"Watch me."

Light arched from his hand; its hue startlingly familiar. I dodged on instinct, even as my mind whirred. If Eva and Tobias hadn't gotten far enough, if they hadn't ended up at the Sagray's and been thrown into the Faewilds...

I needed to give them every second I could.

Flinging myself behind my rapidly charring couch, I threw the chest behind it open, drawing my sword. But the second my hand touched the hilt; all I could see was Adrian.

Adrian, bowing as he asked for my name with a smile that had never stopped making my heart race. The look on his face that first time I had raised my sword against him to fight him for it. The taste of his lips when I kissed him for the first time. The moonlight in his hair that first night we had come together. The scent of him—like home, like belonging. The way he had held our children, one cradled in each strong arm, his lilting voice always the cure for our babies' cries.

The lack of our bond felt like a void spearing toward my heart, intent on taking me with it. Because my world had stopped turning the second his heart stopped beating.

My every breath hurt, but my grip tightened as I regathered my resolve as though my home, my life, wasn't literally crumbling around my ears. Footsteps slowly stalked toward me, barely audible over the crackle of the fire around me. But I would wait for the right moment.

Hold, I could almost hear Adrian whisper in my ear, his arms tightening around me. Tears sprang to my eyes unbidden, and I blinked them away.

A fiery beam fell from the ceiling as I sprang from behind the couch where we had spent so many family nights together. My blade hit home, and the False King hissed out a grunt of pain as I slashed it across his stomach.

He drew his sword, light flaring above him as the house groaned. If I could just keep him here long enough, perhaps the fire would do my job for me.

I darted forward, but he was ready for me. His sword clashed against mine, sparks flying around us. He reached for me, but I was faster. A bloody line opened down his sword arm as I spun away, and I smiled grimly.

Our blades met, the clang of metal against metal lost in the roar of the flame.

"It's almost a shame I have to kill you," the False King drawled.

I kicked out as I spun away. My foot found its mark—the deep gash I had carved into his stomach spraying blood—and he let out a hiss of pain. "Can't say the same."

He was backing me toward the flame with each parry, his size and strength formidable, especially as my own power waned. And he was Celestial, a light wielder too. But as to who was stronger…

As if my thoughts had conjured it, light flared up his sword. I poured mine into my own to match it. He smirked, like he knew something I didn't. Our swords collided, but this time, as his light flew down his blade, something about it made me pause.

My distraction cost me. Or perhaps my time had finally run out.

His light wrapped around my wrists like searing shackles. I jerked back, but his hand flattened against my heart—

I screamed.

Light tore from me, my magic flowing from my chest, my hands, my mouth. All I could hear was his laugh as he took and took and took, the pain overwhelming.

I knew what he was. And, far too late, it became clear exactly why he needed my family. Why he had targeted my daughter specifically.

My body slackened in the False King's hold, even as I coughed helplessly against the smoke, gasping for air. The world around me became a burning blur of light and flame, as the last of my magic was ripped from me, my life force draining right with it.

I closed my eyes.

Estelle.

That familiar, lilting accent filled my ears. Citrus and anise—a scent I thought I would never smell again—wrapped around me like an embrace before his arms followed.

Then there was nothing at all.

CHAPTER 50
BASH

There was only defiance on Eva's face and written upon the tense lines of her body as she disappeared through the mirror.

My legs almost failed me as I tried to run toward her, as I rasped, *"No."*

I couldn't lose her. I wouldn't.

Quinn was helping Yael to her feet as Tobias's magic held a wall of soldiers off. Blood matted Yael's dark hair to her head. Blue light still streamed from Quinn's hand, obviously knitting the wound back together.

"Rivan. He needs—"

An icy blast nearly impaled me. Shadesong's dusky blade just barely knocked it aside, my reaction more instinct than thought.

I raised my sword, locking blades with an oncoming soldier before thrusting my dagger into his side. But another one was there in his place, fire blazing in one hand, a curved blade in the other. I nearly screamed in frustration, my eyes darting to the violently rippling mirror. Fire blazed toward me. I raised a trembling shield of shadow just in time, throwing my dagger at my opponent's heart. She dodged—right into my sword as it slashed across her throat.

"Tobias."

He had seen. Was already trying to get to her just as I was, desperately trying to force his way through the mass of bodies in between us and the ancient mirror.

My shadows shot forward, trying to clear a path. But my magic was too drained from what Rivan and I had done, my shadows as impermanent as smoke as soldiers ran right through them. My sword flashed, my ears faintly ringing as I surged forward, cutting down anyone foolish enough to get in my way. A weak band of shadows wrapped around the wrist of one about to throw an ax. It fell to the floor as he was taken down by one of Yael's arrows.

"*Bash.*"

Tobias was almost to the mirror, his light twining up his sword so brightly I could barely look at him as he battled his way through a mob of soldiers.

"The mirror!"

As I looked to where Tobias was staring, my stomach sank like a stone. The ripples in the mirror had calmed, its edges already dark and dull. That stillness crept inward, its pace accelerating.

My heart stuttered to a stop in my chest.

The mirror was…closing.

And I wasn't going to get there in time.

"*No.*"

The whisper was lost to the din of the battle before it even got past my lips.

Tobias was shouting something as his light flared over and over. Then a blast of air knocked the soldiers in front of me to the side, forcing an open path down the middle.

"*GO,*" Yael yelled from behind me, her gaze fixed on the darkening mirror. "I'll cover you."

I was racing forward before she finished speaking, my heart lodging in my throat as the mirror closed in on itself.

My muscles screamed as I flew forward, faint shadows streaking past as though they could reach her without me. I would make it—there was no other alternative. Just because I knew she could, didn't mean I would leave her to face him alone.

Not again.

Not when I was so close.

With my bloody hand outstretched, I leapt—

And crashed into the enchanted glass a second before Tobias did. The entire mirror shuddered as we ricocheted back onto the stone floor, even the glowing blue glints surrounding it fading away. I was back on my feet in an instant, my shadows already searching for a way through.

Because there had to be. I wouldn't lose her again.

There was a ringing in my ears. Tobias's magic was barely holding the soldiers behind us back even as Yael fought her way through them. Quinn was nowhere to be seen. I could only pray she had heard the urgency in my voice when I yelled Rivan's name, and deciphered the danger he was in.

Tobias swore loudly next to me, splaying his bleeding hand wide against the closed gate. Light streamed underneath his fingertips like he could force the glass to open.

His arms dropped to his sides, his shoulders slumping, even as his light kept the soldiers surrounding us away. As he took one step back, then another, he looked at me with those anguished eyes so like Eva's.

Eva who was now trapped on the other side of the mirror. Alone with Aviel.

My own terror seemed to reflect back at me as I stared at him. My own helplessness.

I didn't recognize my own voice as I rasped, "We're too late."

CHAPTER 51

EVA

It felt like I was trapped between worlds. Like when I passed through the fake castle wall back in Morehaven; the shifting stones pressing in against me and yet not. The same blue glow from that horrible night flashed all around me in sporadic bursts like the fading brilliance of dying stars, its presence oddly comforting.

My breath crystallized in front of my face, the frozen fractals gleaming strangely in the thick, fractured darkness. It wasn't air, exactly. It was something untenable, pulsing with power. Something that felt foreign and familiar all at once. It silently burrowed under my skin, sweeping through me like an invisible wave as if it were parsing out all my secrets. A blinding force pushed against my magic, overwhelming me as I prayed to pass through.

It was everywhere, until it wasn't. And as it retreated, two figures appeared in the endless darkness, softly glowing with a blue aura I barely noticed.

Because the sight of my parents' faces struck me like a dagger to the heart. Greedily, I took in all the small details I had nearly forgotten. The way my mother's eyes crinkled before she gave in to a smile, the perennial lavender scent of her wafting toward me as her simple black dress swayed in a non-existent breeze. The devilish glint in my father's golden-brown gaze, the one-sided dimple forming that matched mine. Or would, if my mouth wasn't hanging open in unadulterated shock.

They didn't look like they had the last time I saw them on the day they died. They looked like the painting in Solara—young and almost painfully vibrant.

I couldn't seem to make a sound. Tears slid down my cheeks as I stared at them, trembling from the violence of a grief that had never fully abated.

"You've been so brave, Evangeline," *my mother whispered, pride filling her tone. Her lips curved in that soft, devastatingly familiar smile.* "But you won't need to be much longer."

"So brave, sweetheart," *my father said, and I wiped away more tears at the moniker I hadn't heard from his lips in far too long. He reached out as if to stroke my face but seemed to think better of it, his hand dropping to his side.*

My voice was hoarse as I asked, "Is this...magic? Or is this real?"

I found myself almost afraid of how badly I wanted it to be the latter.

My father's eyes crinkled, and I let his laugh wash over me. "Why would one exclude the other?"

I stared at him, trying to preserve every part of his smile, his laugh, that feeling of him, into my memory.

"Evangeline."

My head snapped to my mother, my voice breaking as I managed to whisper, "Hi Mom."

"It's time now," *she said, the crowns in her eyes glinting.* "To right a century of wrongs. To claim your birthright. And to stop that bastard once and for all."

I knew I needed to go, but I didn't want to leave them, not yet. But I nodded, furiously blinking my tears away as I desperately tried to drink them in one last time—unwilling to let their blur impede upon my attempt to commit every last piece of them to memory. Wanting to stay suspended in this wrinkle in time for just one more minute, one last heartbeat before they were gone again forever.

"We'll be with you," *my father promised, sensing my devastation.* "Even if you can't see us. We'll be there, right beside you, until the end."

"Remember," *my mother said, reaching out as if to brush my tears away. Her hand stopped abruptly, coming to hover a hair's breadth above my left hand. Her index finger dipped downward to where the shadowy ring that had once been hers shimmered strangely.* "The only way out is through."

"I love you," *I said, looking into eyes that were the mirror of my own as I said the words that had once been too late.*

And it felt real.

CHAPTER 52

EVA

I was falling. Until I wasn't.

There was a familiar tingle on my palm. Silvery words that brought me back to reality all at once.

Come back to me, hellion.

Shaking, I reached up to wipe my eyes. But my face was now dry, as if that pocket in between reality never existed. And yet, I knew it had. At least in the ways that mattered.

The mirror I had just stepped through was built into the obsidian stone of the wall, the twin to its counterpart within Adronix. It was dark and still, the blue glints dimming as its very glass seemed to fade into the shining black wall, seamlessly integrating into the surrounding stone.

I turned to find myself in the heart of a colossal cavern. A massive, bioluminescent cave so immense, I couldn't see the end of it. Glittering stalactites hung above the gleaming azure lake before me, the jagged obsidian dotted with those glowing blue stones. A trove of more blue rocks sparkled on the cave floor, flowing out into the lake like a sea of sapphires. Every surface swam mesmerizingly from its glimmering light.

There was a whole universe in this cave. I was momentarily stunned at how familiar this place felt, though I had never been here before. It might even feel like a haven, had Aviel not been at the shore.

Adrenaline flooded through my veins even as dread pooled in my gut, my heart attempting to beat out of my chest in panic. My own personal nightmare knelt at the edge of the underground lake, his back still to me. The water swirled with that bioluminescent light as he dipped his fingers into it, a bluish ether flowing through him.

Stealing the magic of the land.

My stomach hollowed out as his cold blue eyes snapped to mine, a shudder going through me at the phantom touch of his gaze. It was everything I could do to keep my breathing even.

I should strike now, before he could gather even more power...

My scalp prickled as he stood up, a slow, sinister smile spreading across his face as the undulating glow cast him in an eerie light. I refused to back away, even as my heartbeat thundered in my chest.

"Took you long enough."

The sound of Aviel's voice sent another jolt of terror down my spine. My jaw clenched. He *had* been waiting for me in case he needed to use me for whatever came next. It was yet another ambush, even if it was one I couldn't have avoided.

And I'd run right into it.

"It's only fitting that it's you and me at the end, darling." He smirked. "Just as I always planned."

Bile rose in my throat. That dread had turned into fear, and I was drowning in it.

I reached for my bond with Bash yet found it blocked, as though this place was entirely disconnected from space and time. Even if Bash and Tobias did find a way to follow me through the closed mirror and bring the stone that would siphon Aviel's stolen magic...I couldn't wait for them to save me.

My fingers dug into the scar on my palm, the familiar feel of it grounding. It was the mark his obsession with me had caused so long ago after finding myself in a trap I had yet to escape.

Steeling my spine, I stared Aviel down, trying not to let him see the effect he had on me. "If you think you're going to take anything else from me, you are sorely mistaken. This is *my* birthright." It was the first time I had used that term, the first time I had truly claimed it as mine—my mother's certainty ringing in my words. "Even if it wasn't, you don't deserve to live in this realm after all you've done to it, let alone rule it."

My grip tightened on Nightshade as I let my power flow down the sharp edges of my blade, my darkness imbuing every inch of it.

Aviel chuckled cruelly, those pale blue eyes flashing with malice. "That story I told you about my parents was true, you know. When I told you about my mother leaving my father after realizing the true depth of his ambition for this realm. She tried to take me away from him to stop what was already in motion."

"What happened to her?" I was blatantly stalling as I assessed what to do next. But there wasn't a crown waiting for me, nor some magical instructions written into the stone. No sign of how to beat Aviel to our shared goal without defeating him first.

He shrugged. "I killed her, but not before she killed him. If she had loved us like I loved her, she would have wanted to find a way to bend the realm to our will right along with us."

I couldn't keep the horrified disgust from my face at his complete lack of remorse. Aviel's perfect lips twitched as he took another step closer. "We're not so different, you and I. Orphans, outsiders to this realm. Both granted the power to rule it."

As if he wasn't the very reason I had been orphaned. Fury pooled from my palms in dark torrents, twisting around me like an asp waiting to strike.

"It was too late for her. But *you*...you'll learn to bend to my will. Will learn to love me. You *will* be my queen." His smile was endlessly cold, those pale eyes flat. "And I will crush everything and everyone in this realm until they all learn to bow to me too."

The shudder that ran down my body had nothing to do with the coolness of the cave.

"But first..." His face twisted in a frown, annoyance filling his tone. "I've been to this lake many times. I don't understand how this could be the test. The Choosing. Unless..." Those pale eyes fixed on me. "Unless I need *you*."

This was the Source? Something dropped in my stomach at the realization that we only needed to go beneath Morehaven all along.

Though perhaps the journey was part of the destination, the drive and determination to reach Adronix a trial in itself.

Aviel stepped toward me, hands still glistening with that blue light. I took an instinctual step back. He drew his sword, smirking at me as his stolen magic streaked down it almost mockingly. I bent my knees, settling into my stance.

He lunged forward almost faster than I could track.

My blade met his from a long, ingrained instinct, connecting with a resounding clang. Embers of magic flew around us from the force of our collision and lingered in the air. Our swords crossed, and my knees began to buckle as Aviel used his height and weight against me, shoving downward just as I swiftly jumped back. He countered my next strike with a low parry, the tip of his blade drawing a line of blood across my upper thigh. With a swift upward slash, I tried to catch him off guard, but he was already there, blocking me. Thwarting each advance with uncanny speed and evident ability.

I jerked my head back as the arc of his sword sliced a red line across my chest, cutting straight through my leathers. The gleam of lust in Aviel's eyes twisted my stomach as the wound bled into the line of my cleavage now visible through the tear.

With a cry, I threw myself at him. The force of his counterattack was staggering, so powerful I nearly lost my footing as I skidded backwards on the slick rock. *This* was the warrior who had torn apart the faerie realm. I could barely keep pace with his relentless onslaught despite my training, his centuries of skill all too obvious as I fought to merely hold my ground.

"I have lifetimes on you, darling," Aviel sneered, reading my mind as our swords met in a clang that I felt down my entire body. "Decades solely spent training my body into a weapon to cleave this realm apart. Years where I pictured this very moment—when I finally receive everything I so richly deserve."

He smiled as his next thrust forced me back another step, a gasp of pain slipping from my lips.

He's toying with me, I realized. *Wearing me down for his own ends.*

I wasn't going to beat him like this.

Aviel stepped back; his gaze predatory. "Give into me now, and I'll consider letting your *anima* live. If only to give you an incentive to behave."

Cold rage flooded through me. Darkness coiled under my skin, begging to be fully unleashed. If he took my magic, it would be nearly impossible to stop him. But I didn't see another way but to try.

Thrusting out my hand, I gave in. My magic shot forward in a blast of pure night—like ink shooting from a well. But Aviel was faster, his blue-tinged light forming a shield in front of him. My magic split to the sides, cracking a stalactite in half.

Before I could try again, he lunged at me. Our swords locked, sparks flying as he bore down, my knees nearly buckling beneath me. I attempted to spin away, but he seized my wrist with his free hand, yanking me back against him.

His grip seared into my skin as my darkness fought against his hold. I gasped as his light wrenched my fingers back one by one, struggling to no avail as my sword fell from my grasp. Aviel kicked it away, the dark glow disappearing from the blade as it clattered uselessly against the rocks behind us.

Shackles of light locked around my wrists as I fought and failed. The pain was nothing compared to having him this close to me. I knew what was at stake if he was able to take my magic from me again, stripping me of my last defense.

Aviel leaned forward, so close his breath brushed my lips. Then he grabbed me by my throat. Kicking out blindly, I only hit empty space as he lifted me off the ground. I struggled for purchase, drawing blood as my nails bit into the flesh of his forearms. His hand only tightened, cutting off my air.

Then all I felt was pain as he pulled my power into himself.

I was being ripped apart from the inside out. My body seized at the onslaught as Aviel tore away at my magic, taking what didn't belong to him. I couldn't move, couldn't fight. Couldn't even close my eyes as darkness filled them. My vision cut out like the world was coming apart at the seams, my cries echoing throughout the cavern, tearing from my throat as I found myself unable to out-scream the pain.

Time seemed to slow as I fumbled for the hilt of my dagger, feeling its faint hum against my hip. Aviel stole it from me before I could close my fist around it, its black stone glinting as he raised it above me.

My blood felt like it was thickening in my veins, my struggles barely a whimper. He had taken too much, and my body, my very thoughts, were reacting far more slowly than they should.

"Your magic...and your blood," Aviel murmured, almost clinically.

I watched him stab my dagger downward as if in slow motion.

But I couldn't move. Couldn't so much as twist away as my own dagger pierced my stomach, the black jewel in its pommel glinting up at me.

White-hot agony exploded in my gut. It took a moment for me to realize the scream that cut through the silence was mine.

My blood fell far too quickly as Aviel withdrew the blade. He let me go, and I fell to my knees, gasping for air. I could hear my ragged breathing in my ears, each breath burning like they did in every nightmare.

Then I knew nothing but pain as the darkness took me.

CHAPTER 53

EVA

Pain woke me as quickly as it had dragged me under. I tried in vain to breathe through it, my vision hazy as I forced my eyes open.

Aviel wrapped my braid around his fist, dragging me into the water.

I struggled, trying to dig my feet into the black stone, fighting against the bands of light searing into my wrists. But Aviel was far too strong, and my magic was only a whisper. He pulled me into the gleaming lake, its water soaking through my leathers, lapping at my blood. I realized a second too late what he was about to do when his hand moved to the back of my neck.

Convulsively, I sucked in half a breath before he pushed me under the water. My bound hands slipped frantically against the glowing rocks, their cerulean gleam all I could see. I thrashed, losing my fight against my panic, but his hold was too firm. Bubbles streamed around me as I flailed, the urge to breathe consuming me.

There was a flash of silver in the corner of my vision, and I realized my dagger had fallen into the shallows beside me, its slender blade refracting strangely through the clear water even as my gaze fixed on the black diamond on its hilt.

I needed to breathe. Couldn't hold on much longer—

There was blackness on the edges of my vision when Aviel yanked me back above the surface. I wheezed, my chest heaving as I drew in gasping gulps of air.

Everything blurred, but I could make out a blazing golden light ahead, hovering over the lake. I blinked rapidly, losing my breath entirely when I realized what it was.

A leisurely spinning crown floated slowly toward us, flecks of gold rising above it like embers flying above a fire. It looked like it had been woven together from delicate strands of gold, each whirling around the other in ethereal swivels before tapering into elongated points that dissipated into the darkness. It hung above the lake as if suspended by an invisible string, the tiny stones embedded into it reflecting the luminescence of the cavern around us.

There was something about it that drew me in like it was calling to me —something as undeniable as it was destructive. I pressed my hand against my stomach, breathless from the pain as my blood slipped between my fingers.

As I looked down at the dark swirl of my blood in the water, I realized *I* had summoned it. My blood. Because this was the Choosing, and I was the rightful ruler of this realm.

Which meant I needed to get to that crown first.

But Aviel's light chained my wrists before me. His hand tightly gripped the nape of my neck, holding me in place at his feet where I knelt in the shallow water. I pulled against my bonds, only succeeding in wrenching a moan of pain from my throat as they seared through my skin.

Aviel had the magic of the land on his side. I had foolishly thought I would be able to beat him this time when it mattered the most.

Stubbornly, I forced that thought from my head. There had to be a way.

I will not give up. I will not let him win.

As the crown moved closer, I repeated those words over and over in a silent mantra. And for a second, I felt...something. Something that shouldn't be there.

I closed my eyes, trying to tunnel into the power that should've been entirely drained. Yet somehow, it no longer felt that way. There was a warmth moving through me, a magic that felt like an old friend as it traveled through my bones.

And as I reached for a force I didn't entirely understand, I abruptly realized what it was. That bioluminescent glow had gathered around me, dotted streams clustering around every part of me that touched the Source. Dewdrops of bright blue light lifted from the lake, brushing against my skin as they twirled in an unearthly dance. The magic of the land—my birthright—bequeathed to *me*, not the pretender before me.

As it sank into my veins, it felt like I could finally exhale. Pure, raw power crackled through me, licking across my lips, binding around my wounds, flitting along my knuckles like a row of ringless jewels. Pulsing under my skin in a current that very well might sweep me away. But I hadn't stolen the land's magic like the monster beside me. It had given it to me, chosen me, imbuing it into its rightful ruler.

I greedily drew on it, letting it fill me as Aviel stood above me unaware, his gaze still fixed on the rotating crown.

He may have been able to force the magic from this land, taking it as he had done to me—but this power was always meant to be mine.

Aviel's eyes were locked on the crown mere feet away now. But perhaps sensing the change in me, he glanced down, then froze.

I knew what he would see. The bands of light chaining me had slipped down my glowing skin, no longer able to contain me. My hair had broken free from my braid, spreading around me in a halo of chestnut waves, each strand entwined with threads of blazing blue. And I knew the twin crowns around my pupils matched the color of the crown he was trying to steal from me, as if they had always known this exact moment was coming.

I didn't bother going for my blade.

My head went quiet, everything seeming to still. Then my magic detonated like an explosion. Darkness merged with light, wisps of night mixing with the blue. Aviel's body slammed back against a stalagmite, slumping against it. A smattering of rocks showered him as he gaped at me.

Shaking with the sheer force of the power within me, I got to my feet, retrieving my fallen dagger. A wave of stolen darkness surged toward me. I didn't even look up as a bright shield appeared to stop it.

Snarling, Aviel stalked forward, closing the distance between us as I walked to the water's edge.

Raising my dagger, I said with a lethal calm, "That is *not* your crown."

The stone in my dagger emitted that familiar hum as my palm brushed against it. And suddenly, it clicked. I might never know exactly how, but the last gift my parents had given me, the dagger my mother had made for me, had also been a gift from another mother. One who couldn't have possibly known her son would be linked to its recipient.

Somehow, the same power that had removed the band from my neck was imbued in the black stone of my blade. Perhaps fate had intervened in more ways than one.

Aviel laughed mockingly, bringing me back to the present. "Oh, Evangeline. You know all I have to do is drain you of this power too? And then both realms will be mine."

Our magics clashed again. This time, neither of us seemed able to get the upper hand as that blue light fought against its twin. I just needed to get close enough...

I smirked at him as light flared in the corners of my vision, so different from my usual darkness. "Afraid to fight me hand to hand again, Aviel? After all, I would've beaten you last time if you hadn't used my power to cheat."

His face contorted with rage before smoothing out in a cold smile. "I see I'll have to beat you before I break you."

I pointed my dagger at him in overt challenge—the one I had no intention of discarding—even if part of me was convinced he could see through the ruse. But Aviel released his barrage of magic just as I let go of my own, wisps of steam rising in the air between us in its absence.

Aviel sheathed his sword in a practiced movement. "I'm afraid someone took the dagger I've grown accustomed to in recent years. Perhaps it's time I took it back."

He was fast, so fast I barely dodged as he came at me.

"I'm happy to stick it *exactly* where it belongs."

I let out a battle cry as I thrust my dagger toward him, angled in what would be a fatal strike. He laughed as he parried it, then lunged forward, grabbing for me again. I drove my blade between us, aiming up toward his ribcage in another would-be fatal blow, but he knocked my arm away, kicking out in a rebuttal that nearly flung me back into the water.

Panting, I raised my dagger once more. I couldn't let this go on much longer, not with the blood loss starting to make me feel lightheaded despite the magic now keeping my wound closed.

"I don't want to kill you, darling," Aviel purred. "Though I'd be lying if I said your disobedience didn't make me want to punish you."

His next attack found its mark, my side screaming at the blow. But my defeat of him wouldn't be through skill alone, nor magic, old or new. It would be because of the gift I had been given long before I knew what it truly was, and through exploiting Aviel's own surety in his victory.

I clutched my stomach, swaying. Letting my dagger hang limp in my hand. Giving Aviel an obvious opening as he charged toward me—

My dagger embedded into the shoulder he had left exposed, digging in deep. He had expected me to go for that fatal blow yet again. But I didn't need to kill him, nor did I want to with his link to me.

Not when I needed only to drain him.

Aviel's face twisted in a smirk as his hand engulfed mine where it was wrapped below that black diamond. His fingers dug into my skin, about to pull my blade out, when his eyes bulged. My opposite hand covered his, holding him against the humming stone.

Stolen magic ran in rivulets along his skin into the device that I had finally recognized for what it was. Taking his power from him, like he had from so many others.

His free hand fastened around my throat. The power I had borrowed from the Source spilled out of me in an excruciating torrent, even as what he took from me disappeared into Bash's mother's invention.

The diamond flared impossibly bright, blue light streaming between our splayed fingers. Then the stone cracked right down the middle, shattering into nothing.

No.

A shockwave of magic burst from my broken dagger, bits of darkness mixing with the blue. I stumbled back, taking the blade with me as I stared at the oval hole where my salvation once lived, Aviel's blood dripping down into its ruined, melted pommel.

I didn't have time to regroup. Aviel sprang forward, and I twisted away too late. Shock and blood loss made my movements sloppy. His fist drove directly into the wound on my stomach, the edges of my vision blurring as pain threatened to pull me under.

My back hit the rock. Then Aviel pinned me to the ground in an echo of my worst nightmares.

I couldn't help my strangled cry as a slither of his magic came to take the last of my power a second time. My lungs protested; the taste of blood filled my mouth.

Numb acceptance consumed me as I looked down on myself as if from far away. Like I was watching someone else struggle, her options dwindling into one—and one alone.

Because I knew what I had to do before Aviel could succeed. What I had known all along since that moment in the dark woods by that faerie mound.

There had never been a chance that I would survive this. Even with the magic of the realm on my side, Aviel had stolen too much of the same power for me to wield it successfully against him. And if he reached the crown first...

We would lose.

For a heartbeat, I saw that future I had once dreamed of—my future with Bash, and the life we would have lived together. All those things I so desperately wanted to experience with him. Exploring the realm, rebuilding it with our friends by our side. Getting to know the kingdom I had been born into. Catching up on those stolen years with my brother and my best friend, our trio finally reunited. One day growing our families in a world of peace and laughter.

Simple, lovely dreams. All the things I would never get to do now.

I love you, I thought, fervently hoping Bash could feel an echo of the force of it across our muted bond. That the depth of my love for him could cross time and space, realms and universes to reach him one last time.

I should've said goodbye.

With what felt like the last of my strength, I shoved my hand hard into the center of Aviel's chest. Not expecting it, he reared back, falling off me. Clumsily, I rolled to my side, crawling away. My head swam dizzily, my body screaming in protest as I forced myself to my knees, then my feet, standing between him and the crown by the water's edge. I refused to die kneeling before him.

When I looked at him, a gleam of something entirely too pleased flashed across his face. Confirmation he had been toying with me yet again.

He wouldn't be smiling for long.

The worst part might be that ever since the moment I learned of this damnable choice in that faerie glen, something deep inside me had accepted my fate. Knew it in my bones from the moment of the sprite's proclamation. But my stupid, stubborn heart had refused to admit defeat. Refused to give in.

Until now.

There was no other way. And I would rather die than let him win.

The truth of what I was about to do settled under my skin, the weight of it unbearable. My pointer finger fell against my scarred palm, the hilt of my ruined dagger clenched tightly in the other. I didn't look down as I quickly scrawled my final message; the three words that meant everything. It was all the goodbye I could offer him.

There were tears in my eyes. I hastily blinked them away.

Aviel laughed softly. "What, exactly, do you think you can do against me now?"

In answer, I brought my dagger against my throat. It cut into the pale, thin line where he had forever marked me, a trickle of blood tracing a warm path between my collarbones. My eyes narrowed as I stared him down, living on the razer's edge between two fates.

Aviel froze, his eyes flaring wide. For a deranged second, I wondered if his horror was only due to our bloodlink—or if his obsession had crossed the line into what he thought was love.

"How did you…You can't—"

"You made a mistake when you linked our lives," I hissed, my resolve unwavering even as my fear multiplied. "When you took my blood." My hand was shaking so hard, my dagger dug in deeper, the slice stinging against my skin as my blood slowly dripped its way downward. Adding to the white scar banded around my neck as if I had never escaped that collar, its presence taunting me with what would happen if I didn't go through with this. "And now, I'm going to end us both."

Aviel's hands fell to his side, fear twisting his face. "*Evangeline.*"

My mouth twisted into a savage grin as I took in the panic in his voice. "You thought you'd use me. Instead, all you've ensured is our mutually assured destruction."

Steeling myself, I took a deep breath—

A woman's laugh echoed through the chamber. Aviel spun around just as an explosive blast of flame encircled him. Despite my shock, I took advantage of the opening, stepping back into the lake. Blue stones swirled around me, the magic of the realm answering my call. I was merely a conduit for the Source as it funneled into the inferno enclosing the False King, cerulean mixing with the amber of Alette's mounting fire.

She stepped toward me, the gray dress she wore torn and filthy. I kept my dagger firmly where it was—too afraid that if I moved my arm away, I wouldn't have the strength to raise it again.

"Eva." She said my name in two syllables, sung like a haunting melody. "You don't want to do that."

"Alette," I replied, unable to dredge up a hint of surprise. "I should have known you would be hiding around here somewhere."

She let out a dark laugh as she eyed the blade at my throat, skipping toward me like she didn't have a care in the world. Then held her hand out, as if expecting me to hand it to her. "Come on, little bird, we don't have time for this."

"I have to do this to stop him." My voice splintered despite myself, even as I tried to find it in me to simply cut my throat and be done with it.

Because I could save them. I could save this entire realm, could save my brother, could save my friends who had become my family...and I could save *him*, even if I couldn't save myself.

Bash would survive my death, the breaking of our bond. He had to.

"We won't hold him for long," Alette said in a singsong, breaking into my thoughts. "Already he is leeching what is ours."

I could feel it, the steady drain on my borrowed power. Aviel bleeding away the magic used to contain him faster than I could replenish it as he grew even more powerful.

Again, Alette gestured for the dagger with an impatient flick of her wrist. "Put it down. Killing yourself won't solve anything."

Something about the way she said it had alarm bells ringing in the back of my head. "It's the only way. I—why are you even here? What do you think you're doing?"

"Fixing your fate."

Her words made me pause, even as I knew Aviel couldn't be contained much longer. The only reason we had been able to hold him this long was due to how much the broken stone had been able to drain him before it was destroyed.

Beads of perspiration ran down my forehead as I sank to my knees. "He took my blood. It has to be me."

"Your life is not the cost, little bird." Alette's tone was casual, her eyes glowing like embers. "He trusted me to drug you, and he trusted me to drain you. But he didn't realize then that I was no longer his. That I didn't give him your blood for the link." Her smile radiated pure triumph. "Instead, I gave him *mine.*"

My face slackened. Shock rippled through me as I gaped at her, barely managing to keep my grip on my fleeting magic. She had...*she* had—

Of course, Alette had been the one to bring him my blood. And she had the forethought to thwart Aviel's plan to hijack the Choosing before I had even known it existed.

Changing destiny's a weighty business. Though there is something...strange. Perhaps it is not yet set in stone.

Had the sprite seen Aviel's intent but not the flaw in his hubris? That someone he had deemed so far beneath his notice, even after what he had done to her, would be responsible for altering our future?

A faint tremor ran through me. "Alette. You..."

"Me." That smile turned cruel. "After what he did to me, he handed me the tools to his own destruction—*my* revenge and salvation and redemption all in one little glass syringe. I've been waiting here for him, so I can end things before he can. Hiding in the walls after what I did to his pretty, perfect castle." She let out a maniacal laugh. "It looks better scorched. He gave up looking for me long before I came down here. But I knew he would come to me, eventually. I wanted him to see who was responsible for his undoing: the placeholder he thought unimportant." Her eyes flickered as she tilted her head at me in that unnerving angle. "I was hoping we'd have the chance to say goodbye first though."

My teeth chattered at the power channeling through me, scorching through my veins as Aviel stole it nearly as quickly as I used it against him. I couldn't sustain this much longer.

A shard of blue light escaped from the fire, its jagged bolt reflecting in the ripples of the water. Aviel's power was starting to break through the cocoon around him, a second sharp beam of light slicing through his fiery cage.

I knew we only had moments before he broke through.

"You don't have to do this," I begged, suddenly bereft at the thought of Alette sacrificing herself. At taking on the task I had long since accepted as my own.

She smiled even as she shook her head. For a second, I caught a glimpse of the person she might have been before misery and madness had molded her into vengeance incarnate.

"There's nothing he can do to undo what he's done," Alette said almost pityingly. "And so, there's nothing that'll save him."

The cavern tremored. Alette's eyes burned a molten, fiery red.

"I'm sorry," I choked out.

"We don't let him win." Alette's voice went hoarse as she repeated my own words back to me, the same ones I had once prayed would sway her to save me. Smoke began wafting from her hands, her bare feet, a fiery orange glowing in her throat like a dragon about to breathe flame.

I realized with growing horror that she was going to burn herself from the inside out. And take him with her.

Bursts of flame shot from underneath her skin, her fingernails. Her dress turned to ash, her entire body starting to bubble and blacken.

There was a voice screaming at me to run. But I knelt there, frozen. Unable to do anything but watch. As if witnessing what was about to happen would somehow help, as Alette made the sacrifice I had thought would be mine.

"Fly away now little bird…" Alette's voice was fire and flame as she sent a burst of embers toward me, chasing me toward the mirror. "Your fate is your own."

I shot to my feet in a burst of pure adrenaline. But the crown was gone, the space where it had floated now empty. My stomach sank. Had I somehow failed the Choosing?

The cave groaned, shaking from the force of the magic at war inside it. An ember burned my cheek, and I ran, every thought eddying out of my head except the need to survive. Shards of rock shredded through my leathers, tearing into my skin as they shook loose from the high ceiling above.

Agony flared from the stab wound in my gut, stealing my breath. I stumbled, falling to my hands and knees. The air had grown dangerously thin, like Alette's approaching eruption was burning right through it.

A massive stalactite crashed down in front of the mirror, blocking it from view, only adding to the already insurmountable distance.

I had to get back. To my friends, to my family. To my *anima*.

Because he was mine. And I'd promised him forever.

I forced myself toward the mirror, crawling, every inch of me screaming as I hauled myself over the suddenly scorching rocks, their serrated edges slicing through my palms. Not looking back even as I sensed Aviel break free, sucking the power from his temporary prison. Not even when I heard his echoing scream of rage.

I was so close—

But I wasn't going to make it.

A whip of Aviel's stolen fire wrapped around my leg, burning through my leathers as it tried to take me back to him. I screamed, my fingers clawing against the black rock, knowing I was far too drained to stop him.

My fingers slipped as I was yanked backward. Then a stalactite fell inches from my face, shrapnel barely missing my eye. I wrapped my arms around it. Gritting my teeth, I dragged myself forward, refusing to give up.

Even if I was meant to be this realm's High Queen for only a flicker in time, I wouldn't end my reign without a fight.

This was my realm to protect, powerless or not.

I was distantly aware of a weight settling atop my hair as if in confirmation. My head snapped around, looking back at the lake, even though I knew that golden crown wouldn't be there.

Flame licked at my feet, real for once, and Aviel's hold on me slipped, his screams echoing throughout the cavern. I reached up, feeling the warm metal encircling my head, those flecks of gold I thought might burn brushing almost excitedly against my palm.

I had come through the Choosing victorious. Despite Aviel's schemes and maneuvers, the crown chose *me*. Perhaps it too could sense intent. By choosing the good of the realm over everything else, I had won its allegiance—and, apparently, the right to summon it.

Smoke curled around the black stone ceiling like storm clouds. I coughed, my eyes streaming as I tried to make out a glimpse of the mirror where it had been blocked by an avalanche of obsidian.

I had to get back to Adronix. I had to.

As I tried to stand, I fell hard, a rush of dizziness overtaking me. I had nothing left, that well of power inside me entirely drained, and the Source too far to draw from. Yet that feeling of magic still remained, perched on one finger.

Where my mother's ring seemed to tremble in anticipation.

For a second, I thought I imagined it. But no…there was a vibration of magic, a familiar ripple from the stone glimmering at me as if happy I had finally realized the truth that seemed so obvious. One that I might have figured out sooner had it not been for every distraction since.

After all, my mother had told me the answer before I even knew the question.

The only way out is through.

The boon the sprite had given to me, the ring that had once been my mother's, pulsed frantically. My bloodied finger pressed against it almost unthinkingly.

The gray diamond split in two, disappearing in a wisp of Celestial power that felt like my own. A tiny, oval mirror lay beneath it, its rippling surface unmistakable.

A way out.

There was no way this could work...but this was magic. Just because I hadn't thought of the possibility, especially since every gate I had mirrored through had been enormous, didn't mean it *wouldn't*.

Hope felt too dangerous. But I was out of time to do anything but believe.

I let out a hysterical laugh, unable to stop it. The thing that had scared me all this time had been perched on my finger all along, its power hidden until I needed it the most.

My mom had saved me one last time.

I didn't question it, the final gift she had left me. Not as my ears hollowed out, the air turning thin. My breath dragged from my lungs toward the fiery cyclone that was now Alette, her explosion imminent.

Only death lay behind me, the rest of my life waiting on the other side of the mirror. If only I could reach it.

The Seeing Mirror, I thought as I pressed my finger against it, willing this to work with every fiber of my being. *Adronix. Bash.*

That deadly heat raced toward me, oblivion beckoning as I fell through.

CHAPTER 54

BASH

Aviel's remaining soldiers lay dead across the ancient stone before the Seeing Mirror, the few who had surrendered unconscious and bound in a corner. The stench of battle, of fear and sweat and blood, permeated the cavern.

Pari had sent a stained piece of parchment letting us know they had returned after the avalanche, killing or capturing the soldiers that remained now that their numbers had been so greatly reduced. They had been working to burrow their way to the buried doorway, attempting to blow, move, and melt away the snow that had covered the entrance to the mountain far below.

I was having a hard time caring about the rest of the realm. Not when all I could focus on was her.

Trust that if I have any choice in the matter, I'll come back to you.

My heart crawled further up my throat with each passing second. Beating its way out of my chest, as it had been ever since Eva had followed Aviel through that mirror. As she fought him—the monster who had stalked her for her entire life—alone.

The purgatory was unbearable, my every muscle remaining on high alert. I couldn't stop my mind from racing through every possible scenario my *anima* could be enduring, every single way Aviel might be torturing her while I couldn't reach her, each more horrifying than the last.

I should have gotten there sooner. And even if I trusted her ability, her courage...she shouldn't have to face him without me yet again. Not with the unspeakable cost of her backup plan, the one I knew she wouldn't shy from should all else fail.

She didn't need to be saved, but I couldn't help but beg the gods to bring her back to me.

As I traced the dark, cold edges of the mirror, I silently pleaded for it to open. Trying in vain to feel her through our bond, the link between us far too unsubstantial. There was only damning silence, not a hint of what she was going through.

All that was left was the absence of her, the aching nothingness where Eva was supposed to be.

A frenetic energy was building under my skin. My shadows curled against the glass as they tried and failed to break through.

I can't lose her. I can't—

But there was nothing I could do but wait. Wait and breathe in the same four-count Eva had demonstrated so many times it now felt unconscious to slip into it.

If he hurt her, I would never forgive myself.

She had been unstoppable, a force of nature as she raced through the battle—soldiers falling in her wake without her even raising her sword. Inevitable as she had fallen through the mirror that was her destiny.

Had the Choosing known she was the rightful queen despite Aviel's treachery? Or had she been too late?

Would I even know if she sacrificed herself?

I forced down my sudden nausea, the spiraling weight of my own helplessness. Even after all the ways I had pleaded with her to forget that option, she had still deemed herself expendable—as if the world would keep turning without her in its orbit.

My hand balled into a fist, and I slammed it into the stone wall next to the mirror. Welcoming the pain if only not to wallow in my own powerlessness for one more torturous moment.

There was a low groan. Immediately, I spun to where an unconscious

Rivan lay with his head on Yael's lap. Quinn's magic flowed into him in a slow trickle, her remaining power all that was tying him to life. She had brought him here after finding him half-dead in the stairwell. From where she said she found him, he must have dragged himself halfway up the mountain, following our path through the dark before his inevitable collapse.

Blood leaked sluggishly from a particularly deep cut on Tobias's chest as he paced in front of me, a bruise purpling half his face. His eyes were bleak as he stared unblinkingly at the mirror.

I knew I didn't look much better. An Elemental had burned through the leathers covering my back and shoulder, fusing the leather to my skin before I killed him. The smell of burnt flesh only added to the stench of this purgatory. But it would heal, eventually.

At my attention, Tobias glanced at me, one eyebrow raised. "Can you sense anything?"

"Still nothing," I grunted. Our bond was as silent as when Eva had been collared, a thought that made my stomach plummet.

"I think at least one of us would be able to tell if she were...If she—" His voice broke, and I was selfishly glad he hadn't been able to finish his thought.

Because what if she was already dead? If she had given her own life to stop him, and neither of them would ever return.

No. I would feel it. She couldn't be, and I wouldn't even allow myself to entertain the possibility. Because if she was...

"She's stronger than that," Yael said firmly, her voice still hoarse from the battle. "She's stronger than him."

I nodded. "She is. She—"

But I lost my words completely, my heart lodging in my throat, as three words appeared on the palm I had barely stopped staring at. Three words that felt frighteningly like goodbye.

Fear like I had never felt flooded down my spine until I was drowning in it, dragging me under as my world narrowed to the *I love you* hastily penned in Eva's looping scrawl.

Yael and Tobias were saying my name, concern and panic coloring their voices. Wordlessly, I held out my shaking hand before the iridescent letters faded away—and watched as their faces went as bloodless as I knew mine must be.

I couldn't lose her. Not now—not like this. Not helplessly sitting by as I had done with my mother, waiting to feel my heart break along with our bond. Not when we were so close to this war finally being over, so achingly close to being able to have the life we dreamed of together.

She had to survive this. I had plans for us—a future that seemed to dim, perilously close to disappearing.

Please, hellion. Don't let this be the end.

Her message faded, only the ghostly shiver of her handwriting still on my palm.

"What is it?" Quinn demanded. "What's wrong?"

Rivan's head lolled to the side in her lap. He was unconscious, unmoving, but still clinging to life. Another person I loved that I couldn't help, couldn't save. Even from here, I could hear the labored cadence of his breathing, could see the panic in Quinn's eyes as she fought to keep him here.

"She wrote '*I love you*'," Tobias rasped.

Quinn's lower lip trembled as she looked at him. "Then she's still alive. Still fighting him."

Tobias let out a hollow-sounding laugh, closing his eyes like he couldn't bear to look at her. "That wasn't the update of someone winning that fight."

The silence that followed was deafening. Then Quinn let out a quiet, shuddering sob.

Tobias's eyes flew open, his gaze immediately zeroing in on the tear tracking down her cheek before storming up to the dark mirror, his magic flashing from his fingertips like bolts of lightning. "This can't be it. Waiting for her to win or to die. This can't be—"

His voice choked off as he leaned his forehead against the mirror, his shoulders shaking.

I exchanged a look with Yael. For decades, we had fought the war against the False King, had lost and grieved together. We had battled only to end up here—utterly useless. It wasn't a feeling I was used to, nor one I could easily accept.

But just because I wouldn't accept it didn't mean I could change anything.

The minutes felt like hours as we waited in silence. My eyes never left the mirror, like I could will her back through.

A flash of parchment broke my focus. Yael plucked it from the air.

"Marin said they're still trying," she whispered, staring down at Rivan's prone form.

"Tell her to hurry," Quinn said tiredly. She wiped a hand across her forehead before placing it back on Rivan's chest.

Her magic was nearly exhausted, I realized, either his injuries too great, or her power too depleted from the battle.

Fear engulfed me, even worse than before.

I was going to lose them both.

Yael caught my gaze. "They're not dead yet. She's still fighting, and so is he."

I swallowed past the lump in my throat. "Eva…"

The mirror rippled back to life, dark and flat one second, then undulating silver the next. I shot to my feet, about to blindly leap—

When, as if conjured by her name, my *anima* hurtled through it.

My cry of relief mixed with a garbled sob as I lunged forward, and she collapsed into my arms.

She was blood-smeared and wet, barely an inch of her unscathed. I took in the sight of the cuts covering her body, her shredded leathers, and the stab-wound in her stomach with a lethal calm before I even noticed the golden crown shining on her head.

Then those brilliant gold and hazel eyes rolled back, and she went limp in my arms.

"*Eva!*"

A sharp, all-consuming fear filled me, my shadows exploding around us. Laying her on the ground, her upper body in my lap, I checked that she was still breathing—my lungs only filling when hers did. Her warm breath against my fingertips was the one thing keeping me from losing it entirely.

Tobias was there before I could even ask, helping me as I carefully ripped her torn leathers back from the wound bleeding in her gut.

"Talk to me," Quinn demanded from where neither she nor Yael had moved from Rivan. "Is she—"

"Through and through," Tobias said between clenched teeth. He lightly traced the burn marks on my anima's wrists, and I flinched at the sight. I couldn't feel a thing through our bond while she was wherever she had gone, but if she had a crown on her head, that must mean...

"She won." Tobias's voice was hoarse as he echoed the words in my head. "Whatever happened, she won. But if she's alive, he must be too..."

His hand tightened around his sword, staring at the mirror as if expecting Aviel to jump through next. Had she somehow incapacitated him?

Eva stirred, her lashes fluttering. Alive, awake, and mine. I put my hand on her cheek, careful to avoid the tiny cuts covering her. She jolted, tensing as if readying for battle, but relaxed when she heard my voice.

"Open your eyes, Eva," I murmured. "You're safe now."

Her eyelids slowly lifted, like she had to gather the strength to open them. The dual crowns around her pupils sparkled, bits of gold flecking off into her irises as if in an endless loop, an echo of the crown still firmly in place on her wild hair.

"He's dead," she croaked.

My eyes flew to Tobias, then Yael and Quinn, their expressions as confused as my own must be. Had the bloodbond been a lie? If so, we had nearly lost her for nothing. But with Eva alive and safe, and the False King finally dead, I could scarcely muster the worry about what might have been as I breathed a sigh of relief.

Tobias's mouth opened and closed wordlessly before finally managing, "*How?*"

Eva's eyes glistened. She shook her head tiredly, her tongue darting out to lick her lips.

Hastily, I brought my half-empty canteen to her mouth. "Don't you ever do that again, do you hear me?"

"Save the realm, you mean?" Eva sounded exhausted, her chest rising and falling in shallow pants. She leaned heavily against me, her strength seemingly drained, wincing as Tobias prodded her stomach. But that fire, that indomitable, unyielding part of her was still there, as fierce as always.

"Save the realm without me," I said darkly.

She smirked, that one-sided dimple gracing her cheek. "It worked, didn't it?"

I growled low in my throat. "Yes, hellion. Though the words reckless and self-destructive come to mind..."

"Did you miss the part where it worked, 'cause—"

I leaned down, cutting off her words with a kiss. "And brave. And fearless. And utterly heroic."

Eva smiled up at me, and I brushed my thumb against that dimple that reappeared, needing to feel it. She tried to sit up, then fell back against me with a pained groan, the intensity of her agony breaking through our muted bond reigniting my panic.

Tobias's eyes met mine, his voice carefully controlled as he said, "We need to stop the bleeding."

I looked down to see a fresh wave of Eva's blood pooling beneath her. Tobias's hand was covered in it where he had pressed it against her stomach.

Eva's eyes slowly closed, her voice weak as she whispered, "It doesn't hurt as much anymore."

My fingers wrapped around her wrist, feeling the sluggishness of her pulse beneath my thumb, noting the increasing pallor of her skin even in the dim lighting. The shortness of her breath like she wasn't getting enough air.

She's losing too much blood.

I tried to ignore the sudden ringing in my ears, the way everything except her and the growing puddle of blood beneath her fell out of focus. Panicking wouldn't help her.

"We need to get you a healer, but with the avalanche..." I trailed off, knowing that help would likely come too late. "And Quinn...Rivan's—"

"Dying." Quinn's voice broke on the word, and my head snapped in her direction. The world went blurry around the edges as I saw her face glistening with tears, her bloody hands trembling. "He's dying. I used too much magic during the battle. To kill, the very antithesis of its purpose, and now...I can't hold on to him. I've been doing all I can, but it's not enough."

My heart stopped as I looked at my brother's ashen face, the slow, shuddering rise and fall of his chest.

They were both going to die. And there was nothing I could do to stop it.

"If you don't help Eva, she's dead too," Tobias rasped.

"I don't have enough left for both of them." Quinn swallowed, staring at the iridescent door as if someone would burst through to help. "I don't know if I have enough for even one of them."

And there was no telling how long it would be for help to come.

Eva went rigid in my arms. *"No."*

She pushed herself away before I could stop her, crawling toward Rivan with strength she shouldn't have possessed. I jolted forward, half carrying her as she determinedly brought herself next to him, leaving a dark trail in her wake.

My hand pressed against her side, warm blood slipping between my fingers.

It took a second to get my voice to work. "Eva, you need to stay still. Let your body heal until help comes."

She ignored me.

Laying her head against Rivan's heart, her hand snaked up, cupping his cheek. A terrifying rattling sound gurgled from his chest. Quinn closed her eyes, the glow of her magic faltering against the death that was so surely coming to claim him. Yael watched in mute horror, her hand stilling in Rivan's hair like she had been frozen in place.

Tobias took a step forward. "There's nothing you can do, Eva. It's too la—"

Her eyes opened. Bright blue gleamed behind those dual crowns of gold, her hair streaming around her head like a halo as she slowly sat up, her hands still on Rivan's heart. Quinn reeled backwards in shock as that power sprang from Eva's fingertips, flowing through her body until the shine of it filled the room. The crown on her head seemed to come alive— a thousand golden flecks flying upwards in a mirror of the crowns in her eyes.

Rivan's chest glowed where Eva touched him. Her hand moved down to cover the wound on his side, that light now too bright for me to make out exactly what she was doing, azure rays spreading out from her every point of contact.

His eyes flew open, his startled gasp ringing through the silence.

All at once, the magic disappeared. Eva went boneless against Rivan, the light in her eyes turning back to hazel before they fluttered closed.

I pulled her into my arms. *"Eva."*

Her eyes begrudgingly opened.

As I took in my *anima*, I realized her injuries had entirely disappeared. Her torn leathers had slipped down her shoulder, revealing her blood-drenched yet unblemished skin. No trace of the myriad of gashes that had been there before, not even a mark left over from the stomach wound that should have killed her.

My eyes flew up to hers just as her face broke into an exhausted yet giddy grin.

I smiled back, unable to find words for how relieved, how grateful, how utterly in awe I was of her. Questions could wait for later. For now, I could only be happy she was alive.

There was a collective gasp from the doorway, and I dimly recognized the murmur of voices as our own forces rushed toward us, a battle-worn Marin in the lead. Our soldiers, my rangers among them, ran in, crowding into the room.

But I could only focus on her.

Rivan's hand flew to his fully healed side, his mouth working soundlessly. Then he laboriously pulled himself up to one knee before bowing his head.

Eva's mouth parted in surprise. "There's no need for—"

Then she stilled, looking around with wide eyes.

And that was when I realized the entire room was kneeling for their High Queen.

CHAPTER 55
EVA

Despite the fact that I had fully healed myself, Bash seemed content to keep me in bed for the foreseeable future—if not forever. We had returned to Soleara to recuperate, though I knew we wouldn't be able to stay hidden away for long. Not when the end of the war left so much to be done. And especially not with the growing list of things I needed to do as High Queen. The rebuilding efforts were already underway in multiple kingdoms, aided by the fact that the curse was finally over.

Phantom whined as I stopped petting him to pick up my water glass from the bedside table, but Bash beat me to it, lifting it to my lips. Firmly, I took it from him lest he have any ideas about holding it while I drank.

"Are you hungry?" Bash was already writing a quick note on a piece of paper, then another—both vanishing in a wisp of shadow. He frowned, then wrote one more. "I'll have something brought up…"

"Bash."

His head swung toward me, ready to do whatever I asked of him.

"If you're not going to let me out of this bed, can you at least join me?" I waggled a suggestive eyebrow. "You're fussing."

Phantom nudged his nose into my palm, and I scratched him behind the ear. He had barely left my side since we had brought him here, his attentiveness only eclipsed by his master.

Bash gave me an exasperated look. "No matter how well healed you are, it doesn't mean you don't need rest after what happened." He swallowed. "Your injuries...the blood loss. What he—" His voice darkened, matching the swirling shadows in his eyes. "What he did to you."

For a heartbeat, I was back there—blood seeping from my stomach, my magic torn away. Bash's shadows reached for me, trailing up my bare legs. One curled around the exact spot where that whip of fire had nearly dragged me back to Aviel, but I didn't feel so much as an inkling of distress.

"I'm okay," I whispered, wondering if I was telling him or myself.

Bash sat on the bed next to me, wrapping his arms around me. His scent enfolded me, that mix of earthy woods and rain and something that made me feel utterly safe.

"I didn't know if I'd lost you again." Bash's voice was raw, shaking like he, too, was back in that mountain. "And then you nearly died. You *were* dying." He let out a low, pained sound in the back of his throat as he pulled me closer, shadows swirling in his eyes. "And I almost lost you forever."

"But we won, freckles," I said softly, taking his hand to break him away from the memory he was lost in. He smiled slightly at the nickname. "And I got a cool new party trick."

Closing my eyes to focus, I grinned as I felt the solid weight of my crown appear on my head. As High Queen, it was mine to summon, along with the magic of the land. I pushed away the thought that claiming it sooner may have saved Alette from giving herself up in my stead—though whether it was fate or circumstance, I doubted there was anything I could have done differently. The only thing I could do now was respect her sacrifice and honor the lifetime she had given me in return by making this realm better for it.

I blinked, and the crown was gone, my darkness trailing around my fingertips as if in outrage I hadn't called for it first. Bash's shadows darted forward, the two swirling together in a mesmerizing vortex.

"I do like that we match," Bash said, staring into my now ever-changing eyes. The flecks of gold within my irises moved in an endless, continuous circuit from my pupils, mirroring the gold specks flying like embers from my crown. Like Bash, it was easy to tell my relative agitation or calm from the rate at which they did so.

I shot him a playful smirk. "I've known that was your kink since the matching tattoos."

He scowled at me even as a hint of wry amusement filled our bond, light and lively.

I'd been so close to losing him. Losing everything.

Bash's expression sobered as he managed to see too much, like always. I could practically feel his questions along with his concern, the ones he had put off while insisting I convalesce. I had told him the barest of details along with everyone else—how my blood had summoned the crown from the Source itself, how Aviel had defeated me, how Alette had saved us all. But I knew he could sense the ache in my heart. Knew he was waiting for me to open up in my own time, even as he quieted my screams from the new nightmares that woke me, where Aviel dragged me back into a fiery death from which there was no escape.

Bash's gaze was so full of worry and kindness that something pricked behind my eyes.

"Tell me what you're thinking, hellion."

I shrugged. "I still can't believe he's gone. That it's over."

"Neither can I," Bash admitted. "When you sent that goodbye..."

I unconsciously touched my throat, though the mark my blade had left there had disappeared without a trace. Bash's eyes tracked the movement, their dual-toned blue and green fading to the gray of his shadows as they reached toward me, tugging my hand away and tucking it into his own.

Pale scars still circled my throat, my wrists, my ankles, that rose still marked on my palm. Aviel's bite mark, however, had faded significantly, as if my enhanced magic had rejected his false claiming. But I was thankful they hadn't disappeared along with my other injuries, the scars a testament to what I had survived.

"I was so close to killing myself," I whispered, looking away. "And it would've been for nothing."

A tendril of shadow lifted my chin, bringing my eyes up with it. "I'm grateful she gave you another choice."

"I wish I could've done the same for her."

It was all too easy to imagine a world in which our places were reversed. Yet Alette hadn't hesitated to change my fate, whether it had been driven by a sense of altruism or her own desire for revenge.

Aviel had underestimated her, just as I had, to his own detriment. The placeholder who had the misfortune to look enough like me to attract his attention. He hadn't even spent his time or energy searching for her after she had nearly brought down his castle.

No one had ever helped her. And she hadn't hesitated to save us all.

I hoped that wherever she was now, she had finally found peace.

"He would have won, if not for her," I murmured, remembering the feeling of him siphoning away even the seemingly endless power I had been granted. Bash must have felt that bleakness because his grip tightened. "He was so close to winning."

"Whether it was fate or just blind luck, he's gone now, Eva. Because of Alette's bravery, and her sacrifice. And yours."

He looked pointedly down at my side, though no trace of the wound in my gut remained.

"I'm okay now," I said haltingly. "I'm more than okay now that he's gone...now that this is over. And I know now that there isn't anything we can't take on together."

Bash let out a long breath, his thumb and forefinger catching my chin as he leaned in. "As long as you never forget that again, hellion."

The door creaked open. "Are we interrupting something?"

Yael and Marin stood there, each holding a tray of food. I breathed in the scent of something freshly baked, my gaze immediately zeroing in on the glazed brioche rolls dusted with powdered sugar next to a mouthwatering assortment of charcuterie and fruits.

It was almost ridiculous how ravenous I had been lately. Quinn had told me it was my body regaining its strength, and I was happy to listen to it. Grinning at them, I quickly exclaimed, "Come in."

I started to pull away—or tried to, as Bash's arms tightened around me.

He let out an exaggeratedly contented sigh. I gave him a look that brought a smirk to his face.

"I have no intention of letting you go, ever again," he murmured into my ear.

I turned my head to graze a kiss against his jaw. His arms loosened, just slightly.

Yael sat at the foot of the bed, plucking a berry from the tray she placed in front of her. Phantom quickly repositioned himself beside her, rolling over as she scratched his belly. Marin set down her tray on my bedside table, then came up next to me.

"May I?"

I nodded, and she placed her fingers on my temples. The warm hum of her magic spread over me, and I slowly let out a breath.

"She's fine," Marin said, looking at her brother.

Bash arched an eyebrow. "Shouldn't you be telling *her* that?"

Marin snorted. "Eva already knows that. You're the one acting like a mother hen."

I smirked, chuckling under my breath. Marin picked up her tray and put it on my lap. Bash smiled as he watched me quickly demolish one of those rolls before digging into a clay pot of eggs baked in a savory tomato sauce. A dollop of fresh cream lay on top of the bowl of berries, and I scooped some up with a raspberry before putting it in my mouth.

"You rang?"

Rivan walked into the room, also bearing a tray. I raised an eyebrow at Bash. He had the nerve not to even look embarrassed.

I rolled my eyes. "How much food, exactly, are you expecting me to eat?"

Bash only smiled, swiping a strawberry through the cream before placing it between my lips. I nipped him as I bit down. He yelped as Yael guffawed.

"I wasn't sure who would come the fastest," Bash said dryly, taking a steaming mug from Rivan's tray. He carefully dipped a small metal infuser filled with loose leaf tea into it, then picked up a spool of honey, carefully twirling it before adding the exact amount I liked. "But now we get to all enjoy a meal together."

I pouted at Rivan. "If I'm stuck in bed, you should be too."

Rivan placed his tray on the bed, winking before scooting underneath the covers beside me.

Bash carefully blew on the mug of tea before passing it to me.

Yael grinned. "I see he's still fussing."

I shook my head. "You have no idea. He won't even let me—"

"LA-LA-LA," Marin cut in, putting her fingers in her ears. "This *is* my brother you're talking about."

I snorted. "I was going to say, 'get up by myself'. Get your head out of the gutter."

There was a tingle on my palm, warm from the mug.

No, you weren't.

A blush crept up my cheeks. Bash leaned over, spearing a bite of egg with a fork before placing it in my open mouth. His knuckles lightly grazed my cheekbone before he pulled away. Rivan reached forward, snagging a jam-filled pastry from Yael's tray.

"Hey, stick to your own," she teased.

"According to her majesty, I should be bedridden too," Rivan exclaimed through his full mouth. "Besides, someone had already taken all the pastries by the time I got there."

I reached over him, grabbing a pastry for myself. "Why is Rivan allowed to be up and about when he was worse off than me?"

Yael coughed something that sounded like, "Debatable."

Marin stabbed some fruit with a fork. "Rivan doesn't have a whole host of new abilities to let his body adjust too. And while that magic healed you both, it didn't entirely replenish the blood loss. Not to mention the fact that you repeatedly burned out your magic."

"You said yourself that I'm fine now." I shot Bash a pointed look. "So I should be *training*. Just like I did the last time I got my magic."

Marin laughed. "In my medical opinion, the only reason Rivan isn't still stuck in bed is because Bash could only focus on one of you at a time."

I took a long sip of the tea—savoring the restorative taste of ginger and turmeric. "It's not like I have an entire realm to run or anything."

"Everything will still be there once you've had some time to recover,"

Marin said placatingly. "Though I can't say I'm not feeling the same pressure hiding out here."

Yael took her hand, using the free one to pick up a pastry. She used it to point at Marin, then me. "Bash is right. We've all been through a lot. And we somehow all made it through alive." Her eyes flickered to Rivan, then back to me. "Even when we shouldn't have." She tugged Marin closer, looping her arm around her waist. "We deserve a break. So let yourself take one before it's time to return to the real world."

She bit into the pastry, somehow glaring threateningly at us all despite the jam running down her chin.

"You're not wrong," I said with a sigh. "It just seems like the to-do list is never-ending...and only getting longer."

"Your steps don't have to be long," Rivan said gently. "They just have to take you in the right direction."

I took his hand, wrapping our fingers together. "How are you feeling?"

One eyebrow twitched. "Absolutely wonderful, as always."

I gave him a baleful look, and he chuckled.

"Honestly." He squeezed my hand. "Whatever you did in that mountain...I'm completely healed. Not that I can make sense of it beyond the fact that it was a magic more powerful than any I've ever experienced."

Bash lifted another egg-laden fork to my mouth, and I gave him a begrudging look as I closed my lips around it.

There was a knock on the open door, and I looked up to see Tobias and Quinn. Both holding trays of food.

Quinn eyed the feast already spread out on the bed, then smiled at Bash. "I see you weren't kidding about the urgency."

"Join us," Yael said with a laugh. A controlled burst of air pushed two chairs up next to us. "Apparently, Bash missed group dining."

Marin giggled. "But apparently not tables."

"I suppose magical cleaning has the benefits of no crumbs in the bed," Quinn mused as she plopped down on the proffered chair.

Bash let out a long-suffering sigh. "I'm not apologizing for taking care of my *anima*..."

The group broke out into loud conversation about the insanity of bonded couples, especially when one was recovering.

I just smiled to myself, stealing the fork from Bash before he fed me another bite. A shadow twirled itself into my hair, brushing lightly against my ear. I could feel his eyes on me as I ate, watching me closely as my family laughed around me. Unhurriedly, I finished my plate, half listening to the chatter. My lips quirked as I raised an eyebrow at Bash in a silent, *Are you happy now?*

He smiled smugly as I pushed the empty tray at him. Then his mouth opened in surprise as I hopped out of bed, using Rivan as a shield before he tried to pull me back.

"Eva..."

"If I stay in this bed another moment, I'm going to scream," I said, then bit my lip as Bash's eyes darkened at the insinuation.

I backed toward the dresser, picking out a pair of leggings and a workout top. Bash looked ready to leap from our bed and carry me back into it.

"Someone hold Bash down while I change."

Bash crossed his arms as the rest of them grinned.

I eyed him as I retreated to the bathroom. "I'm going to train now. If you'd like to come with me, you're welcome to. Otherwise, I'm not above using my new powers to tie you to the bedpost."

Bash smirked, and I could practically read his retort in the sinful look in his eyes, the sensuous feeling snaking down our bond. The one that promised he would follow up on that declaration later.

He shifted, and Rivan made a move as if to block him. Bash gave him a look of pure challenge, and I knew they would soon be dueling it out in the sparring ring.

Then he sighed, raising his hands in defeat.

"Whatever you say, Your Majesty."

CHAPTER 56

EVA

My golden dress crisscrossed across my chest, circling around my neck, leaving a diamond of exposed skin under my breasts before wrapping around my waist. The flowing skirt extended to the floor, but there was a long slit up my leg—perfect to stow my dagger within reach. Though the one strapped to my side was now a gift from my brother, an almost exact recreation of the one I had lost minus the stone, its remains melted down far beneath this castle. Delicate golden ribbons extended across my shoulders and interlaced down my arms, matching the gold strands braided into my hair, the golden liner on my eyelids and the dust of gold on my cheeks.

We had spent the evening meeting with the royal families—not that the new King of Soleara and the Queens of Imyr hadn't been frequent visitors. Tobias had quietly assumed his new role, working to reorient our people in a realm that suddenly remembered them, all while grieving those we had lost in that final battle. Queen Sariyah's sea-green eyes were still haunted after what had happened on her way to Adronix as she thanked me for taking down the one responsible. I had been happy to see Eliav and Noam again, though they also looked bone weary from their own rebuilding efforts.

Both Mayim and Esterra were still dealing with dissenters. Perhaps I had been foolish to think Aviel's end would dissuade those who had supported him from rising again. Their outright attacks had dissipated to whispers about my legitimacy as news had spread about the democratic ideologies I had brought with me from the human realm, never mind the fact that the blueprint was almost entirely my mother's.

The weight of the realm I was responsible for felt just as heavy at peace as it did in war. I wouldn't rule as a figurehead, and I had no intention of being just another monarch. Yet finding a more democratic solution for a kingdom that had always existed without such representation would take time, even with my mother's books of notes and learnings. Even if this group of rulers seemed surprisingly receptive to the change.

Though perhaps after seeing how close Aviel had come to stealing this world for himself, they saw the wisdom in dividing that power. With the checks and balances I proposed, it wouldn't be so easily taken again.

My uncle had pulled me aside to let me know that, despite efforts to locate him, Silvius had disappeared from Morehaven during the post-battle chaos. I knew Rivan had already tasked some of Imyr's best trackers to hunt him down, but the thought of him free and at large after the retribution I had promised him rankled. He was the mastermind behind the magic blocking bands, the serum they had injected me with, and gods knew what else. It wasn't safe to leave him to his own devices, never mind my personal vendetta.

Our talks had lasted late into the night, and I had been relieved when we had been able to retire. Bash led me down the newly painted hallways to our rooms, the sage green a welcome change. He had taken it upon himself to bring bedding from Imyr—its citrusy scent alone went a long way in making it feel like home.

I hadn't needed to refuse to take residence in the room Aviel had once trapped me in, since it was still a pile of fire-scorched rubble. A hole remained visible from the exterior of the castle, where Alette had saved me. But the library down the hall had survived the flames, to my relief. I hadn't yet decided what to do with the tower when the reconstruction was complete, but I had already made the stoneworkers promise to keep the scorch mark on the floor as a testament to the one who had put it there.

After all, it did look better scorched.

While refurbishing Morehaven had hardly been our top priority, we had found ways to make it our own. Carpet now covered the marble floor I would never forget the cruel coldness of; blues and greens and shadowy grays slowly taking over the endless white. While certain hallways and some specific spots still summoned a flash of residual terror when I passed, those places were becoming fewer and farther between. Apparently, banishing the ghosts of the past was sometimes as simple as a fresh coat of paint.

On the days it wasn't so easy—old fears shivering down our bond as I imagined a harsh breath on the nape of my neck—Bash would lift me onto Nisa, and we would ride out over the ridge. Breathing in the fresh mountain air as we trotted together through the patches of earth that had once been gray and dead, now slowly being reborn in the early throughs of spring.

While it seemed strange to call Morehaven home, it was slowly becoming it. Though I had a feeling anywhere could be, as long as my *anima* was with me.

Bash's voice broke through my reverie. "I probably should've given you this before dinner, but I didn't want to share the look on your face."

I looked behind me to see Bash holding a familiar dark sword. One I thought had been lost forever in the cave far below this castle. My mouth dropped open, and I felt his amusement, its reflection almost bubbly across our bond. Just as I knew he could feel my shock and joy like it was his own.

When Bash handed Nightshade to me, I nearly wept as I unsheathed it, taking in the blade I was sure had been lost. My darkness wrapped around it lovingly as I closed my eyes, savoring the feel of its handle as my grip tightened.

I had missed it in my hands.

"It was the only thing I found intact down there, besides the mirror," Bash murmured. I could feel his satisfied contentment increase as my face broke into a smile.

"You went—"

"I wanted to be sure," Bash cut in grimly. "It was one of the first things

I did when we moved in. The sword took a bit to repair after the way it melted in the blast."

"I never thought I'd see it again."

I sat on the bed, my fingers trailing up and down the flat side of my blade as my darkness latticed around it in overlapping patterns.

Peace or no, I had no doubt I would find the need to use this sword again. The thought didn't scare me, not with my family at my side. And despite all that still needed to be done, I knew I was exactly where I was meant to be.

Fleetingly, I wondered where I would be had I never found this realm. Had I never found my *anima,* our friends, my not-so-deceased brother. If I hadn't discovered my long-denied magic, so much a part of me now that I didn't know how I used to breathe without it. I wondered where I would've ended up if I hadn't learned exactly who and what my parents were and the sacrifice they had made for me. Even if I had always known how much they loved me.

I was so lost in my own head that I barely noticed a shadowy wisp wrap around my ankles, jerking my legs out from under me so I fell back upon the bed. A prickle of need I knew he could feel started low in my belly as more wisps trailed up my thighs in lazy strokes, exposing me to him as they pushed my legs open wide.

Teasingly, I pointed my sword at him.

Bash smirked. "I've always preferred you with a blade in your hand. Reminds me of how we first met."

His fingers reached up to toy with the delicate ribbon draping across my collarbone, leaning over me to trail kisses down each golden thread. My sword dropped to my side as I arched against him, needing *more.*

"This dress is torture, hellion," he groaned, brushing his lips against the exposed skin between my breasts. "Take it off for me."

His shadows were already pulling it higher, and I nearly laughed aloud at their urgency. Like we didn't have all the time in the world now.

"Only if you promise to make me scream," I acquiesced, watching his eyes darken in a way that had nothing to do with the shadows swirling within them.

Laughing lightly at Bash's groan of impatience as I started undoing each tie, Bash began to help me in a way that only served to distract us both, his mouth pressing against every new section of exposed skin.

He twirled one of the ribbons around his finger, letting the edge of it brush against my peaked nipple. The light, teasing touch made me moan. "I'm not sure what turned me on more tonight, the way you so effortlessly commanded everyone, or the fact that you were wrapped up like a present. All I wanted to do was bend you over your throne and rip these off one by one."

I gasped as he sucked my nipple into his mouth, his tongue swirling against it. "It's not too late to make that a reality."

His laugh was low and husky. "Oh, I absolutely plan to make that fantasy come true for us both. But not before I get you off first."

Bash pulled my dress off completely, his shadows having undone the remaining clasps and ties without me realizing, leaving only the silver-star necklace gleaming between my naked breasts. He yanked off his jacket, then his shirt, my mouth going dry as he revealed the defined muscles of his stomach. His hands moved to his pants, and my eyes trailed down the hard, vee-shaped lines leading the way to the uncomfortable-looking bulge tenting them.

I whined deep in my throat as his fingers paused. He smirked, then complied with my wordless plea, his cock thick and wanting as he stood completely nude over me. A bead of come glistened at the tip, and I leaned forward with the intent of licking it off.

Bash's shadows pushed me back down, pinning my wrists to my sides. I knew I would be able to get free if I wanted to—knew exactly how safe I was with him—but I didn't so much as try, relishing the heat building inside me as I gave up control.

His fingers caught my chin. "Is this okay?"

My only reply was a loud moan as his shadows slipped between my legs, as eager as I was for this, teasingly sliding into my wetness before moving it around my clit.

Their master didn't move. "You know the rules, Eva. I need to hear you say it."

I shivered with desire as I breathed, "*Yes.*"

Bash's smile was feline. "Then it's my turn first, hellion."

I made a noise of dissent, wanting to taste him, to *feel* him inside me. It was quickly swallowed by my moan as his head lowered between my thighs. He groaned, the rumble of it hot against my core, and I gasped his name.

Those dark tendrils trailed slowly up the midline of my stomach, the sensation of him *everywhere* almost unbearable. They teased against my nipples in time to Bash's tongue until I finally let go, crying out as Bash kept moving, that talented tongue circling insistently to wring out every second of my pleasure.

I should have felt satiated. Instead, it somehow made me feel even more desperate for him. When I had control of my limbs once again, I lunged at him, the shadows holding me back gone in an instant. Bash chuckled roughly against my lips as I pushed him off the bed with one hand to his chest, forcing him to his feet. That laugh died abruptly as I went to my knees before him.

My fingers trailed lightly down over the lines of muscle carving his abdomen...then lower. He let out a full body groan as I took him into my mouth. My eyelids fluttered closed as I flattened my tongue against him, humming with satisfaction.

"Eyes on me," Bash ordered, his low voice curling down my spine.

I obeyed, watching him from beneath my lashes. Those shadow-filled eyes went half-lidded as I sucked him deep into my throat, my cheeks hollowing with each shallow thrust of his hips. My fingers dug into his thighs, urging him deeper. The way I wanted him...it felt like it would never be satisfied.

Darkness flared from me in an echo of his teasing tendrils, one wrapping tightly around his thick base, each stroke timed to the suction of my lips.

"*Fuck.*"

Bash tensed, shuddering. Then he yanked me to my feet, wrapping my legs around his waist as he backed me against the wall. His hands ran down my body, lingering on my backside. I arched against the cool stone, savoring the moment before we were joined—that delicious grind of his shaft against that growing ache between my legs.

"I *was* promised a throne," I objected even as I pressed myself against him, unable to wait another moment. I gasped as the head of his cock aligned with my entrance.

Bash held me there, panting against my lips as he leaned his forehead against mine. "We have all night. And all the ones after that, my queen."

His mouth crashed into mine, then he pushed into me with one slow roll of his hips. I let out a mangled moan at the stretch, writhing against him. One hand tangled in my hair, the other digging into my thigh as he thrust into me, over and over. Rasping my name into the hollow of my neck as he rocked deeper, a shiver of bliss pulsing through me.

I gasped his name in return as he took me unrelentingly, like he couldn't hold himself back. And I didn't want him to, my hips meeting and matching his every thrust—each one adding to the building pressure until I thought I might break.

"Be a good girl and scream for me like you promised," Bash said raggedly. "I want the whole castle to hear you come."

"I seem to remember it was you who—" I sucked in a short gasp as his shadows slipped between my thighs. "...who promised."

He gave me that crooked half-grin that made something swoop low in my stomach. "Semantics."

I canted my hips against him, needing more of him—needing all of him. He angled himself so deep inside me I thought I might come apart.

When I did, I couldn't hold back my scream of pleasure. My body shuddered in a violent spasm as I unraveled, Bash holding me up as I sagged against him.

I barely realized he had flipped me around until my cheek pressed against the stone. He buried himself back inside me, the evidence of my orgasm dampening my inner thighs. When I whimpered against the new, deeper angle, he let out a satisfied growl that sent a shiver of pleasure down my spine.

It felt almost strange that my desperation for him no longer had anything to do with the threat against our lives. Not when we had the rest of them to be together. And yet I was utterly desperate for him, like my need for him would never be entirely sated.

One arm wrapped around my hips, my ass slapping against Bash's thighs as I arched into his thrusts, that aching pressure building yet again.

My darkness whirled around us uncontrollably, turning the stone in front of me black as night though I found myself unable to think about anything but the building heat prickling beneath my skin. His fingers found my clit, and my eyes rolled back, my legs already trembling.

"That's right, hellion," Bash groaned. "Come for me."

I came apart at his command with a cry, his body pinning me to the wall the only thing keeping me upright. I could feel him shudder as he emptied himself inside me, my name falling from his lips.

"Gods, Bash. I..." My words jumbled on my tongue as he slipped from inside me. I was saved by his mouth pressing against mine as he gathered me into his arms, lifting me up like he knew my legs weren't able to support me yet.

He sat me on the bathroom counter, carefully cleaning me. "Throne next, or should we leave something to look forward to?"

My heart felt like it might burst as I added yet another addition to my list of things I wanted to experience with him now that I was assured of the time to do so. Its growing length was a far cry from the empty dreams I had stopped letting myself hope for not so long ago. "I want everything with you, but I suppose I can wait one more day for this particular adventure."

Bash smirked at me. "Who says we're only doing it once?"

He carried me back to the bed, holding me tight against him as his shadows tucked the sheets in around us. I relaxed into him, feeling the rise and fall of his chest as we breathed together. Savoring the happiness I could feel across our bond, multiplying endlessly from both of us.

And I realized that I had found everything I hadn't let myself want, for fear of it being taken away from me again—that home, that safety, the love I had never let myself dream of. That I finally believed in forever.

CHAPTER 57
EVA

The days felt long, but the weeks felt short as we spent our time steadying the realm after so long in chaos. Overseeing plans to rebuild what had been broken in the war, finding homes for those displaced, leaving no ask for help unanswered.

Some days, I would marvel at how long it had been since I had heard my father's voice in my head commanding me to breathe in order to hold myself together. As unconscious as the reflex was, the fact that I hadn't needed it was a sure sign of how safe I finally felt. Other nights, I would wake up from a nightmare with Bash whispering those words over and over as his arms tightened around me, my father's voice blending in with his.

Breathe, Eva. Count each second.

But while the memories I relived in my dreams left me cold and shuddering, they were never the ones where I had to fight my way out. Never the kind that left marks. And Bash's fingers circling steadily on my back as he held me close soon chased their chill away.

It finally felt like I could exhale. Like I could allow myself to revel in the relatively strange sensation of being…happy. At the sense of peace in knowing I was where I was supposed to be, with the people I loved there beside me.

Well, almost.

As the room darkened in the shadows of twilight, I stared up at the portrait of my parents. My eyes zeroed in on my mother's matching pair looking down at me. And for the first time in a long time, I couldn't think of the last time I had been forced to hear the reverberations of her screams.

Instead, a fleeting memory of her infectious laugh seemed to echo in the room, my father's deep one matching it. I wished they could be here with me, like defeating Aviel should have brought them back. But something told me they knew how this all had turned out, even if they weren't here to see it.

Some things couldn't be fixed, but I would spend the rest of my days changing the things I could for the better.

My onyx gown had begun to blend into the gathering shadows when I heard a noise from behind me. Bash leaned a broad shoulder against the doorway, his arms crossed in front of him. I couldn't help but smile at the sight of him with a crown on his head, the deep gold that matched my own somehow not clashing horribly with the auburn of his hair.

"You look exhausted," Bash said, coming up behind me. His arms wound around my waist, tugging me against his chest before moving to massage my shoulders. I let out a small groan. He peppered little kisses along the long line of my neck as his thumbs dug into my muscles below, and I tilted my head to the side to give him better access.

"Gee, thanks," I mumbled. "If I have to review one more plan, I think I might go cross-eyed."

"Is that so?" Bash spun me around, holding me at arm's length as he gave me a wicked grin. "So you don't want to hear *my* plans?"

I blinked stupidly. "*Your* plans?"

"For us."

"Us?"

He shook his head, one side of his lips curving up in that devastating half-smile. Watching me with that same soft wonder as he often did when he thought I wasn't looking. Like he couldn't believe that not only did he find me, but he also got to keep me forever.

I tilted my head at him, waiting. Then let out a surprised squeak as he sat on the bed, pulling me onto his lap.

"Of course I have plans for us," Bash said, somewhat exasperatedly even as a wave of warmth flooded down our bond. "I have nothing *but* plans. I plan to make this kingdom everything it should have been, everything it could be with you leading it. I have plans to build the family you've always wanted—when you're ready, that is—and make sure our children are raised in a realm that only ever knows peace. I have plans to worship you, as my High Queen, as my *anima*, as my lover, as my friend... They start with teasing that little moan I can't get out of my head from those perfect lips of yours and end with us sated and wrapped in each other until we fall asleep and find each other in our dreams."

Bash leaned forward, lifting my hands behind his neck, his light caress down my arms making me shiver. "And I have plans to...what did you say we couldn't have? That night when you didn't see any other alternative?"

He pulled out a small box from his jacket pocket and opened it. Inside there was a ring.

It was familiar, if not almost exactly the same as the boon I had received after learning of what I thought meant my doom. My mother's ring that had saved me. Bash had replaced the ruined stone—the large, oval diamond now an oddly iridescent black, the exact shade of the shattered diamond from my dagger. Like my darkness solidified, as clear as the night we had first met, and radiant with the promise of tomorrow. As though the two stones from my mother that had been destroyed had been melded into one.

My throat was too choked up to respond, Bash's thumb catching the happy tears that rolled down my cheeks before they could fall.

His answering smile was blinding. "Oh, right. My plan is to live happily ever after."

Thank you for reading! Did you enjoy? Please add your review because nothing helps an author more and encourages readers to take a chance on a book than a review.

And don't miss more in *THE MIRRORED TRILOGY* coming soon! Turn the page for a sneak peek!

Also be sure to sign up for the City Owl Press newsletter to receive notice of all book releases!

SNEAK PEEK OF THE FINAL INSTALLMENT OF THE MIRRORED TRILOGY

TOBIAS

The sky feels far too large when you've spent so long in a cage.

My breath snagged, my feet skidding to a stop as if there were an invisible barrier across the stone archway that led from the Solearan castle I had grown up in. The courtyard before me was too open, the pale, blue sky seeming to expand exponentially as I struggled to draw in a breath. My heart pounded in my ears as I tried and failed to force one foot forward.

The sky was too endless, even as something small and trapped inside me berated me that it meant freedom.

Big breath in. Count each second. Breath out. And count the same.

I sucked in a quick, boxed breath—my father's voice speaking that familiar four count in my head just as he had done so many times in that dank dungeon cell. But I was free—free of that awful place, free of that mask whose weight I could still feel on my temples, free of my imprisonment as I had been for months now.

Safe. Free…Why did it feel like I never truly would be?

Five years. That was how long I was in that dank dungeon. No sun, no fresh air, no light. A crisp wind caressed my cheeks, and I closed my eyes with a shudder, hating myself as I reached for the familiarity of that darkness.

I still dreamt of that cell every night. Trapped and unable to find a way out, the slow drip of the dank walls, the endless dark. The torture that was Aviel's draining of my power, over and over and over again. The iron taste of blood in my mouth when he was finally finished, and I had screamed myself hoarse. I had taken to leaving a light on at night after too many times waking up terrified and alone in the pitch blackness, unsure if the memory of my escape was some sort of cruel fallacy my mind had conjured in a last ditch effort to stay sane.

My heart pounding in my ears, I managed a cautious step forward. The world tilted strangely.

With a sharp gasp, I hurried back inside the doorway, my vision narrowing to the stone around me and my shaking hands. Thankfully, I didn't have any observers at this early hour as I pressed my forehead against the side of the archway. My hands grasped at the unforgiving stone, feeling its grounding presence beneath my fingertips. Cold, harsh stone had been the only thing I had felt for so long. Had hated as it leeched what little warmth I had in those dank dungeons even.

And here I was reaching for it instead of embracing the crisp air that whipped around my face as if in reprimand.

Wincing, I made myself let go. I needed to get a hold of this awful, irrational fear, if I was going to be to function as the King of Soleara...or just function, in general. While I had spent days riding horseback to reach Adronix during those final days of battle, readying the Solearan troops and staying by my sister's side, those nights on the road had been spent shaking in my solitary tent, trying to calm my racing heart before the next day began. The slow ride to Adronix had been torturous, much of it in open air. I had focused on the surrounding trees, sucking in air in careful patterns. Trying to focus on my purpose, on my duty, on my revenge. I had been grateful for my horse's solid warmth underneath me, his hooves moving forward when we left the tree cover. Hiding the fact that I was frozen and silently hyperventilating beneath my hood.

But it was Quinn who had always seemed to find me whenever it became too much to bear, taking my mind off my fear with casual conversation. I wondered if she had any idea how much she had saved me time and time again.

And yet it had gotten worse, not better now that I was home and had the option of hiding indoors. Without imminent need moving me forward I had lost whatever inertia had fueled the fleeting bravery that kept my terror at bay. Idly, I wondered if my people thought me reclusive or simply inattentive, holed up in my castle as I was. Pari, Akeno, and Thorin had long since stopped extending offers of companionship, knowing it would only earn them another polite but firm no.

I needed to get over this. I should've already.

The sky seemed to laugh mockingly as if it had heard me as I forced myself to look up into it. Sweat dripped down my back as I made my legs walk forward, despite a growing buzzing in my ears.

I closed my eyes as soon as I reached the practice yard. Trembling, I fell into the familiar motions of a form my body knew as easily as breathing, hoping that balance and movement would chase my demons away. Yet I could feel the taunting caress of the morning sunlight on my cheeks reminding me of the endless openness surrounding me.

Clenching my jaw, I tried to focus on the light itself, not what it meant. There was something about sunlight, something that had always helped me recharge and find some semblance of fortitude even before I knew the connection to my magic. I had always felt my best as the sun rose, usually baiting my grumpy, night owl twin as she woke up bleary eyed and grumbling. But after my capture and imprisonment, in that dark, dank cell with that damn mask blocking even the hint of light available from reaching my face, it felt foreign. A pale imitation of the comfort it had once held, though my magic still rose within me as if aching to reach out the world I refused to reenter.

But my light still felt wrong. Tainted. Like it had been stained by the ways it had been used against innocents and those I loved.

Shaking my head, I forced those thoughts away. I *had* missed this. The fresh air in my lungs. The smell of the earth, the breeze. The ground beneath my feet instead of stone and dripping stone. I missed it all so damn much, even with the ever-present twist to my stomach that now accompanied my experience.

As I reached the final pose, panting far too hard for the casual warmup, light footsteps broke the silence. Reluctantly, I opened my eyes— though I already knew to whom they belonged.

Quinn Sagray smiled up at me, the tight curls of her hair waving wildly in the wind. For one precious moment, the sky seemed to melt away.

My sister's best friend had been mirroring between Morehaven and

Soleara so often I rarely knew which kingdom in which she would spend the night...not that I was keeping track of where she spent the night. But when she was here, she usually stayed in the room down the hall from me, the sounds of her footsteps walking past my closed door somehow distinctive despite the number of visitors at my parents' massive former home high in the mountains. I could usually hear her tinkering with something or another late into the night.

Her room was more mad scientist' lair than sleeping space now, experiments bubbling in beakers I had been surprised she had been able to obtain in this realm. When I had asked her once about them, she had simply arched an eyebrow and said, "We live in a world full of magic and you're surprised I was able to procure a few beakers?"

I had been spending most nights at the castle, giving her space during the daylight hours. But she always seemed to find me when it came time to train, just as she had when we had journeyed to Adronix together.

"I thought I'd get a workout in before it's time to go." Her sunny smile grew wider. "I should have known you would've beat me out here. Can I join you?"

"Sure," I grunted. Inwardly I winced at my eloquence, though even now I wasn't used to speaking at length. After so long wearing a mask that choked off my voice until even my screams were silent...I cleared my throat. "What have you been working on?"

"Just trying to understand more about the intersection of magic and medicine."

I raised one eyebrow, my tone droll as I asked, "Is that all?"

Quinn shrugged. "There are so many diseases in the human realm that could benefit from this sort of research, if it turns out to be successful. Not that disease has been eradicated here either, but the treatments..." Her eyes lit up, and I couldn't help but be utterly charmed by her excitement. "The way the healers here are able to fix things with magic is one thing, but the way they use magic to imbue tonics with those cures... if there were a way to mass produce such a thing, it could be huge. And I didn't spend all those years getting my MD to stop researching now."

Many would have, were they to find themselves in another realm and best friends with the High Queen of all of it. But that wasn't who Quinn was, or ever had been. It was easy to remember the girl I knew before all of this, effortlessly kind and always the first person to offer to help. My sister's best friend but in many ways mine too—our trio inseparable until we were torn apart. It was no surprise that she had found a career that was aimed at helping people, or that her magic revolved around it. Nor was it a surprise she had kept at it, even here.

She tapped her foot impatiently and I repressed a smile. Even when we were kids, Quinn had never been able to stay still.

Quinn's arm brushed mine as she moved past me, the fleeting touch seeming to emanate down my entire body. Her amber eyes sparkled as they met mine, and I almost missed the training sword she tossed at me as I found myself momentarily lost in them.

She raised her own. "Ready?"

I nodded mutely.

If freedom meant having nothing left to lose then I had been so, so foolish to believe I had ever been freed.

Don't miss it. Sign up for Dana Evyn's newsletter at danaevyn.com to receive all the details about the final installment of The Mirrored Trilogy!

ACKNOWLEDGMENTS

Writing a sequel is an entirely daunting task, and I couldn't have done it without the below list of family, friends, and the very best readers who fell through the mirror with me to share in this adventure.

First, a huge thank you to my three-star book group who got me back into reading, introduced me to romantasy, and therefore changed my life forever. My twin sister Sam, alpha reader extraordinaire who read this book first. To Mel, the queen of worldbuilding and the best book recs. To Leah, whose design eye has saved me more than once. To Teresa, who started my love of romantasy in the first place. And to Hope, Stacey, and Minako, for always being endlessly supportive.

To Sav, the very best PA and an amazing friend. I'm so thankful to work with you. And to my wonderful agent, Jackie for believing in me and always having my best interests at heart.

To my author friends who have helped me every step of the way. To Ariella, whose advice and friendship have helped me more than you know. To Jaclyn, my witchy sister whose debut I cannot wait for. To Desirée, for her friendship and bloodthirsty mermaids, and to Leslie, my release day twin. And to Alison, whose advice helped get me where I am now.

To my editor Danielle, the bat is for you! A big thank you to the entire owl team for all your work behind the scenes for this release.

To my street team – the people that took a chance on a debut author with a shadow daddy and a pretty cover. And to Nolani, whose beta read comments still make me cackle.

To the artists who have made my characters come alive – I'm so grateful to all of you.

To my mom, who has been endlessly supportive of her bookworm, fantasy obsessed daughter who never wanted to stop reading. And to the second set, Kate and Charlie, who always brighten my day.

To my husband Shane – I love you, freckles. To my daughters, who are never allowed to read my work, there is nothing sweeter than your support, snuggles, and excitement about mommy's books. To my creatures, Dallas and Mia, for always keeping me company as I write.

And to my readers, without whom none of this would be possible. Thank you for going back through the mirror with me. Remember, the only way out is through.

About the Author

DANA EVYN is a romantasy author who has been lost in her daydreams for as long as she can remember, though she only recently started writing them down. When she's not writing, she's usually reading a good book—especially one with an indomitable female lead, a unique magical world, and a dark twist you don't see coming. She lives in Kirkland, WA with her two tiny humans, ever-supportive husband, giant golden retriever/luck dragon and tiny familiar/kitten.

To sign up for Dana's newsletter, please visit danaevyn.com

[Instagram] instagram.com/danaevyn
[TikTok] tiktok.com/@danaevyn
[X] x.com/danaevyn

ABOUT THE PUBLISHER

City Owl Press is a cutting edge indie publishing company, bringing the world of romance and speculative fiction to discerning readers.

Escape Your World. Get Lost in Ours!

www.cityowlpress.com

facebook.com/YourCityOwlPress
x.com/cityowlpress
instagram.com/cityowlbooks
pinterest.com/cityowlpress

www.ingramcontent.com/pod-product-compliance
Lightning Source LLC
LaVergne TN
LVHW022344151224
799165LV00005BA/1024